the ALTERED HISTORY of
WILLOW SPARKS

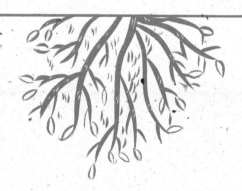

AN ONI PRESS PUBLICATION

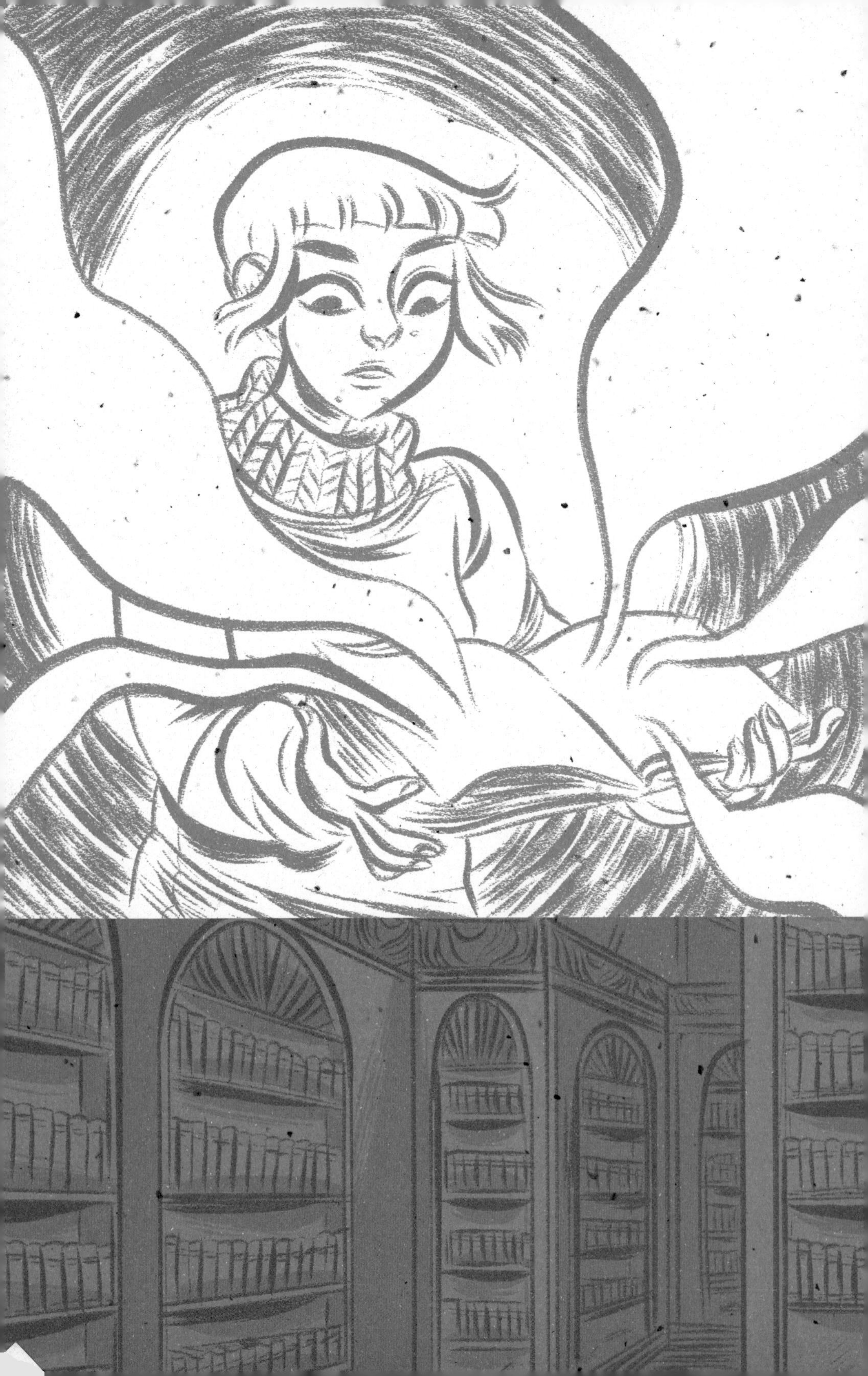

the ALTERED HISTORY of WILLOW SPARKS

BY TARA O'CONNOR

LETTERED BY CRANK!

COVER COLORED BY KATY FARINA

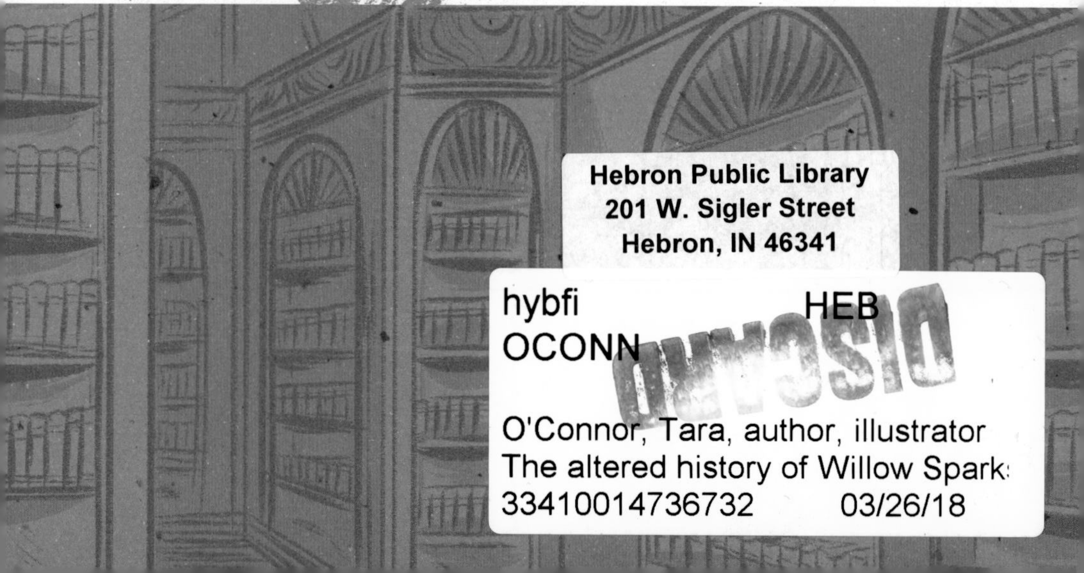

DESIGNED BY HILARY THOMPSON
EDITED BY ARI YARWOOD

PUBLISHED BY ONI PRESS, INC.

JOE NOZEMACK • FOUNDER & CHIEF FINANCIAL OFFICER
JAMES LUCAS JONES • PUBLISHER
CHARLIE CHU • V.P. OF CREATIVE & BUSINESS DEVELOPMENT
BRAD ROOKS • DIRECTOR OF OPERATIONS
RACHEL REED • MARKETING MANAGER
MELISSA MESZAROS MACFADYEN • PUBLICITY MANAGER
TROY LOOK • DIRECTOR OF DESIGN & PRODUCTION
HILARY THOMPSON • GRAPHIC DESIGNER
KATE Z. STONE • JUNIOR GRAPHIC DESIGNER
ANGIE KNOWLES • DIGITAL PREPRESS LEAD
ARI YARWOOD • EXECUTIVE EDITOR
ROBIN HERRERA • SENIOR EDITOR
DESIREE WILSON • ASSOCIATE EDITOR
ALISSA SALLAH • ADMINISTRATIVE ASSISTANT
JUNG LEE • LOGISTICS ASSOCIATE

ONIPRESS.COM
FACEBOOK.COM/ONIPRESS
TWITTER.COM/ONIPRESS
ONIPRESS.TUMBLR.COM
INSTAGRAM.COM/ONIPRESS

@TARAOCOMICS
TARAOCOMICS.COM

FIRST EDITION: JANUARY 2018
ISBN 978-1-62010-450-7
EISBN 978-1-62010-451-4

LIBRARY OF CONGRESS CONTROL NUMBER: 2017905078

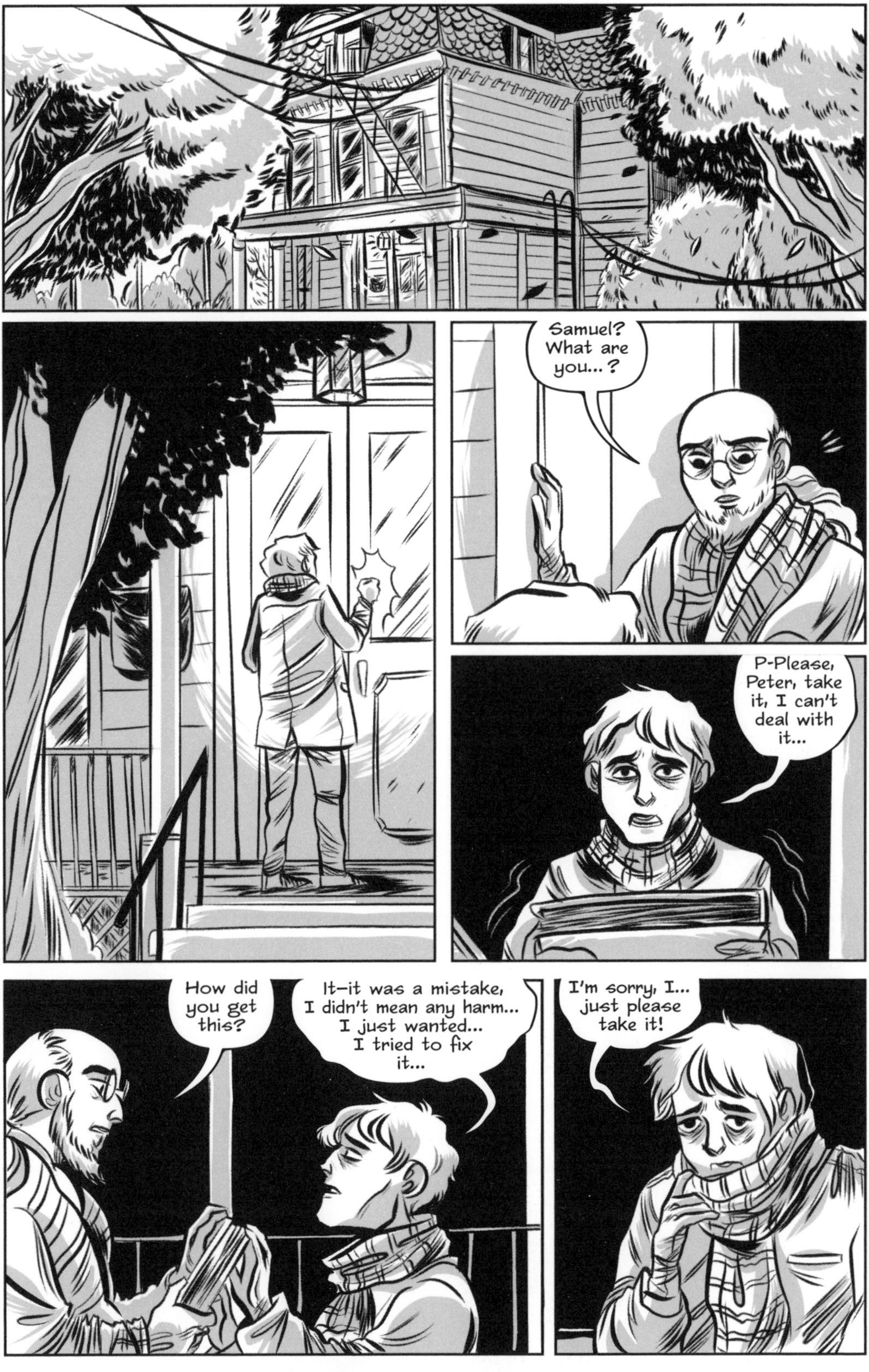
Samuel? What are you...?
P-Please, Peter, take it, I can't deal with it...
How did you get this?
It-it was a mistake, I didn't mean any harm... I just wanted... I tried to fix it...
I'm sorry, I... just please take it!

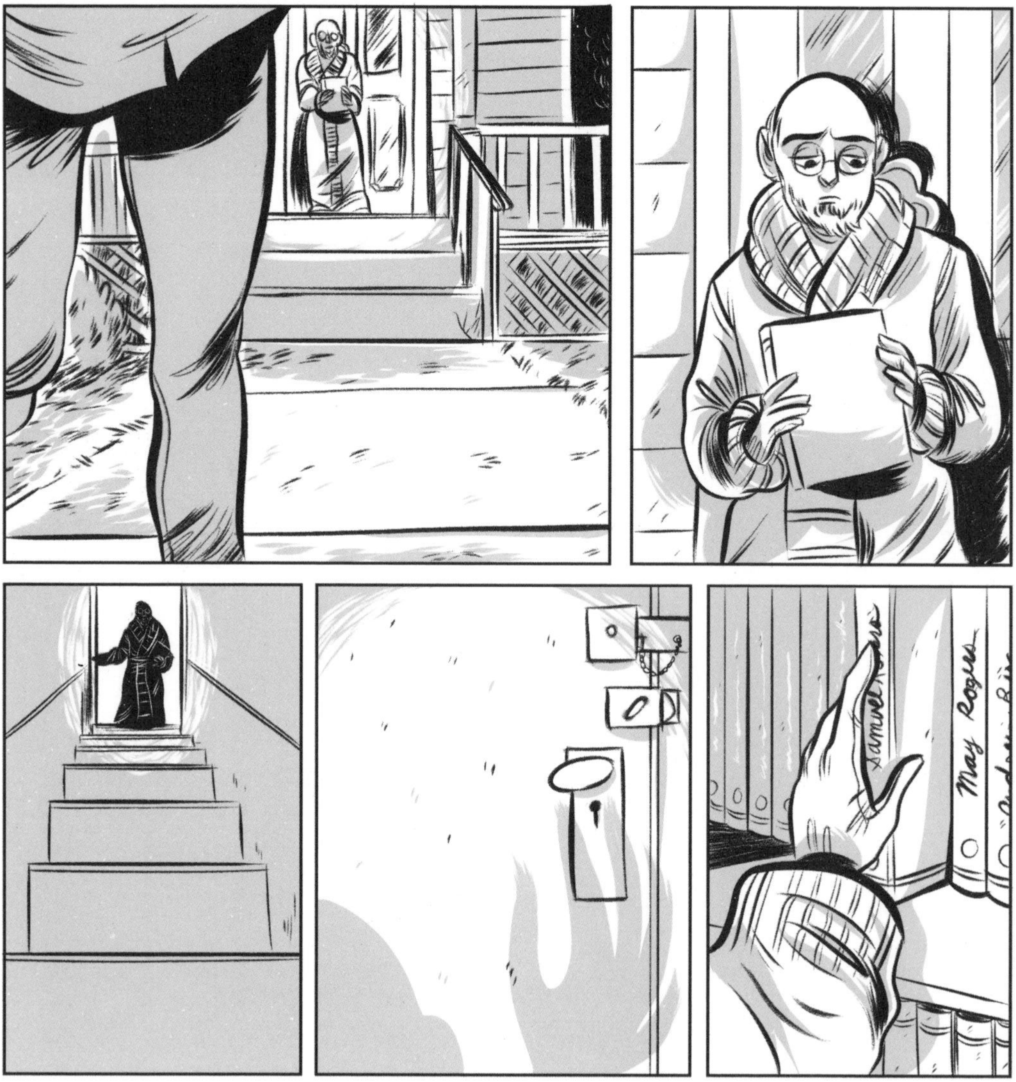
May Rogers

the ALTERED HISTORY of WILLOW SPARKS

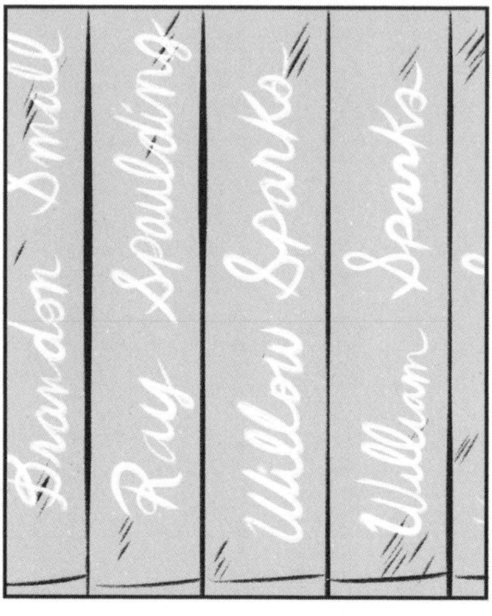
Brandon Small
Ray Spaulding
Willow Sparks
William Sparks

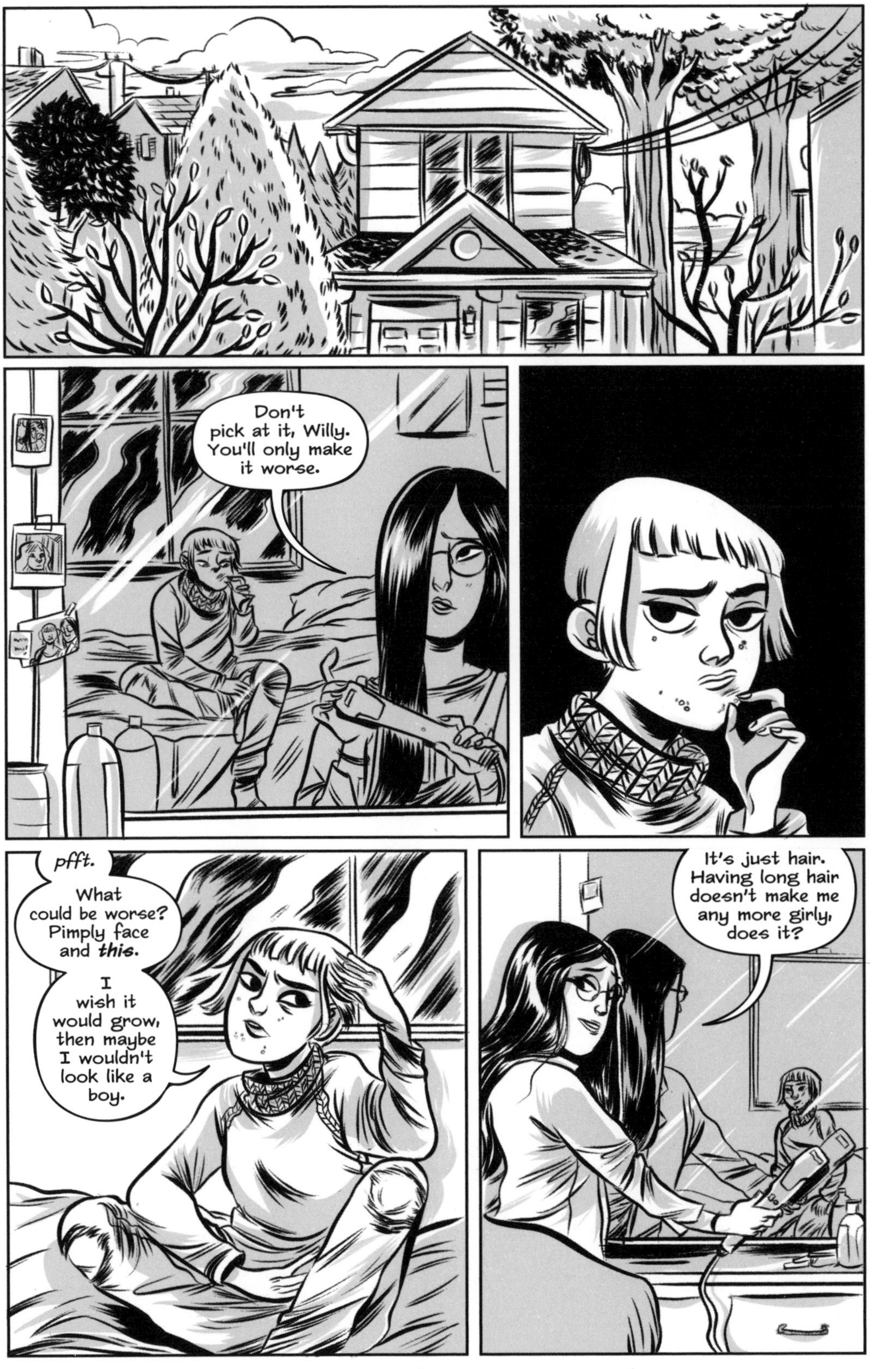
Don't pick at it, Willy. You'll only make it worse.
pfft.
What could be worse? Pimply face and *this*.
I wish it would grow, then maybe I wouldn't look like a boy.
It's just hair. Having long hair doesn't make me any more girly, does it?

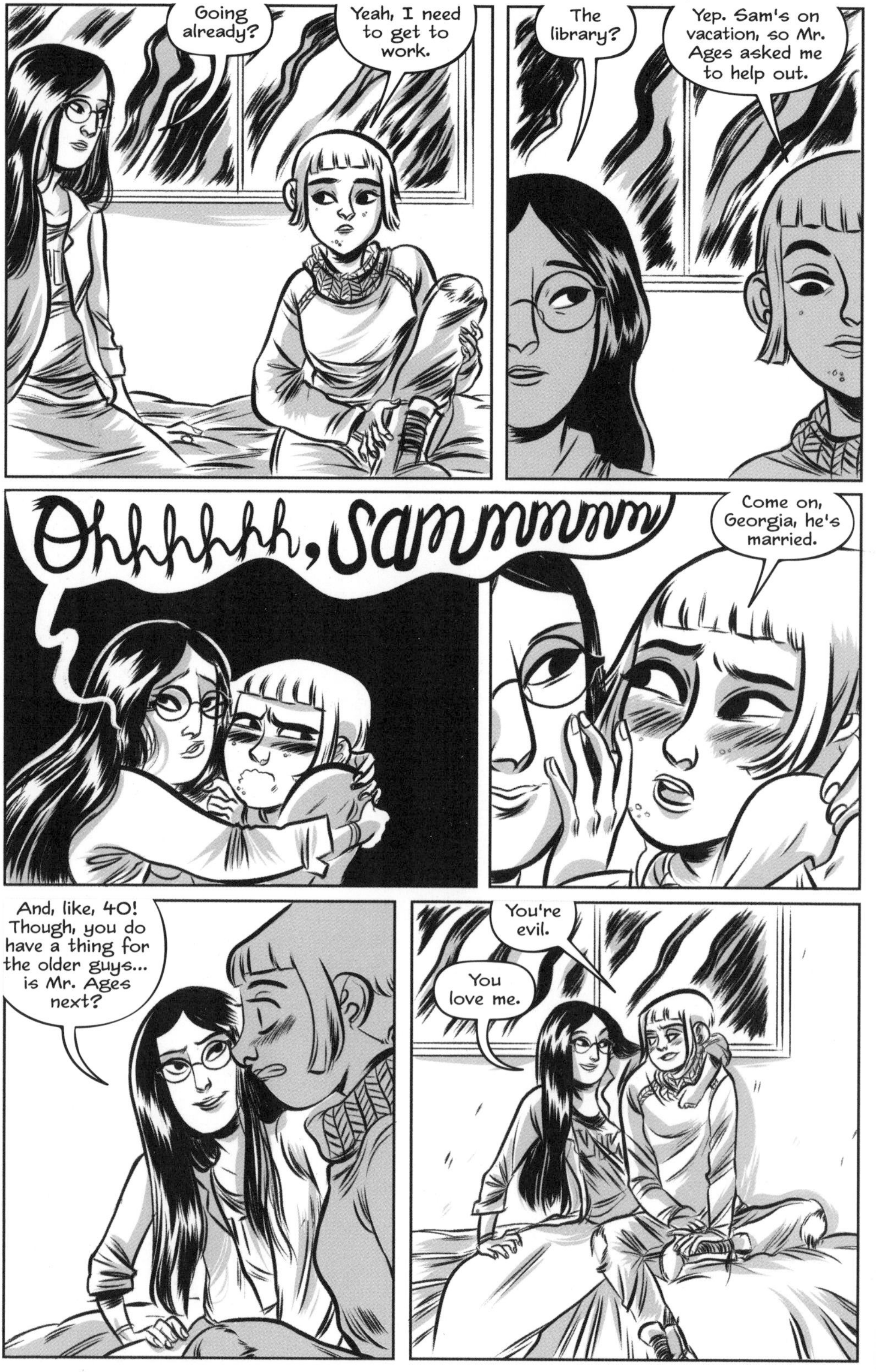
Going already?
Yeah, I need to get to work.
The library?
Yep. Sam's on vacation, so Mr. Ages asked me to help out.
Ohhhhh, Sammmmm
Come on, Georgia, he's married.
And, like, 40! Though, you do have a thing for the older guys... is Mr. Ages next?
You're evil.
You love me.

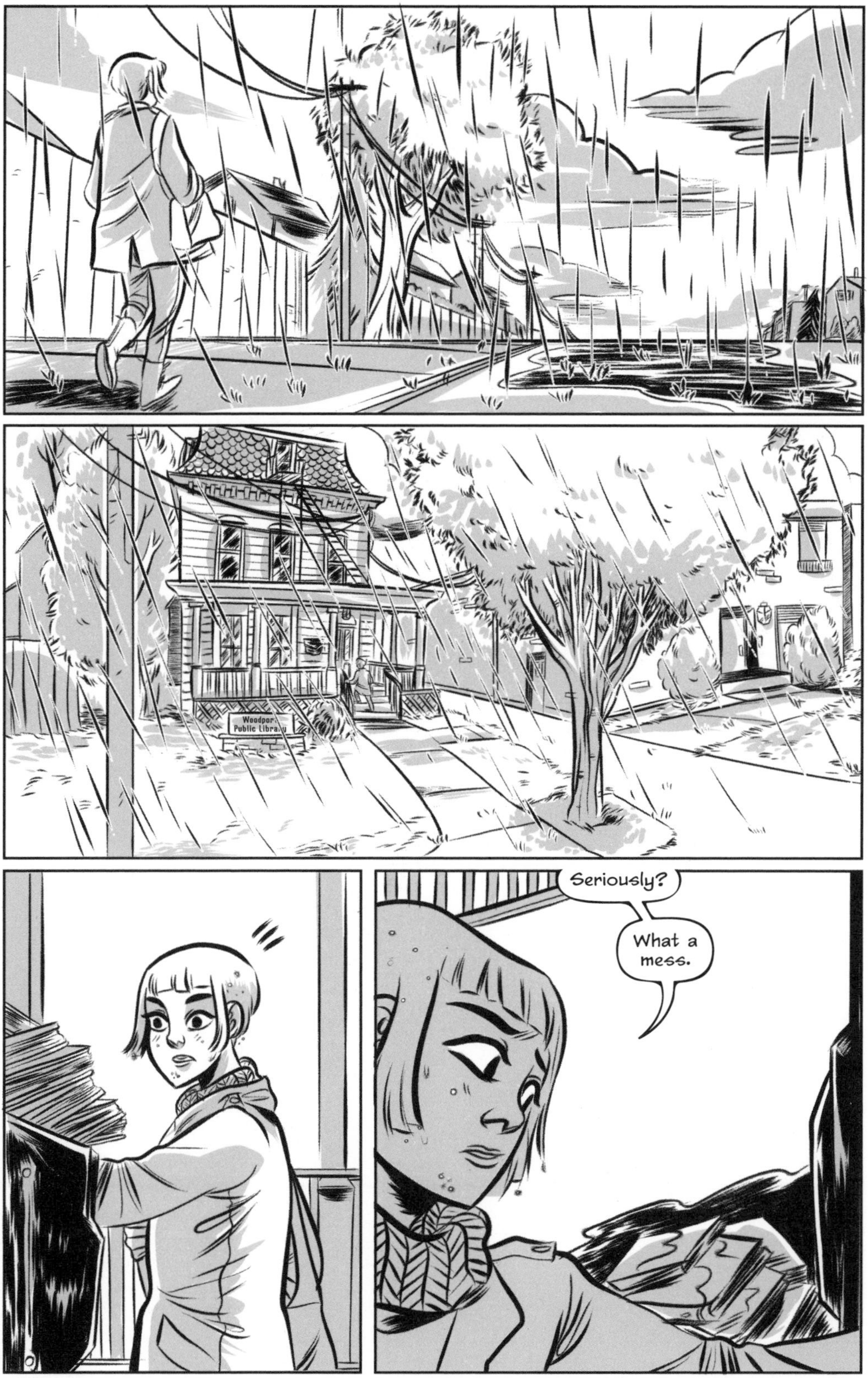
Seriously?
What a mess.

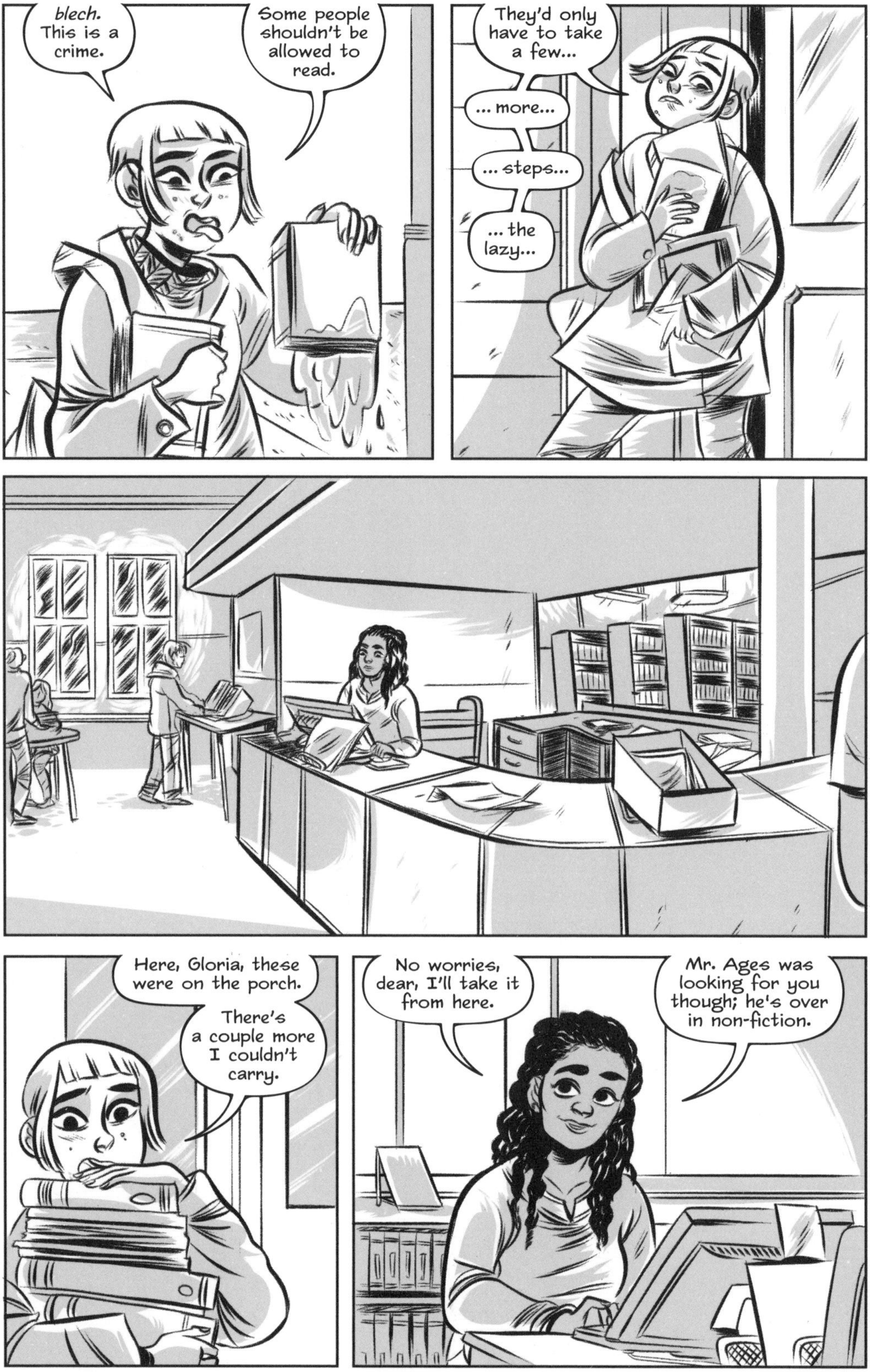
blech. This is a crime.
Some people shouldn't be allowed to read.
They'd only have to take a few...
... more...
... steps...
... the lazy...
Here, Gloria, these were on the porch.
There's a couple more I couldn't carry.
No worries, dear, I'll take it from here.
Mr. Ages was looking for you though; he's over in non-fiction.

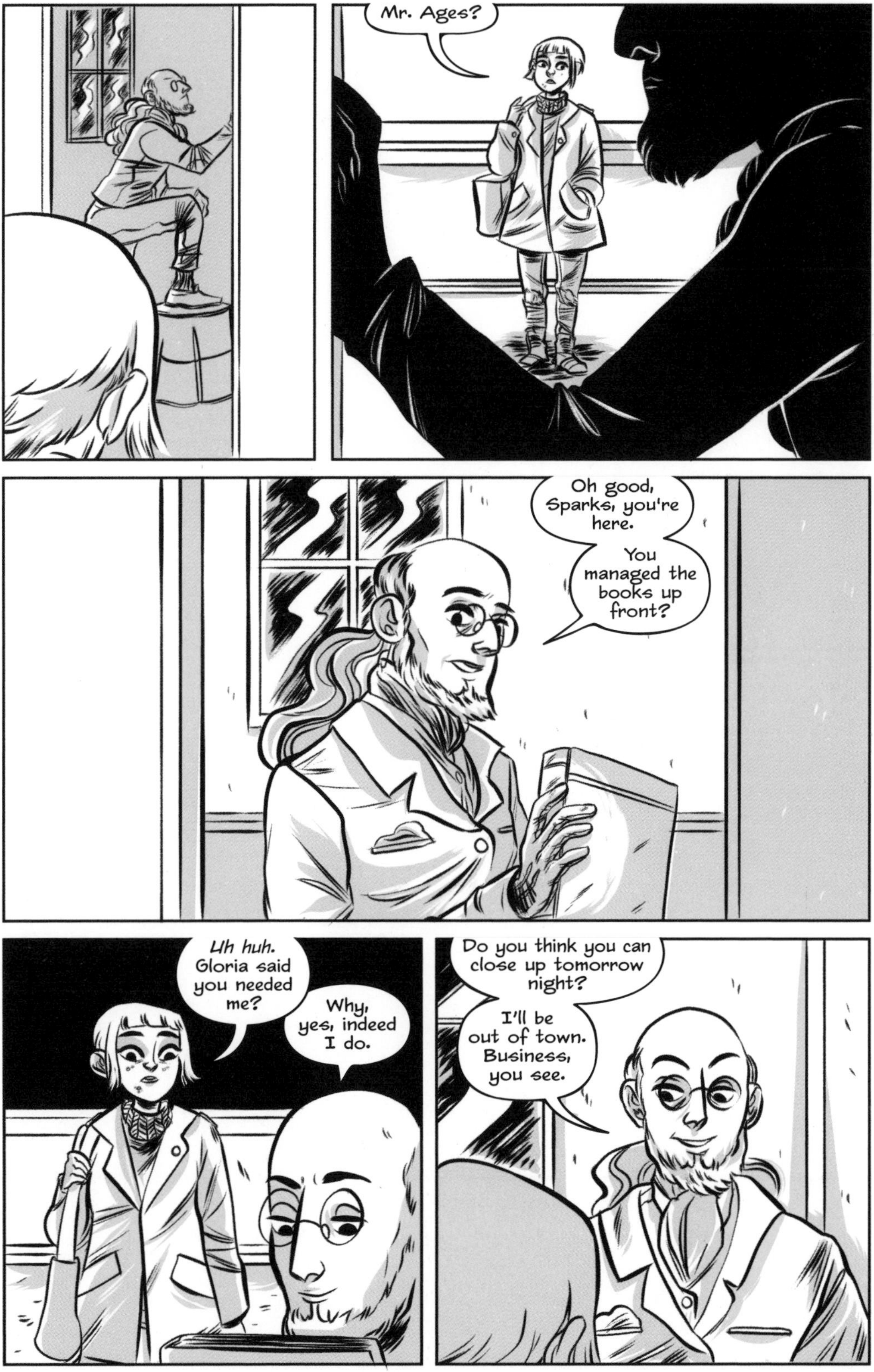

Mr. Ages?
Oh good, Sparks, you're here.
You managed the books up front?
Uh huh. Gloria said you needed me?
Why, yes, indeed I do.
Do you think you can close up tomorrow night?
I'll be out of town. Business, you see.

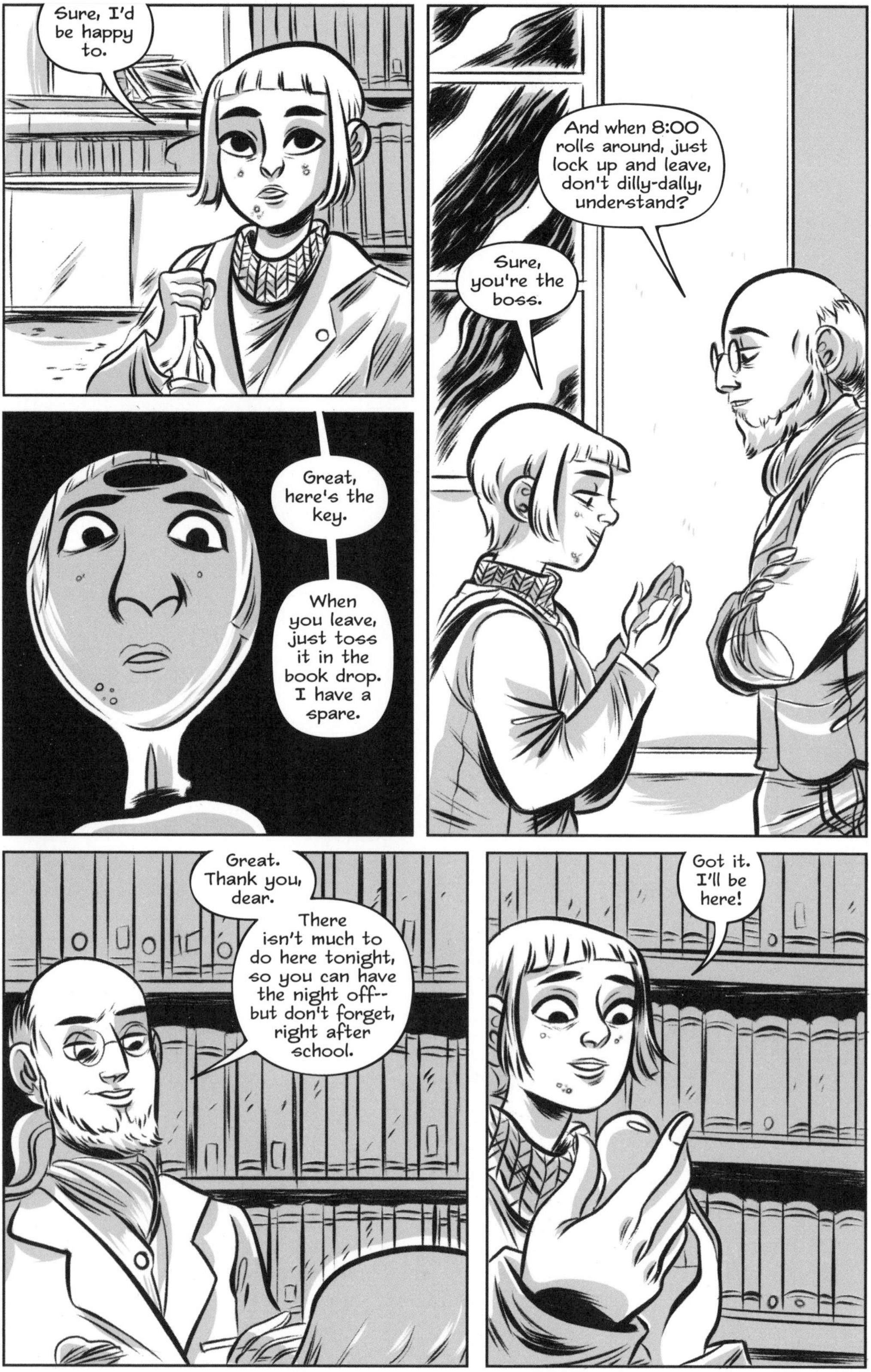

Sure, I'd be happy to.
Great, here's the key.
When you leave, just toss it in the book drop. I have a spare.
And when 8:00 rolls around, just lock up and leave, don't dilly-dally, understand?
Sure, you're the boss.
Great. Thank you, dear.
There isn't much to do here tonight, so you can have the night off-- but don't forget, right after school.
Got it. I'll be here!

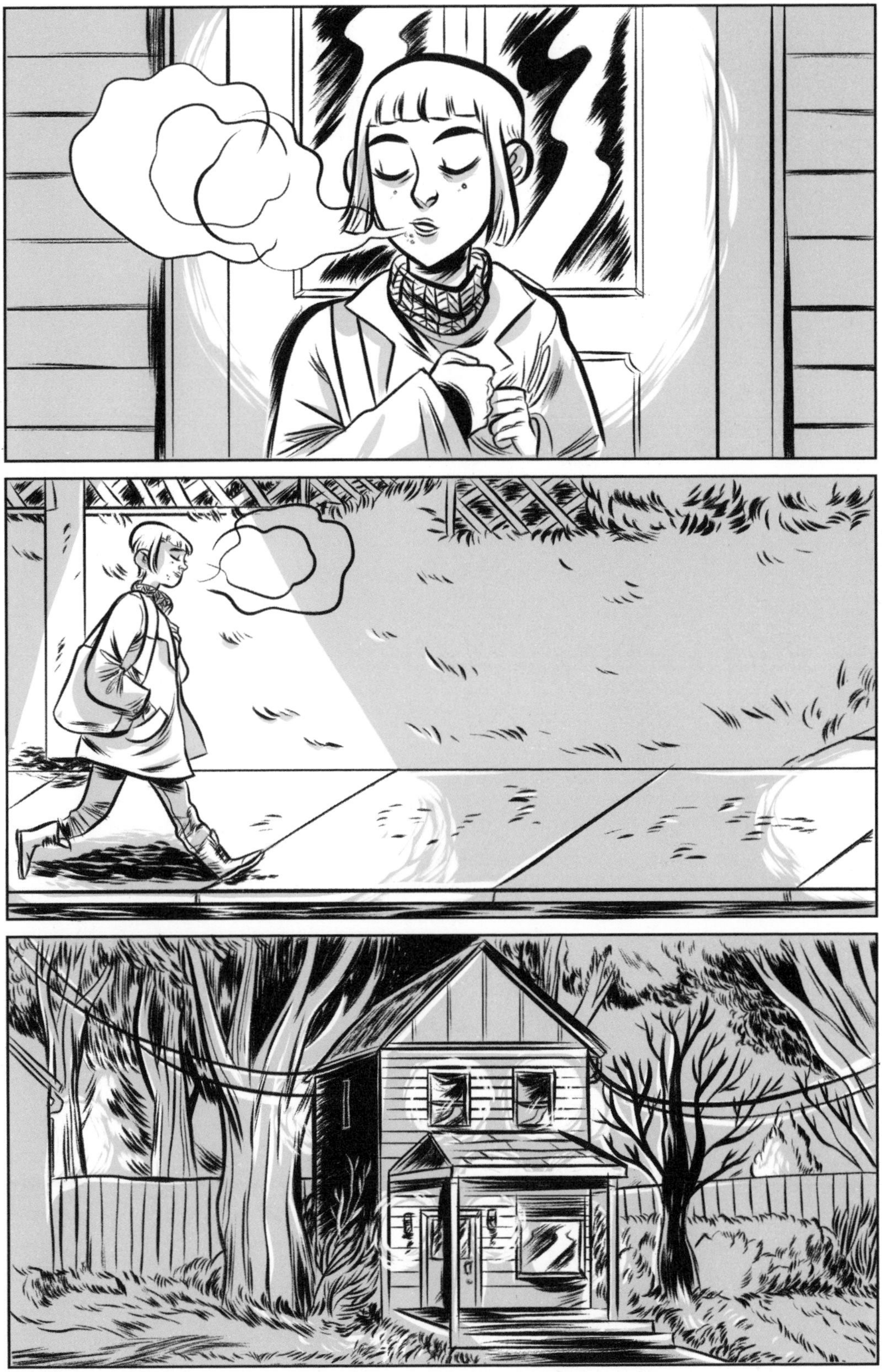

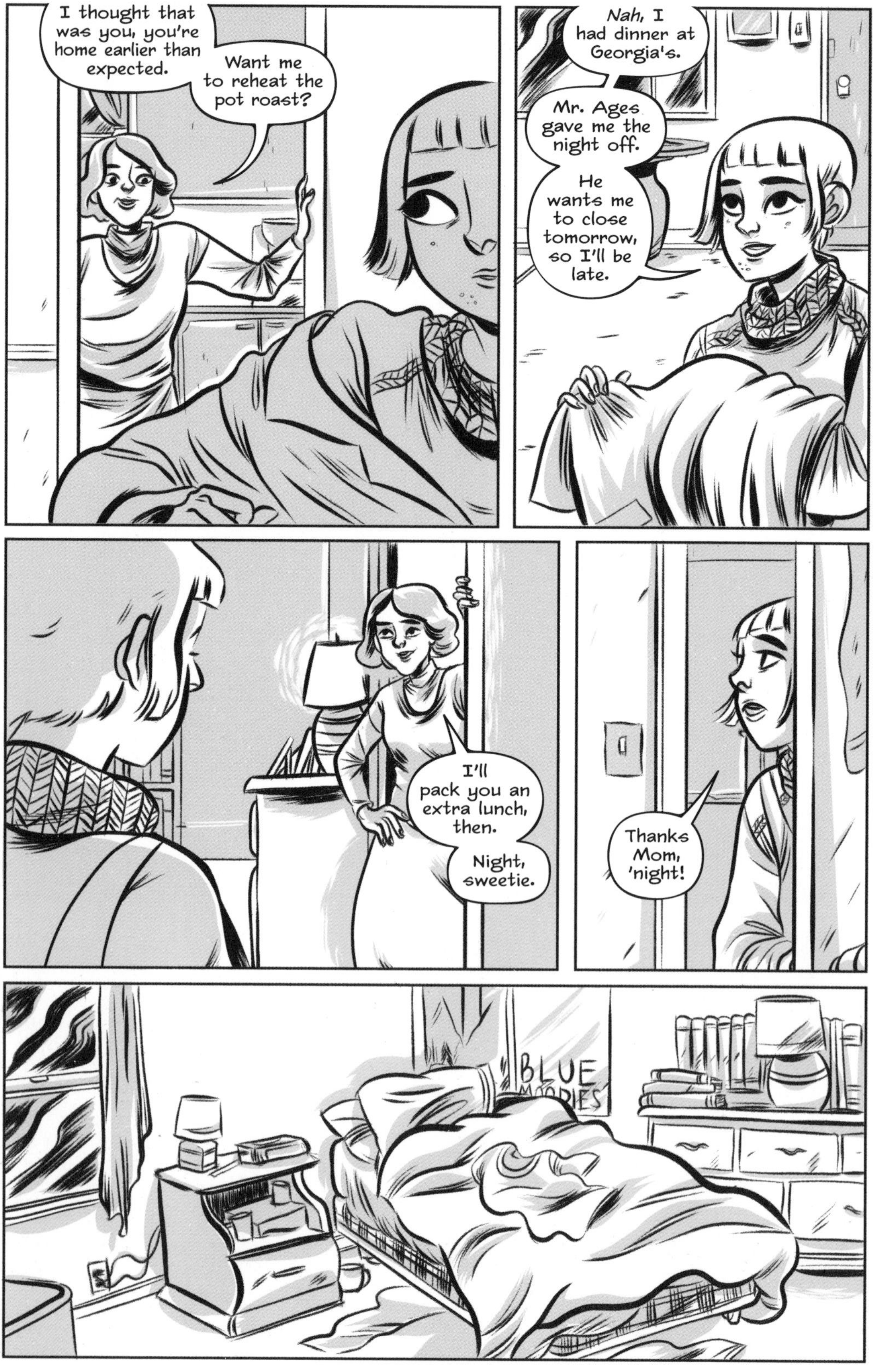
I thought that was you, you're home earlier than expected.
Want me to reheat the pot roast?
Nah, I had dinner at Georgia's.
Mr. Ages gave me the night off.
He wants me to close tomorrow, so I'll be late.
I'll pack you an extra lunch, then.
Night, sweetie.
Thanks Mom, 'night!
BLUE MOODIES

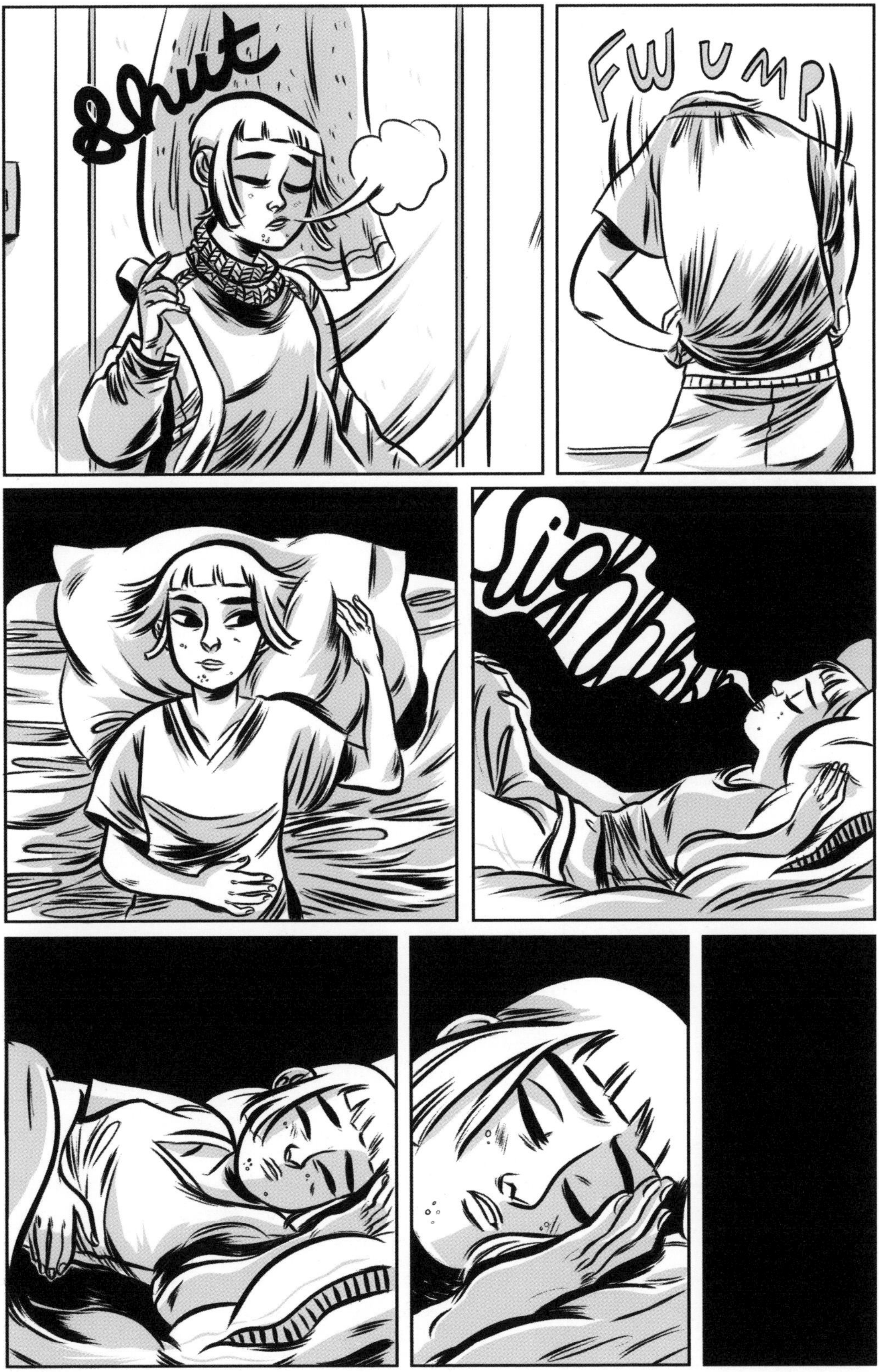
Shut
FWUMP
Sighhh

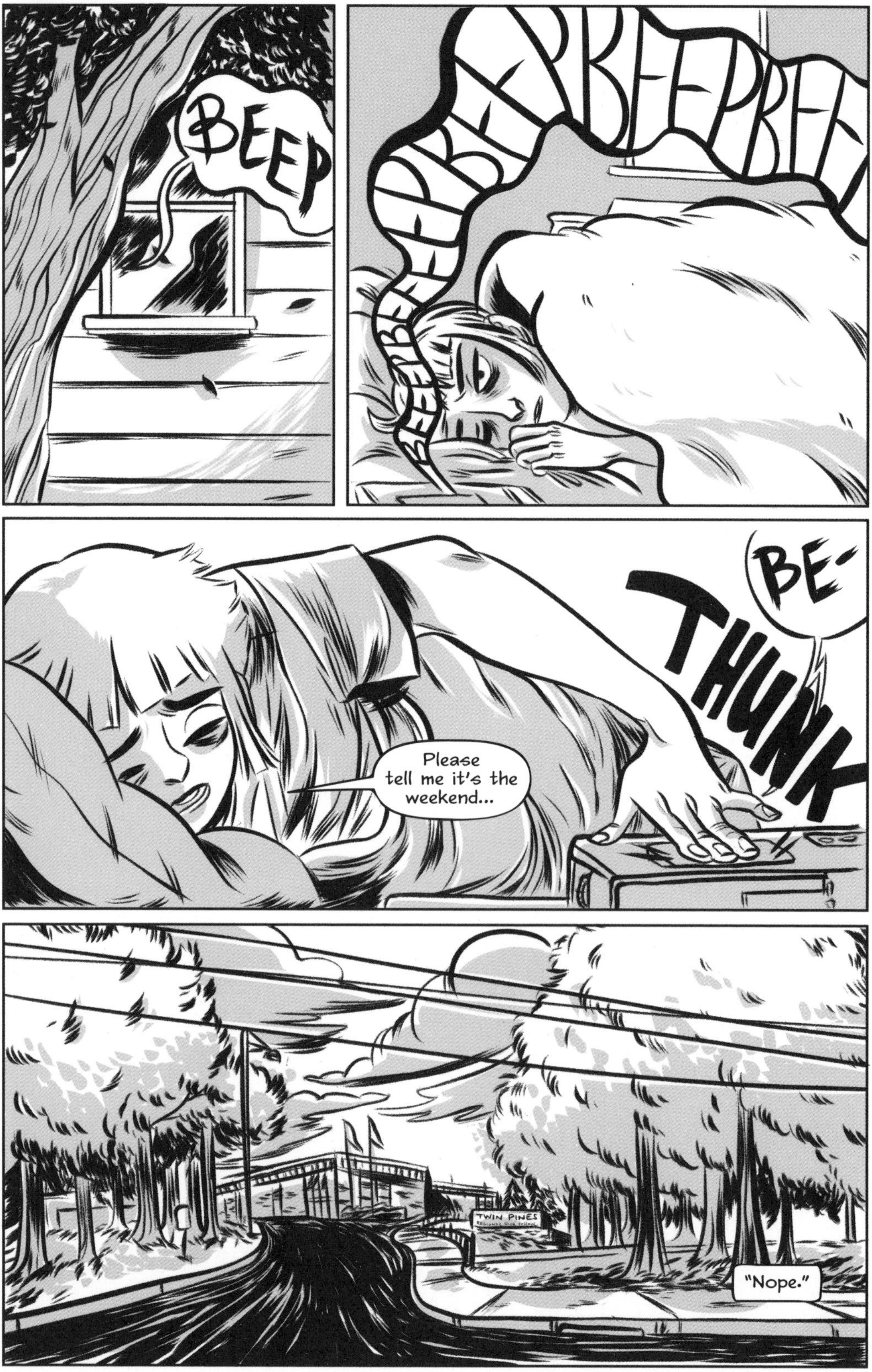
BEEP
BE-THUNK
Please tell me it's the weekend...
TWIN PINES
"Nope."

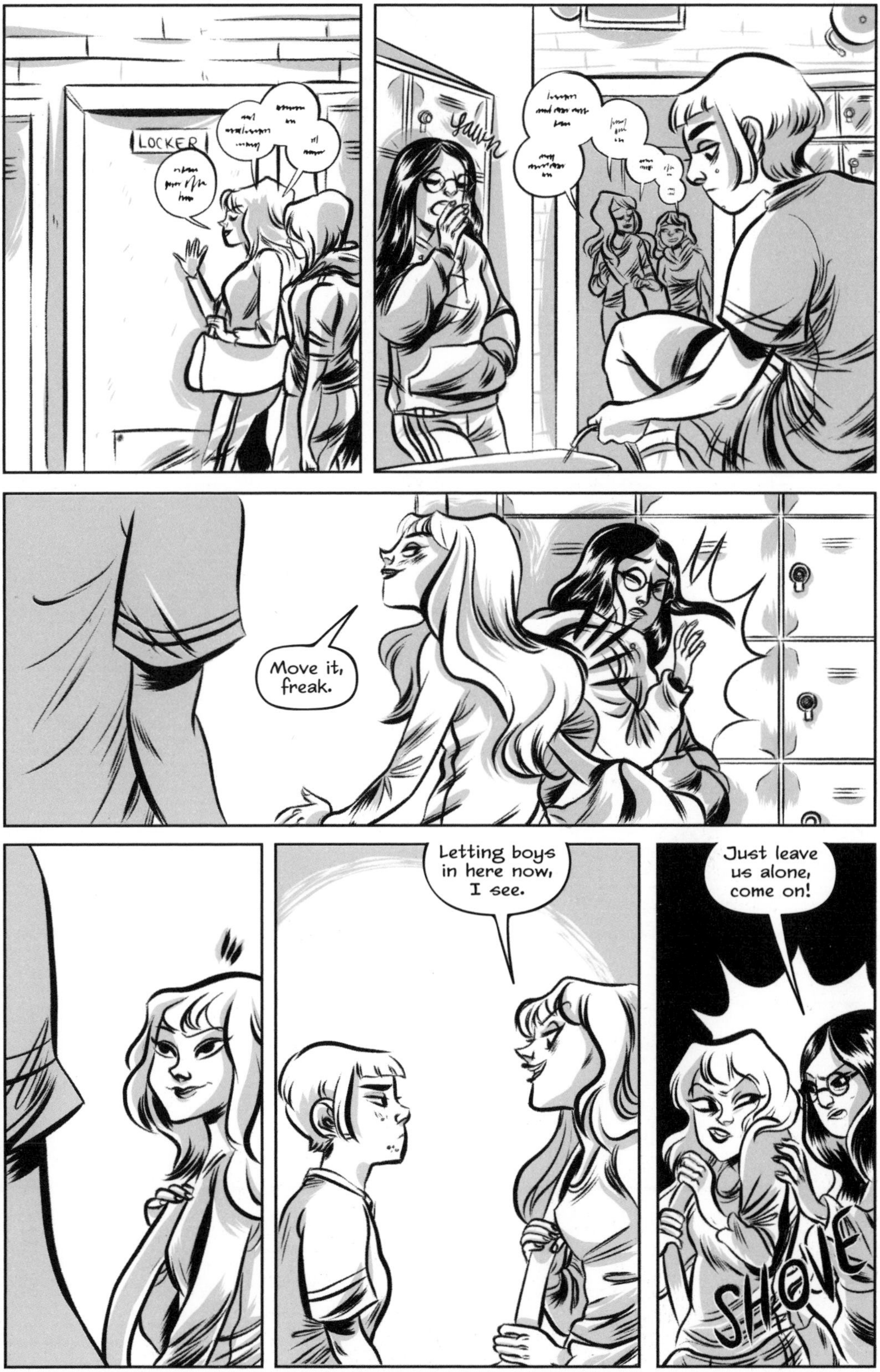

LOCKER
YAWN
Move it, freak.
Letting boys in here now, I see.
Just leave us alone, come on!
SHOVE

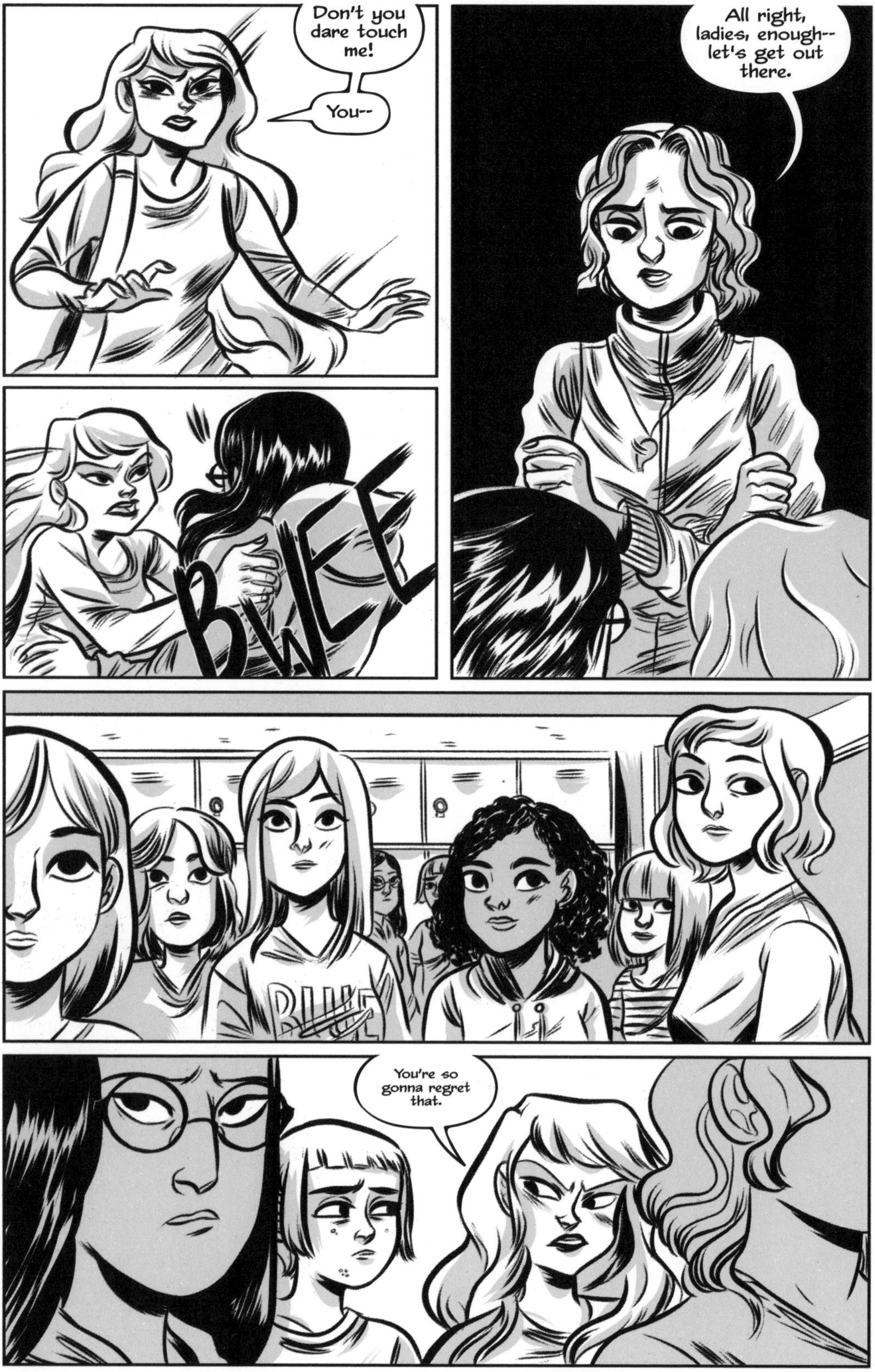
Don't you dare touch me!
You--
BWEE
All right, ladies, enough--let's get out there.
You're so gonna regret that.

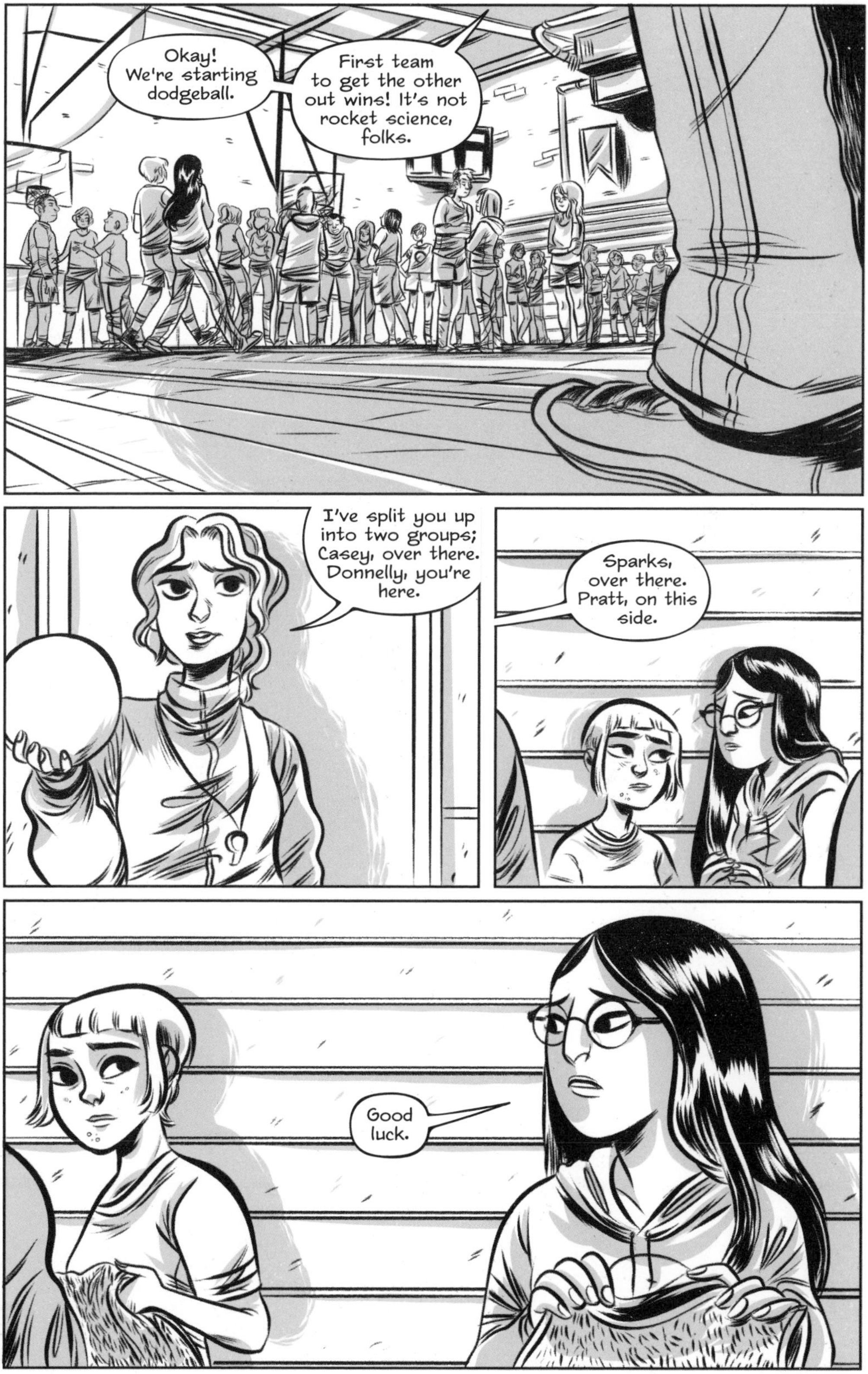
Okay! We're starting dodgeball.
First team to get the other out wins! It's not rocket science, folks.
I've split you up into two groups; Casey, over there. Donnelly, you're here.
Sparks, over there. Pratt, on this side.
Good luck.

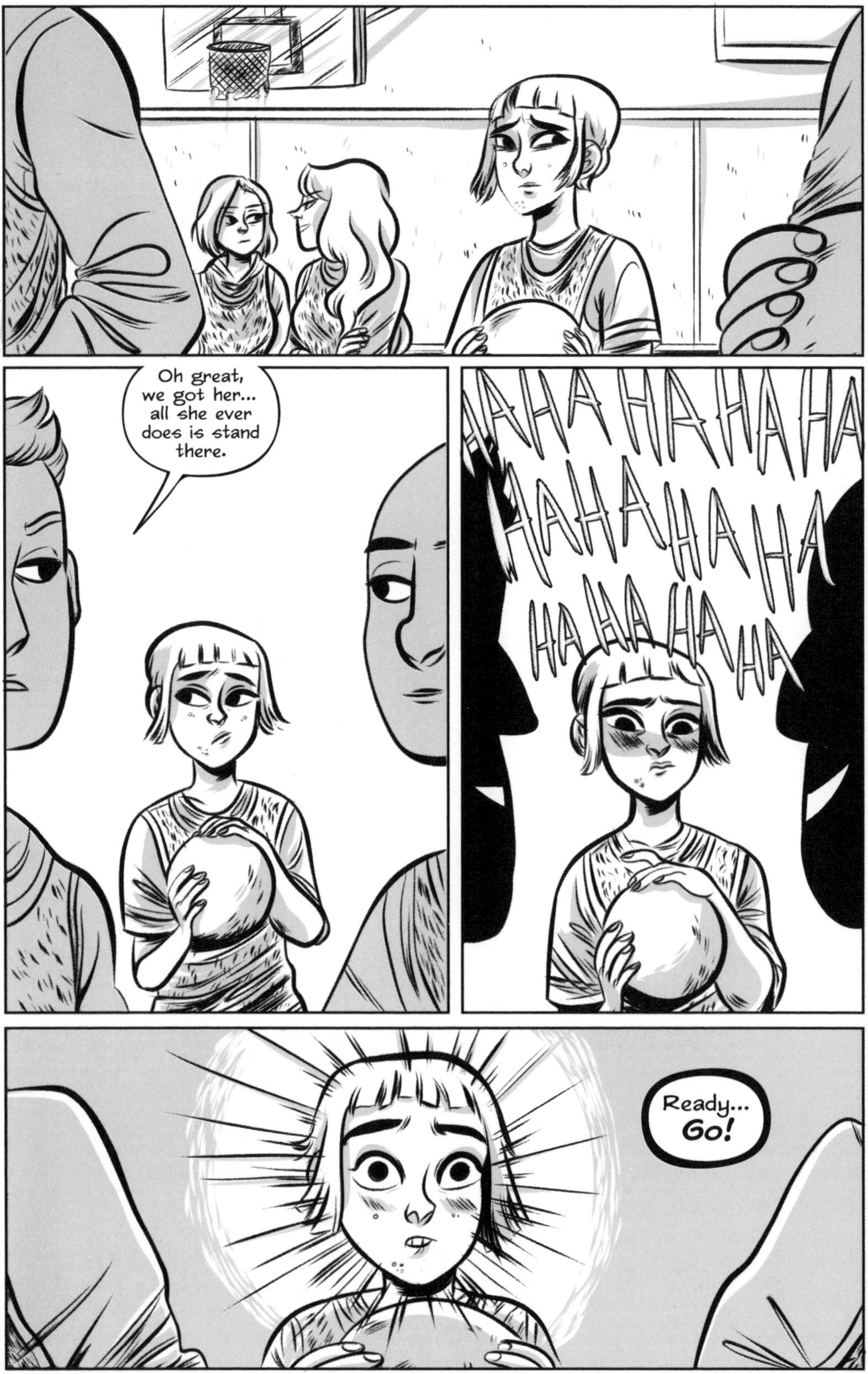
Oh great, we got her... all she ever does is stand there.
HA HA HA HA HA HA HA HA HA HA HA HA HA HA HA HA HA HA HA
Ready... Go!

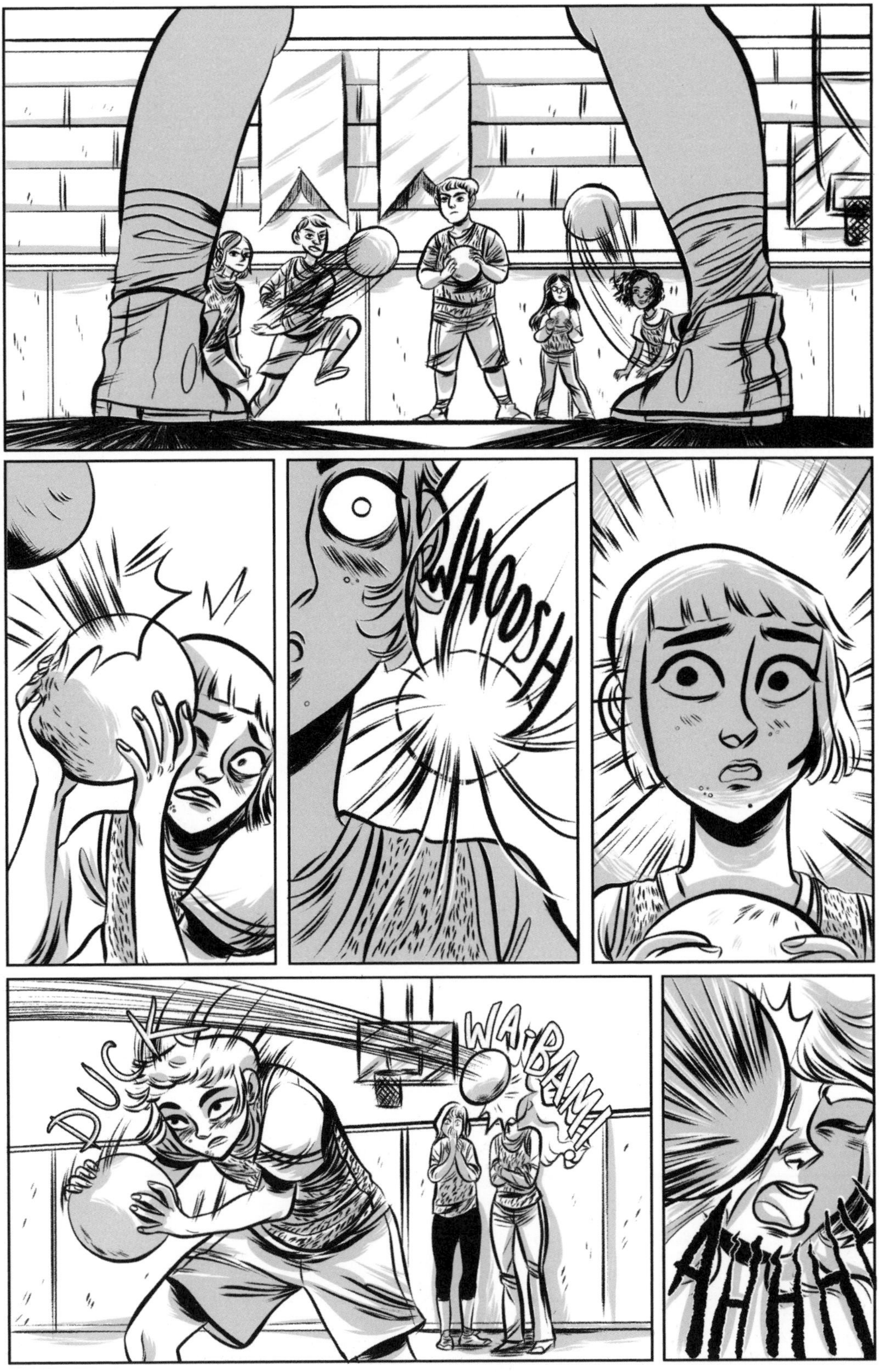
WHOOSH
DUCK
WA-BAM!
AHHH

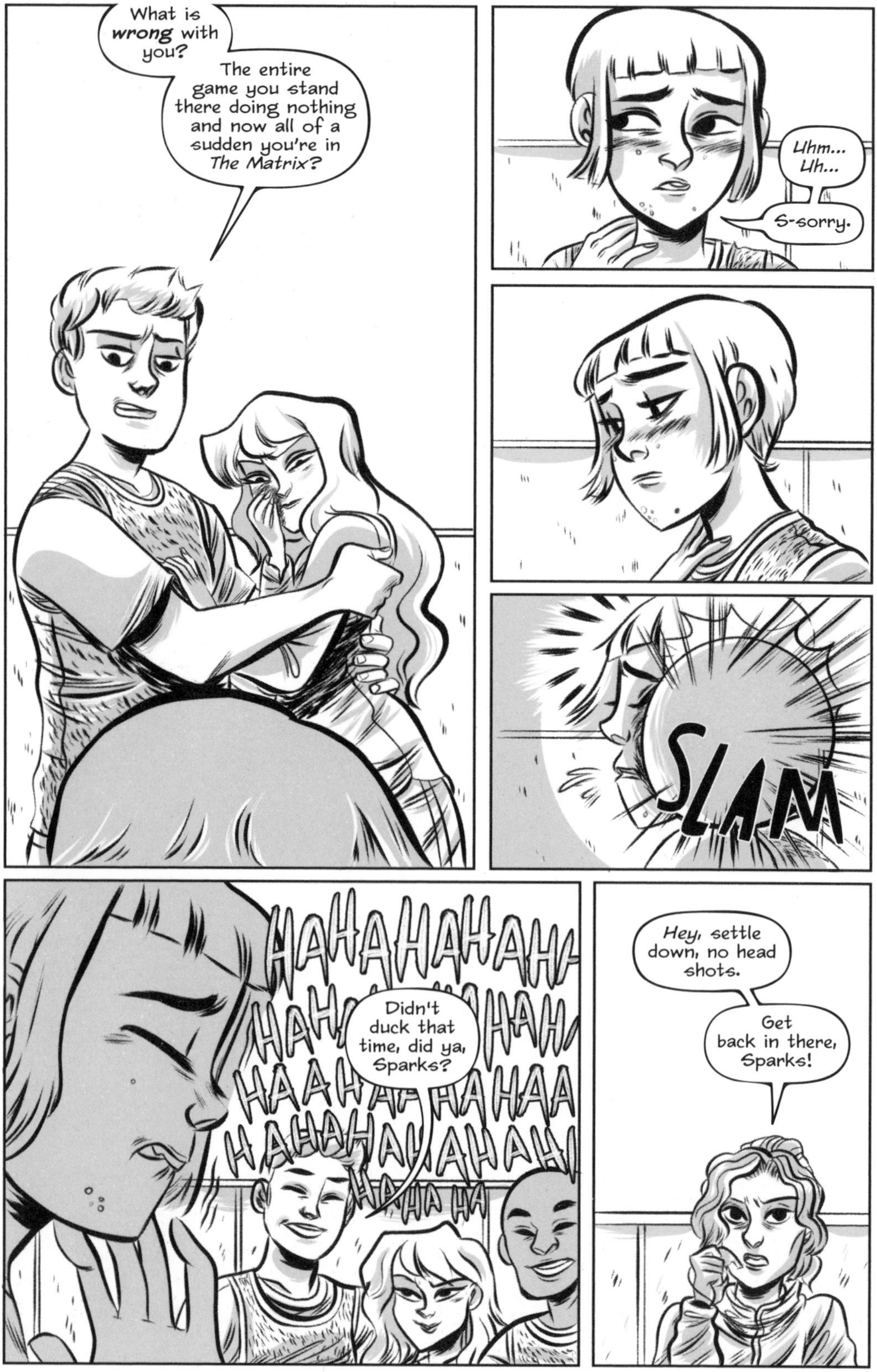
What is ***wrong*** with you?
The entire game you stand there doing nothing and now all of a sudden you're in *The Matrix*?
Uhm... Uh...
S-sorry.
SLAM
HAHAHAHAHAH HAHAHAHAHAH HAAHAHAHAHAA HAHAHAHAHAHI HAHA HA
Didn't duck that time, did ya, Sparks?
Hey, settle down, no head shots.
Get back in there, Sparks!

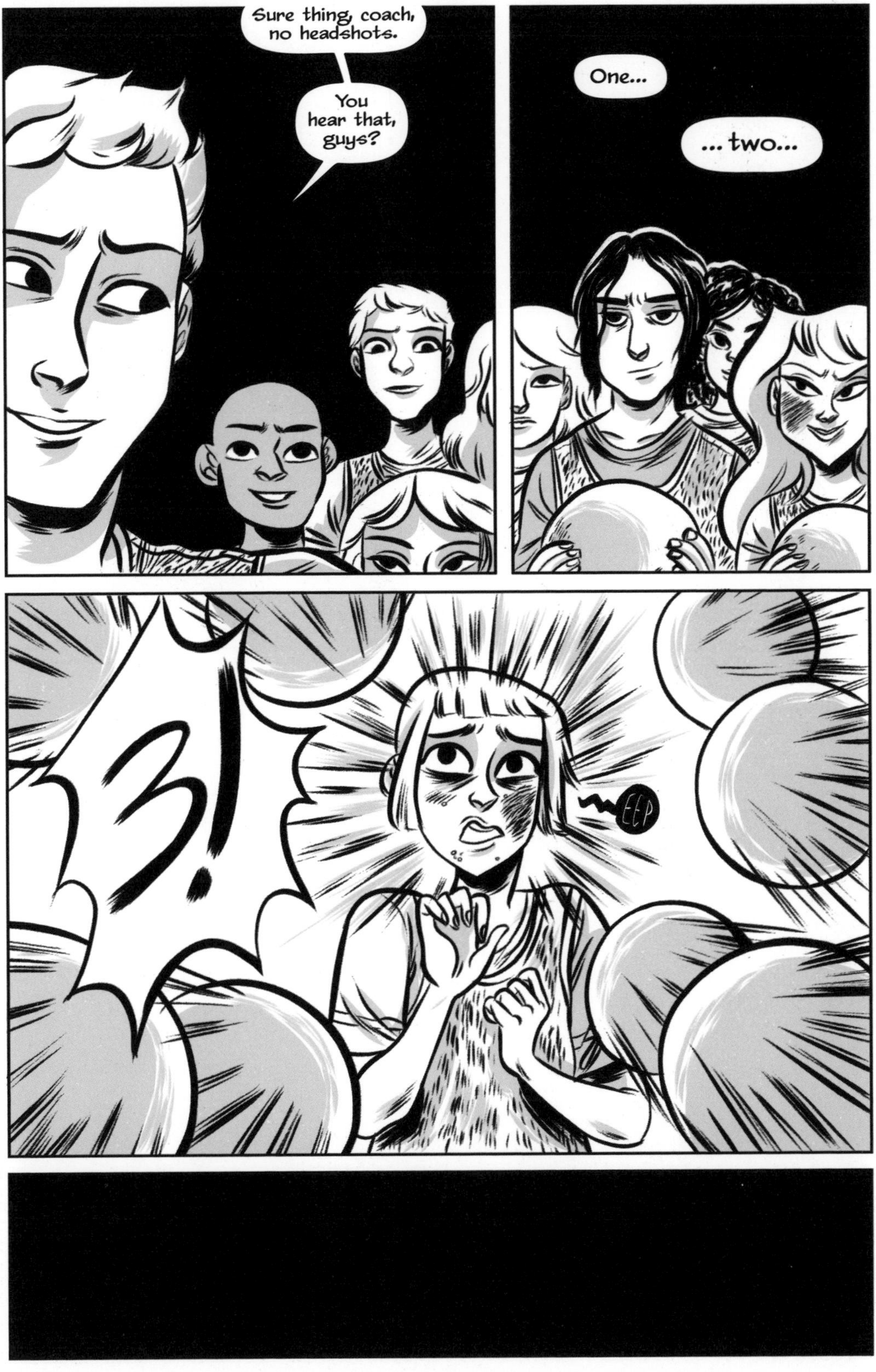
Sure thing, coach, no headshots.
You hear that, guys?
One...
... two...
3!
EEP

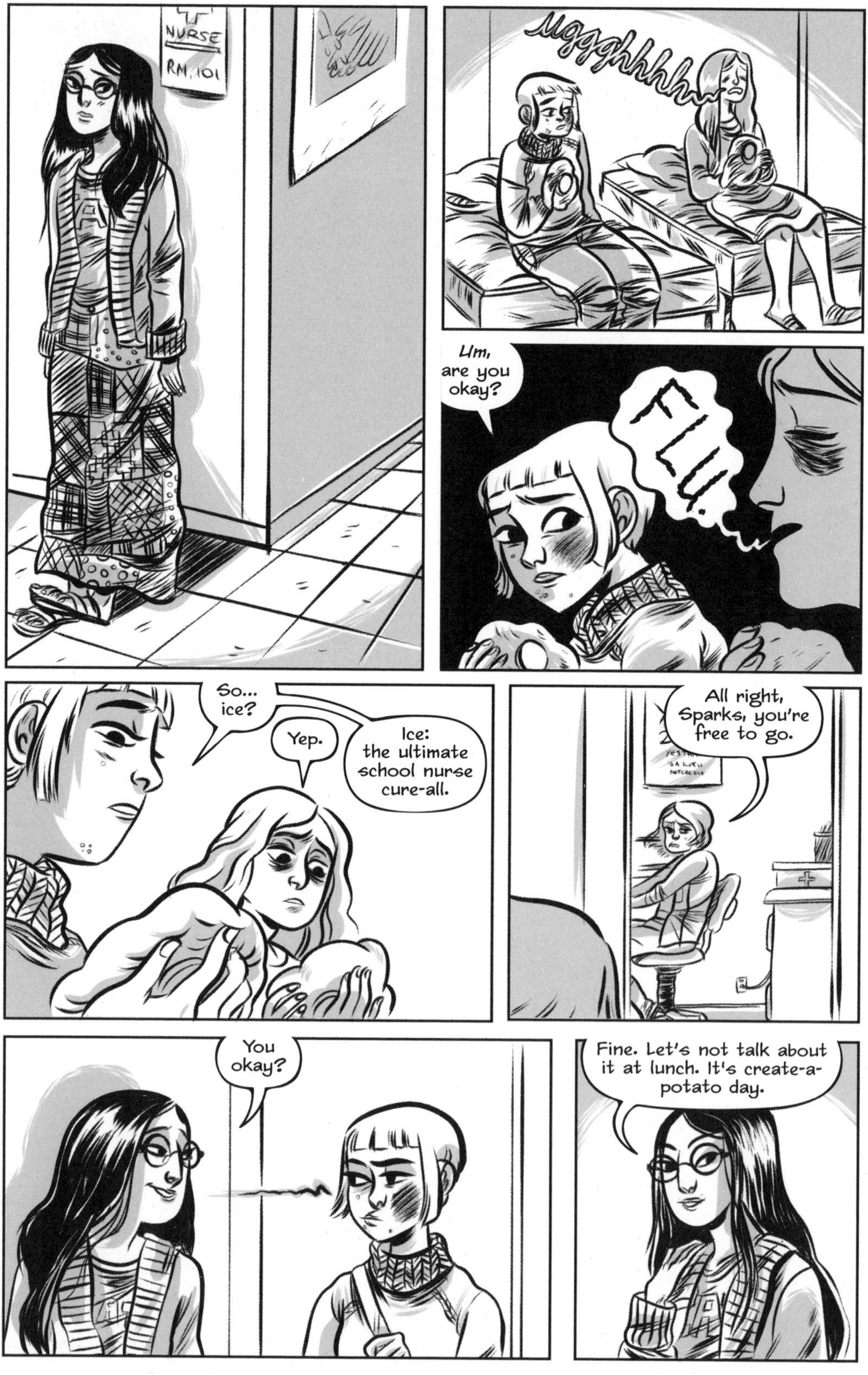
NURSE
RM. 101
ugggghhhhh
Um, are you okay?
FLU.
So... ice?
Yep.
Ice: the ultimate school nurse cure-all.
All right, Sparks, you're free to go.
You okay?
Fine. Let's not talk about it at lunch. It's create-a-potato day.

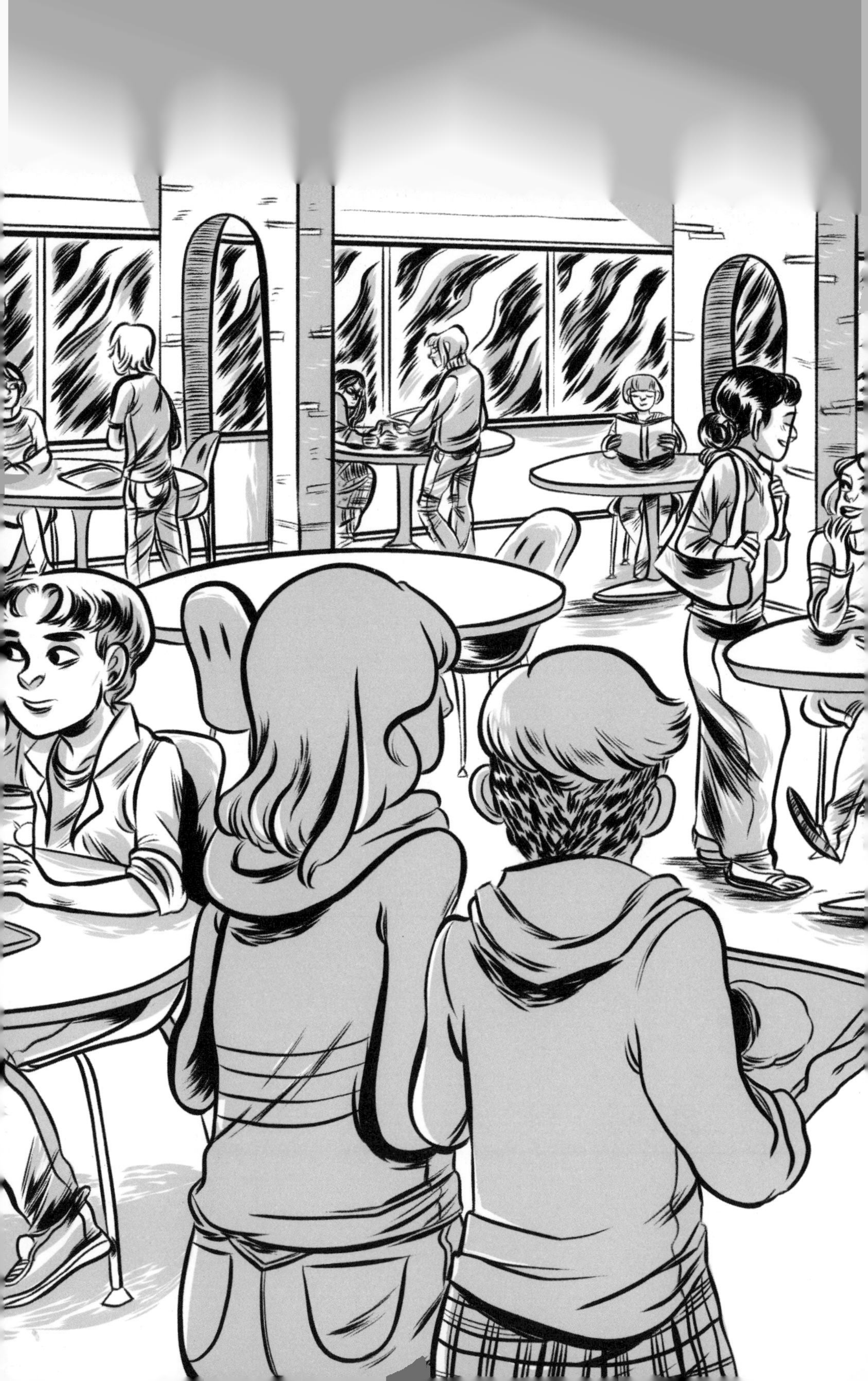

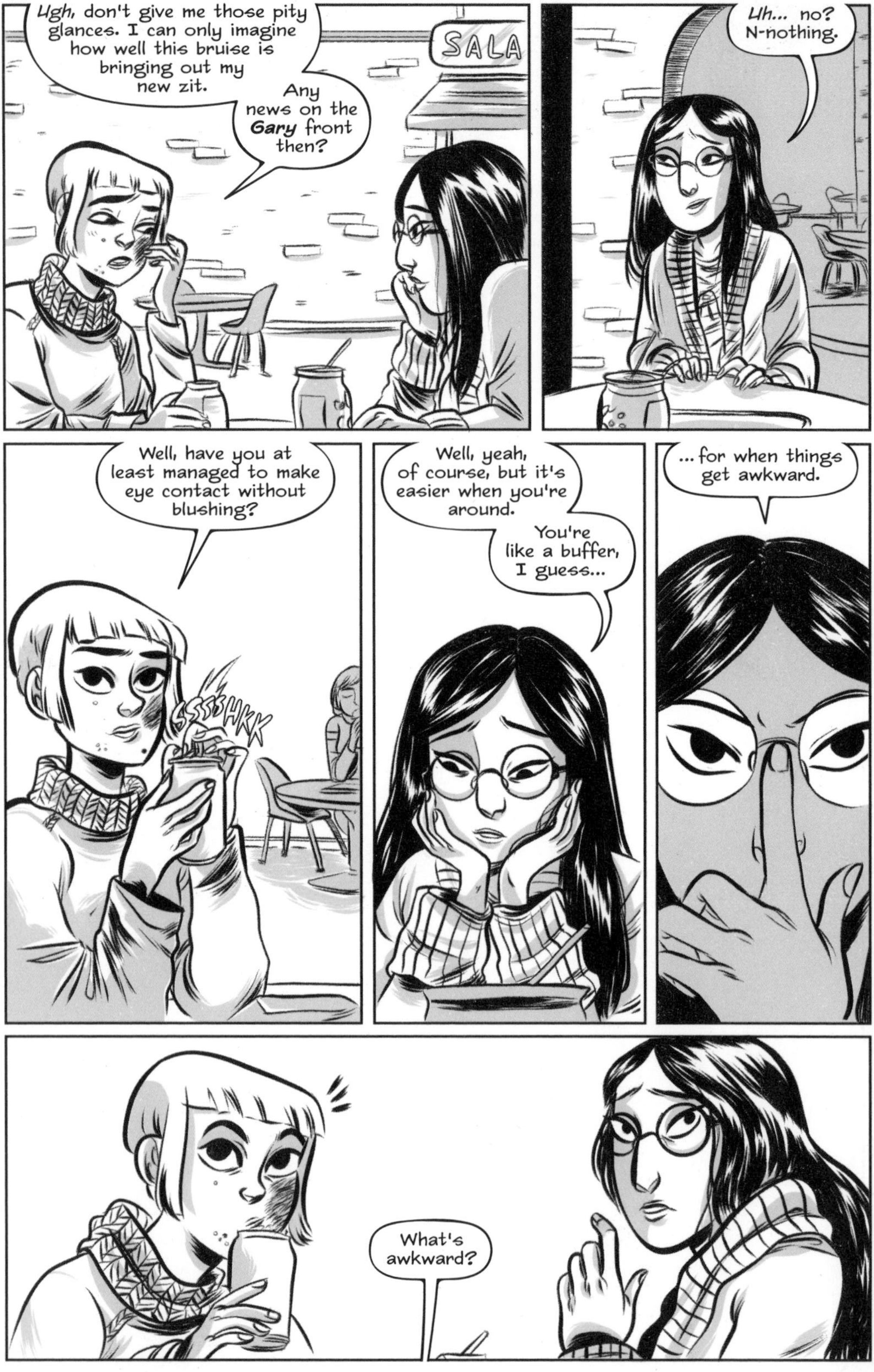
SALA
Ugh, don't give me those pity glances. I can only imagine how well this bruise is bringing out my new zit.
Any news on the Gary front then?
Uh... no? N-nothing.
Well, have you at least managed to make eye contact without blushing?
SSSSHKK
Well, yeah, of course, but it's easier when you're around.
You're like a buffer, I guess...
...for when things get awkward.
What's awkward?

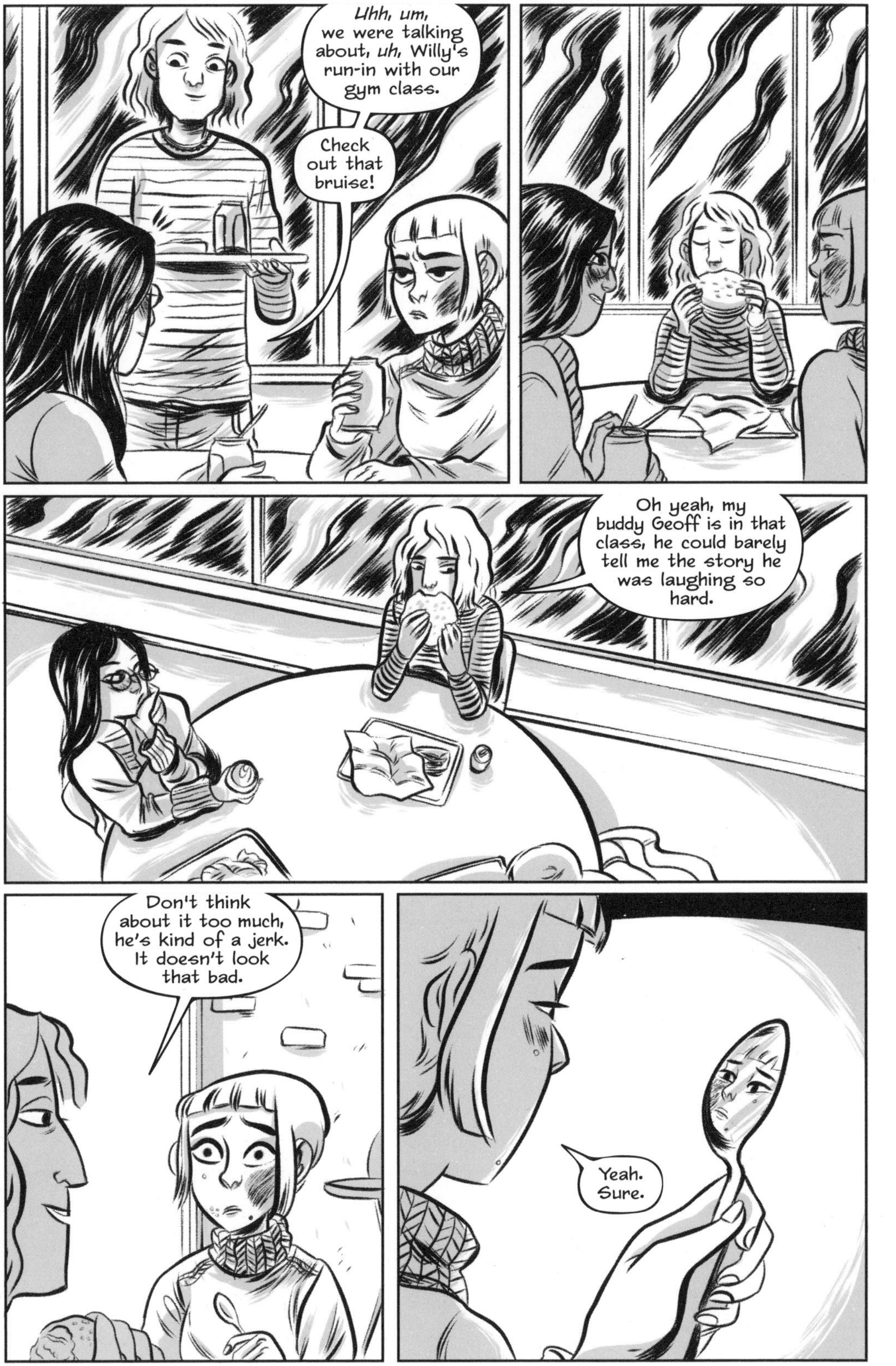

Uhh, um, we were talking about, *uh*, Willy's run-in with our gym class.
Check out that bruise!
Oh yeah, my buddy Geoff is in that class, he could barely tell me the story he was laughing so hard.
Don't think about it too much, he's kind of a jerk. It doesn't look that bad.
Yeah. Sure.

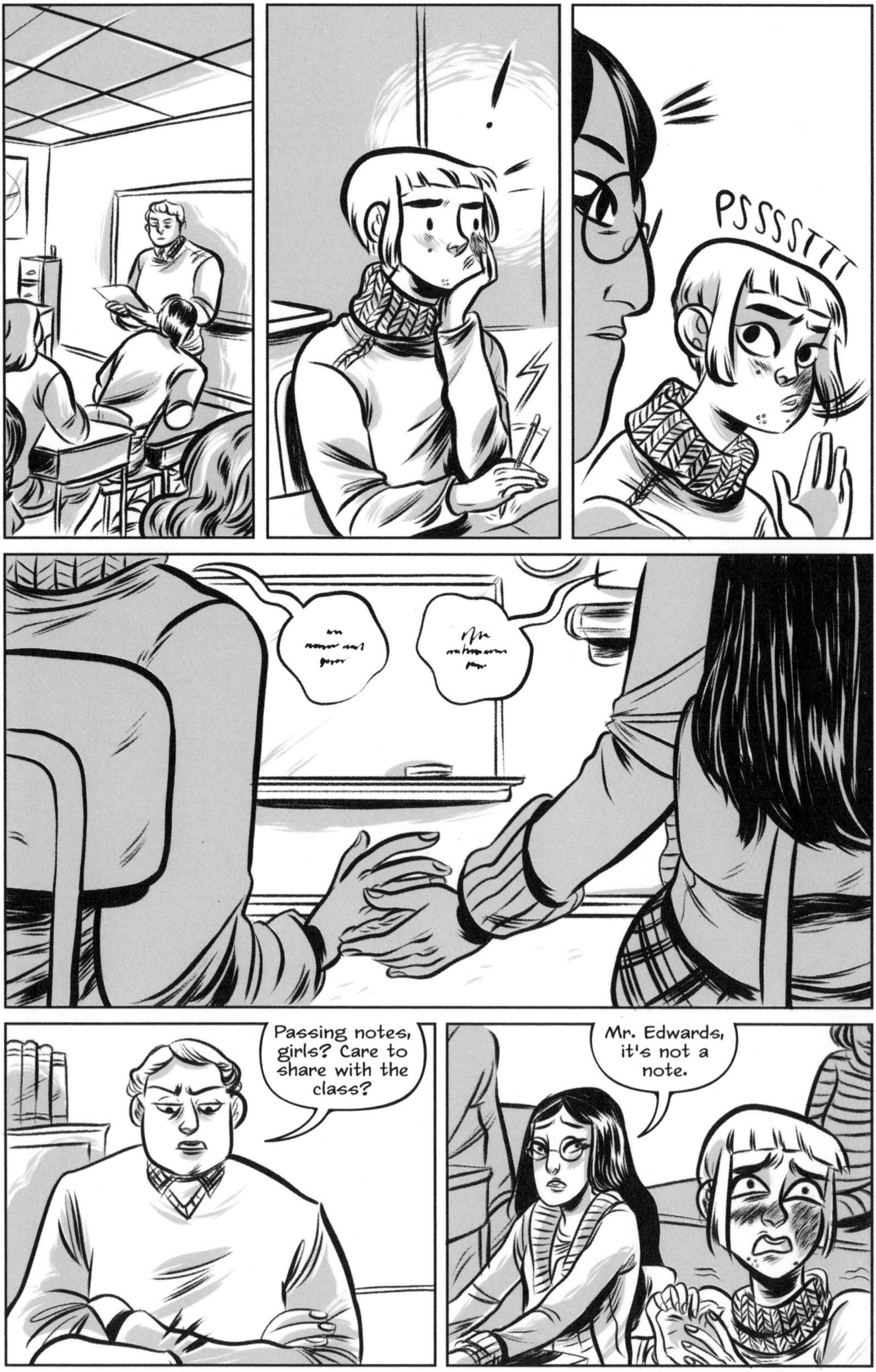
PSSSSTTT
Passing notes, girls? Care to share with the class?
Mr. Edwards, it's not a note.

Thank you, Miss Pratt, but I believe I can handle this.

Well. Hand it over.

Sir, please... it's--

Now.

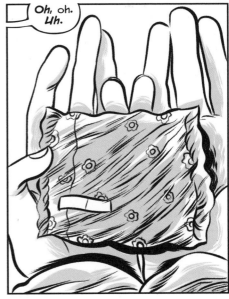

Oh, oh. Uh.

HA HA HA HA HA HA HA HA HA HA HA HA HA HA HA HA HA HA HA HA HA HA HA HA HA HA HA HA HA HA HA HA HA HA

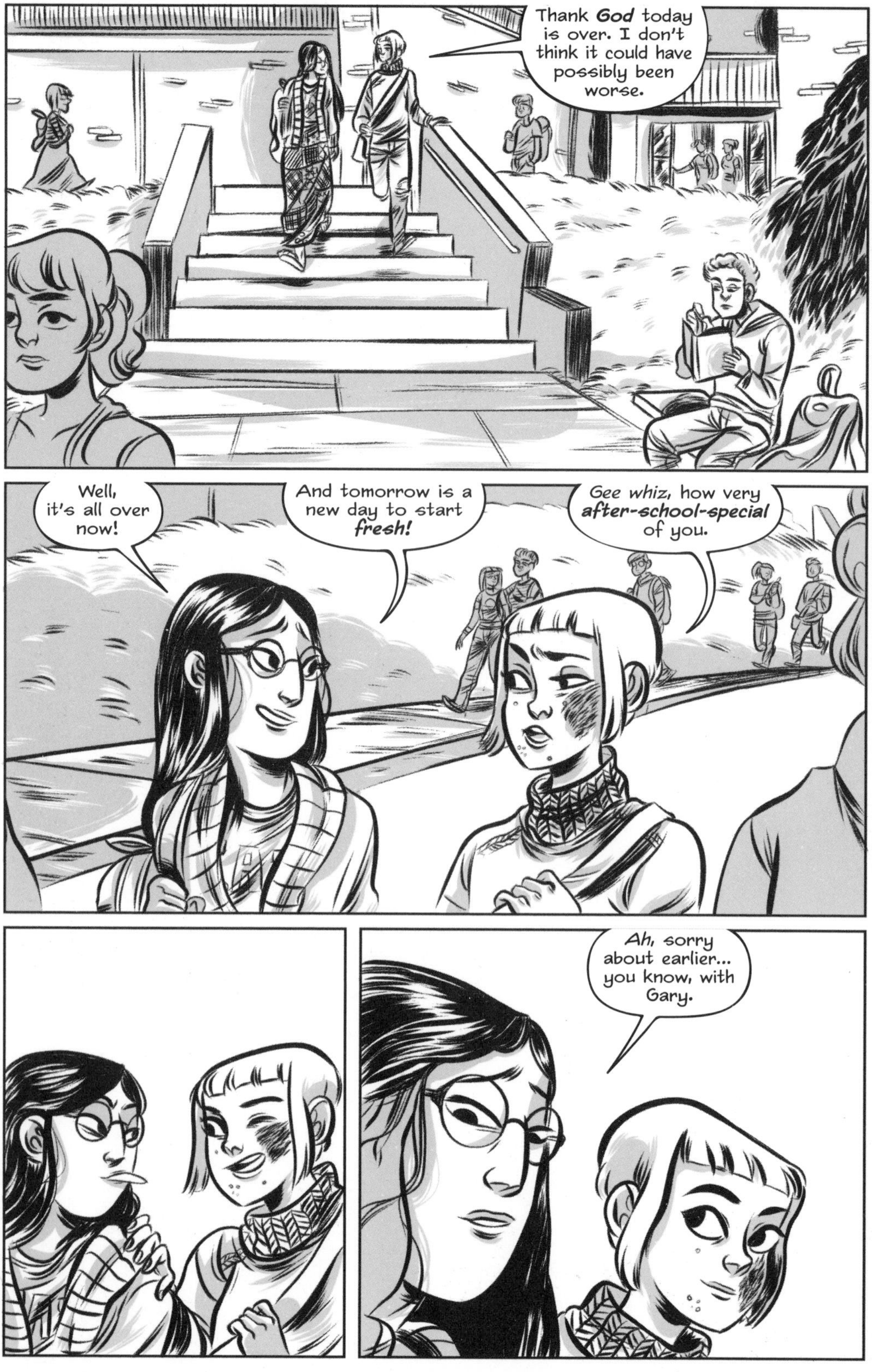
Thank **God** today is over. I don't think it could have possibly been worse.
Well, it's all over now!
And tomorrow is a new day to start ***fresh!***
Gee *whiz*, how very ***after-school-special*** of you.
Ah, sorry about earlier... you know, with Gary.

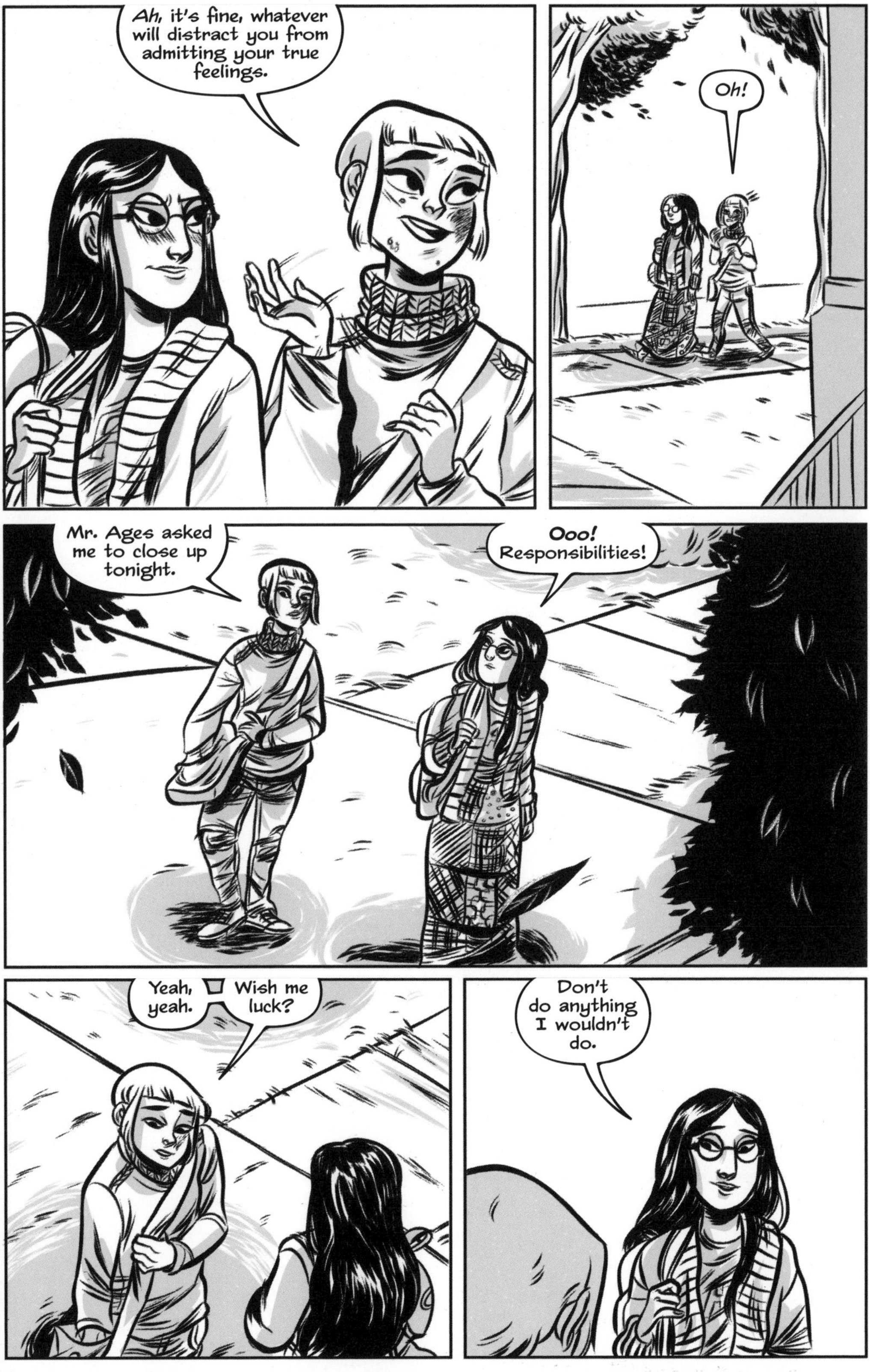
Ah, it's fine, whatever will distract you from admitting your true feelings.
Oh!
Mr. Ages asked me to close up tonight.
Ooo! Responsibilities!
Yeah, yeah.
Wish me luck?
Don't do anything I wouldn't do.

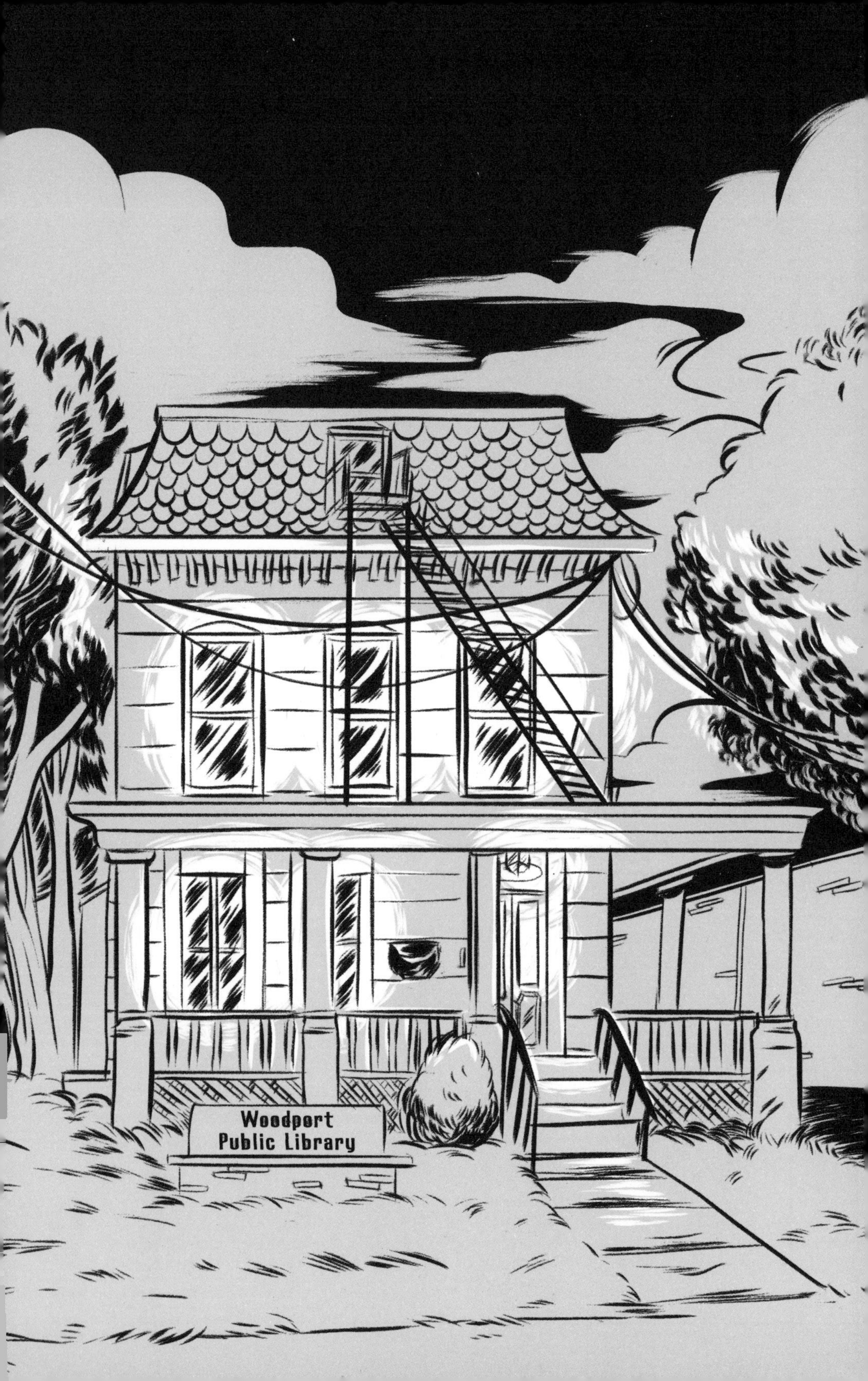
Woodport
Public Library

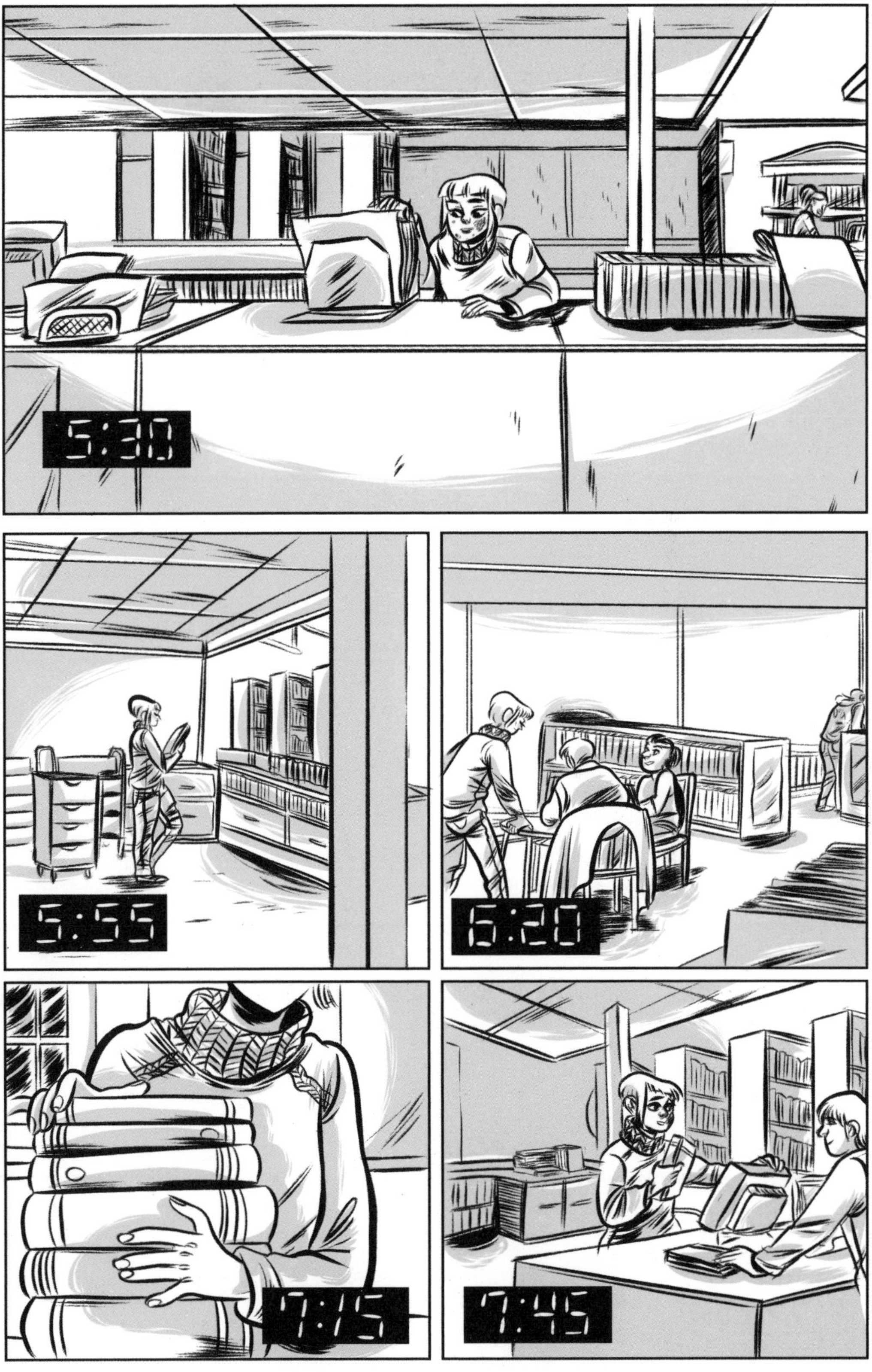
5:30
5:55
6:20
7:15
7:45

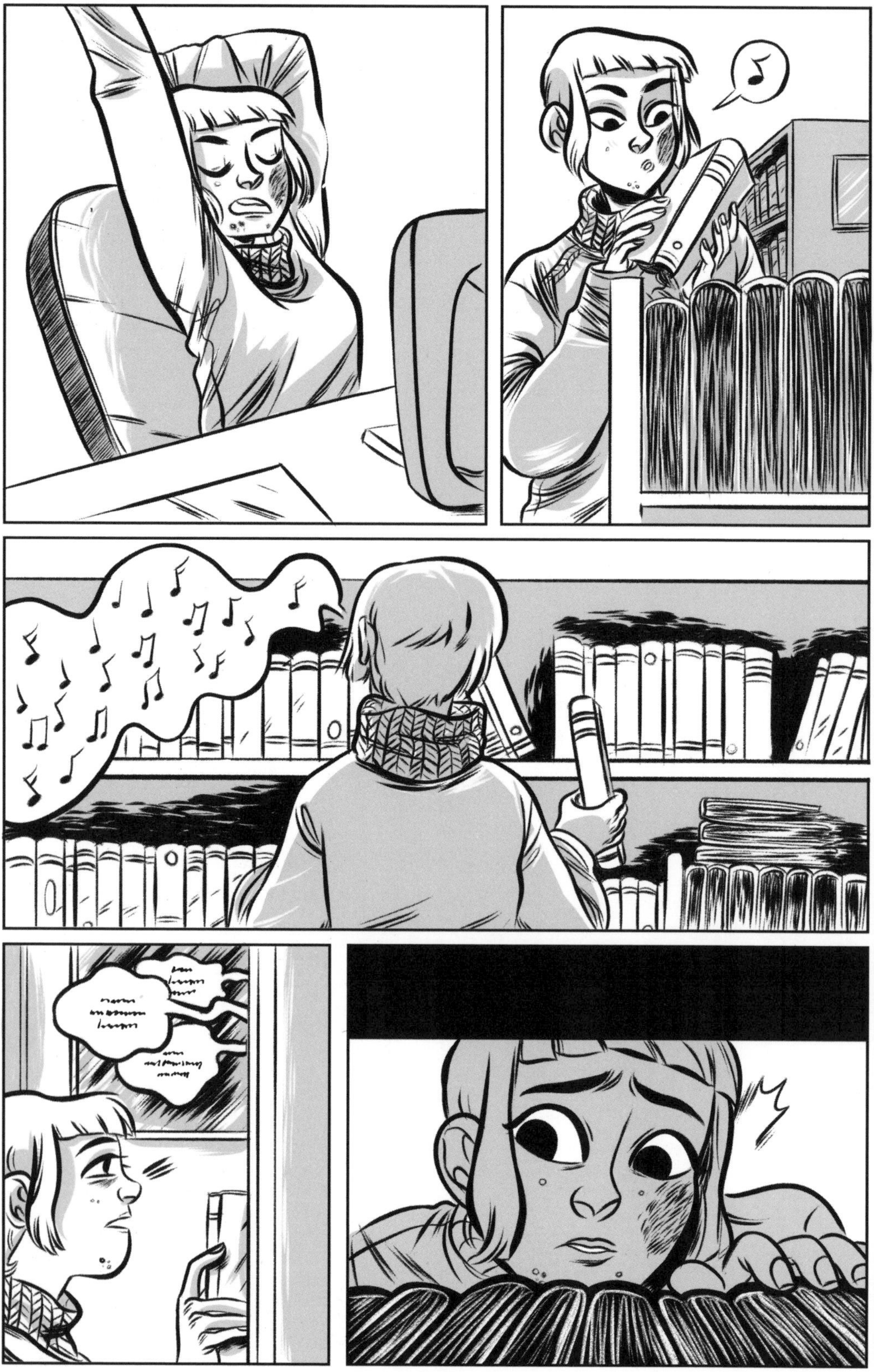

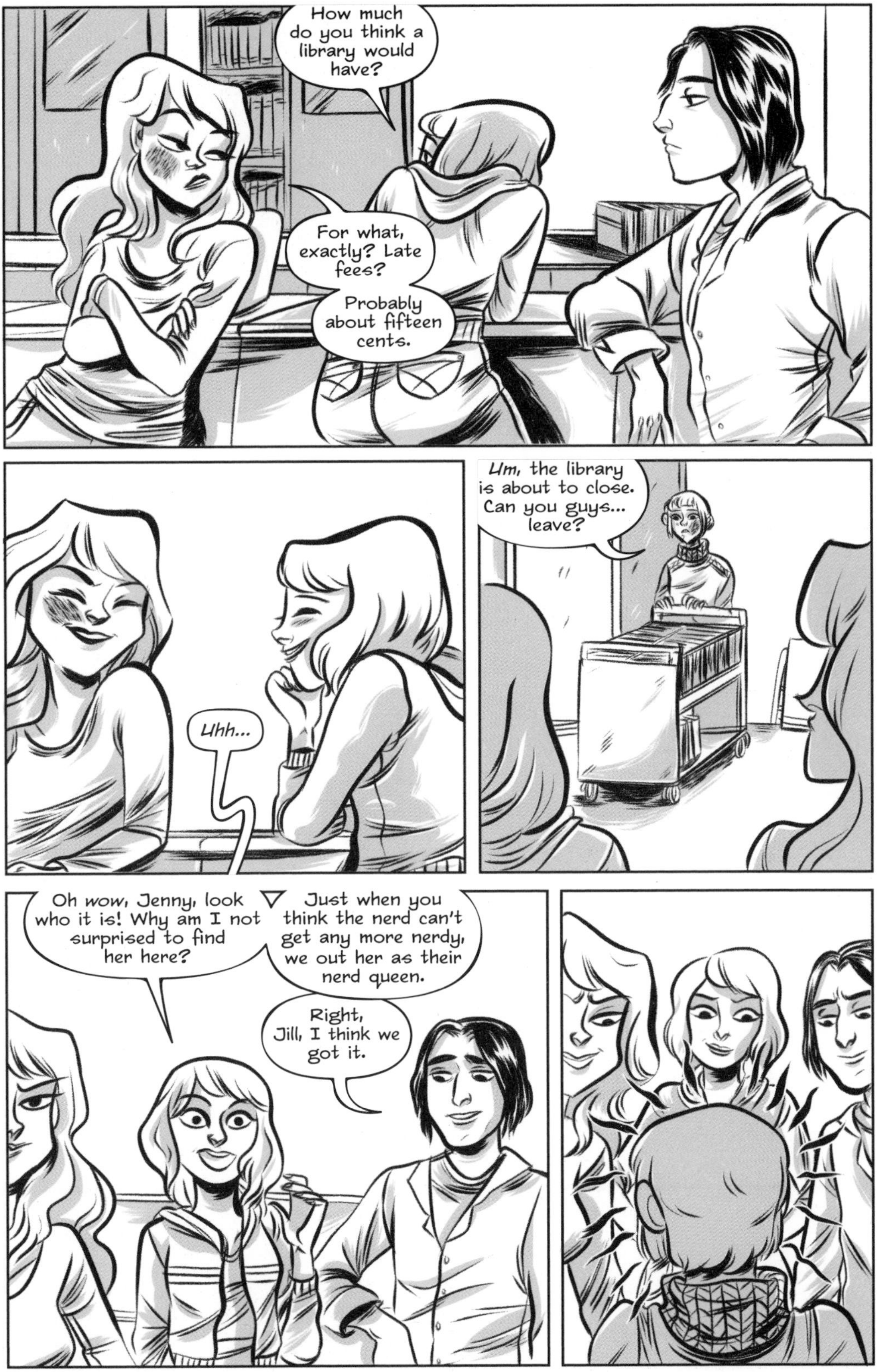
How much do you think a library would have?
For what, exactly? Late fees?
Probably about fifteen cents.
Uhh...
Um, the library is about to close. Can you guys... leave?
Oh wow, Jenny, look who it is! Why am I not surprised to find her here?
Just when you think the nerd can't get any more nerdy, we out her as their nerd queen.
Right, Jill, I think we got it.

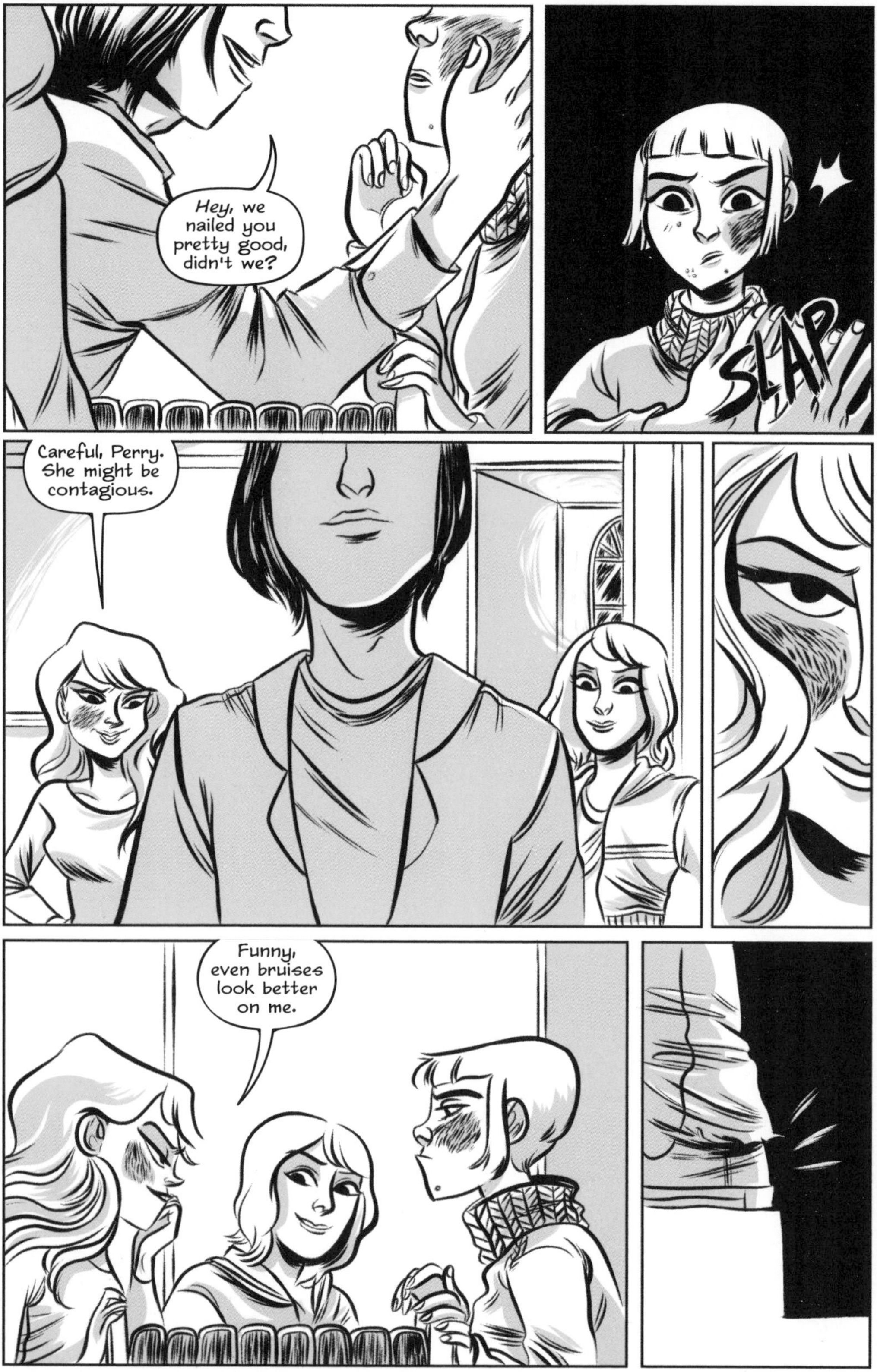
Hey, we nailed you pretty good, didn't we?
SLAP
Careful, Perry. She might be contagious.
Funny, even bruises look better on me.

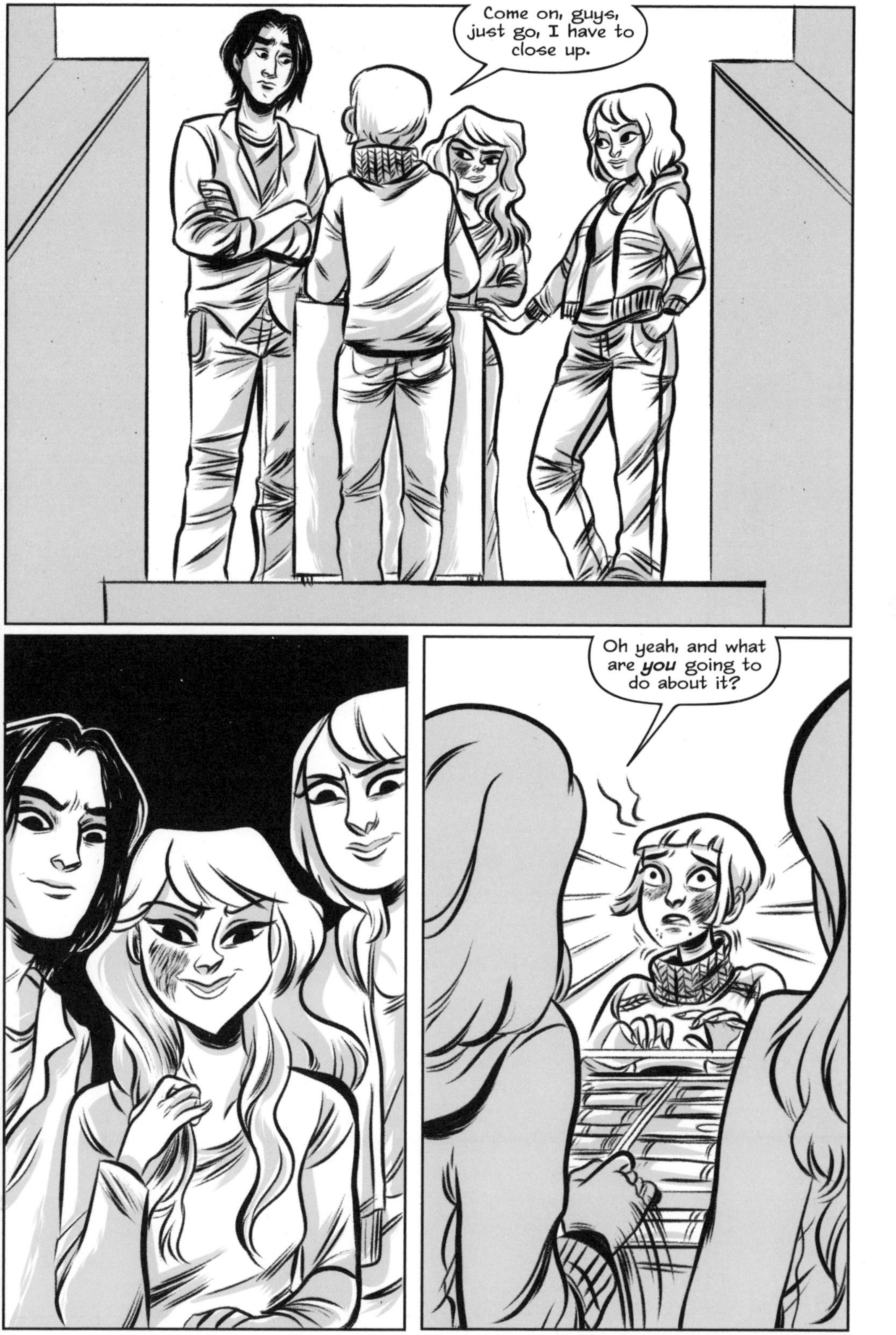
Come on, guys, just go, I have to close up.
Oh yeah, and what are *you* going to do about it?

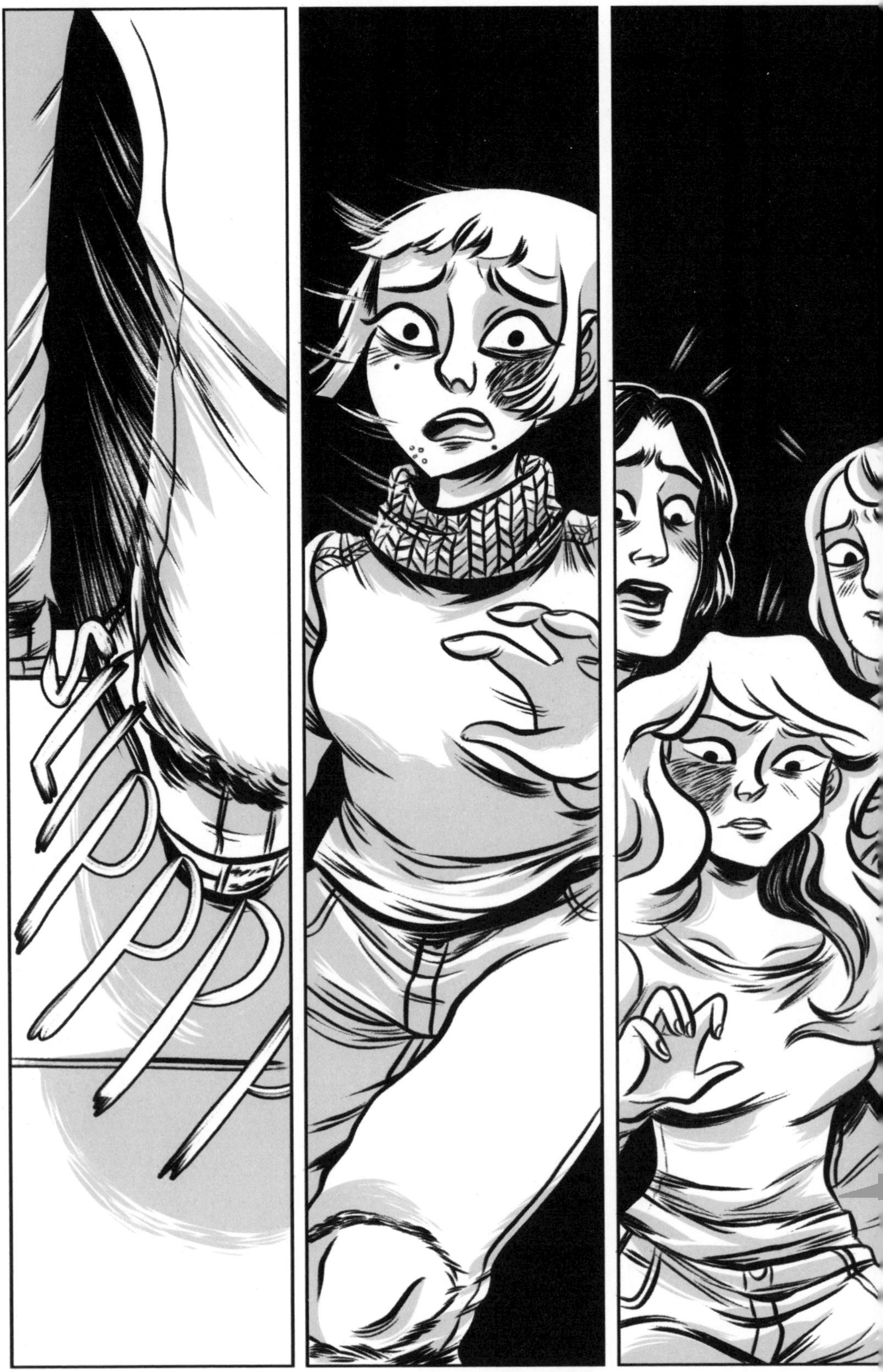

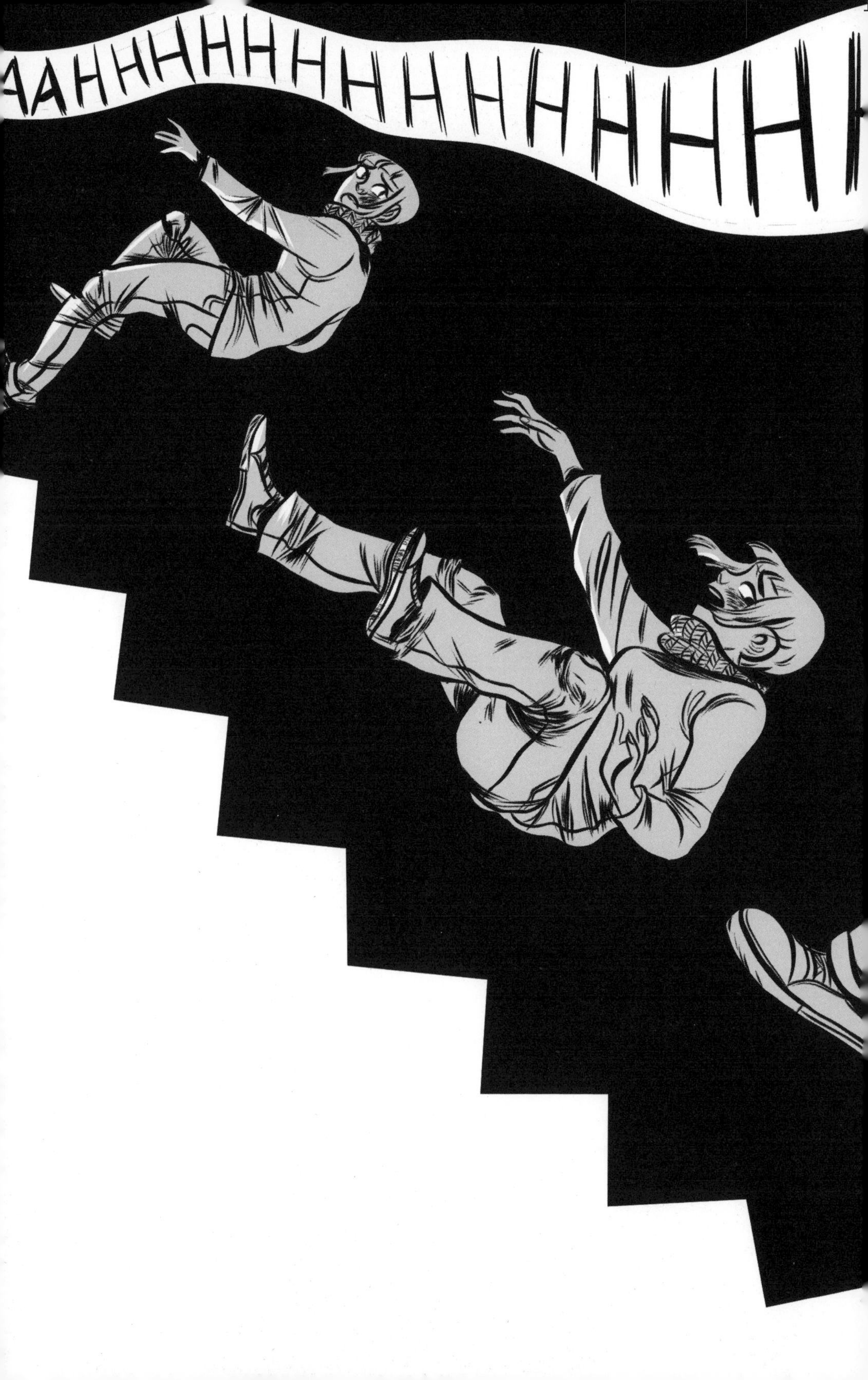
AAHHHHHHHHHHHHHHHH

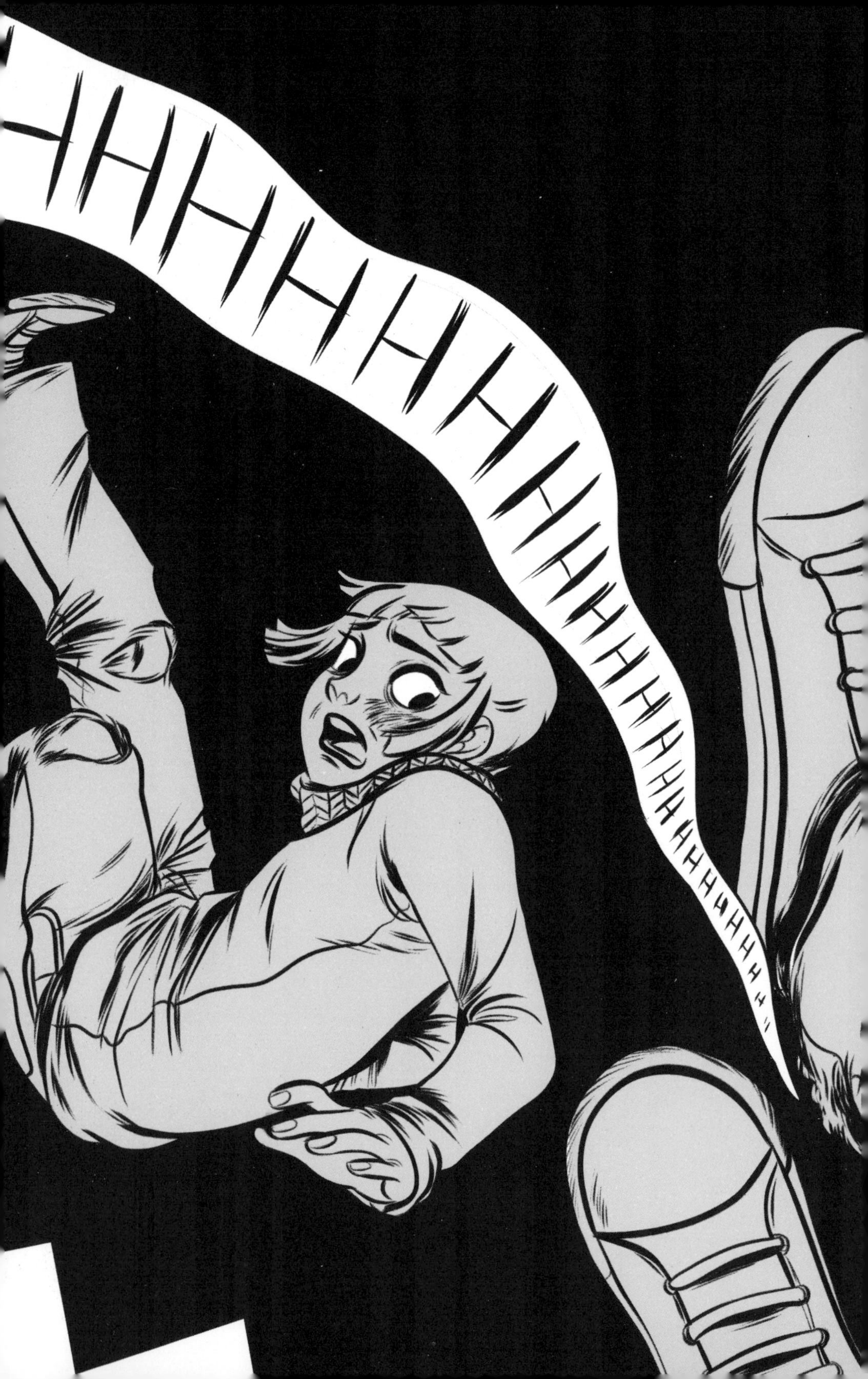
HHHHHHHHHHHHHHHHHHHHHHHHHHHHHHHH

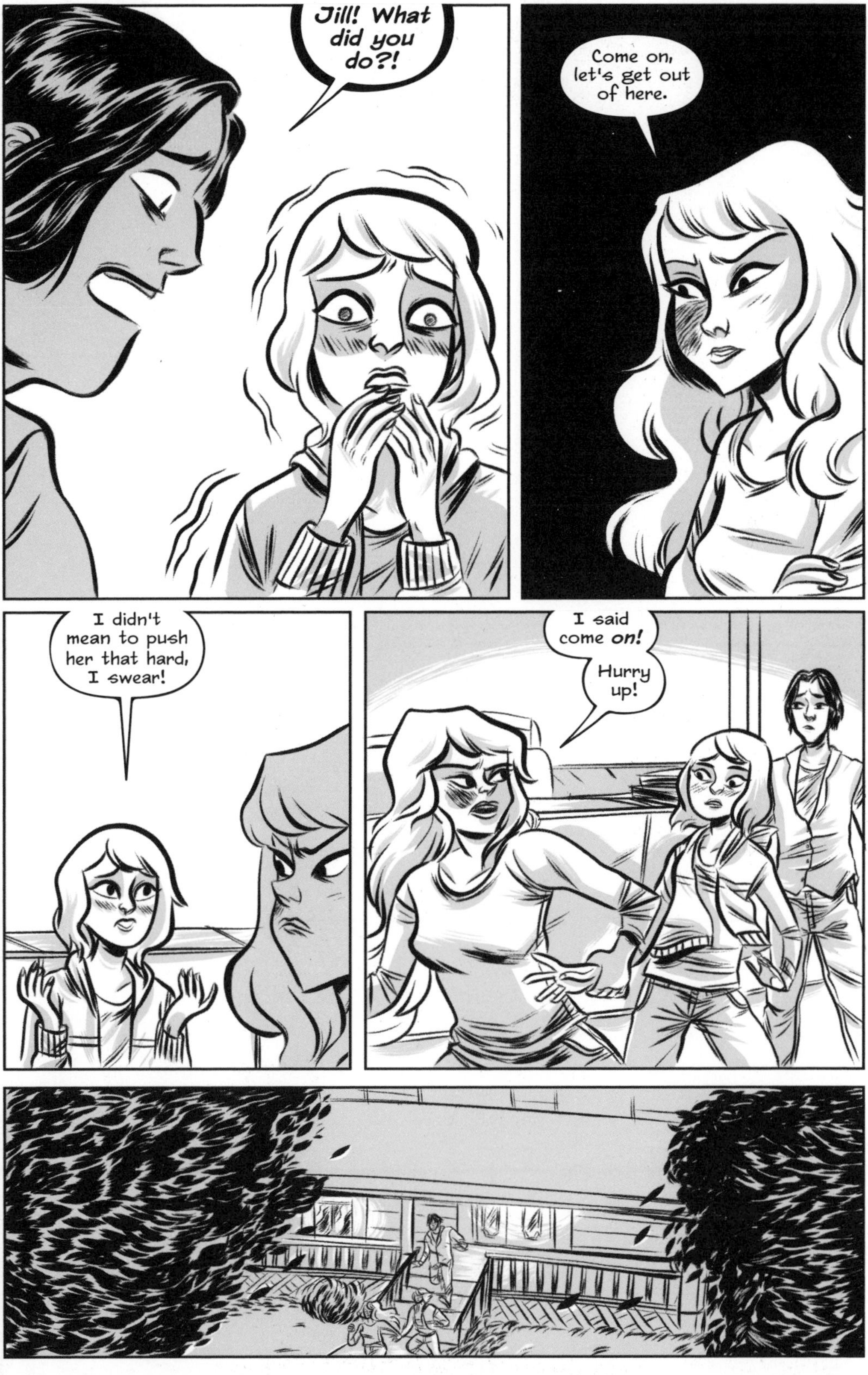
Jill! What did you do?!
Come on, let's get out of here.
I didn't mean to push her that hard, I swear!
I said come *on!*
Hurry up!

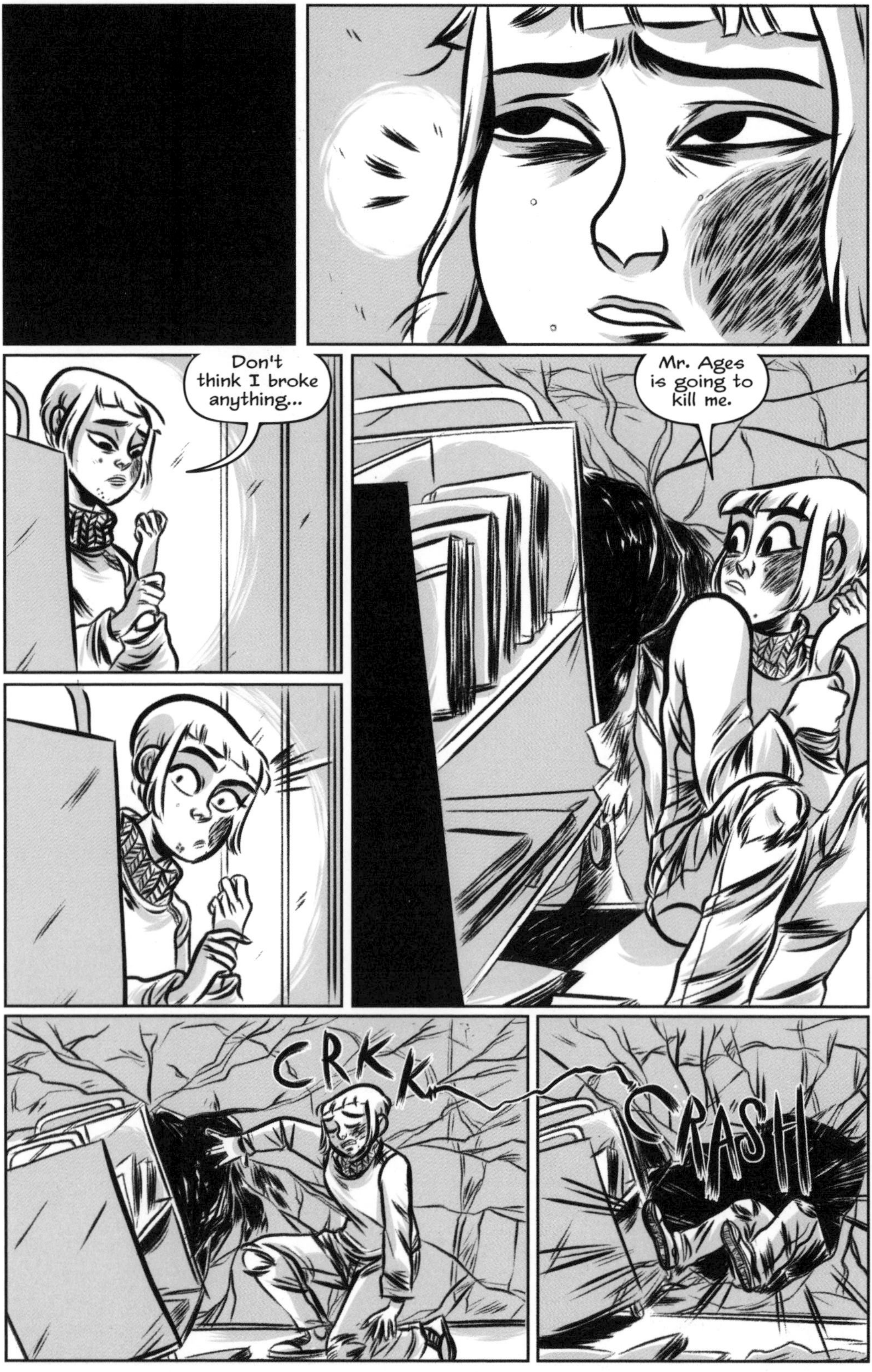
Don't think I broke anything...
Mr. Ages is going to kill me.
CRKK
CRASH

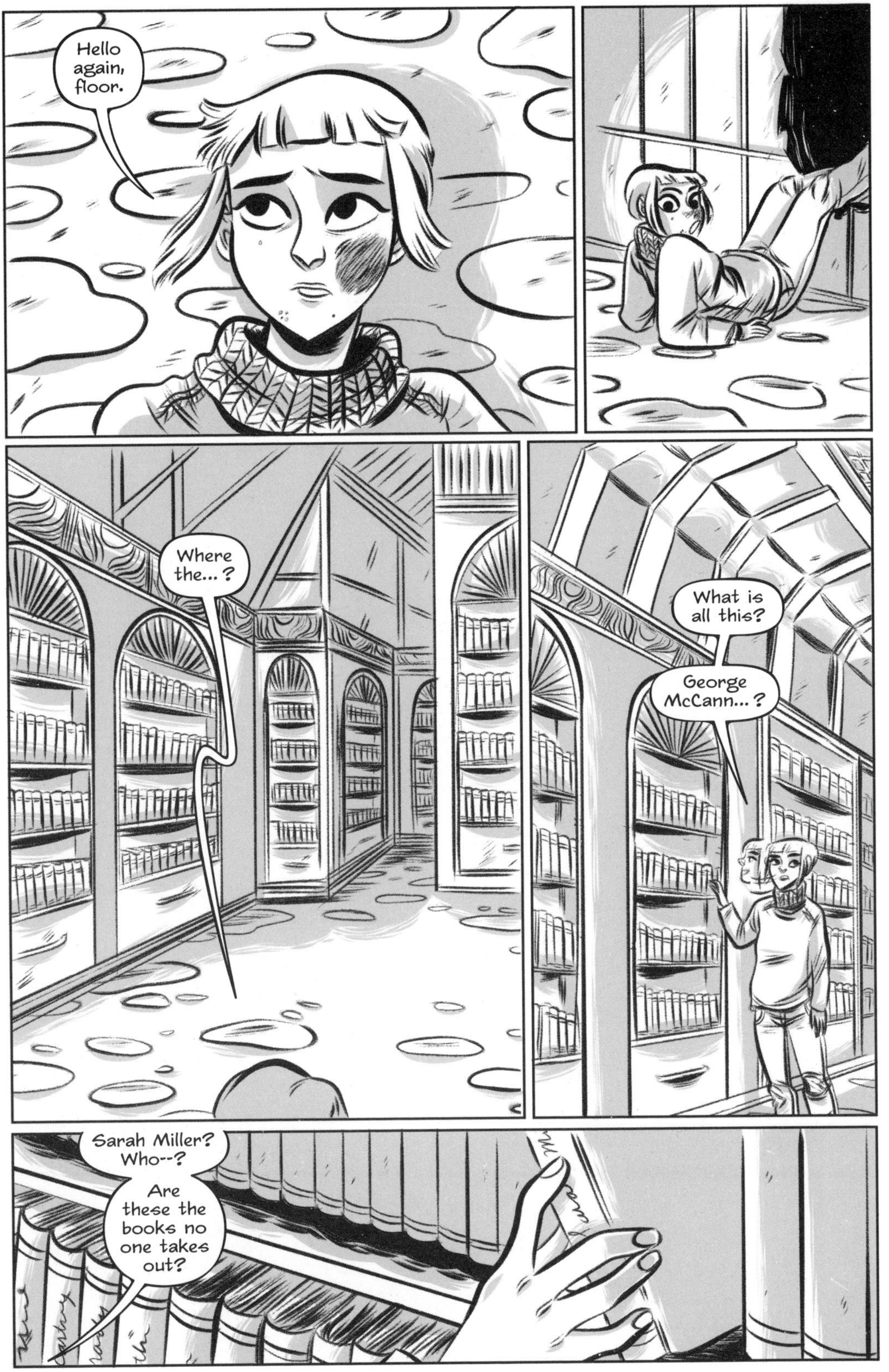

Hello again, floor.
Where the...?
What is all this?
George McCann...?
Sarah Miller? Who--?
Are these the books no one takes out?

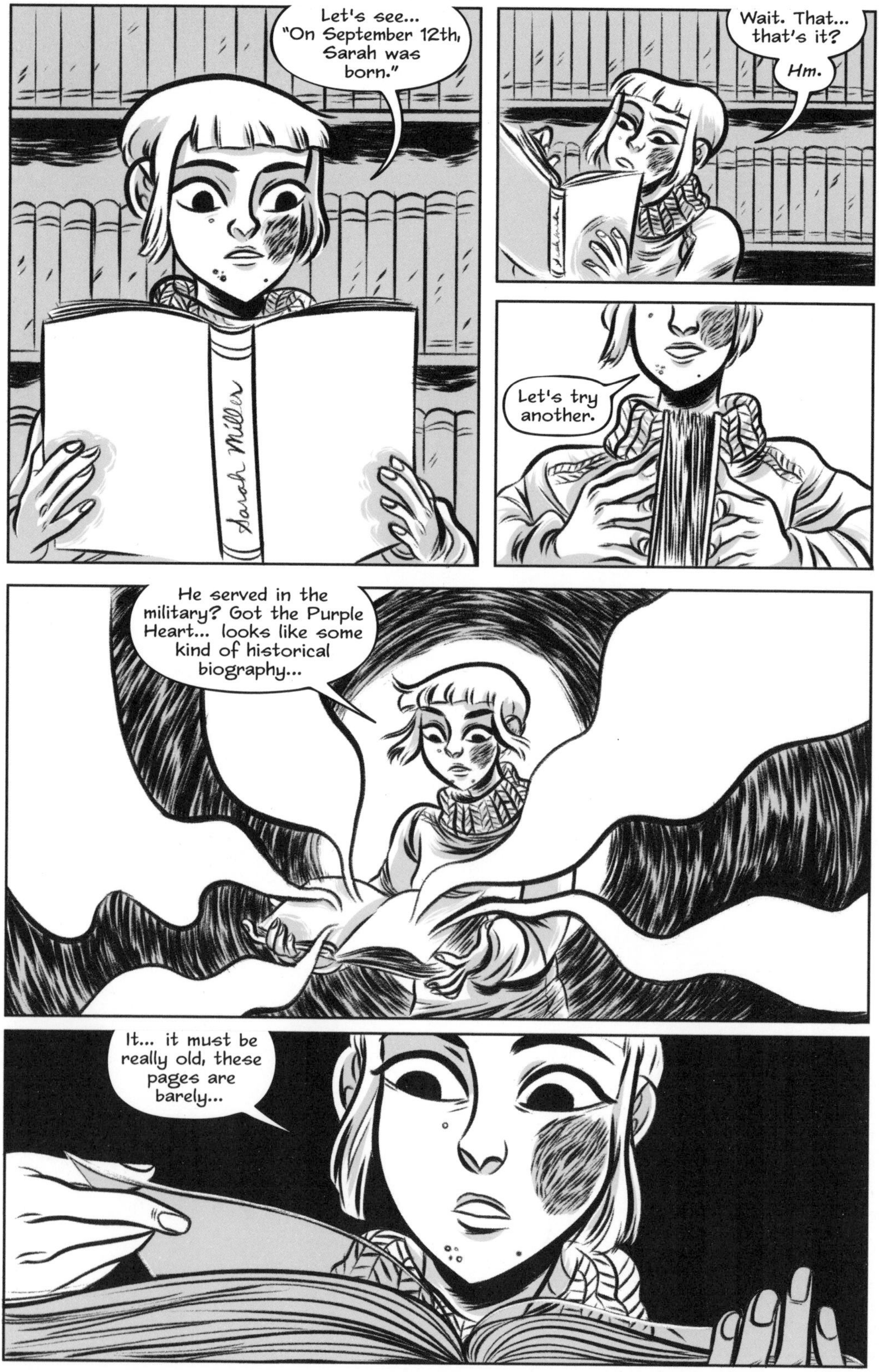
Let's see... "On September 12th, Sarah was born."
Sarah Miller
Wait. That... that's it?
Hm.
Let's try another.
He served in the military? Got the Purple Heart... looks like some kind of historical biography...
It... it must be really old, these pages are barely...

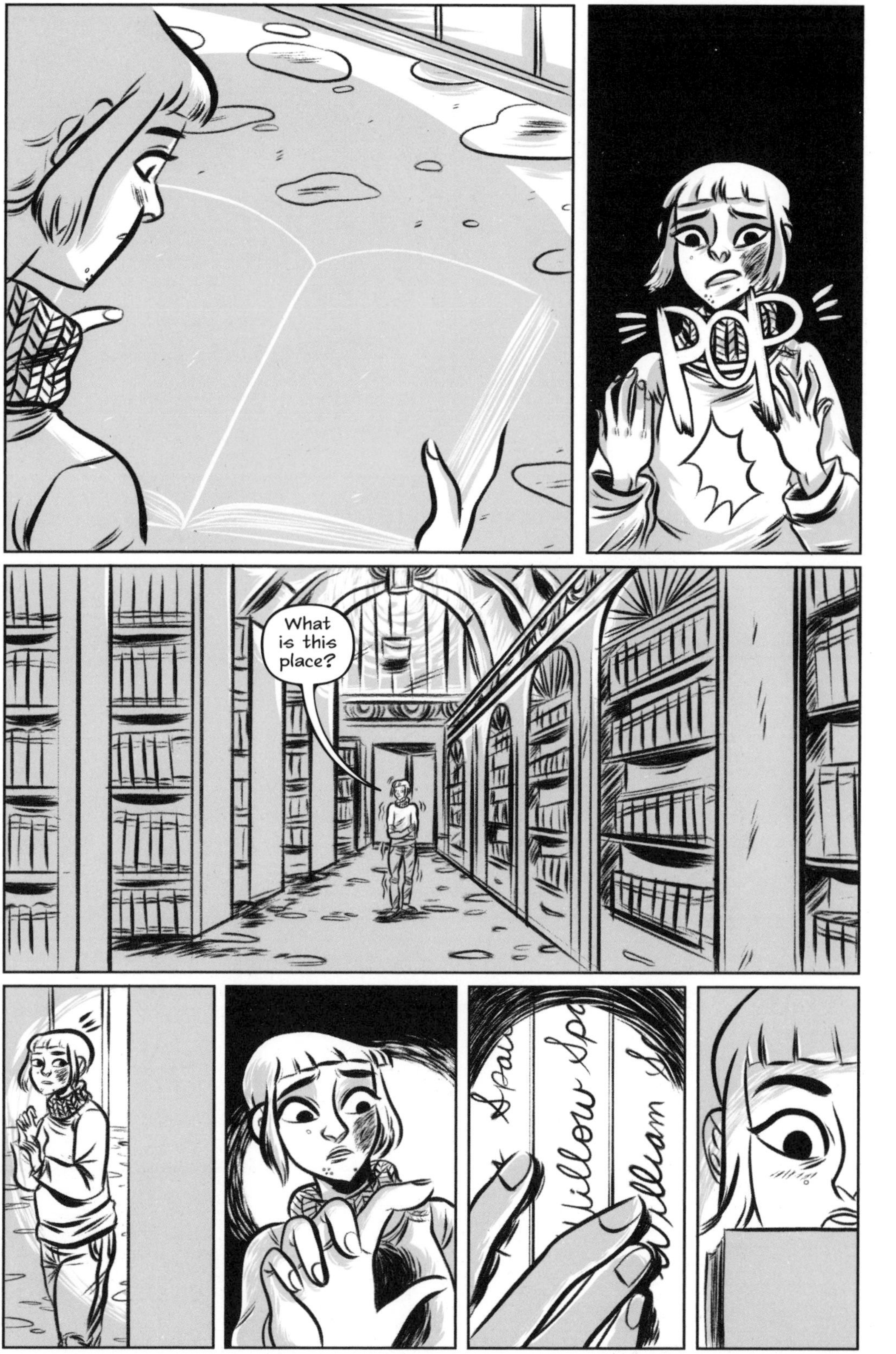
POP
What is this place?
Willow
William

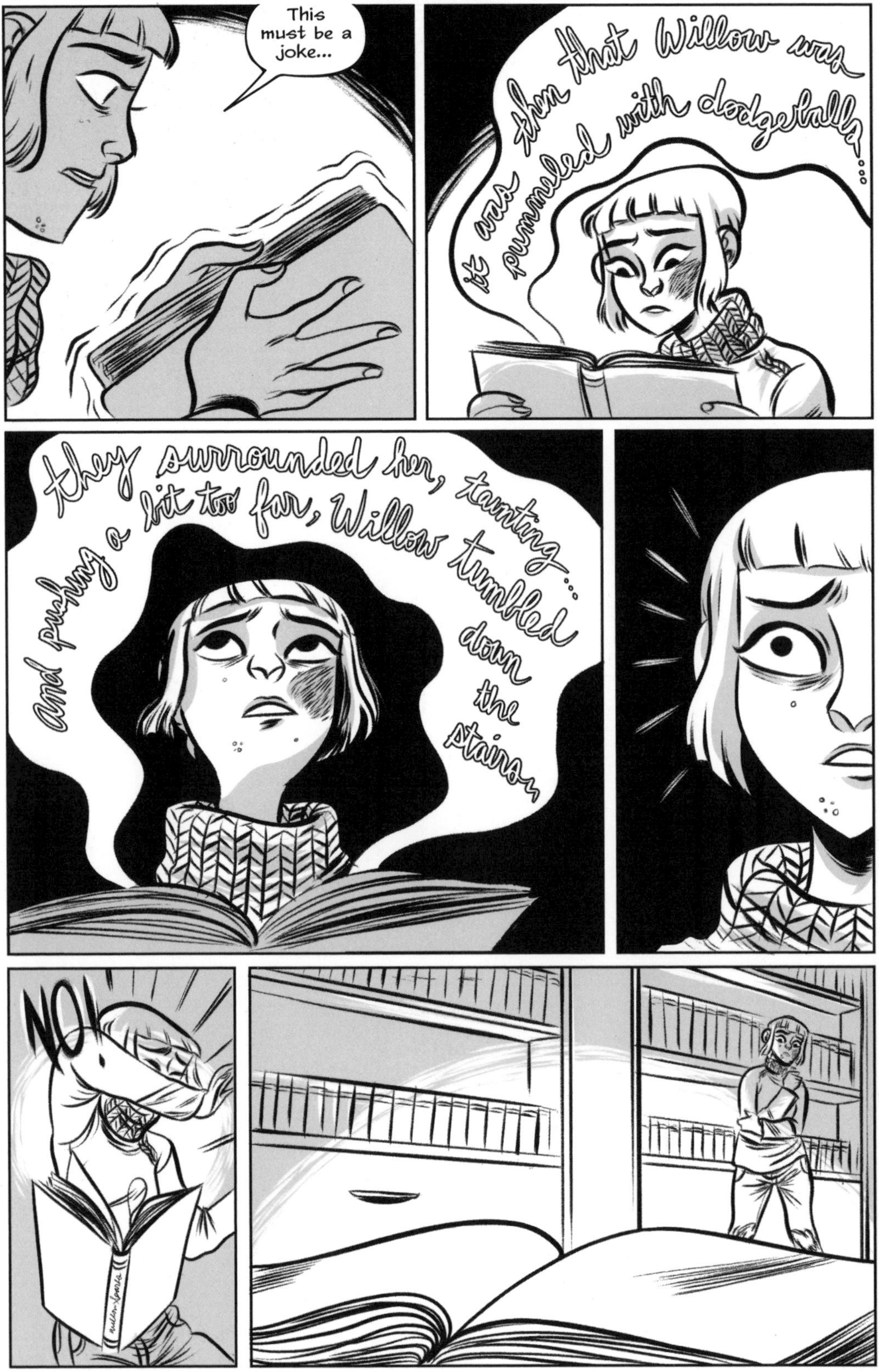
This must be a joke...
It was then that Willow was pummeled with dodgeballs...
They surrounded her, taunting...
And pushing a bit too far, Willow tumbled down the stairs.
NO!

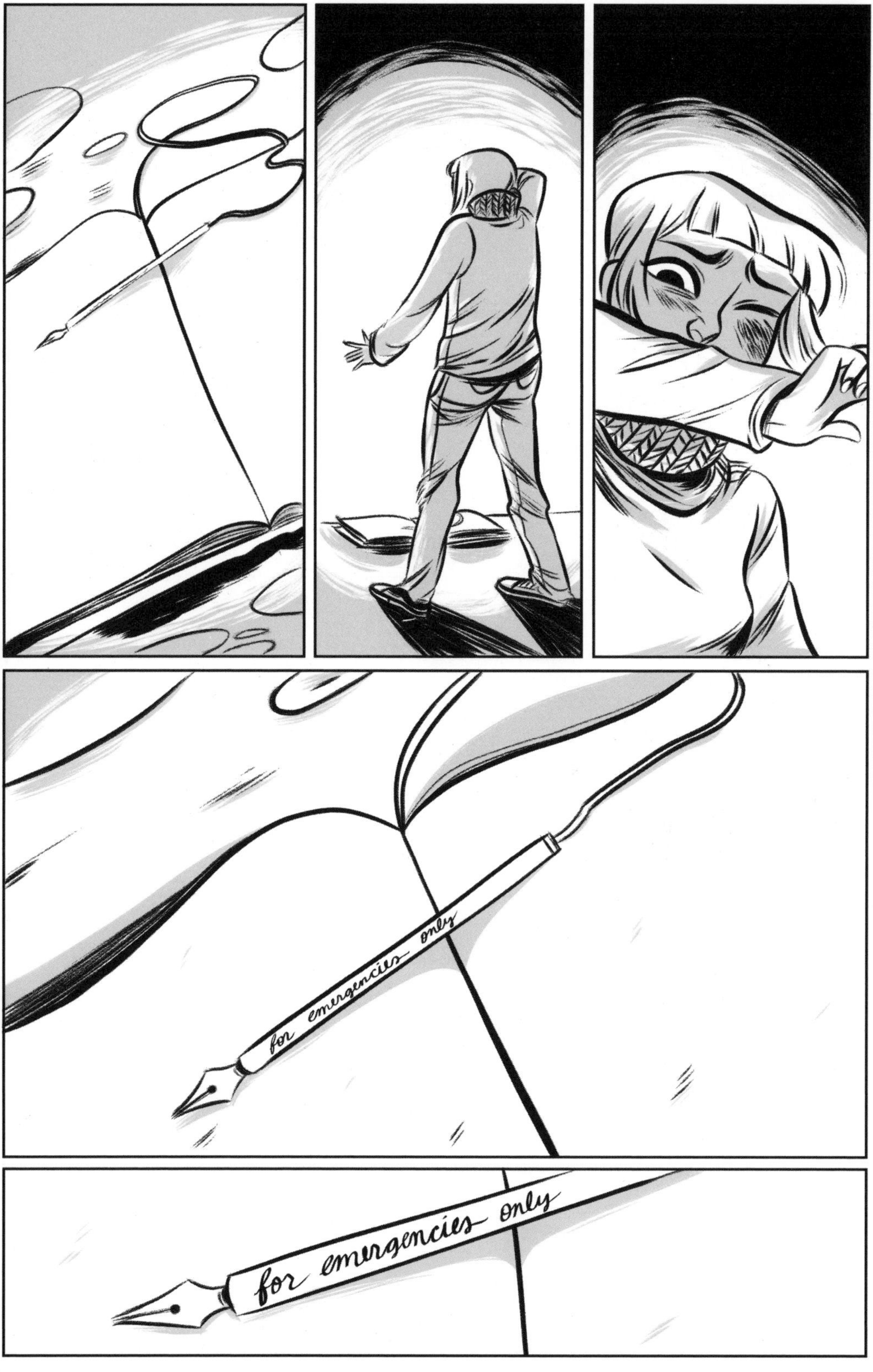
for emergencies only
for emergencies only

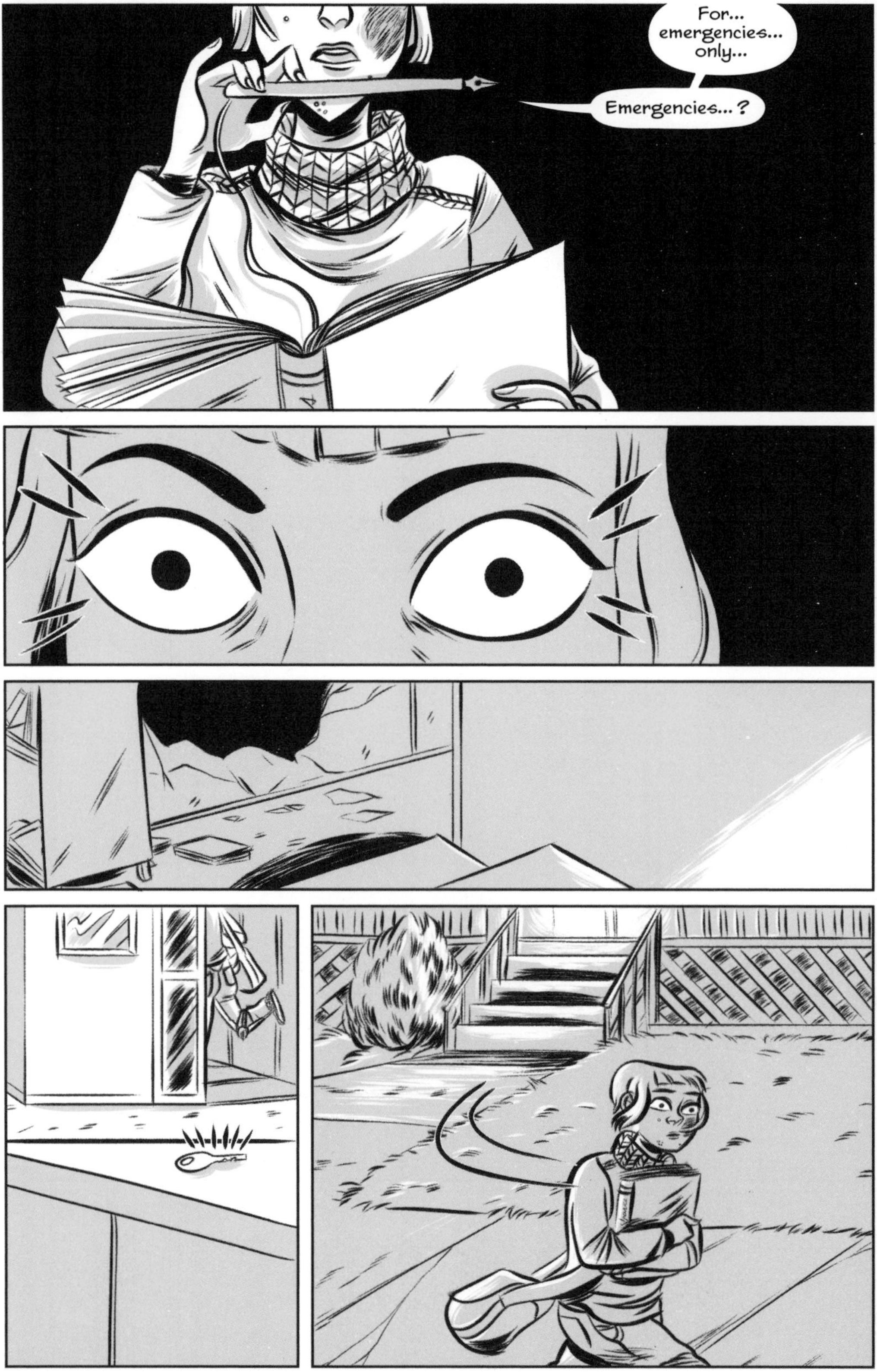
For... emergencies... only...
Emergencies...?

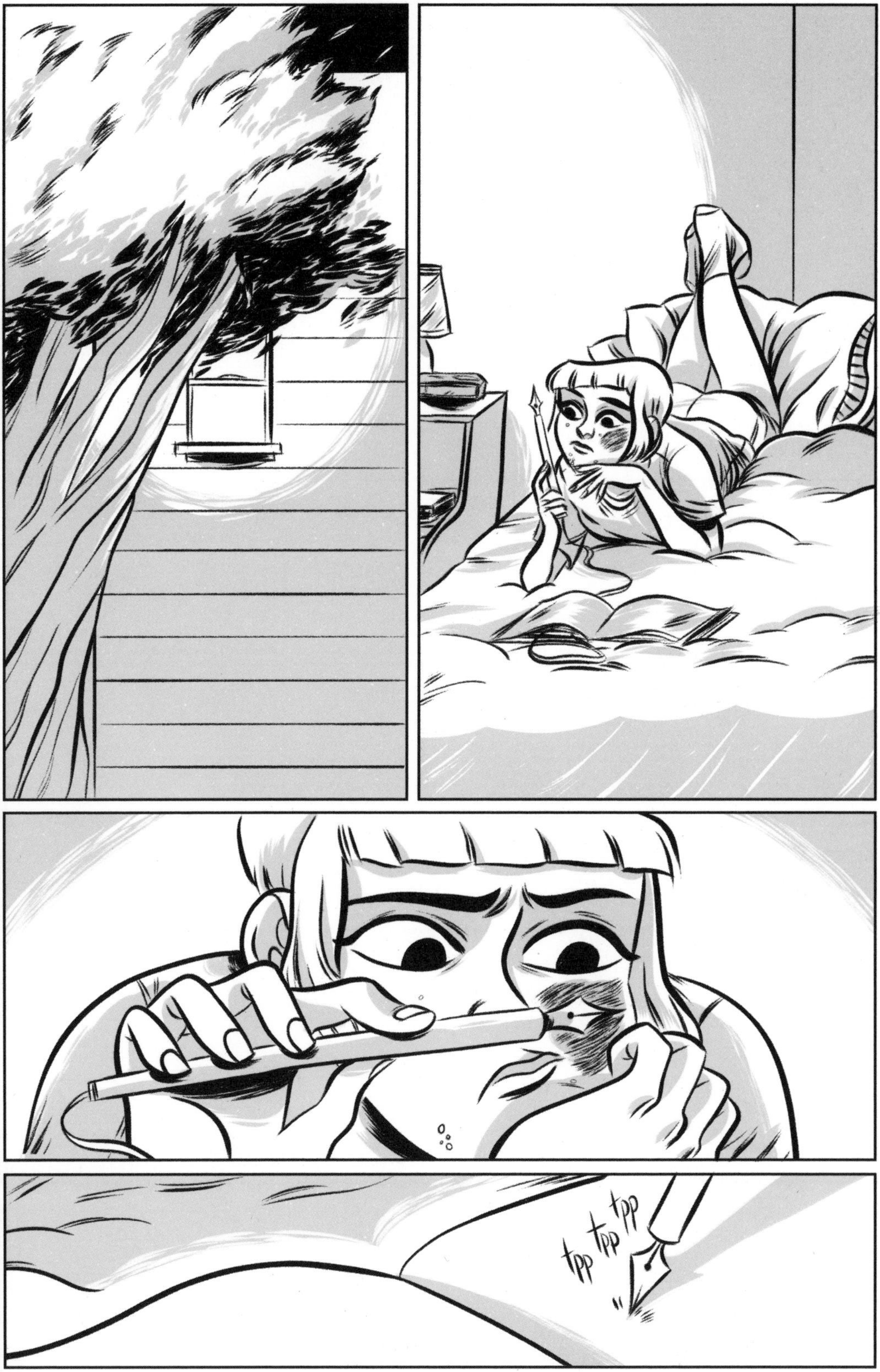
tpp tpp tpp

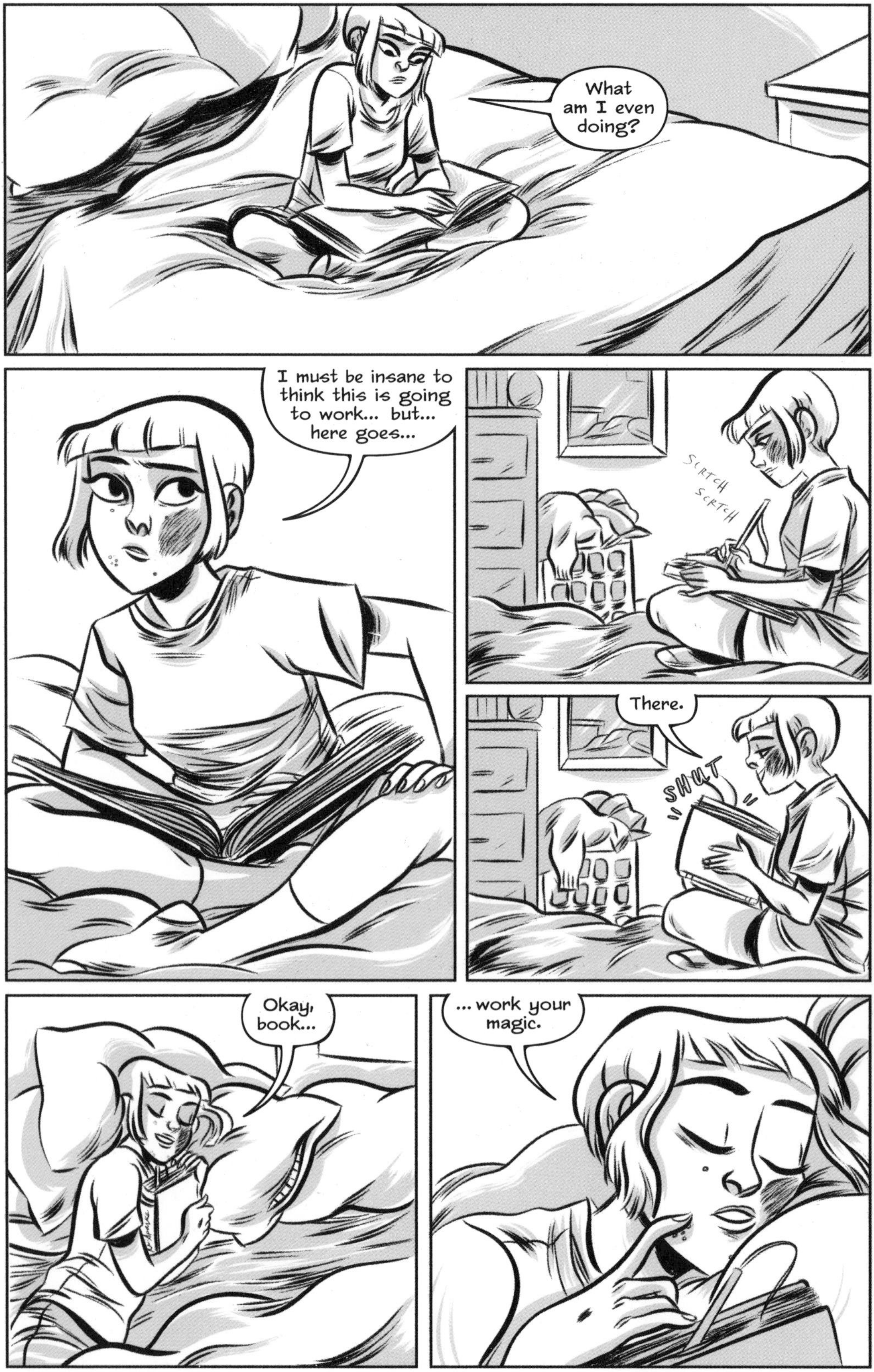
What am I even doing?
I must be insane to think this is going to work... but... here goes...
SCRTCH SCRTCH
There.
SHUT
Okay, book...
...work your magic.

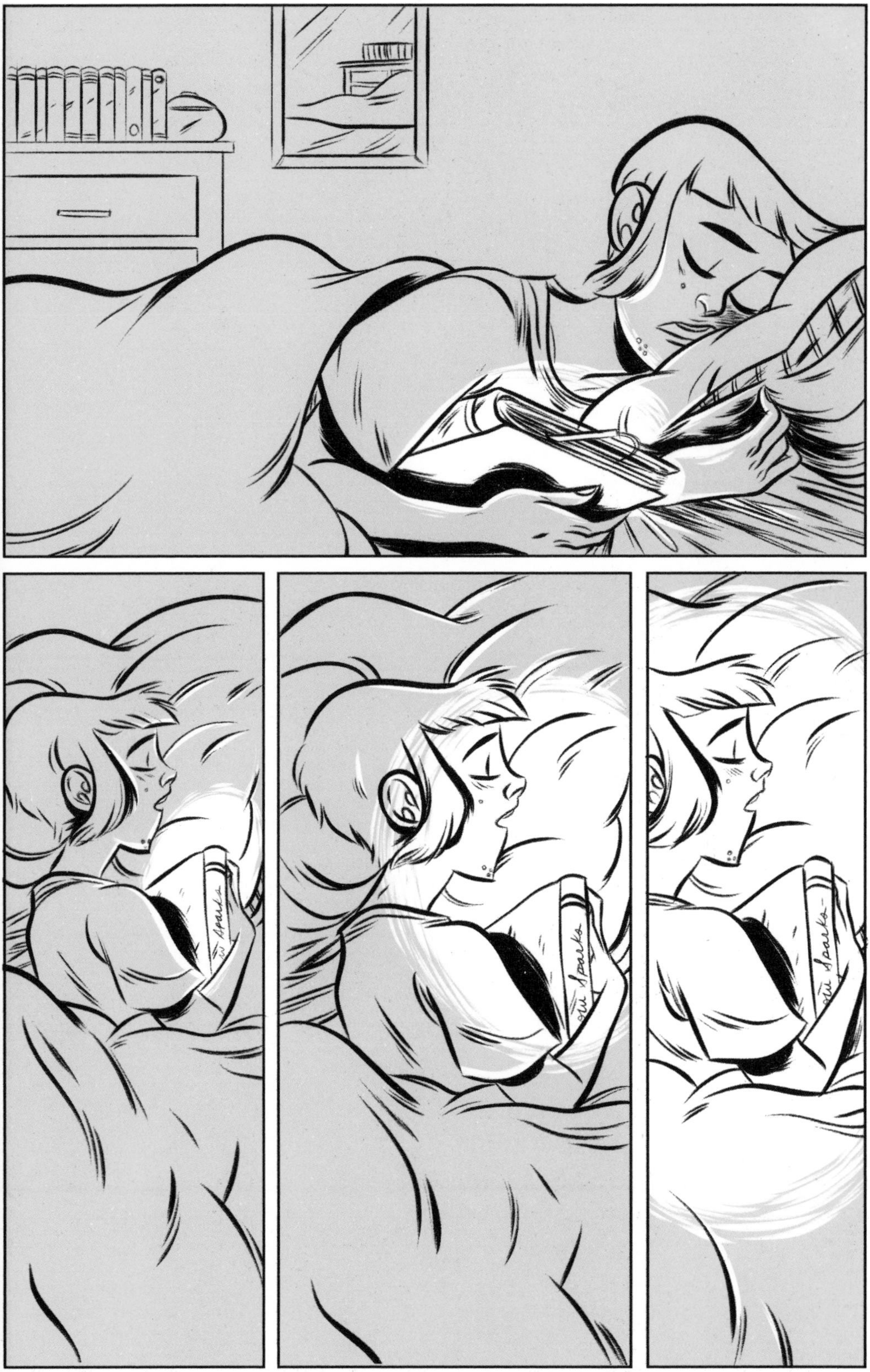
Sparks

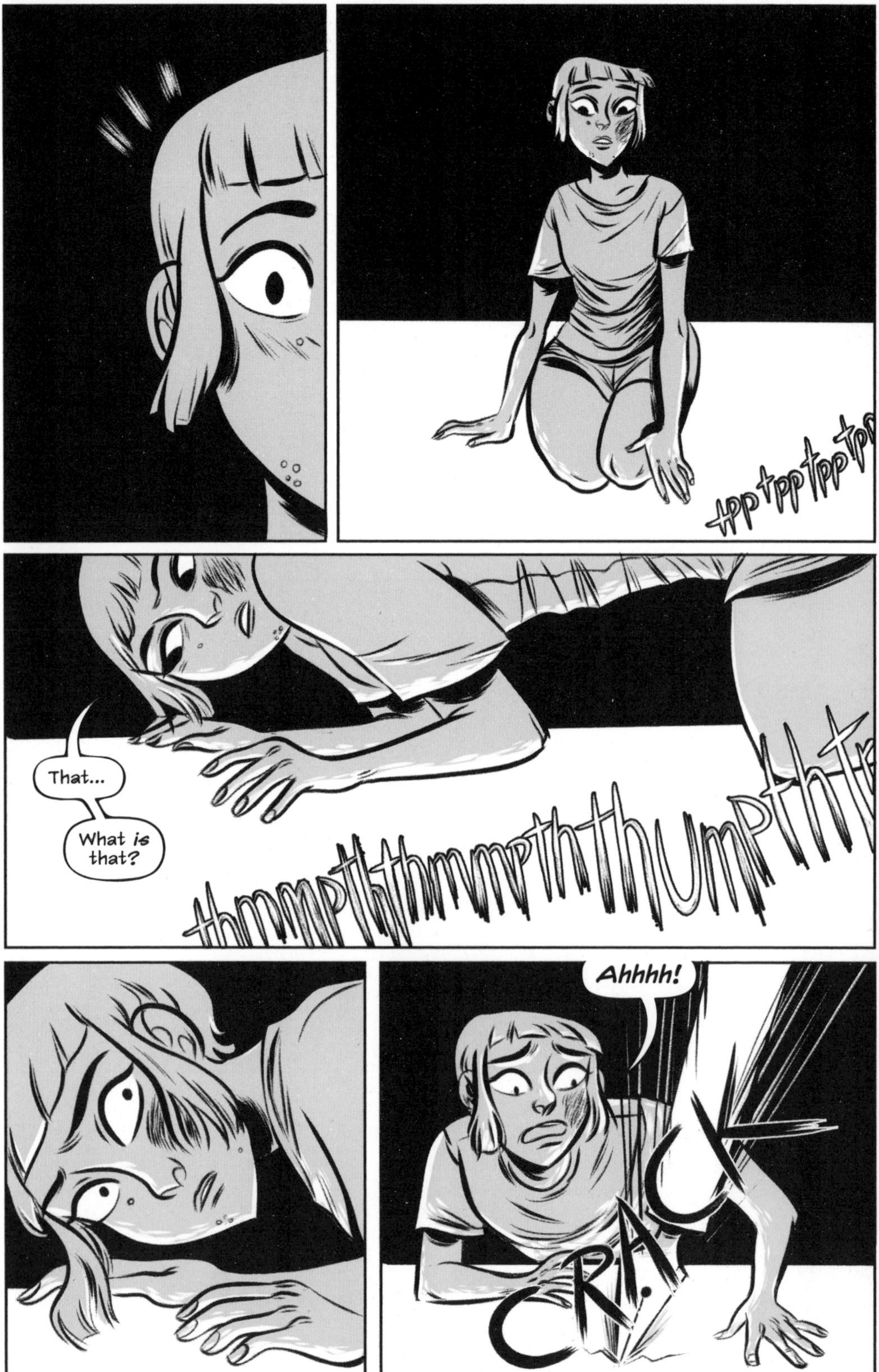
tpp tpp tpp tpp tpp
That...
What *is* that?
thmmpththmmpththUMPthtr
Ahhhh!
CRACK

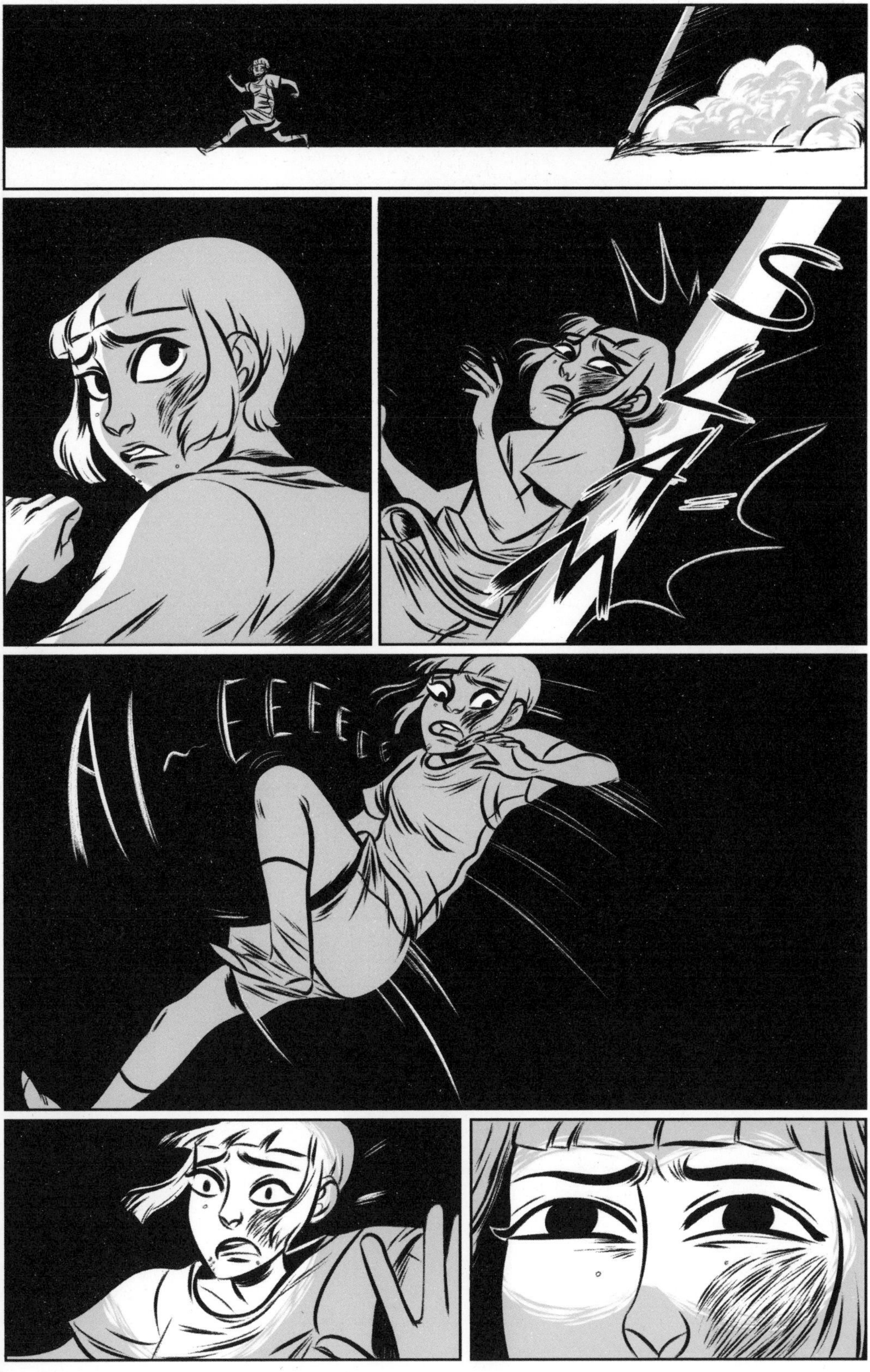
AI~EEEEEE

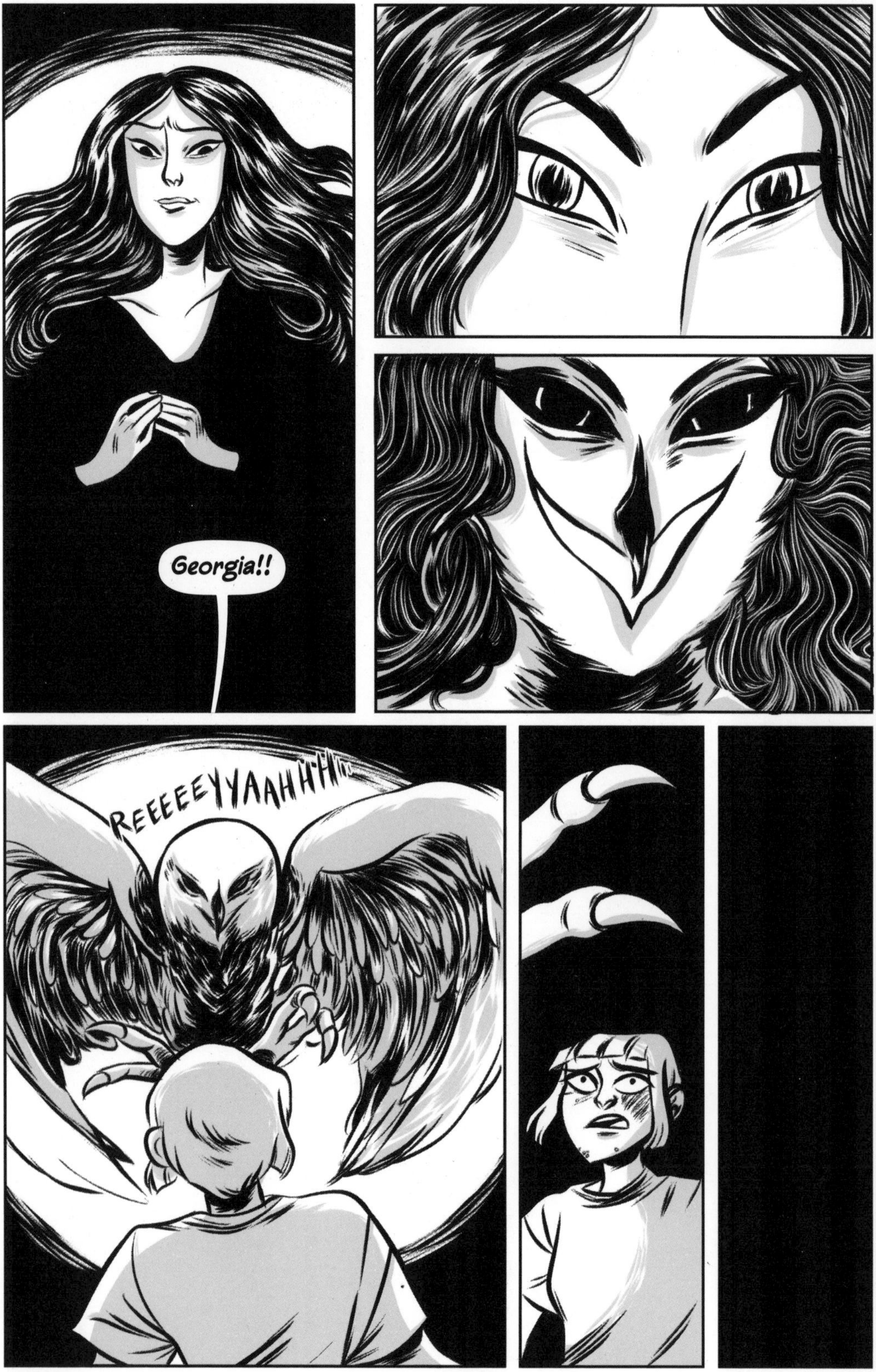
Georgia!!
REEEEEYYAAHHH

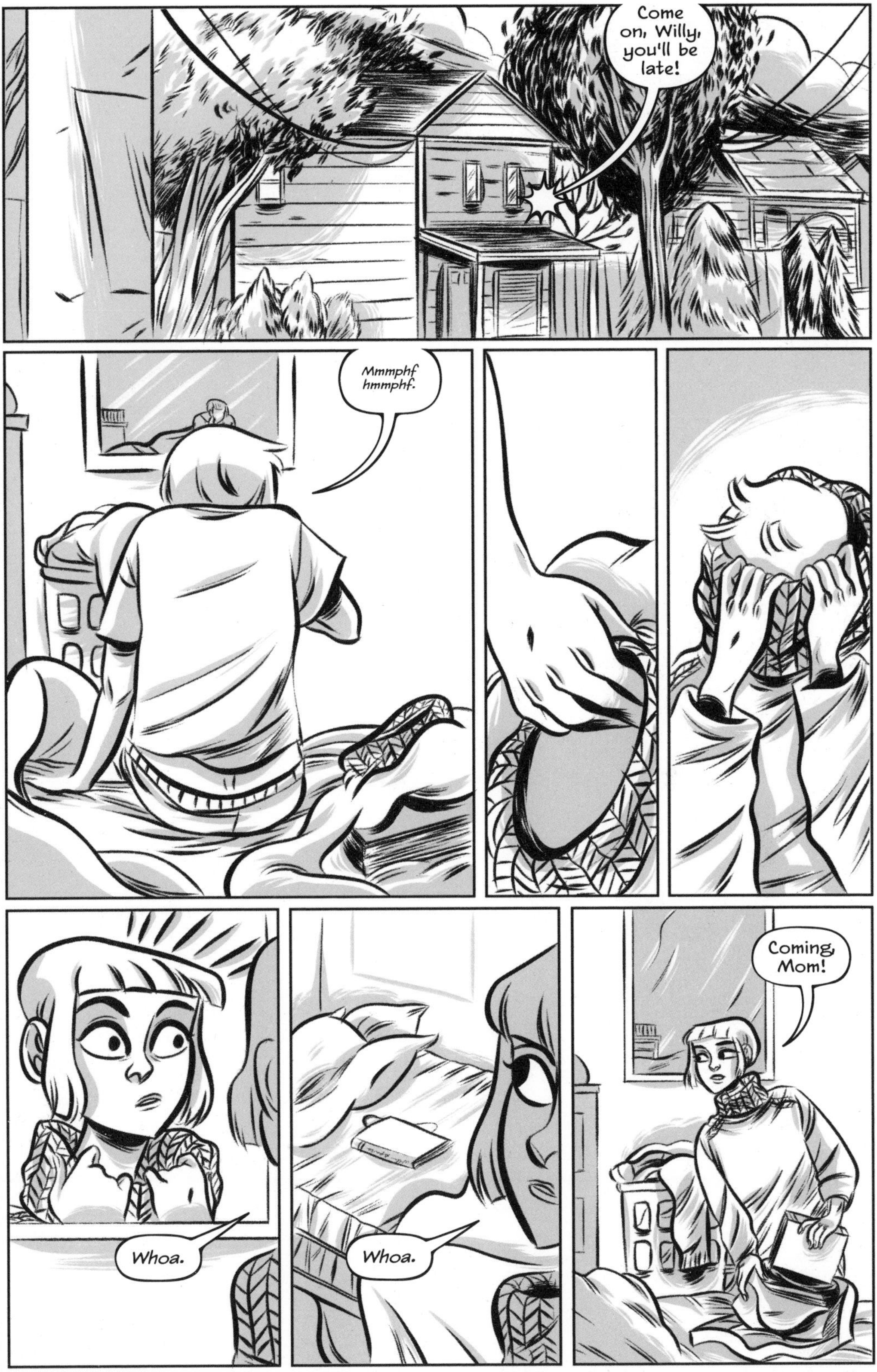
Come on, Willy, you'll be late!
Mmmphf hmmphf.
Whoa.
Whoa.
Coming, Mom!

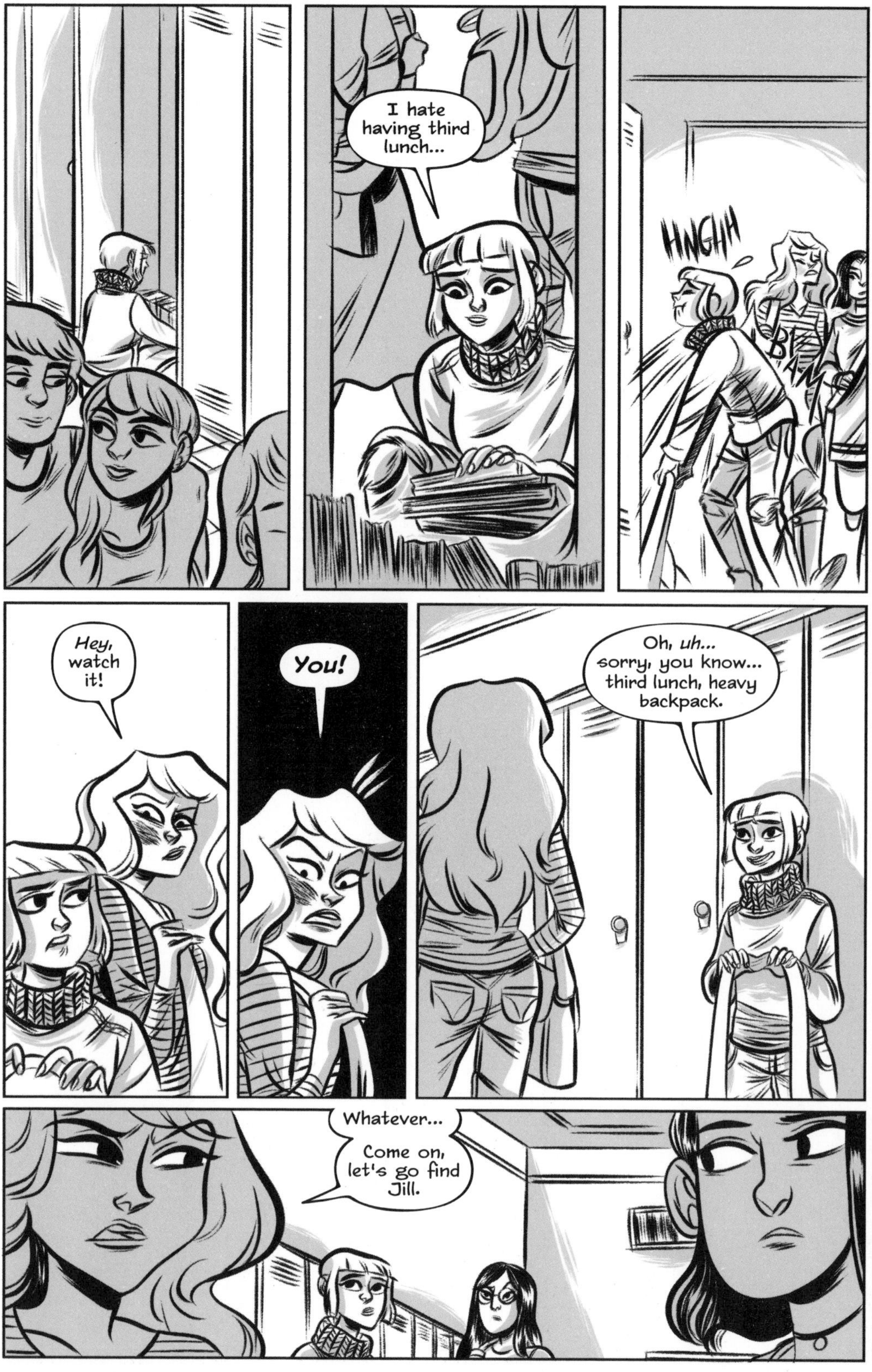
I hate having third lunch...
HNGHH
BAM
Hey, watch it!
You!
Oh, uh... sorry, you know... third lunch, heavy backpack.
Whatever...
Come on, let's go find Jill.

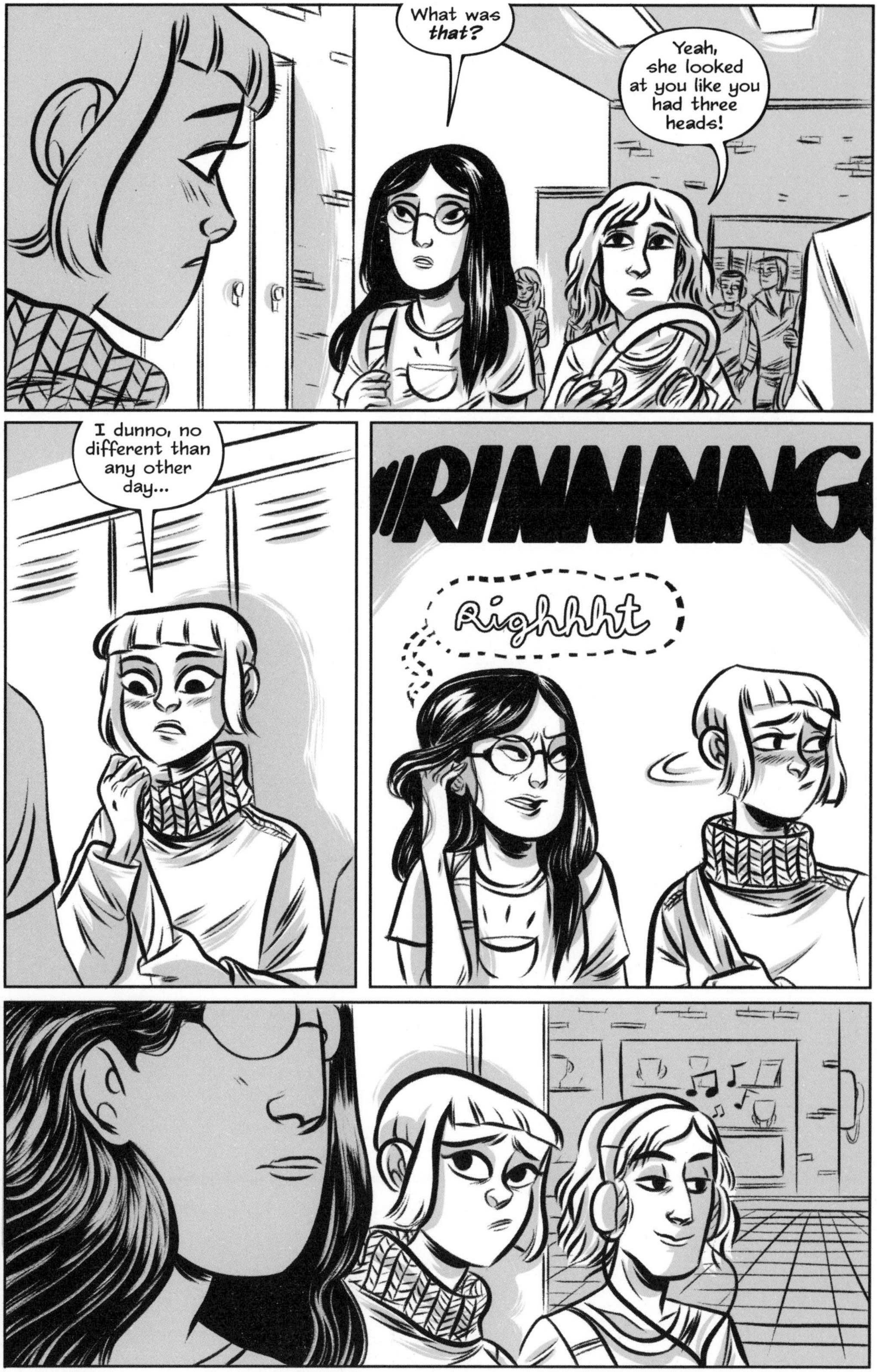
What was *that?*
Yeah, she looked at you like you had three heads!
I dunno, no different than any other day...
RINNNNNG
Righhht

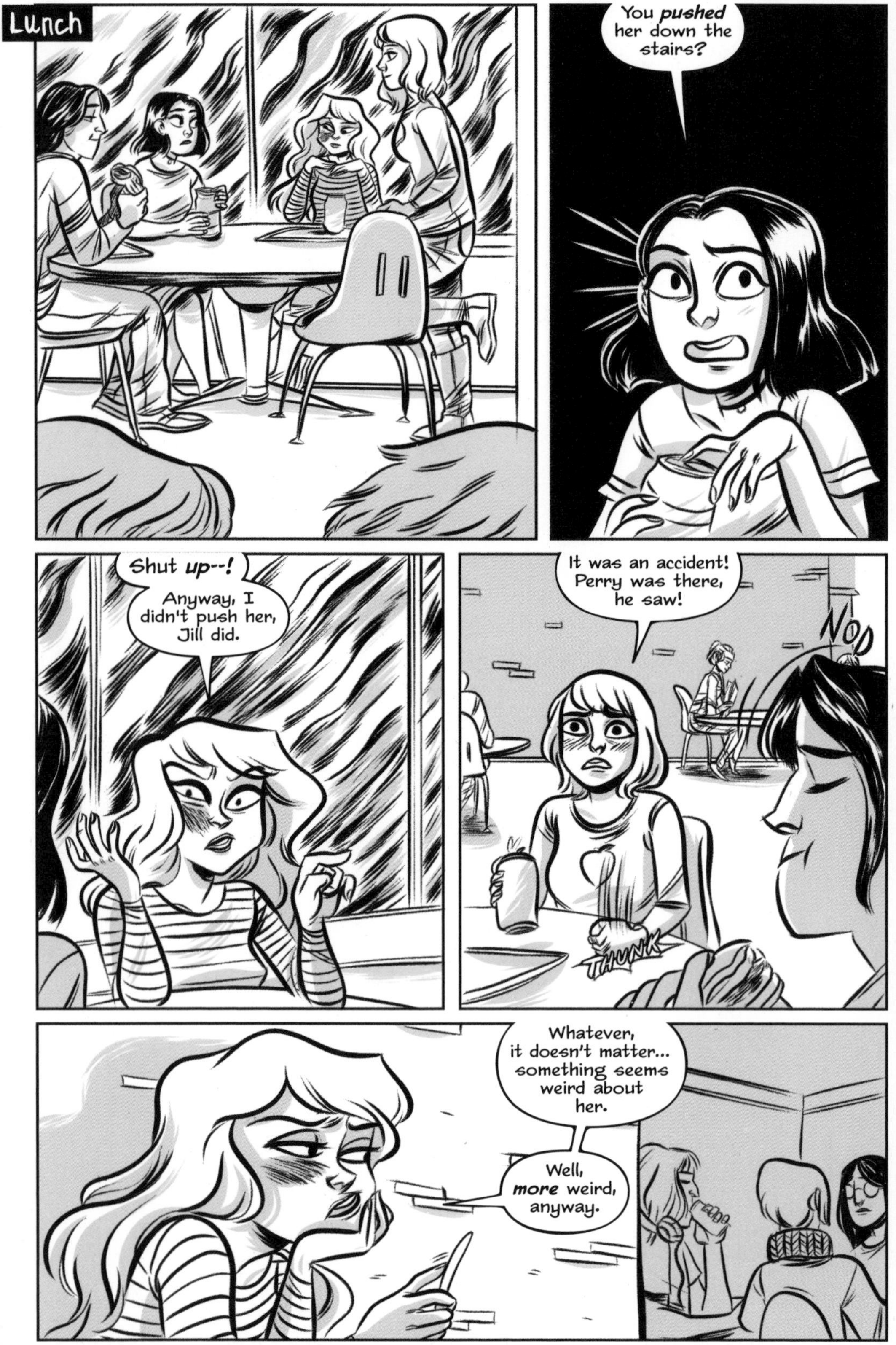
Lunch
You pushed her down the stairs?
Shut up--!
Anyway, I didn't push her, Jill did.
It was an accident! Perry was there, he saw!
NOD
THUNK
Whatever, it doesn't matter... something seems weird about her.
Well, more weird, anyway.

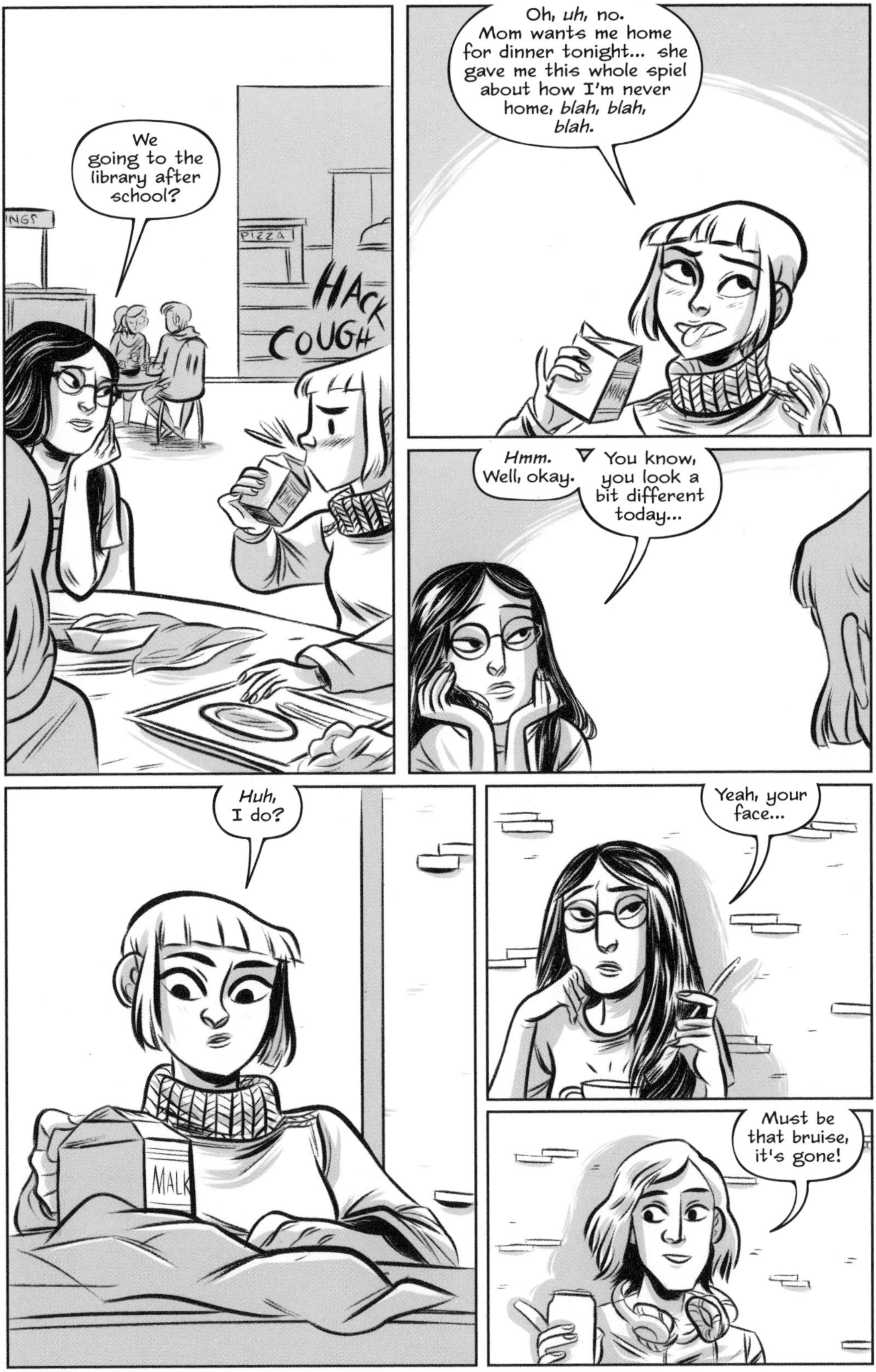

We going to the library after school?
HACK COUGH
PIZZA
Oh, uh, no. Mom wants me home for dinner tonight... she gave me this whole spiel about how I'm never home, blah, blah, blah.
Hmm. Well, okay.
You know, you look a bit different today...
Huh, I do?
MALK
Yeah, your face...
Must be that bruise, it's gone!

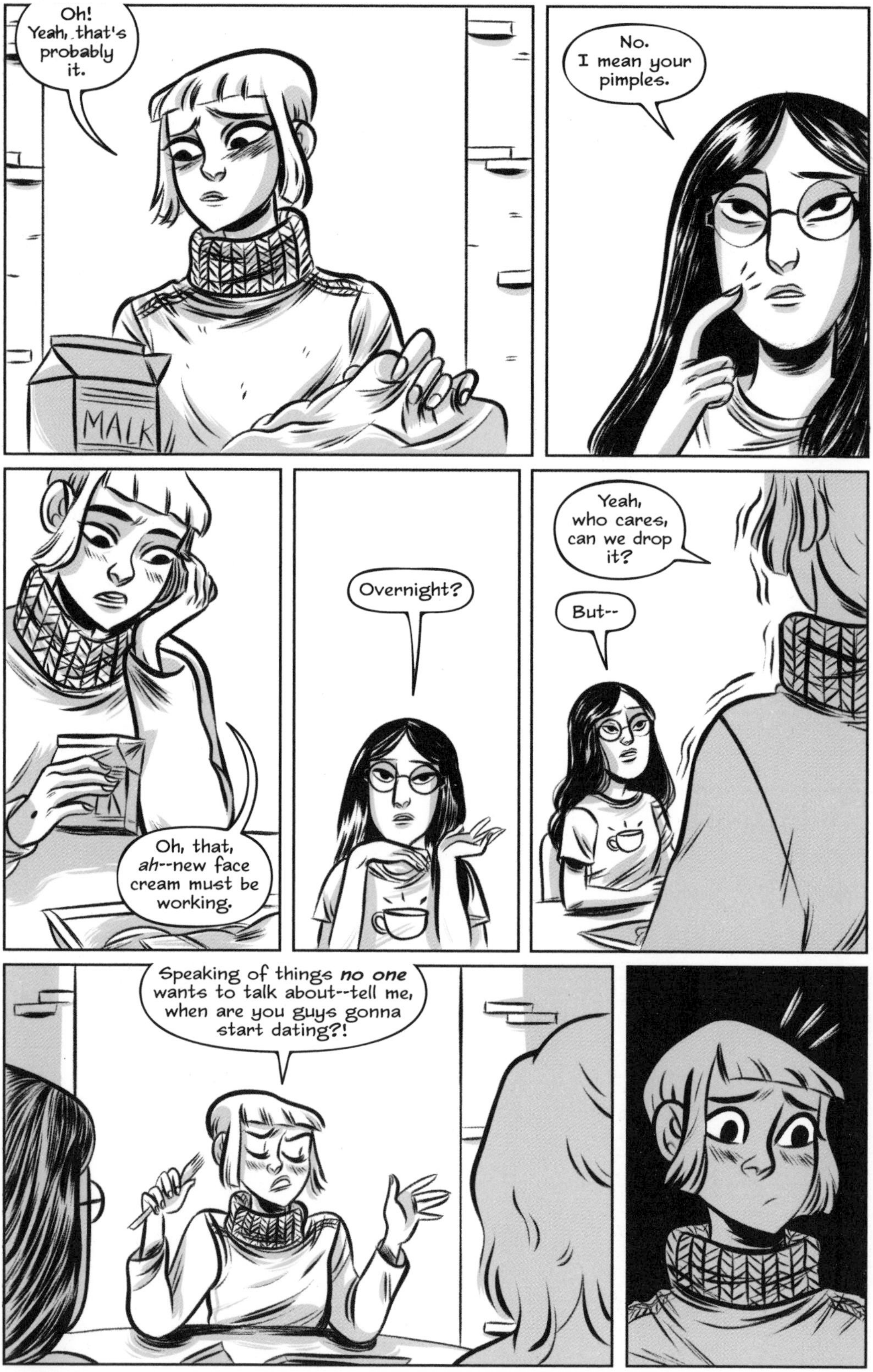
Oh! Yeah, that's probably it.
No. I mean your pimples.
MALK
Oh, that, *ah*--new face cream must be working.
Overnight?
Yeah, who cares, can we drop it?
But--
Speaking of things ***no one*** wants to talk about--tell me, when are you guys gonna start dating?!

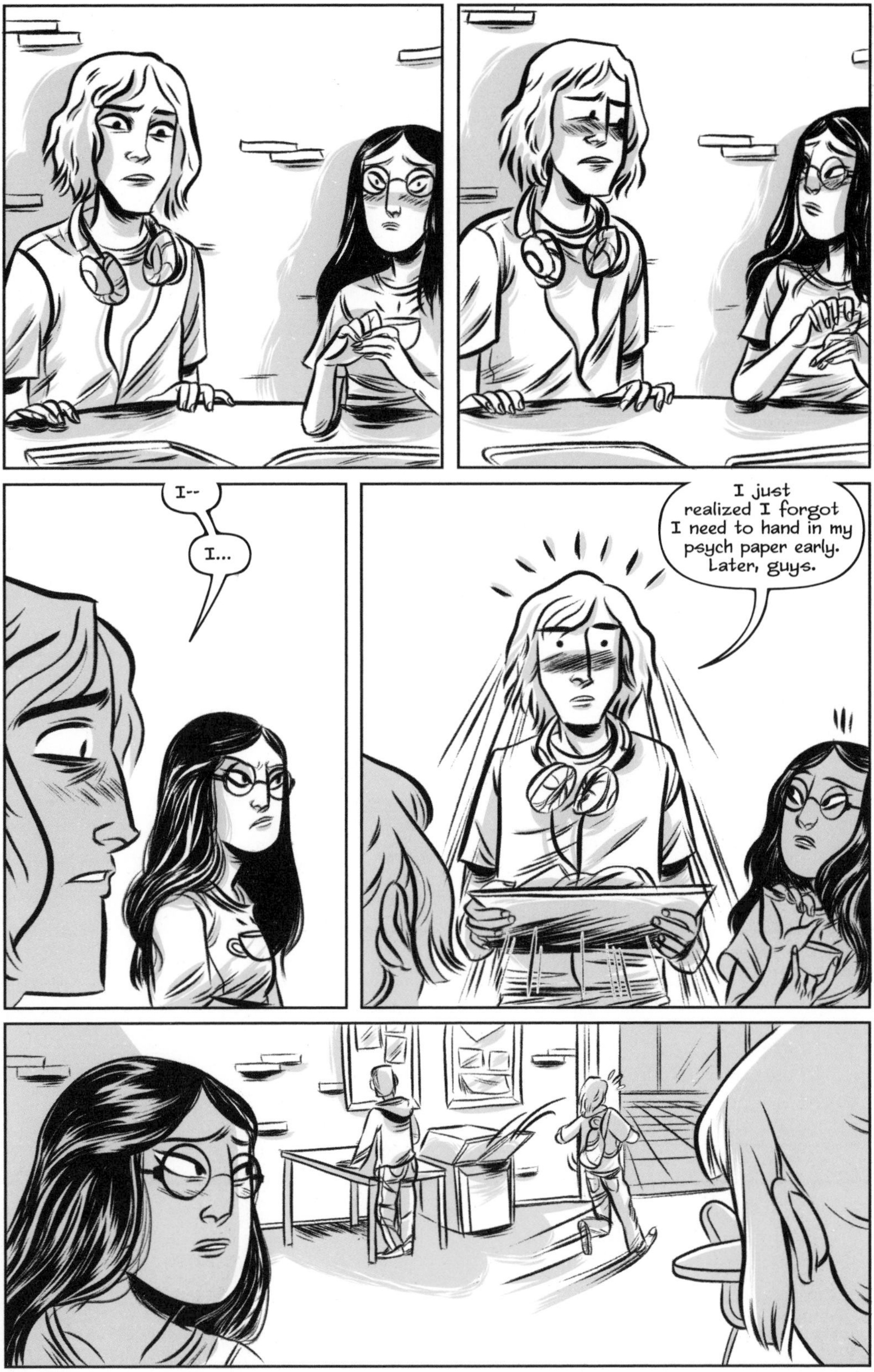
I--
I...
I just realized I forgot I need to hand in my psych paper early. Later, guys.

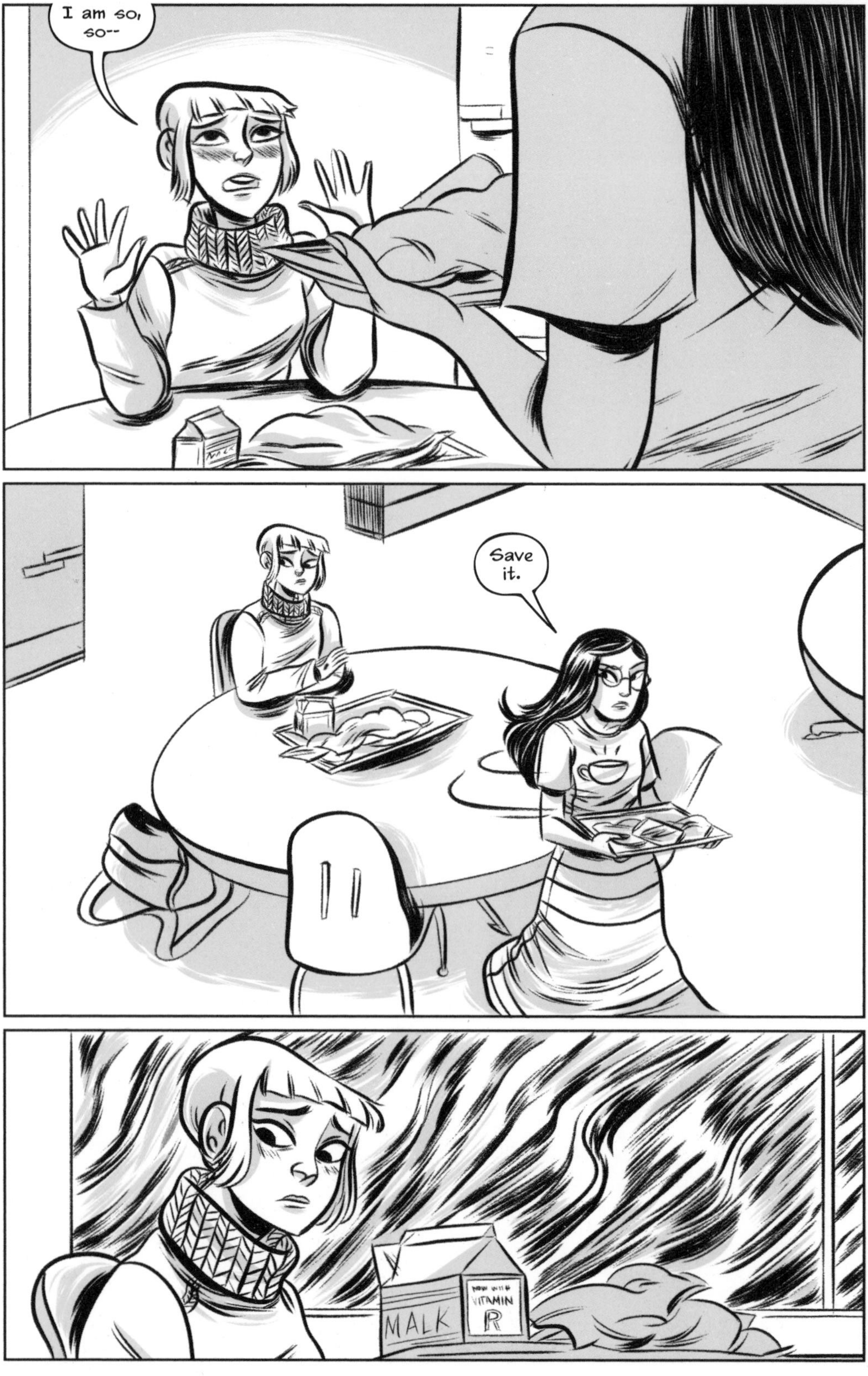
I am so, so--
Save it.
MALK
MALK
NOW WITH VITAMIN R

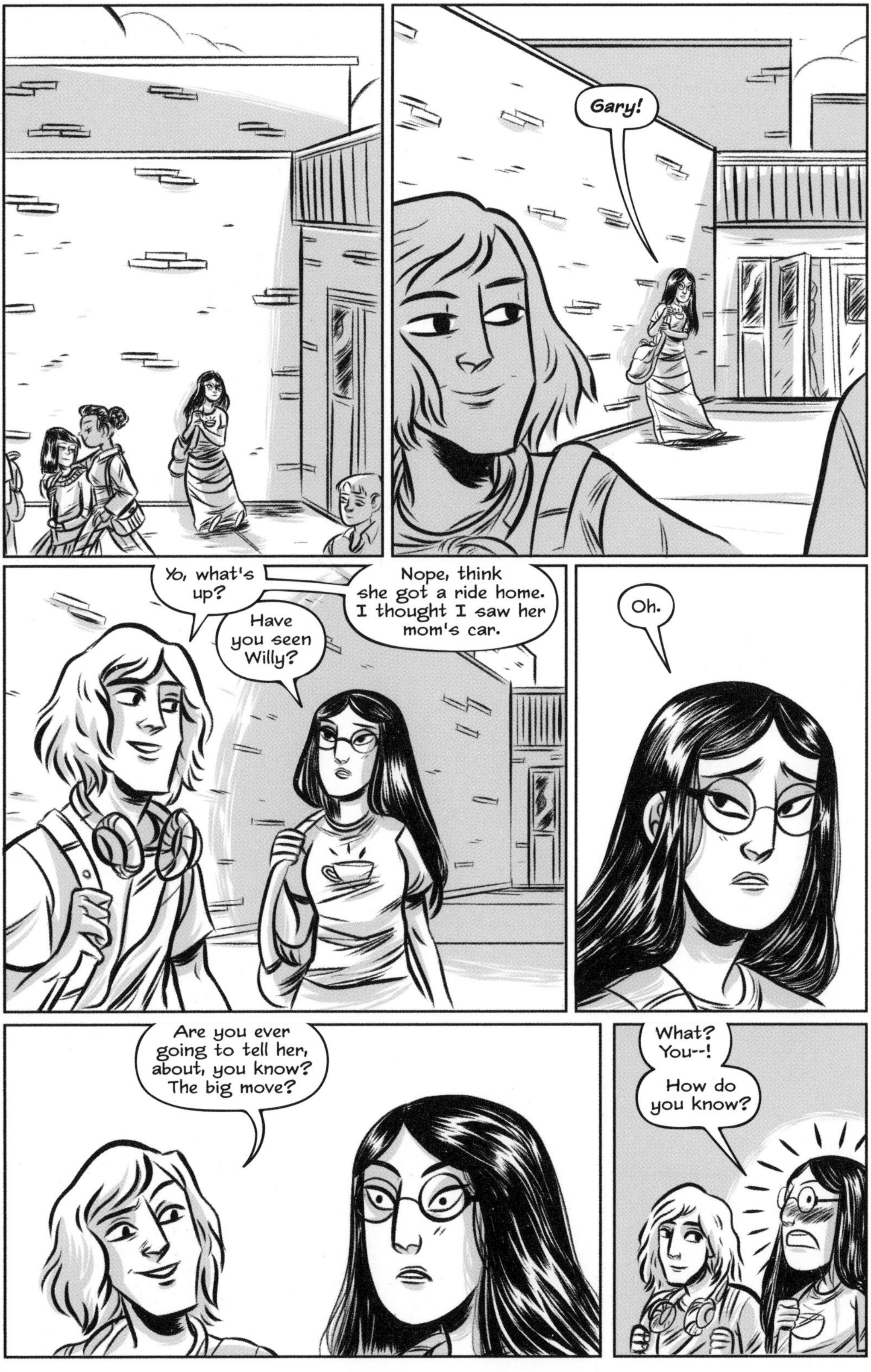
Gary!
Yo, what's up?
Have you seen Willy?
Nope, think she got a ride home. I thought I saw her mom's car.
Oh.
Are you ever going to tell her, about, you know? The big move?
What? You--!
How do you know?

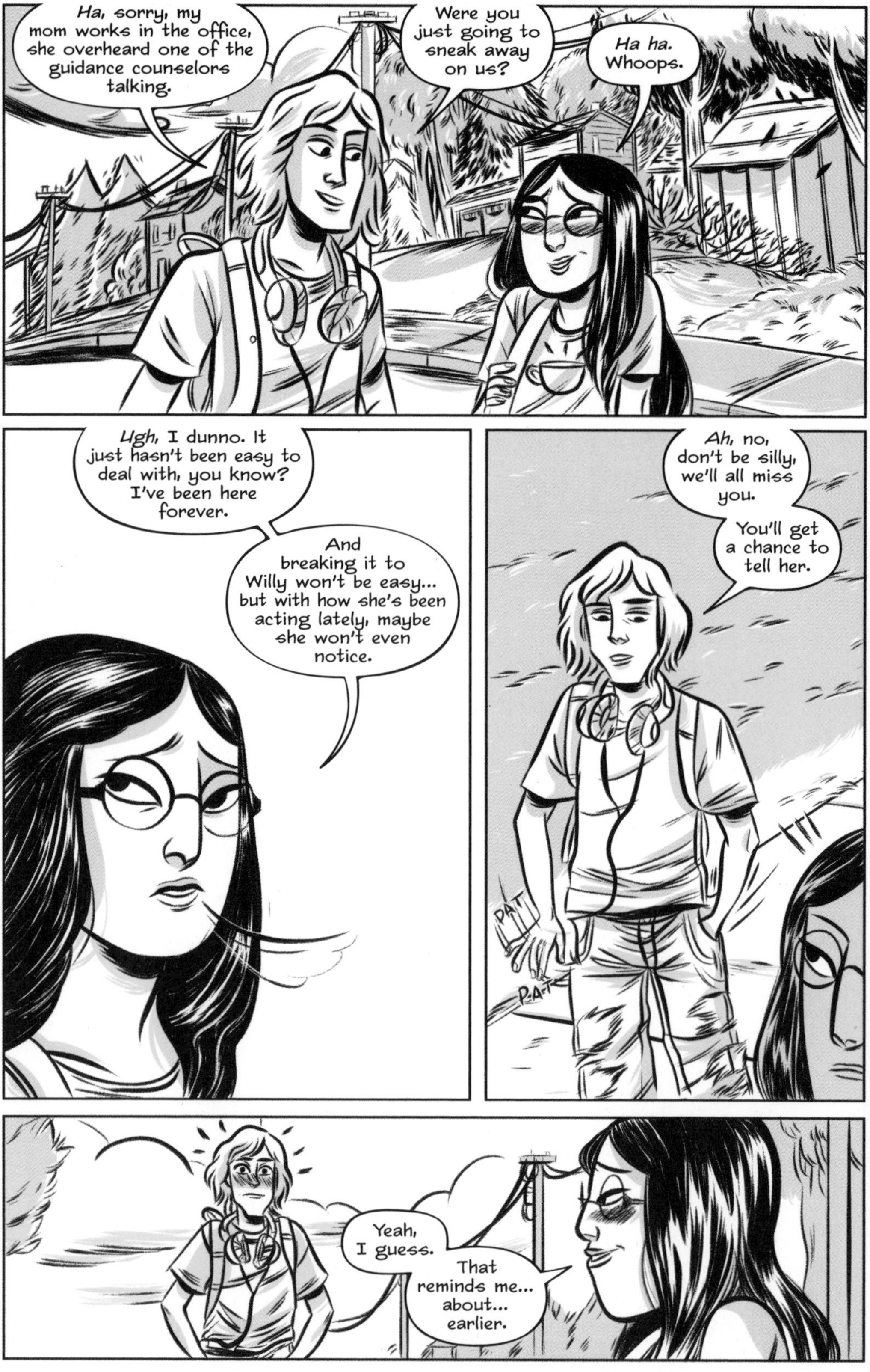
Ha, sorry, my mom works in the office, she overheard one of the guidance counselors talking.
Were you just going to sneak away on us?
Ha ha. Whoops.
Ugh, I dunno. It just hasn't been easy to deal with, you know? I've been here forever.
And breaking it to Willy won't be easy... but with how she's been acting lately, maybe she won't even notice.
Ah, no, don't be silly, we'll all miss you.
You'll get a chance to tell her.
PAT
P-A-T
Yeah, I guess.
That reminds me... about... earlier.

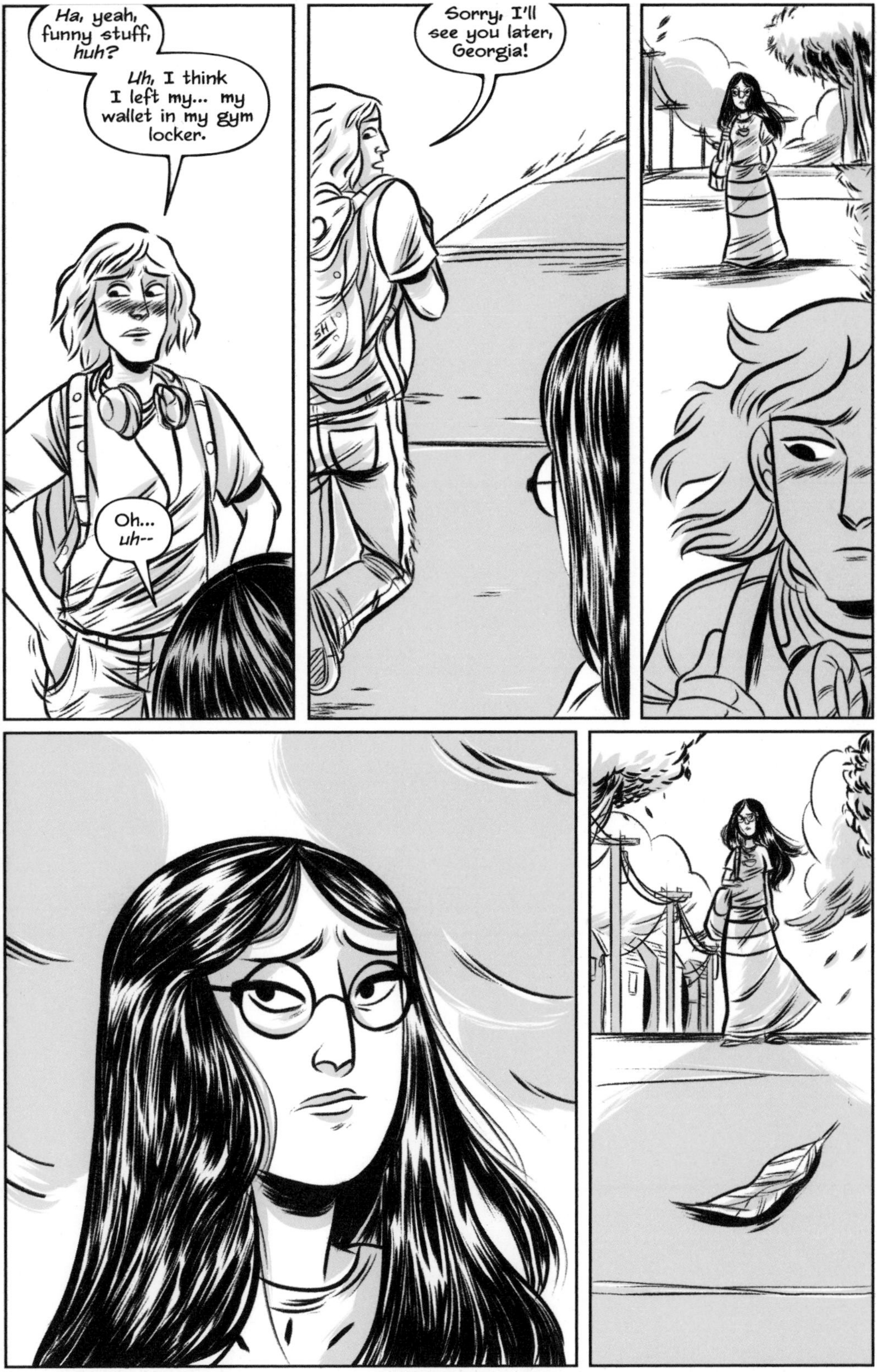
Ha, yeah, funny stuff, huh?
Uh, I think I left my... my wallet in my gym locker.
Oh... uh--
Sorry, I'll see you later, Georgia!
SH

Some potatoes, honey?

Uh. Sure.

THUNK

Willy, how many times do I see you in that sweater?

Maybe you should, I dunno, mix things up a bit?

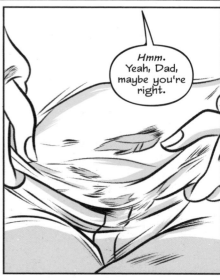

Hmm. Yeah, Dad, maybe you're right.

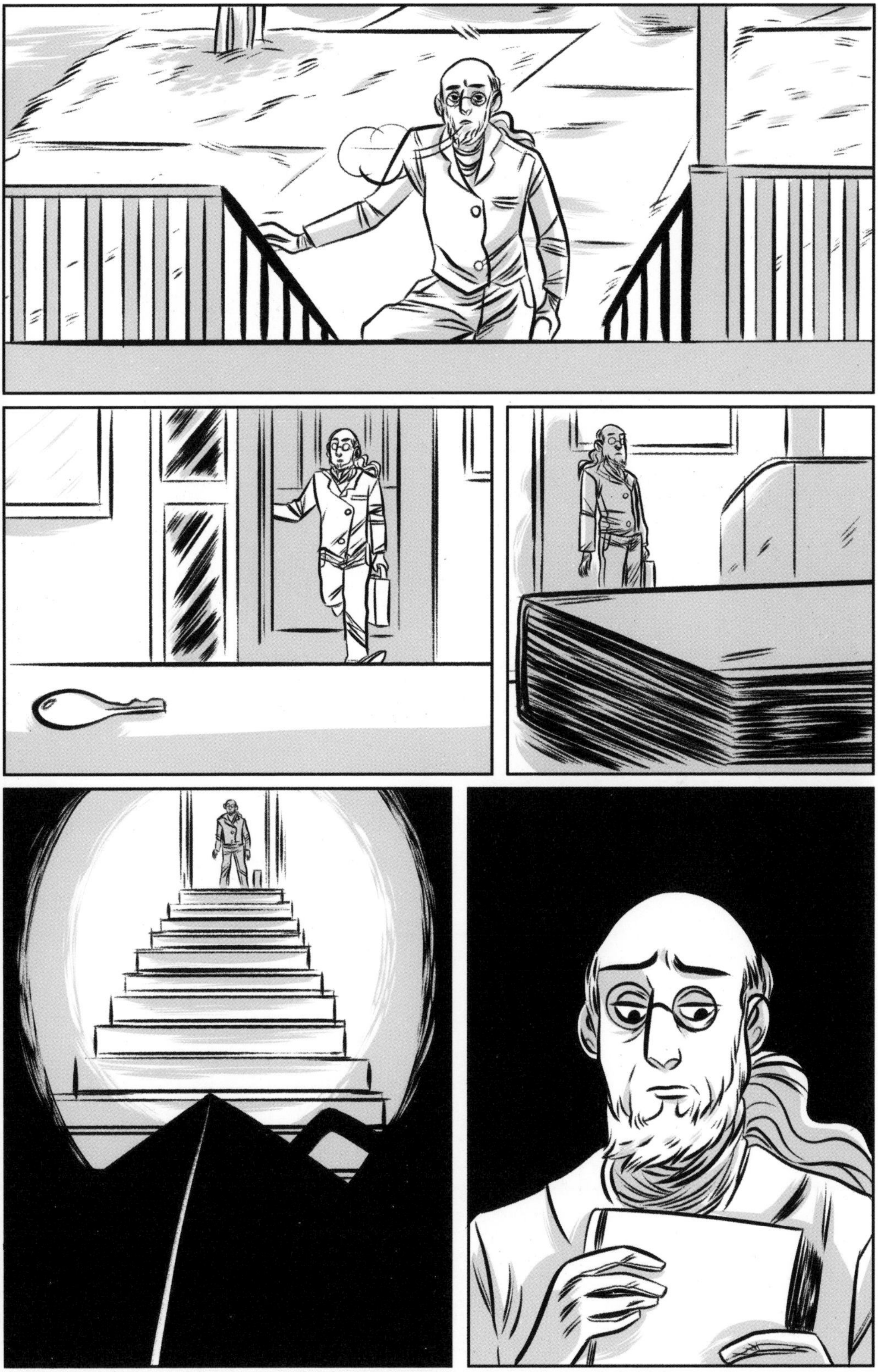

There.

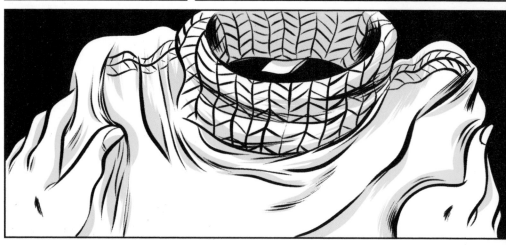

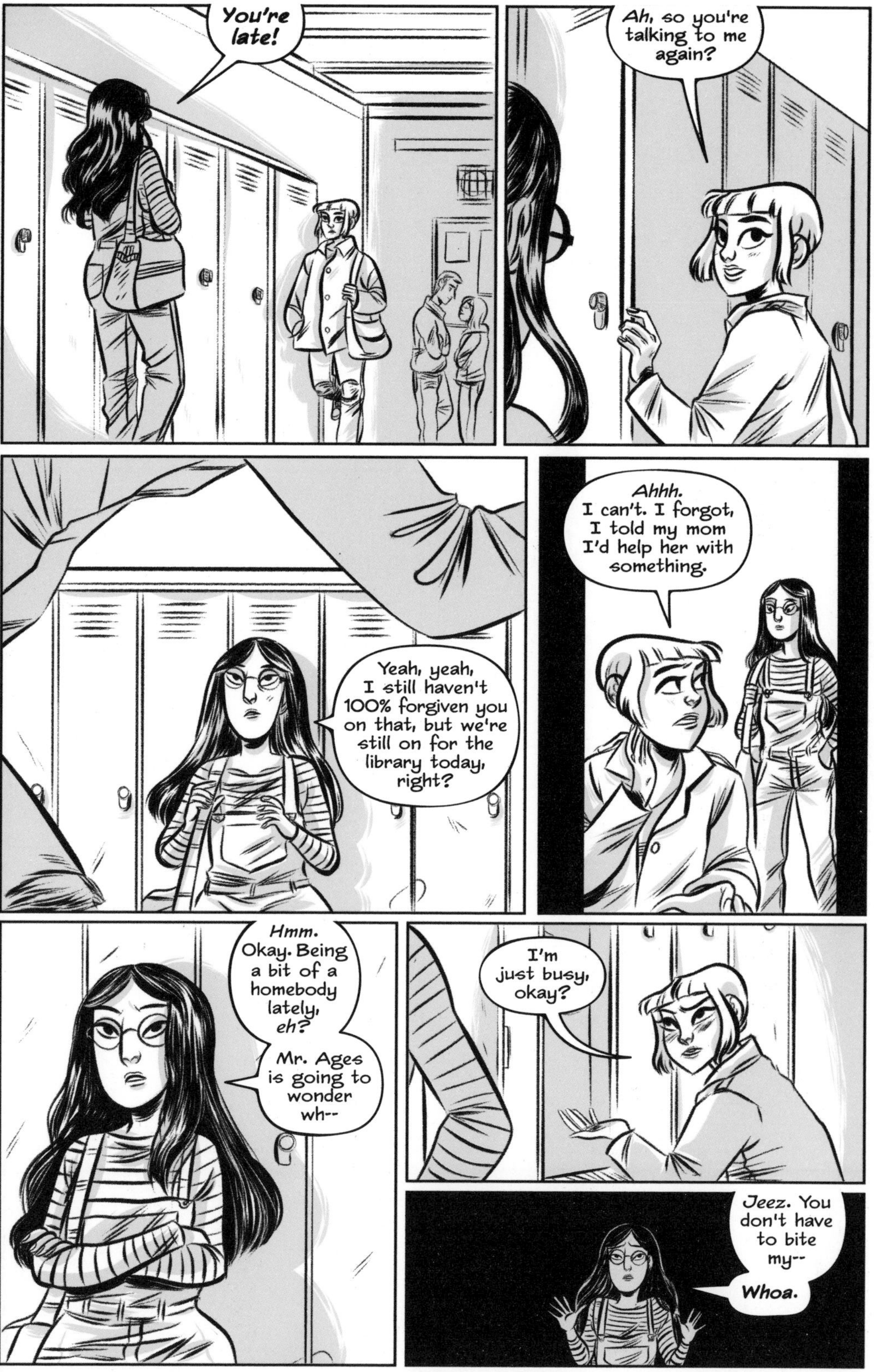
You're late!
Ah, so you're talking to me again?
Yeah, yeah, I still haven't 100% forgiven you on that, but we're still on for the library today, right?
Ahhh. I can't. I forgot, I told my mom I'd help her with something.
Hmm. Okay. Being a bit of a homebody lately, eh?
Mr. Ages is going to wonder wh--
I'm just busy, okay?
Jeez. You don't have to bite my--
Whoa.

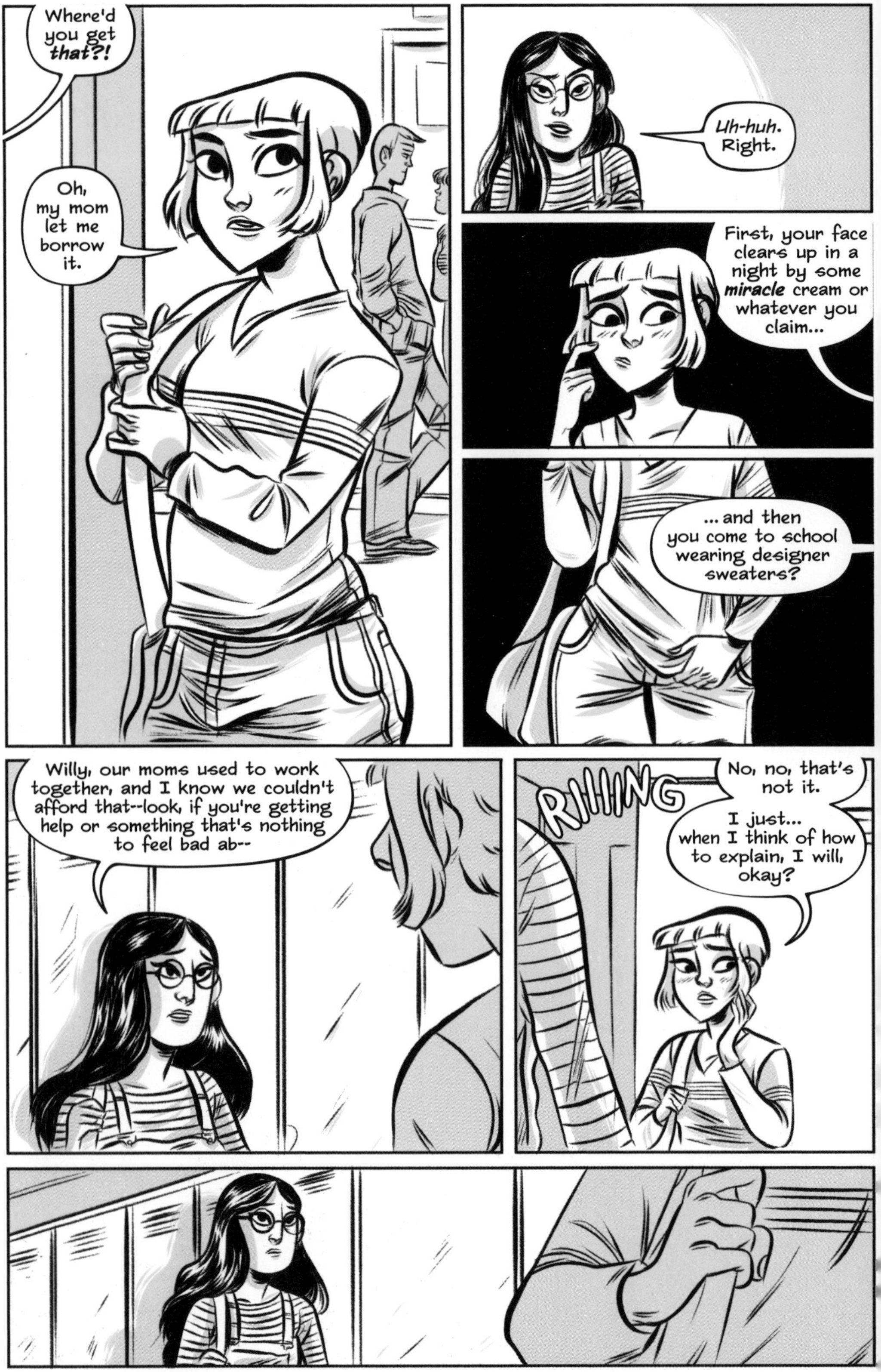
Where'd you get *that?!*
Oh, my mom let me borrow it.
Uh-huh. Right.
First, your face clears up in a night by some *miracle* cream or whatever you claim...
...and then you come to school wearing designer sweaters?
Willy, our moms used to work together, and I know we couldn't afford that--look, if you're getting help or something that's nothing to feel bad ab--
RIIIING
No, no, that's not it.
I just... when I think of how to explain, I will, okay?

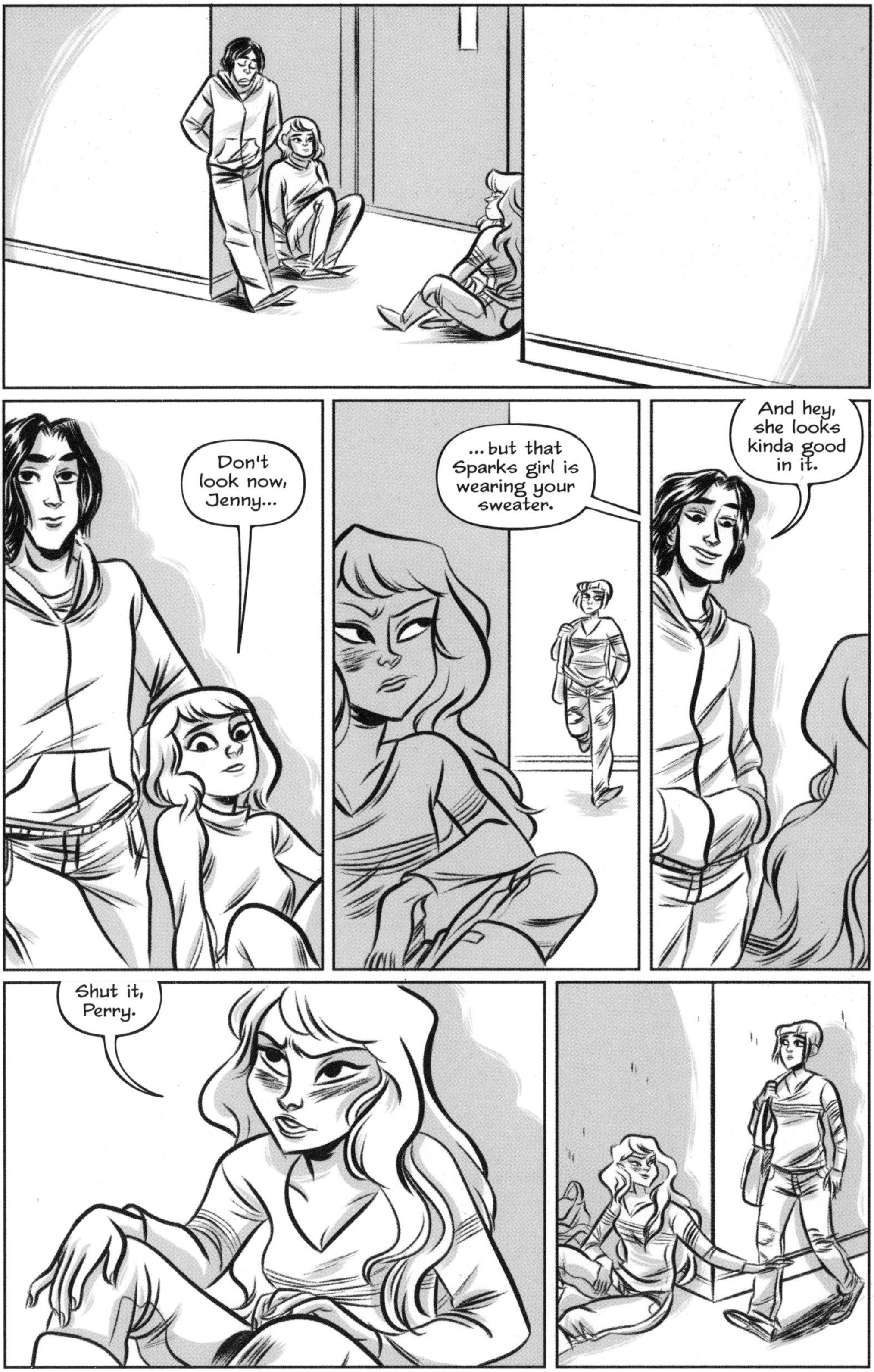
Don't look now, Jenny...
...but that Sparks girl is wearing your sweater.
And hey, she looks kinda good in it.
Shut it, Perry.

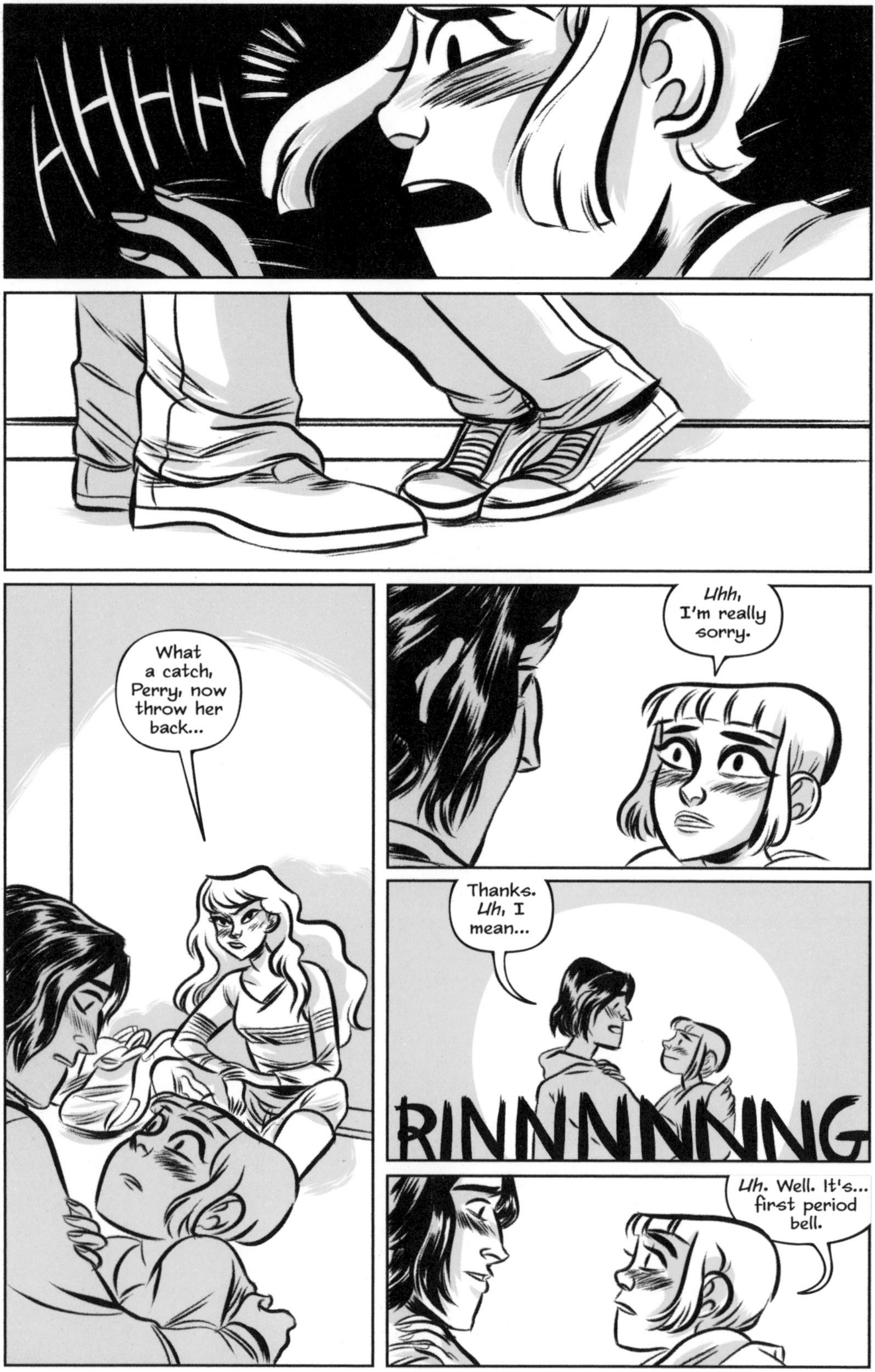
AHHHH
What a catch, Perry, now throw her back...
Uhh, I'm really sorry.
Thanks. Uh, I mean...
RINNNNNNG
Uh. Well. It's... first period bell.

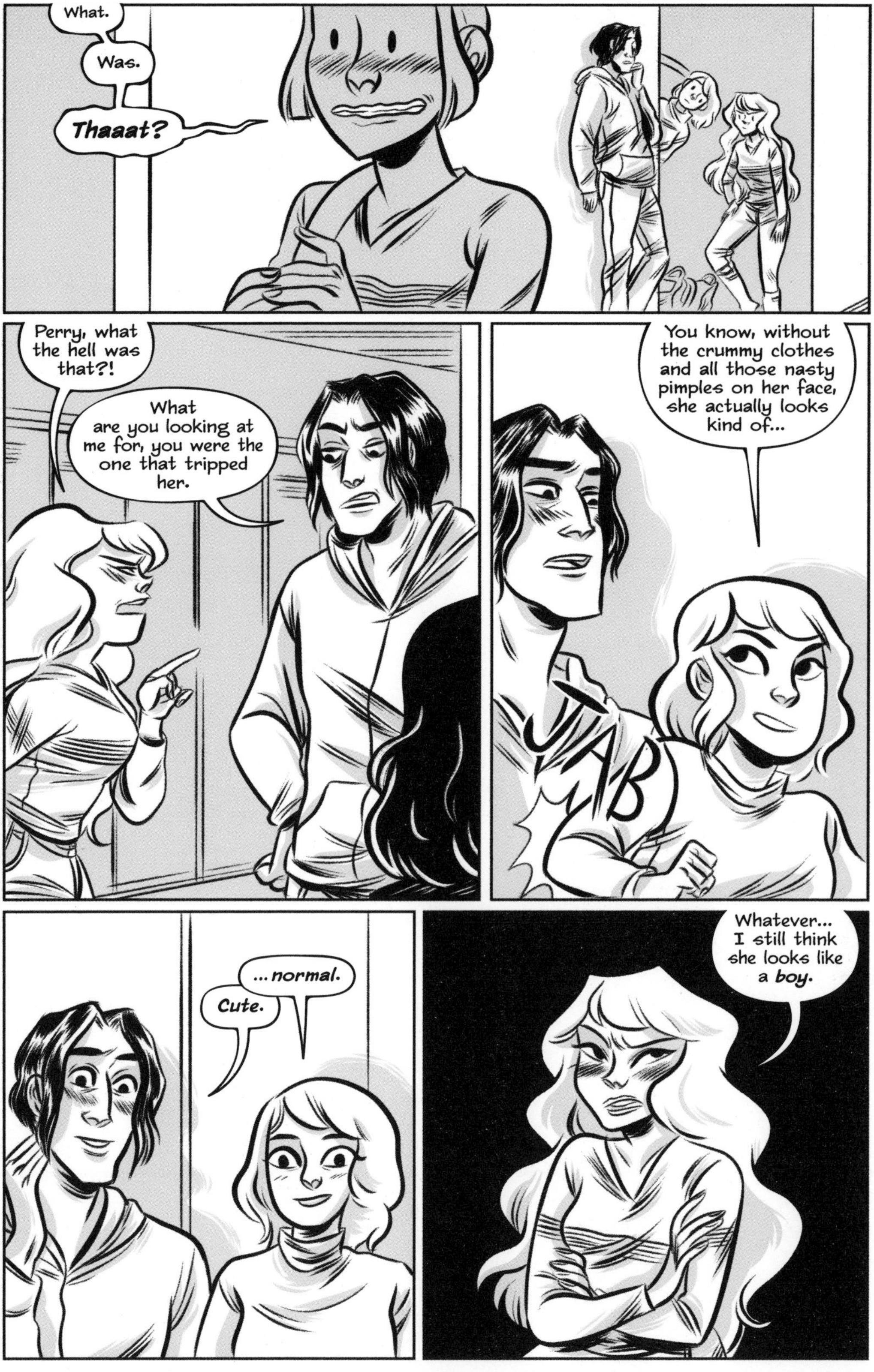
What.
Was.
Thaaat?
Perry, what the hell was that?!
What are you looking at me for, you were the one that tripped her.
You know, without the crummy clothes and all those nasty pimples on her face, she actually looks kind of...
JAB
Cute.
...normal.
Whatever... I still think she looks like a boy.

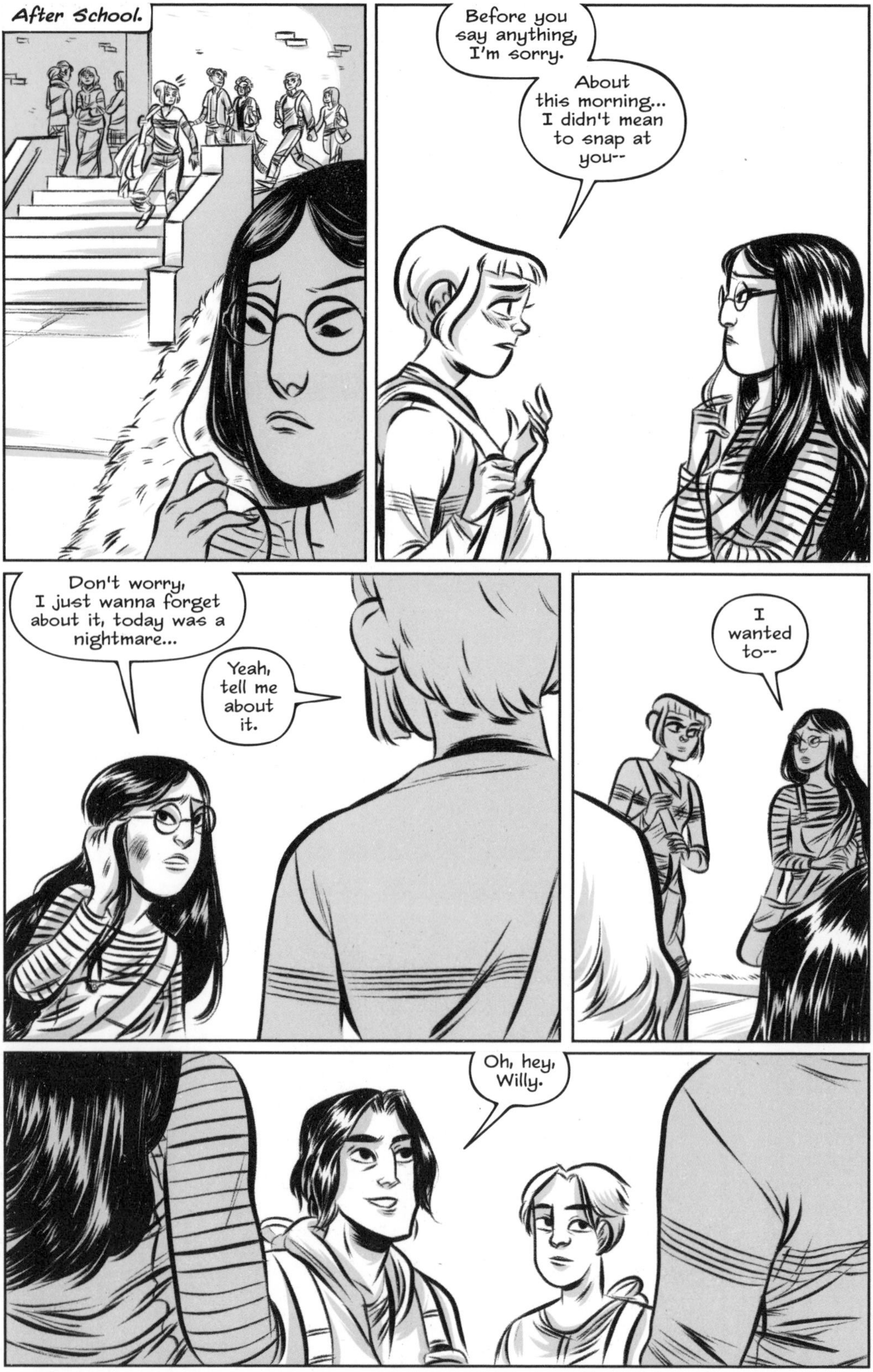
After School.
Before you say anything, I'm sorry.
About this morning... I didn't mean to snap at you--
Don't worry, I just wanna forget about it, today was a nightmare...
Yeah, tell me about it.
I wanted to--
Oh, hey, Willy.

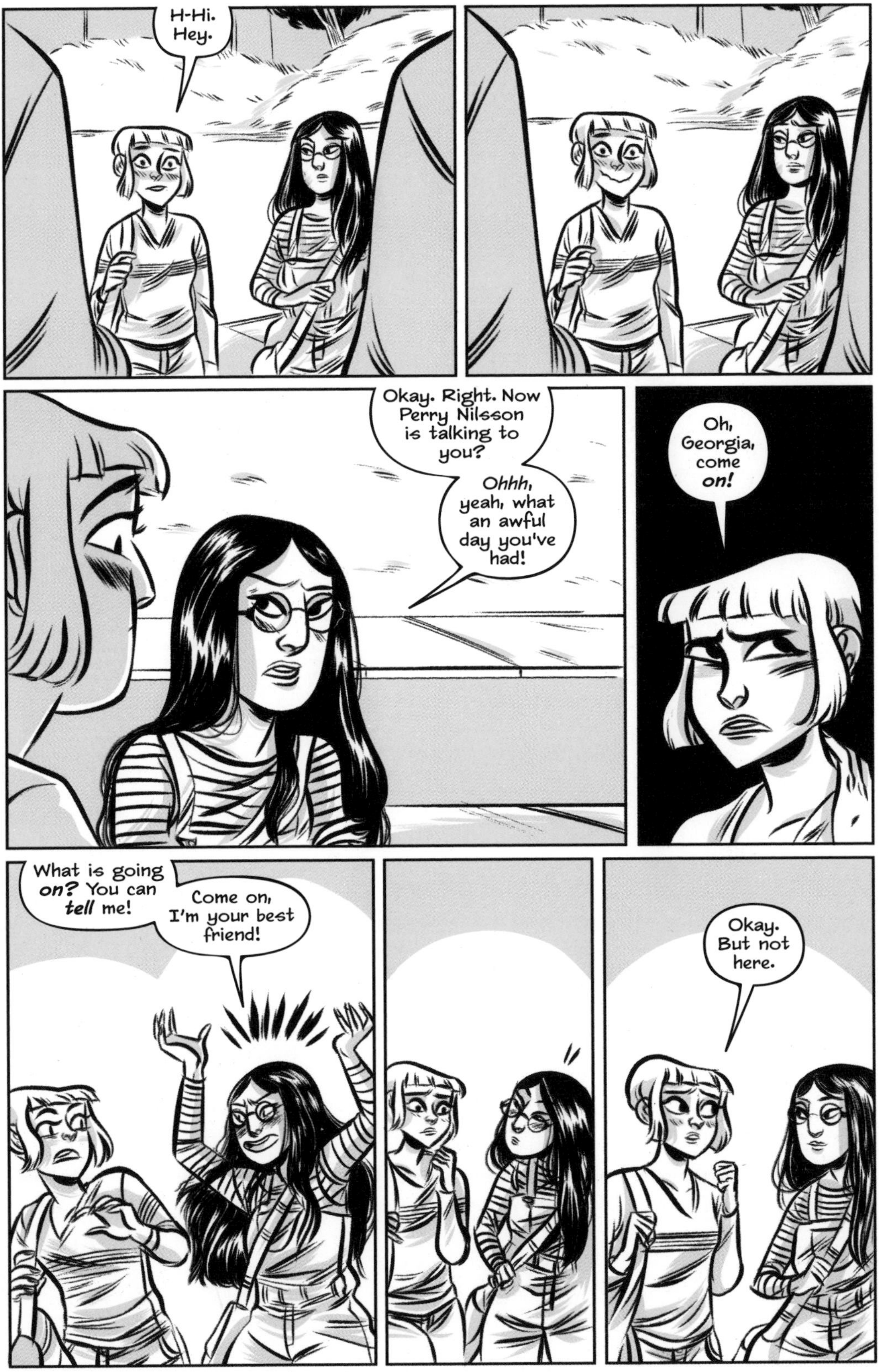
H-Hi. Hey.
Okay. Right. Now Perry Nilsson is talking to you?
Ohhh, yeah, what an awful day you've had!
Oh, Georgia, come *on!*
What is going *on?* You can *tell* me!
Come on, I'm your best friend!
Okay. But not here.

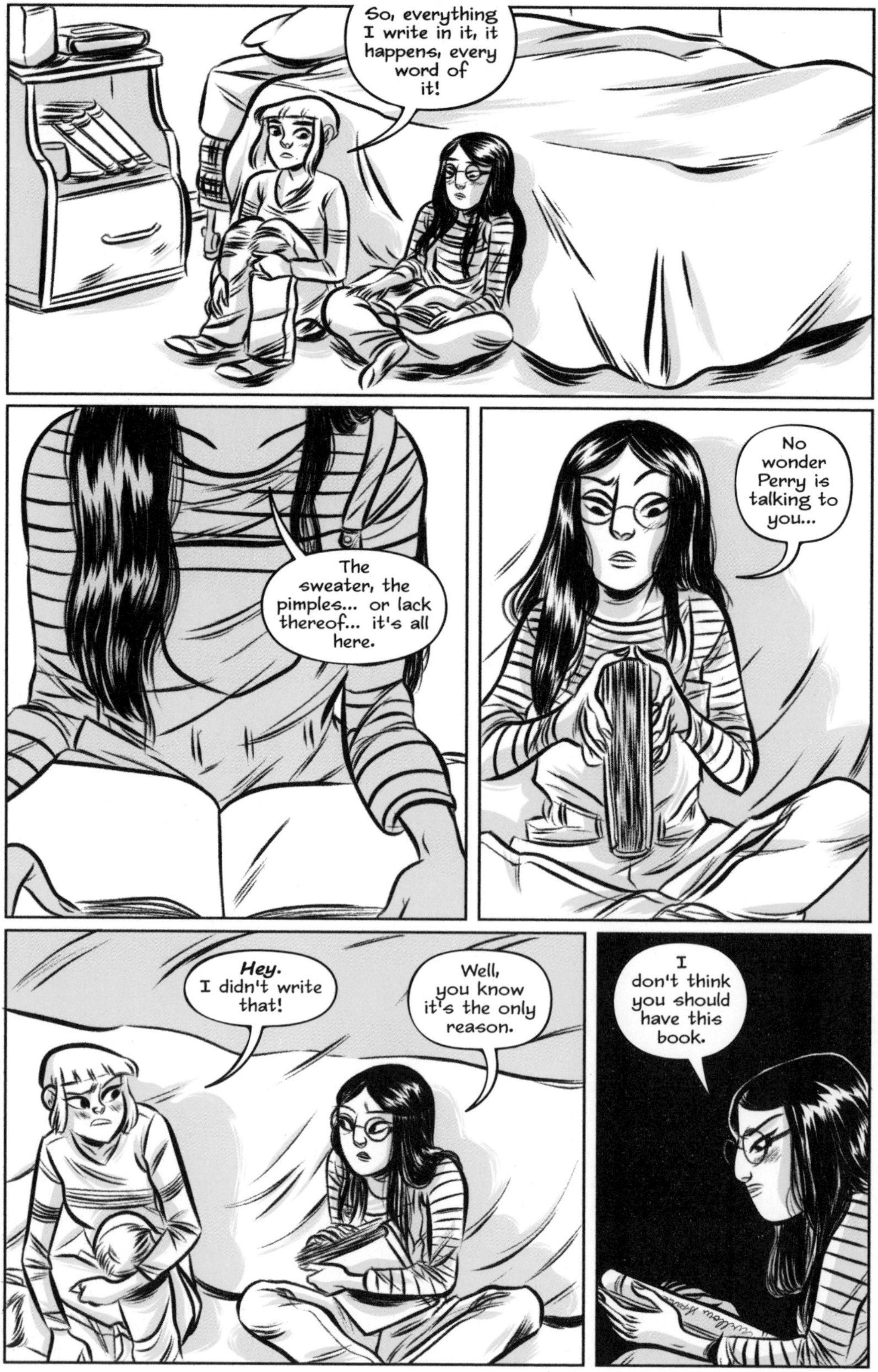
So, everything I write in it, it happens, every word of it!
The sweater, the pimples... or lack thereof... it's all here.
No wonder Perry is talking to you...
Hey. I didn't write that!
Well, you know it's the only reason.
I don't think you should have this book.

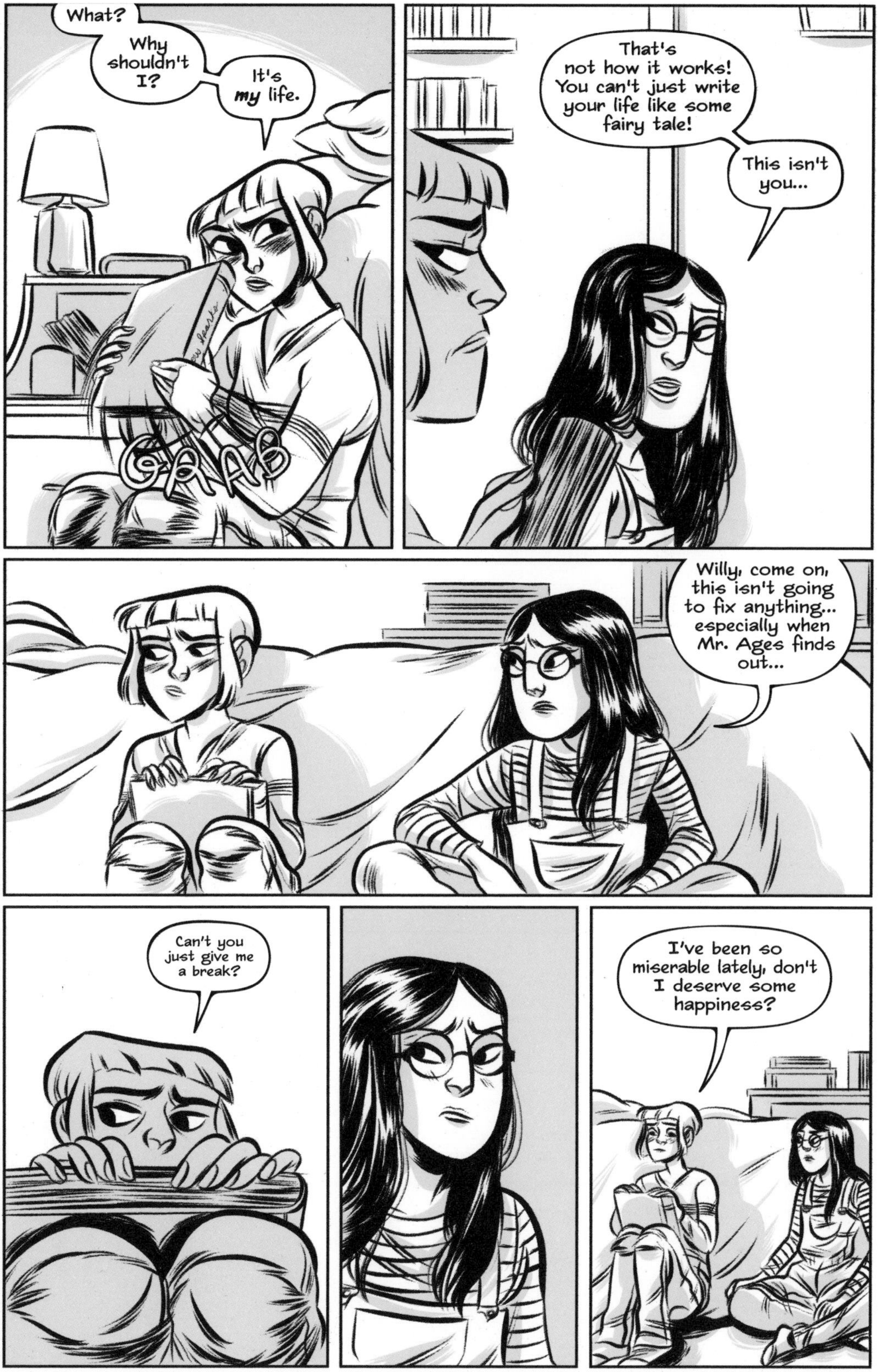
What?
Why shouldn't I?
It's *my* life.
GRAB
That's not how it works! You can't just write your life like some fairy tale!
This isn't you...
Willy, come on, this isn't going to fix anything... especially when Mr. Ages finds out...
Can't you just give me a break?
I've been so miserable lately, don't I deserve some happiness?

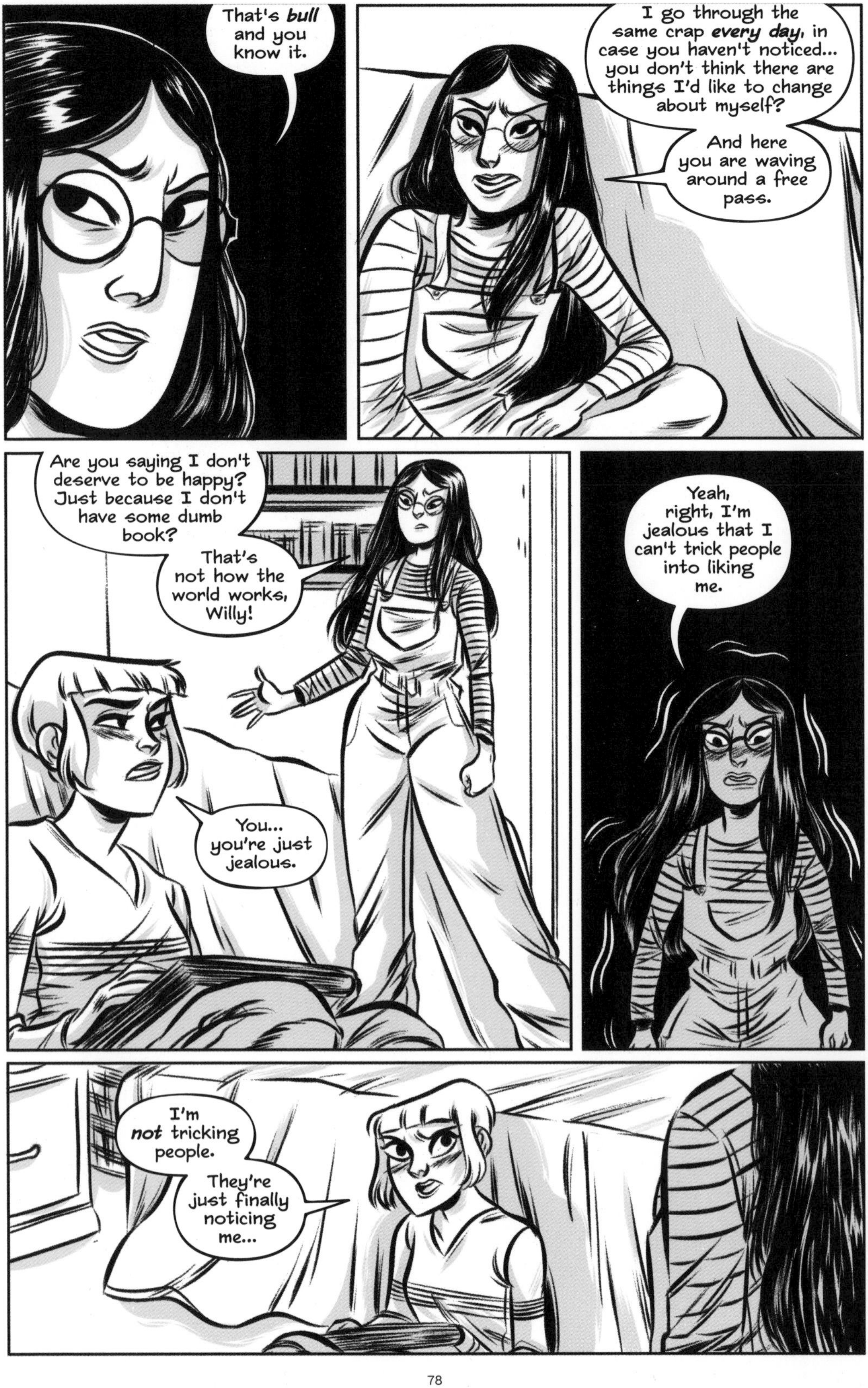
That's *bull* and you know it.
I go through the same crap *every day*, in case you haven't noticed... you don't think there are things I'd like to change about myself?
And here you are waving around a free pass.
Are you saying I don't deserve to be happy? Just because I don't have some dumb book?
That's not how the world works, Willy!
You... you're just jealous.
Yeah, right, I'm jealous that I can't trick people into liking me.
I'm *not* tricking people.
They're just finally noticing me...

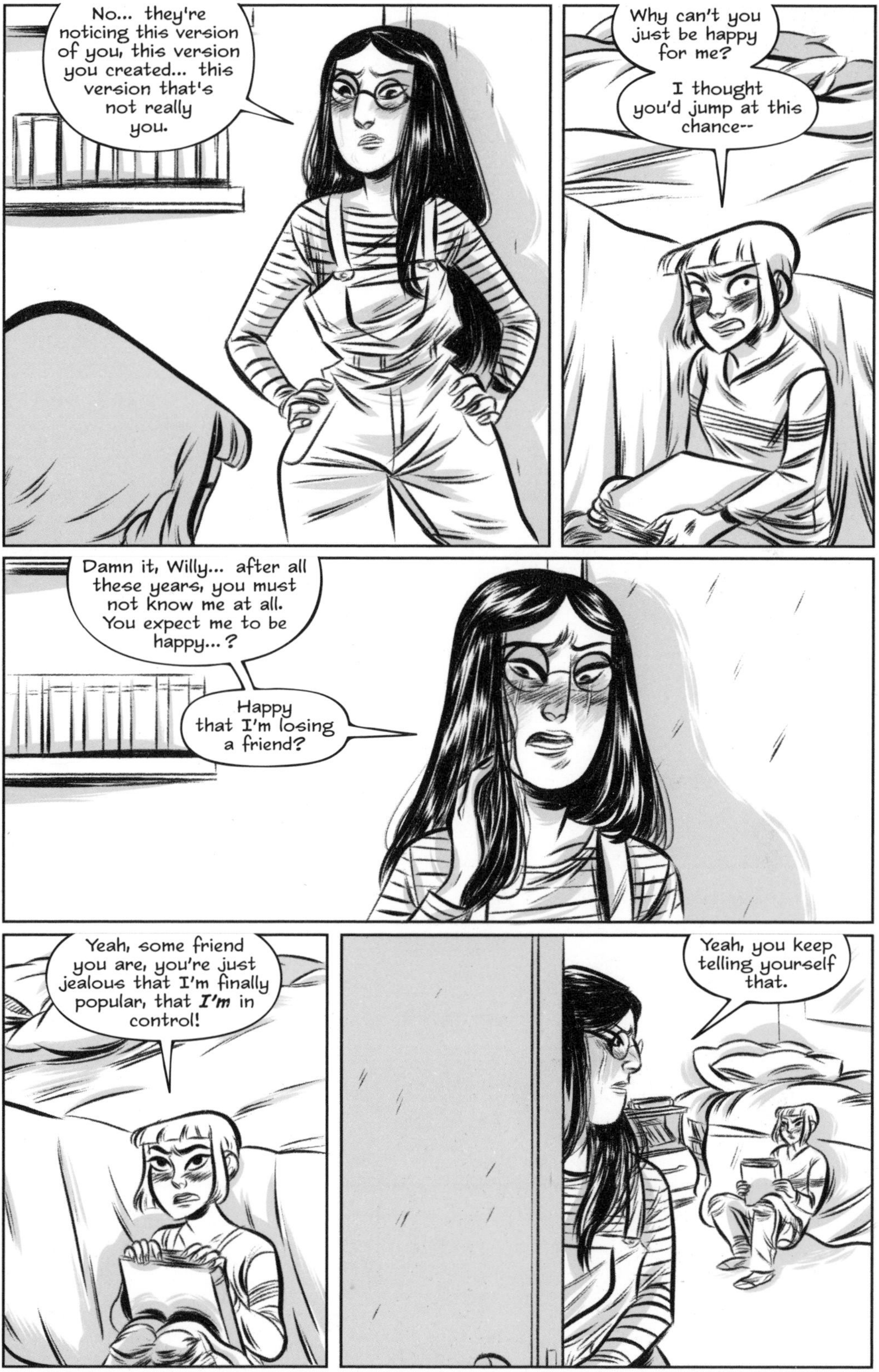
No... they're noticing this version of you, this version you created... this version that's not really you.
Why can't you just be happy for me?
I thought you'd jump at this chance--
Damn it, Willy... after all these years, you must not know me at all. You expect me to be happy...?
Happy that I'm losing a friend?
Yeah, some friend you are, you're just jealous that I'm finally popular, that ***I'm*** in control!
Yeah, you keep telling yourself that.

SLAM
Get!
Out!
Stupid!
Jerk!
Wha?
It's... what is this?
Ink?

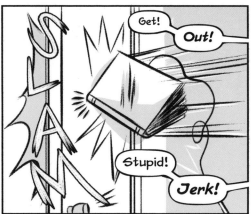

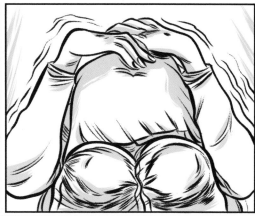

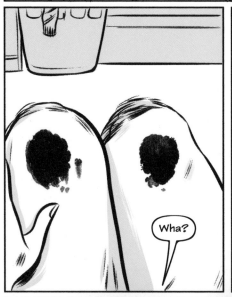

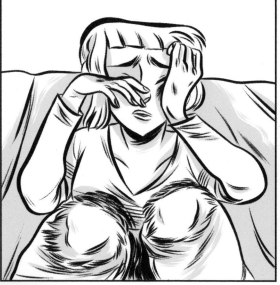

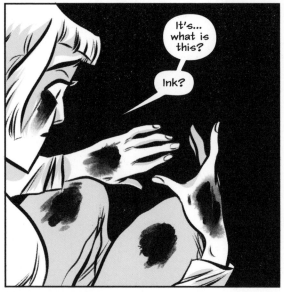

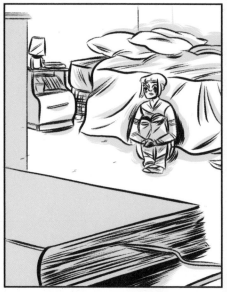

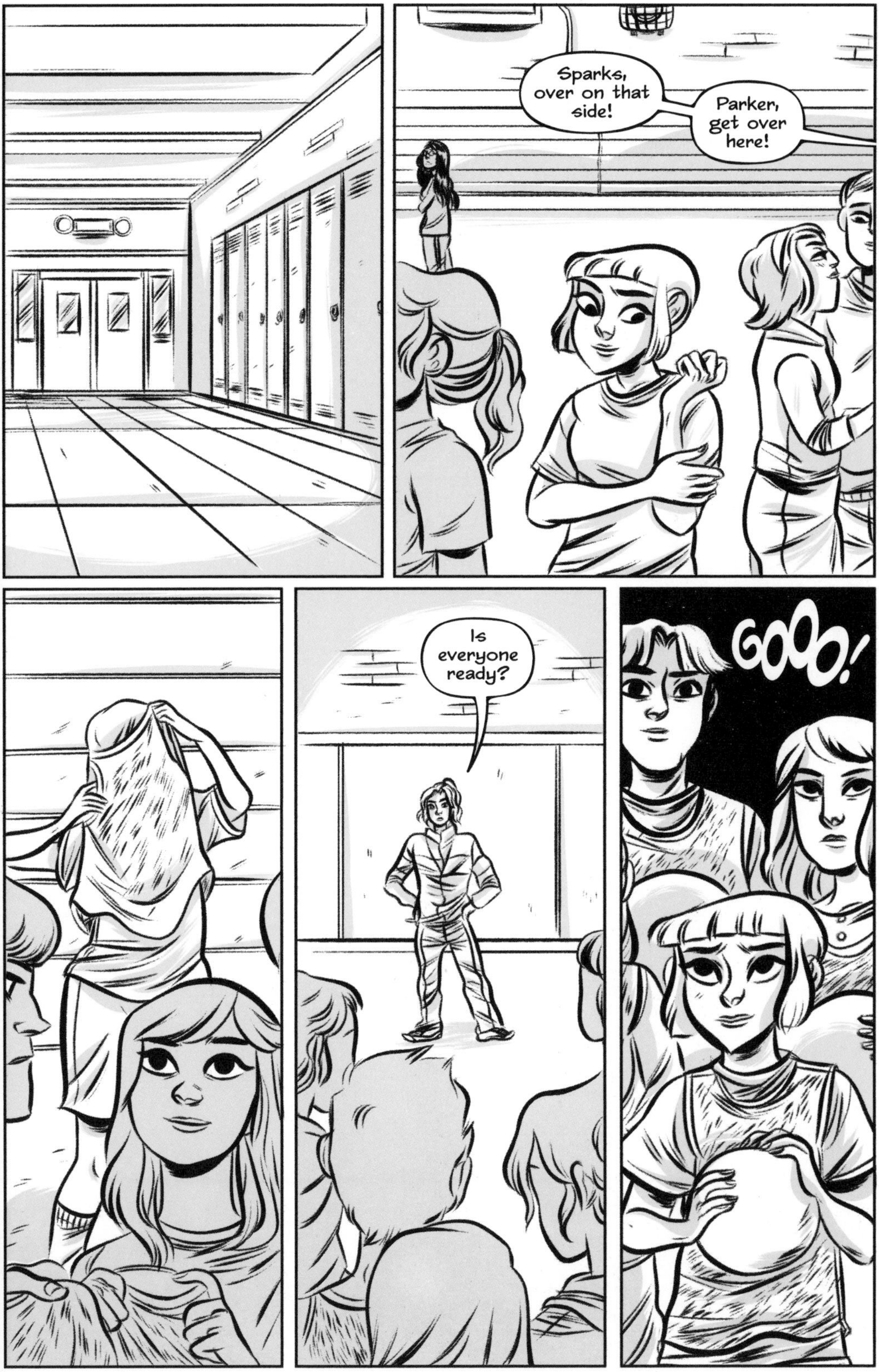

Sparks, over on that side!
Parker, get over here!
Is everyone ready?
GOOO!

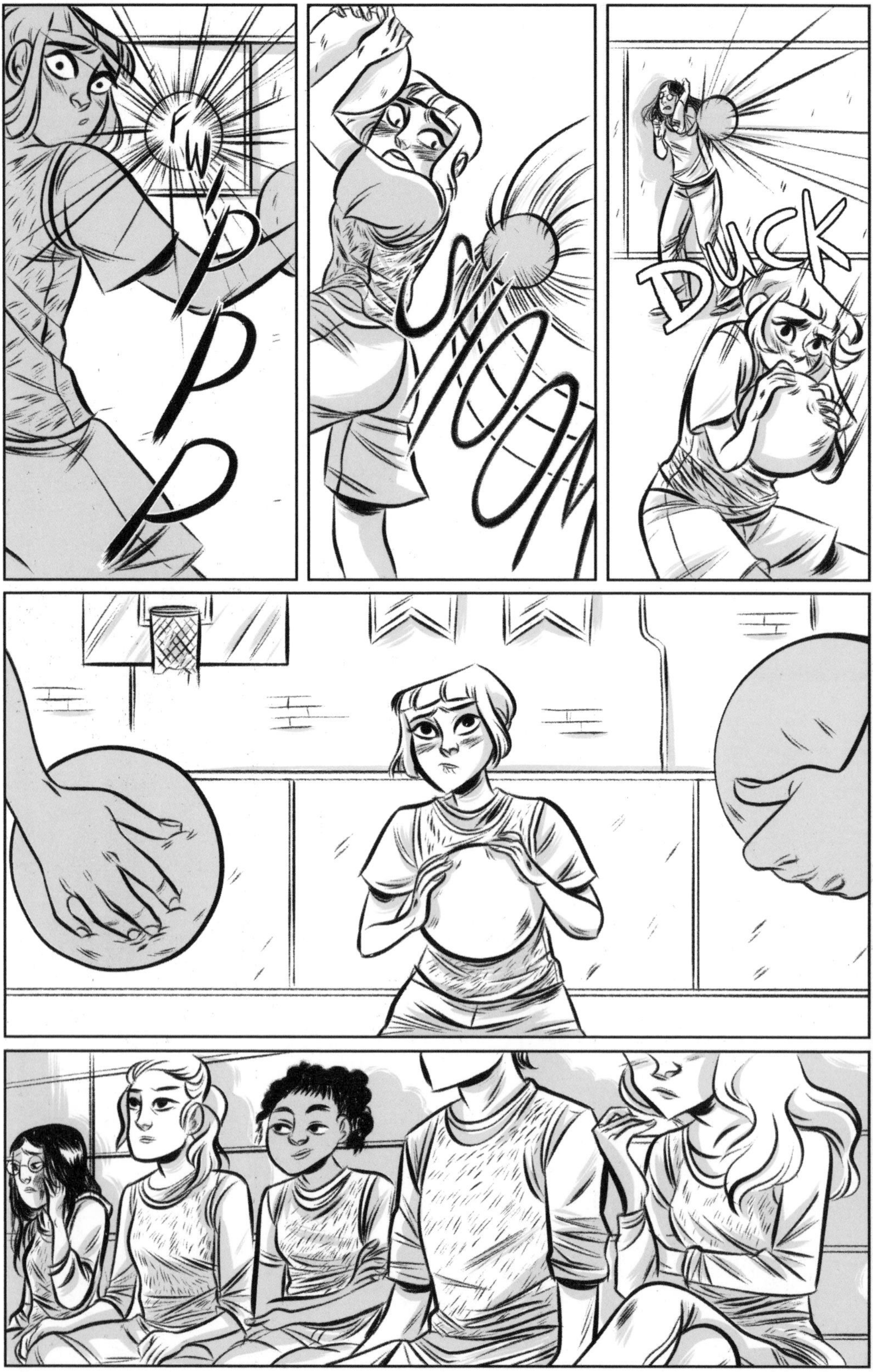
FWIPPP
DUCK

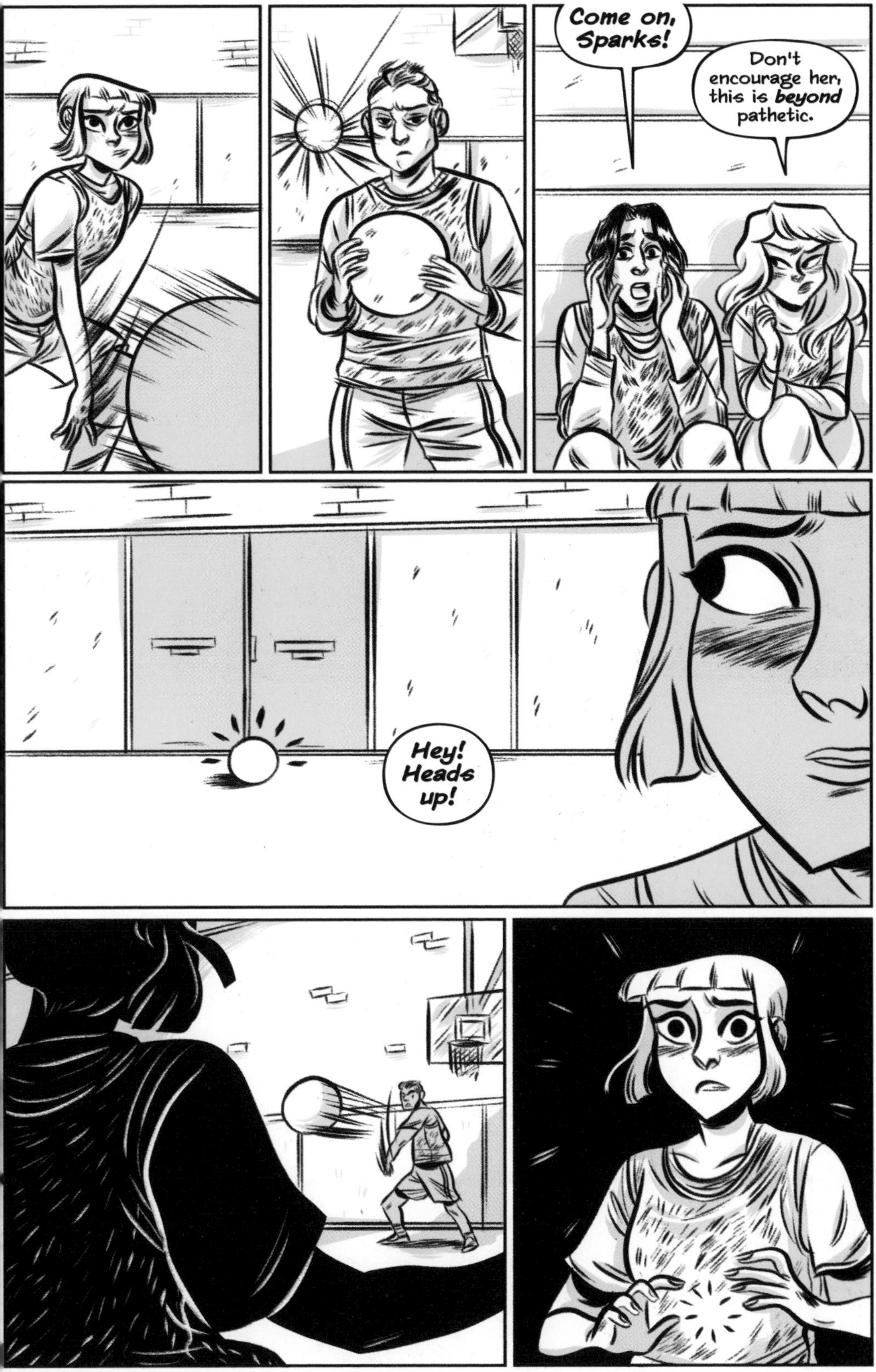
Come on, Sparks!
Don't encourage her, this is beyond pathetic.
Hey! Heads up!

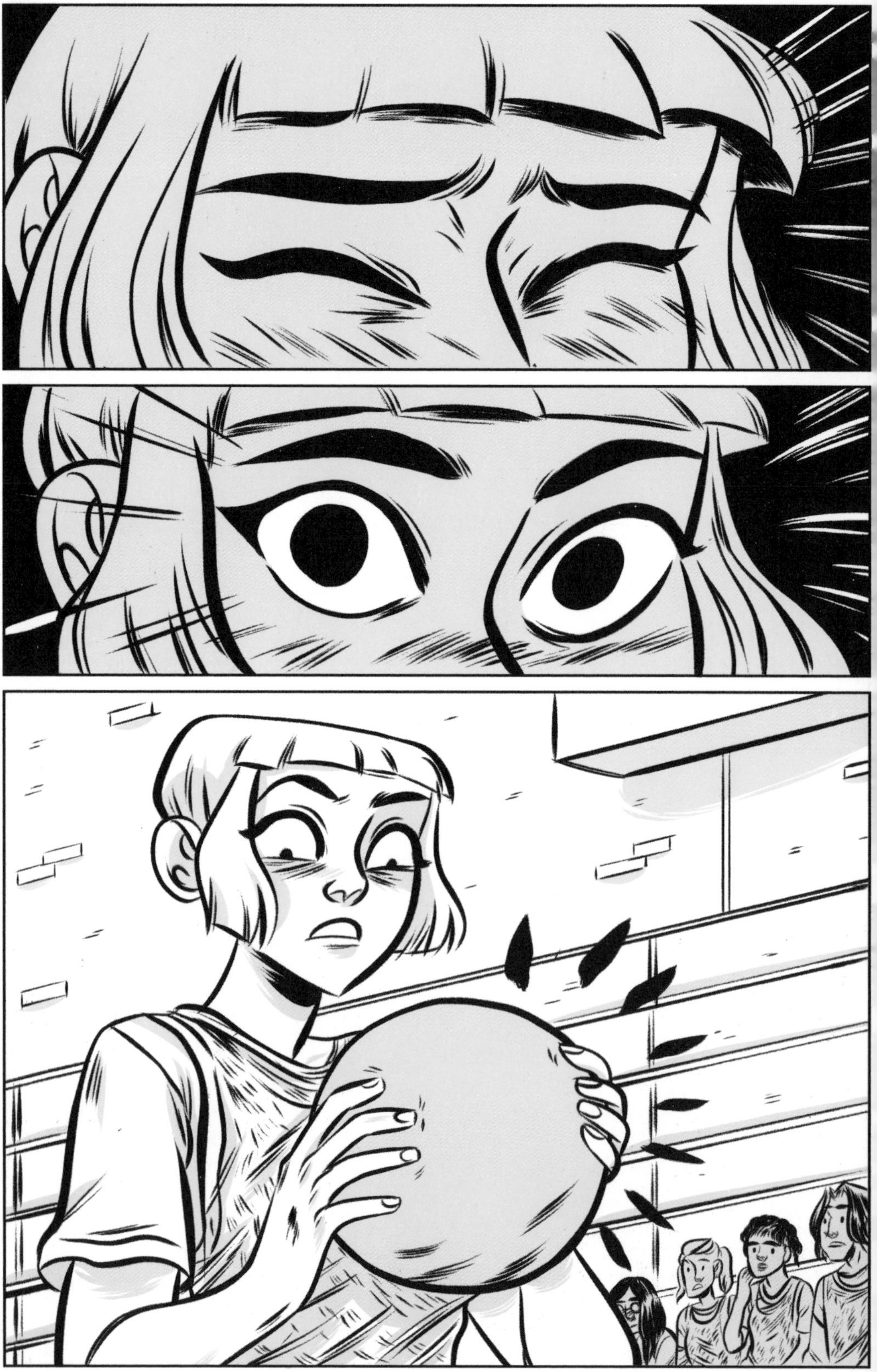

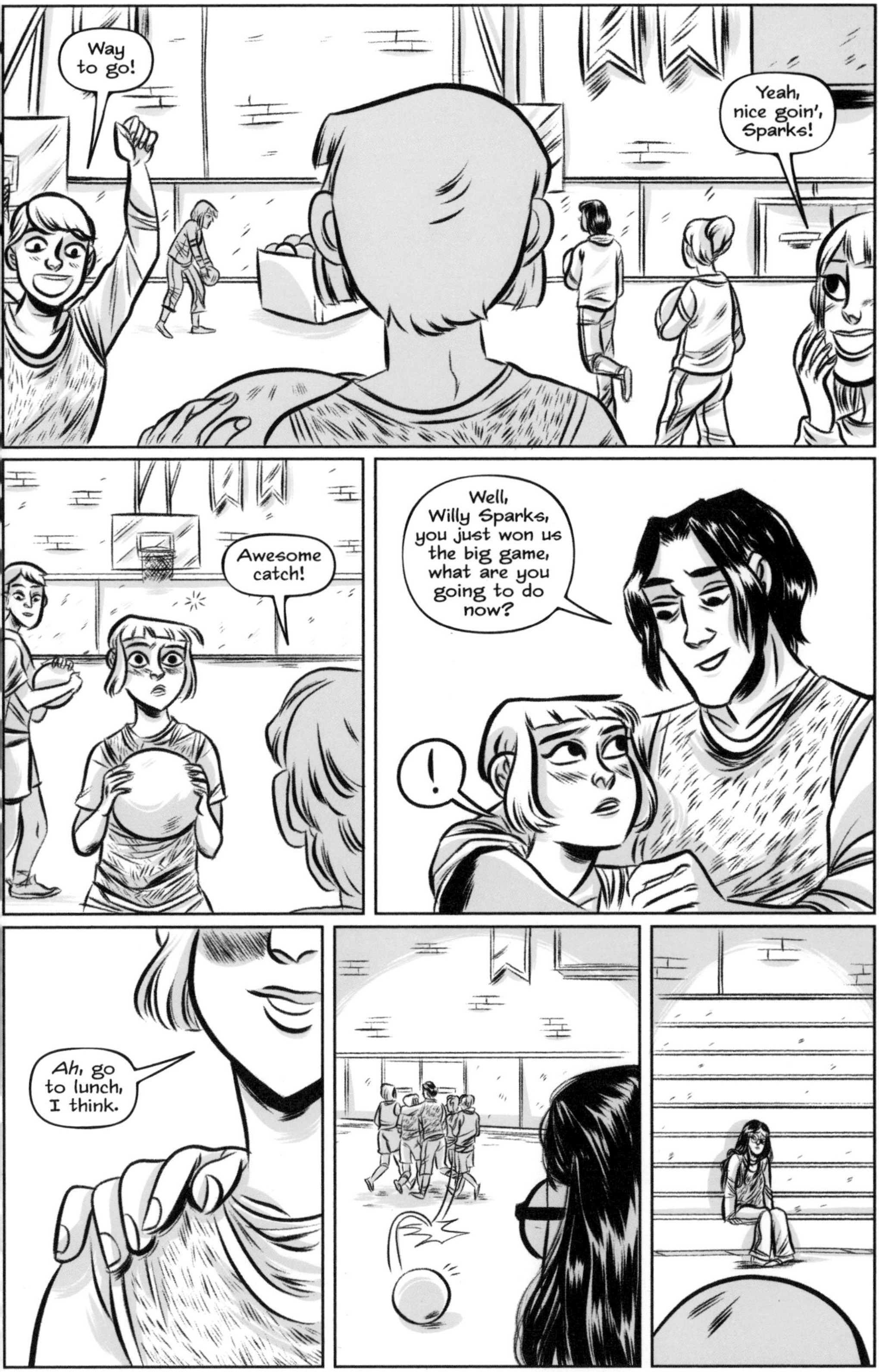
Way to go!
Yeah, nice goin', Sparks!
Awesome catch!
Well, Willy Sparks, you just won us the big game, what are you going to do now?
!
Ah, go to lunch, I think.

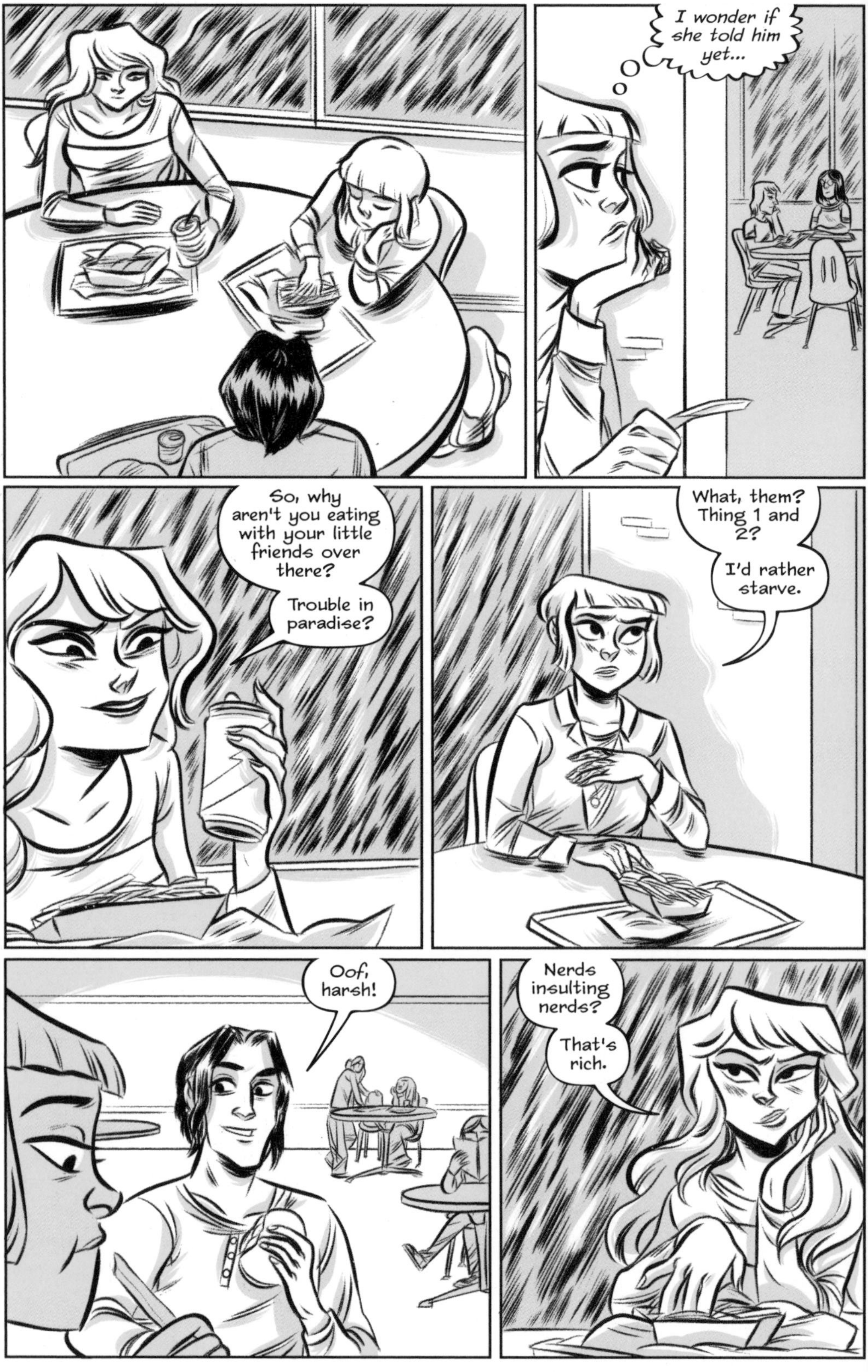
I wonder if she told him yet...
So, why aren't you eating with your little friends over there?
Trouble in paradise?
What, them? Thing 1 and 2?
I'd rather starve.
Oof, harsh!
Nerds insulting nerds?
That's rich.

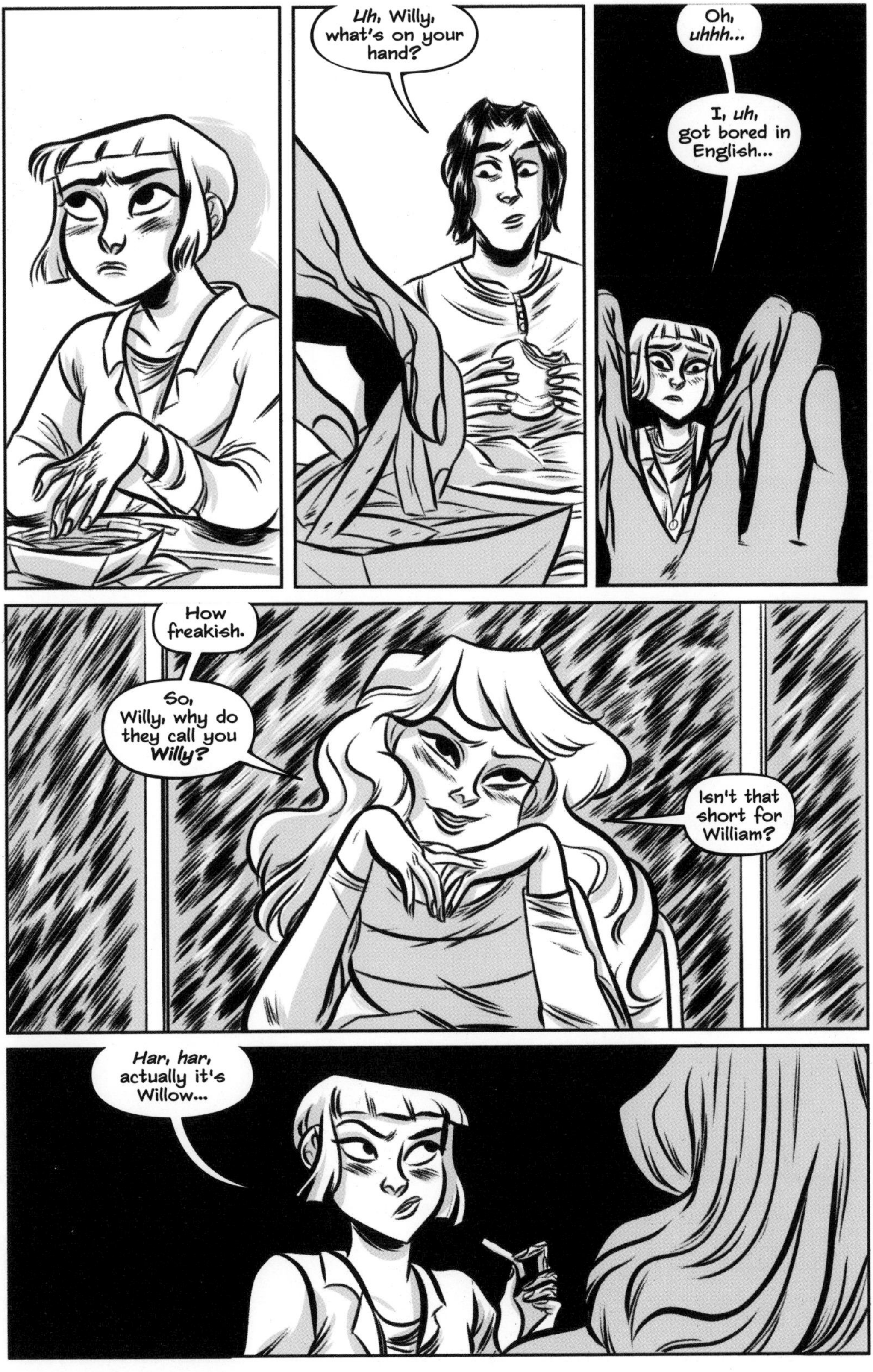
Uh, Willy, what's on your hand?
Oh, uhhh...
I, uh, got bored in English...
How freakish.
So, Willy, why do they call you Willy?
Isn't that short for William?
Har, har, actually it's Willow...

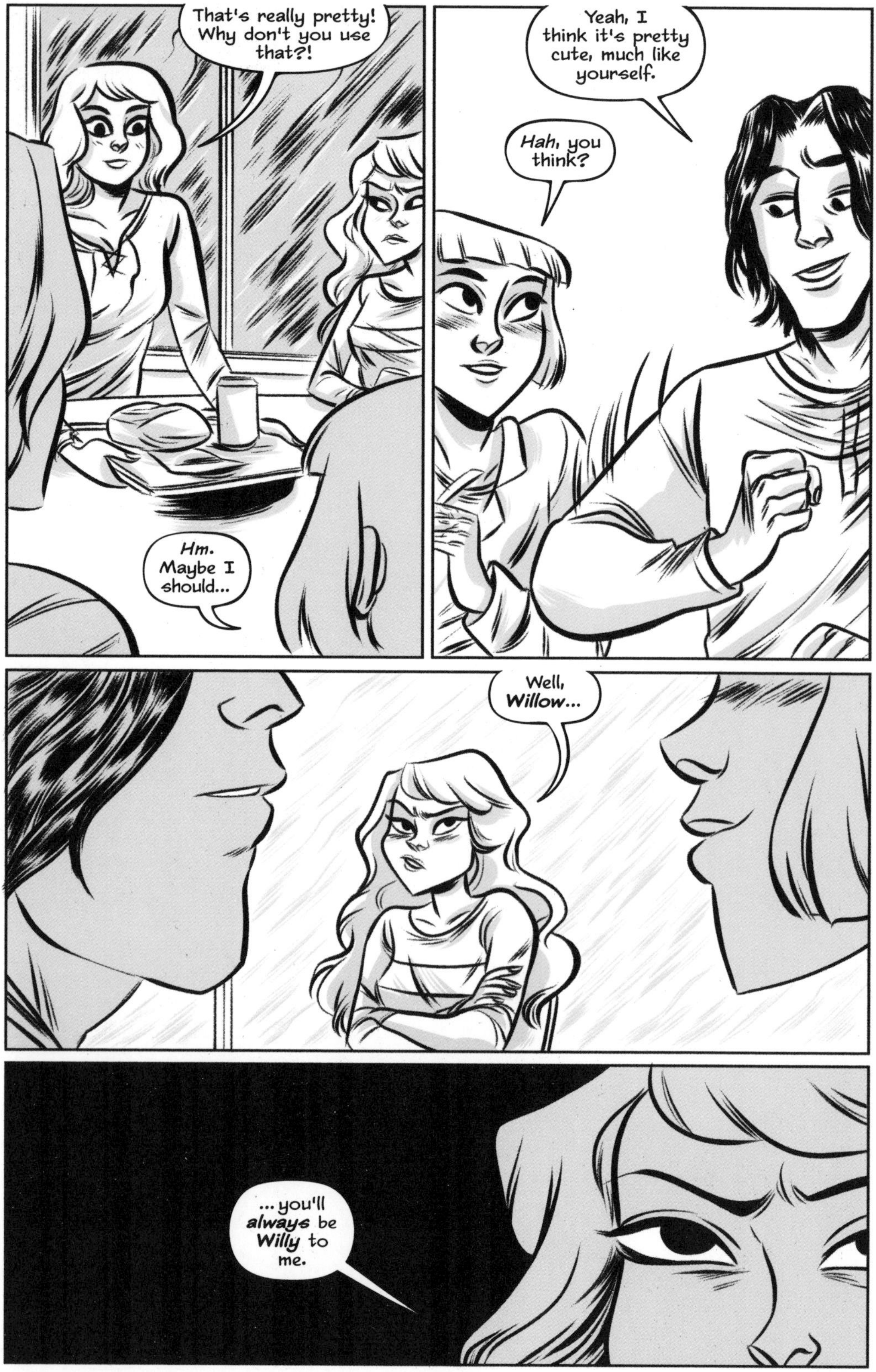
That's really pretty! Why don't you use that?!
Hm. Maybe I should...
Yeah, I think it's pretty cute, much like yourself.
Hah, you think?
Well, Willow...
...you'll always be Willy to me.

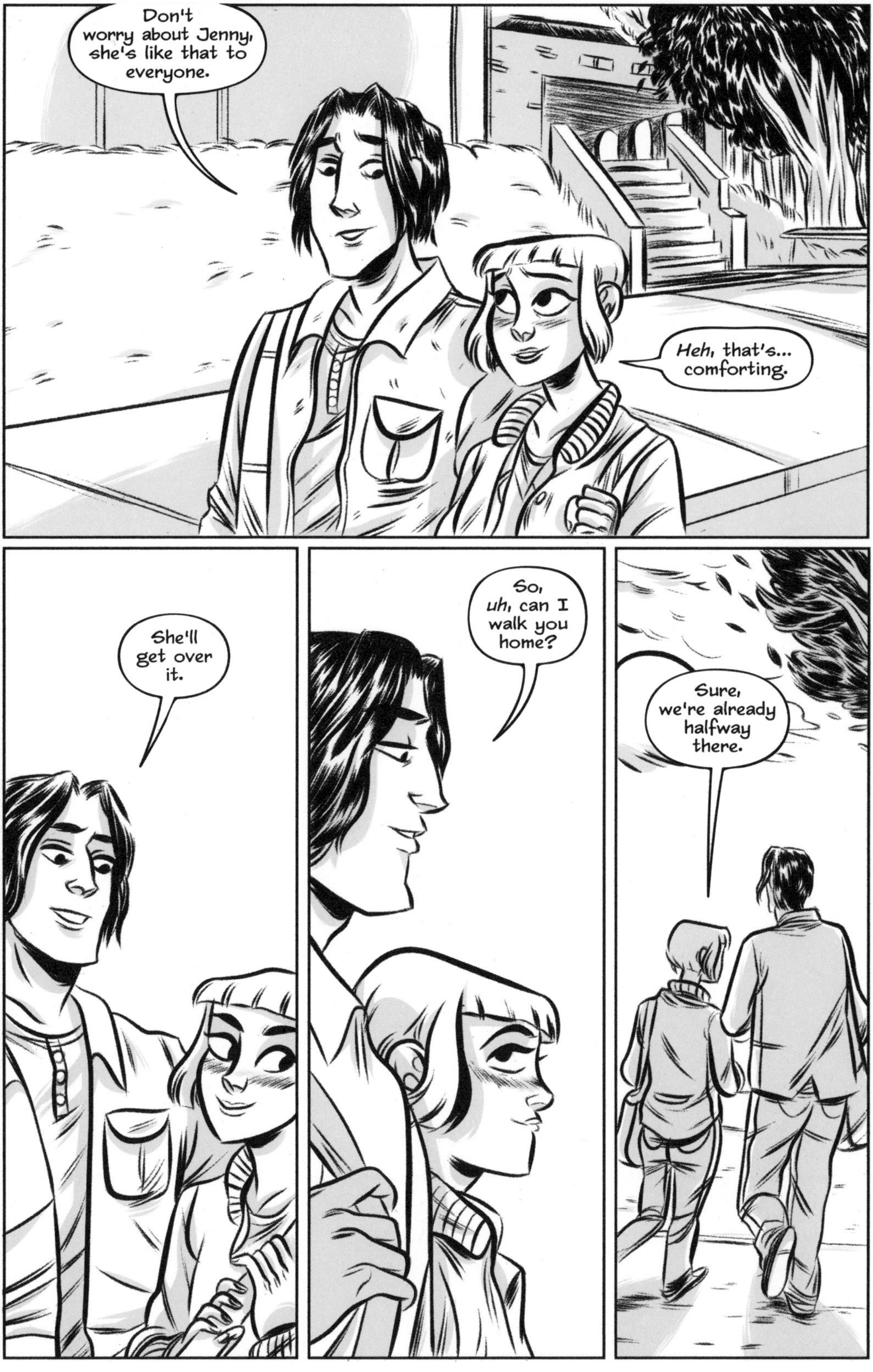
Don't worry about Jenny, she's like that to everyone.
Heh, that's... comforting.
She'll get over it.
So, uh, can I walk you home?
Sure, we're already halfway there.

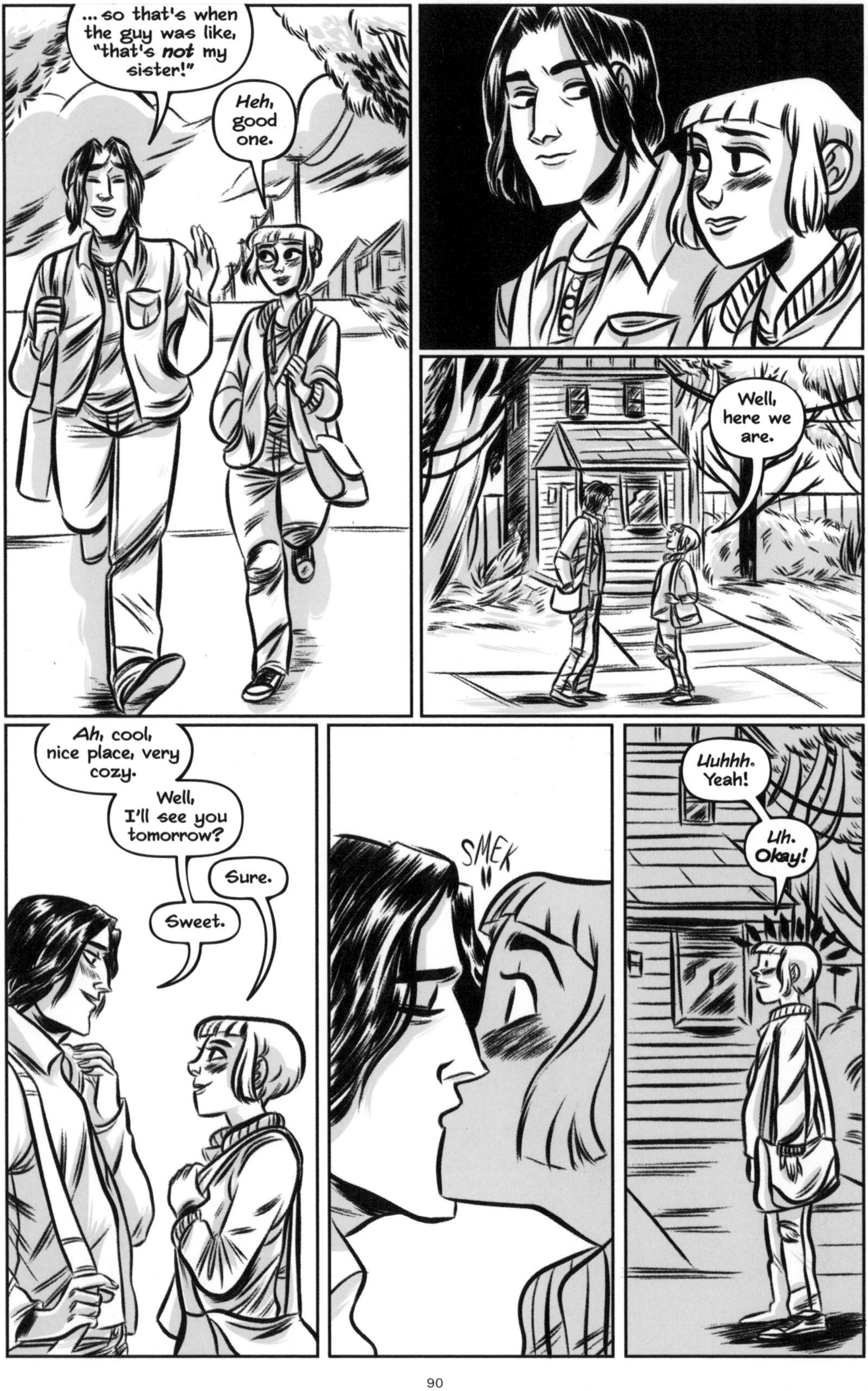
...so that's when the guy was like, "that's *not* my sister!"
Heh, good one.
Well, here we are.
Ah, cool, nice place, very cozy.
Well, I'll see you tomorrow?
Sure.
Sweet.
SMEK
Uuhhh. Yeah!
Uh. Okay!

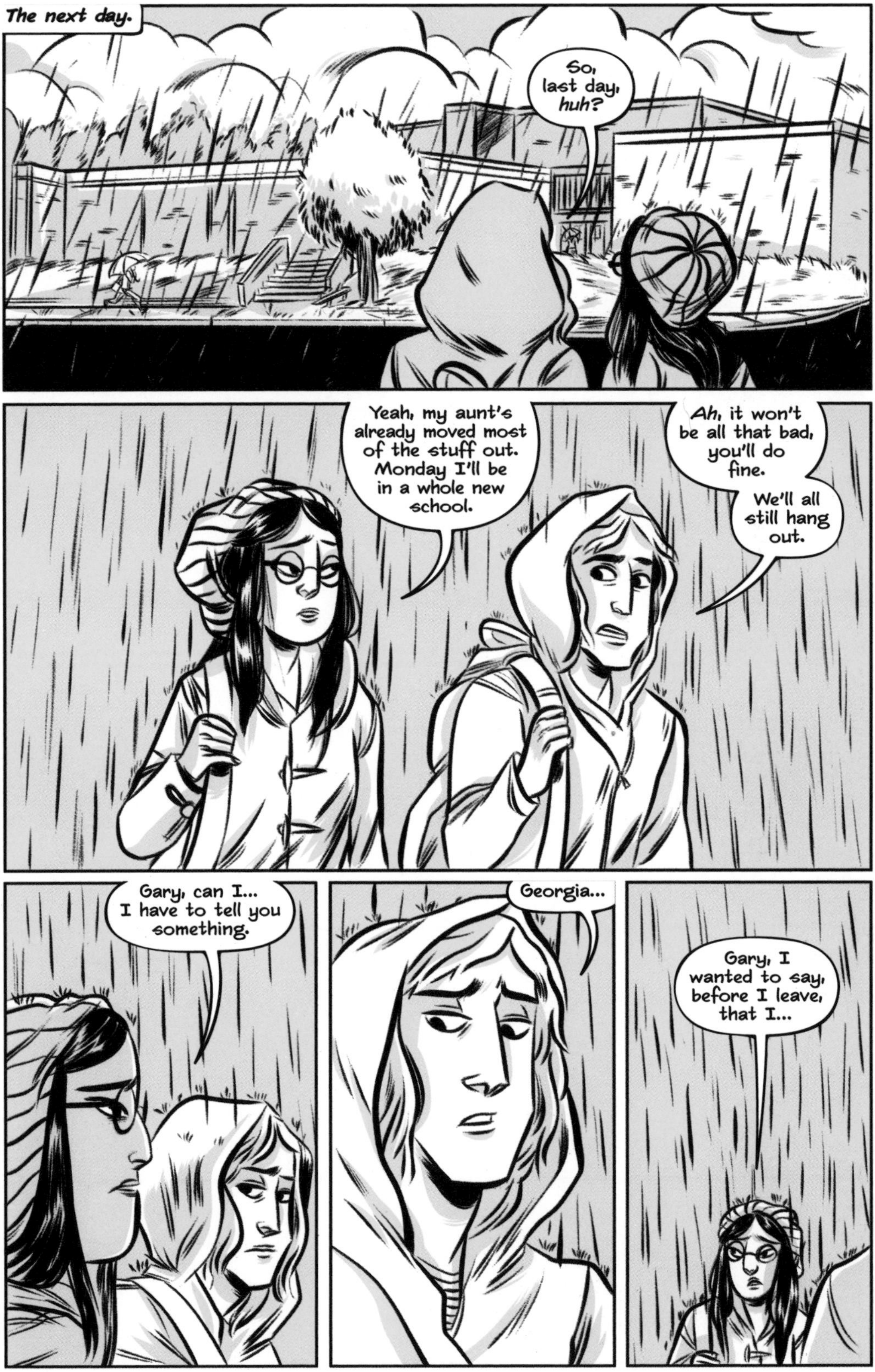
The next day.
So, last day, huh?
Yeah, my aunt's already moved most of the stuff out. Monday I'll be in a whole new school.
Ah, it won't be all that bad, you'll do fine.
We'll all still hang out.
Gary, can I... I have to tell you something.
Georgia...
Gary, I wanted to say, before I leave, that I...

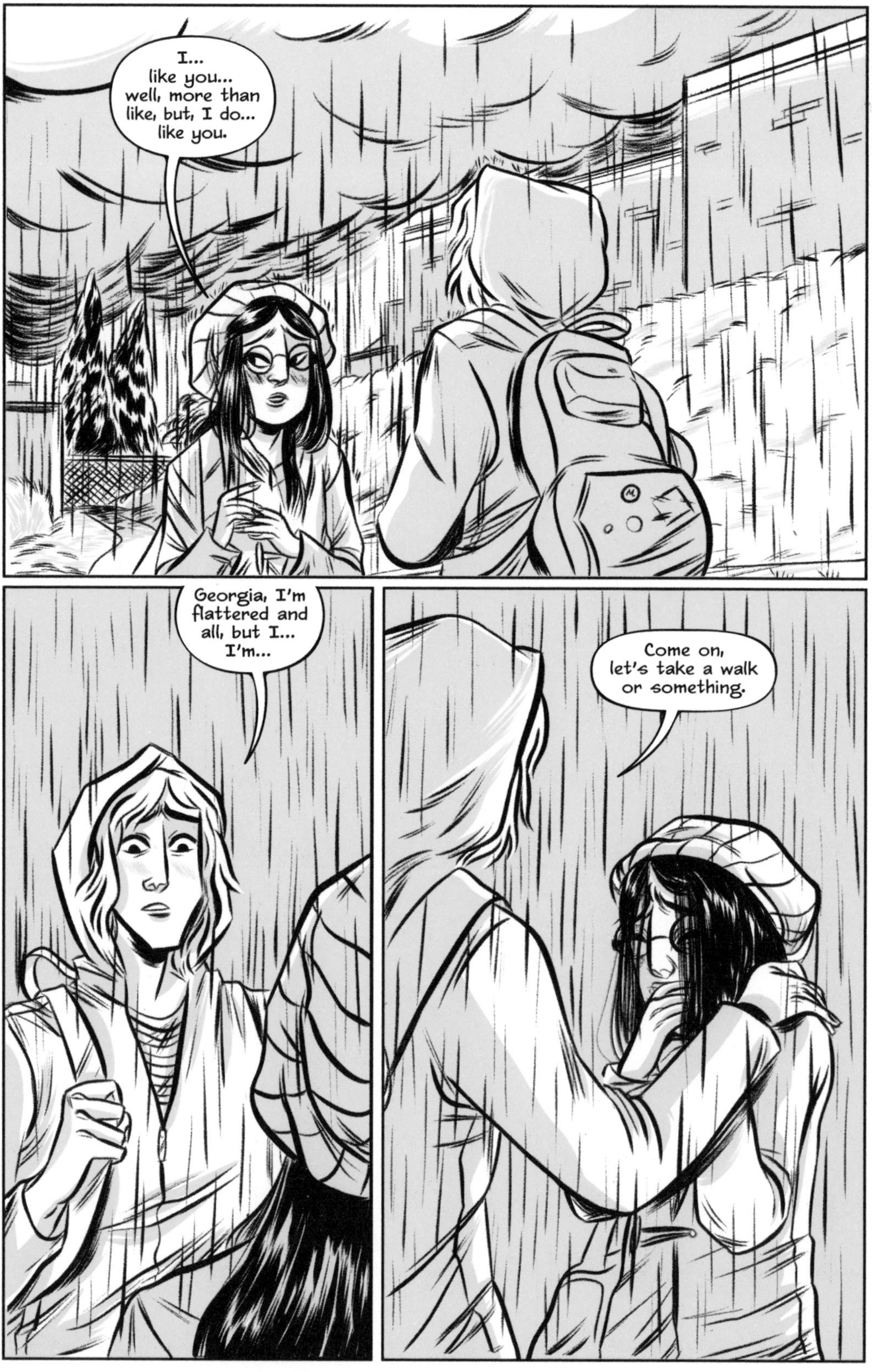
I... like you... well, more than like, but, I do... like you.
Georgia, I'm flattered and all, but I... I'm...
Come on, let's take a walk or something.

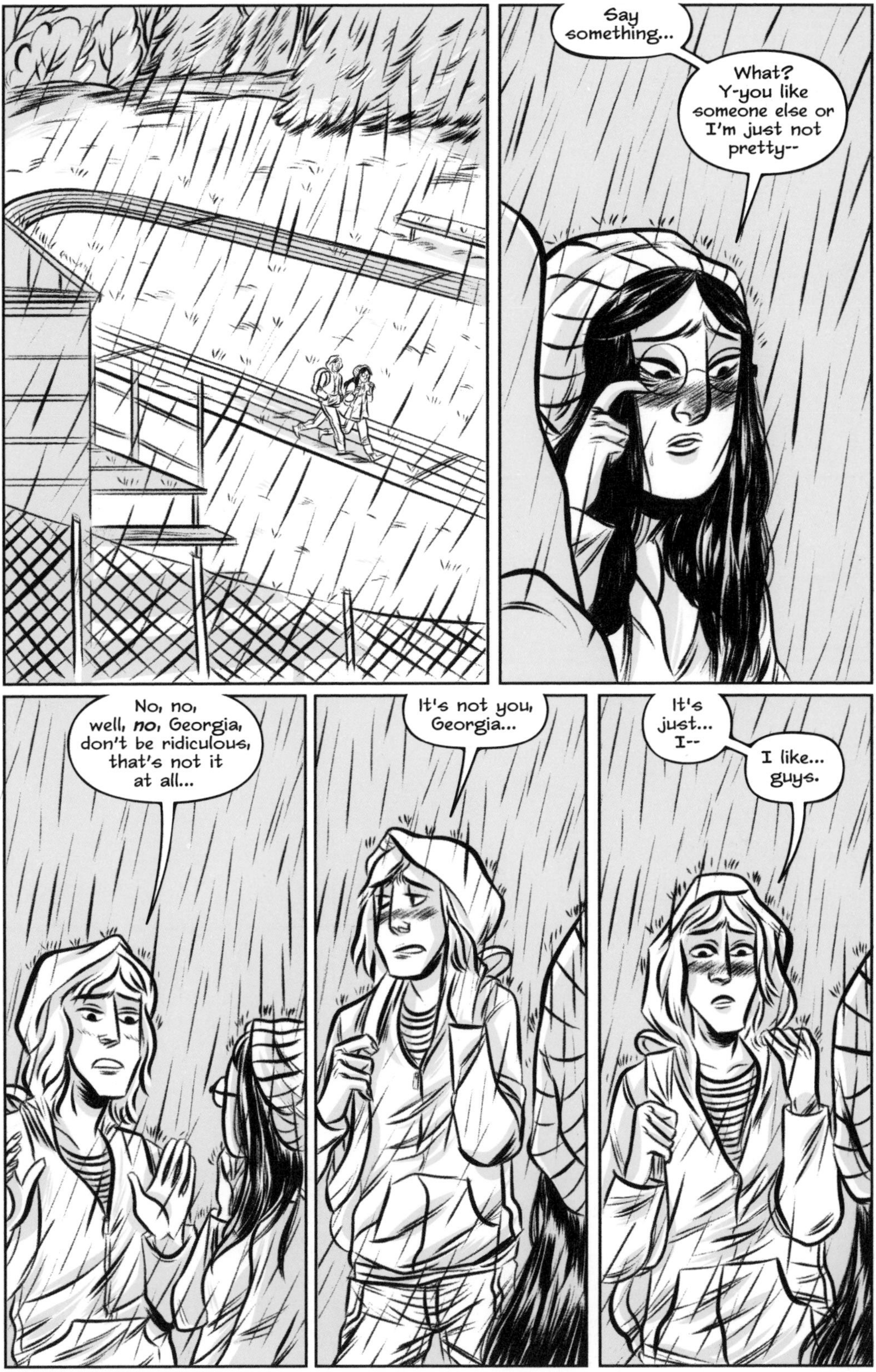
Say something...
What? Y-you like someone else or I'm just not pretty--
No, no, well, ***no***, Georgia, don't be ridiculous, that's not it at all...
It's not you, Georgia...
It's just... I--
I like... guys.

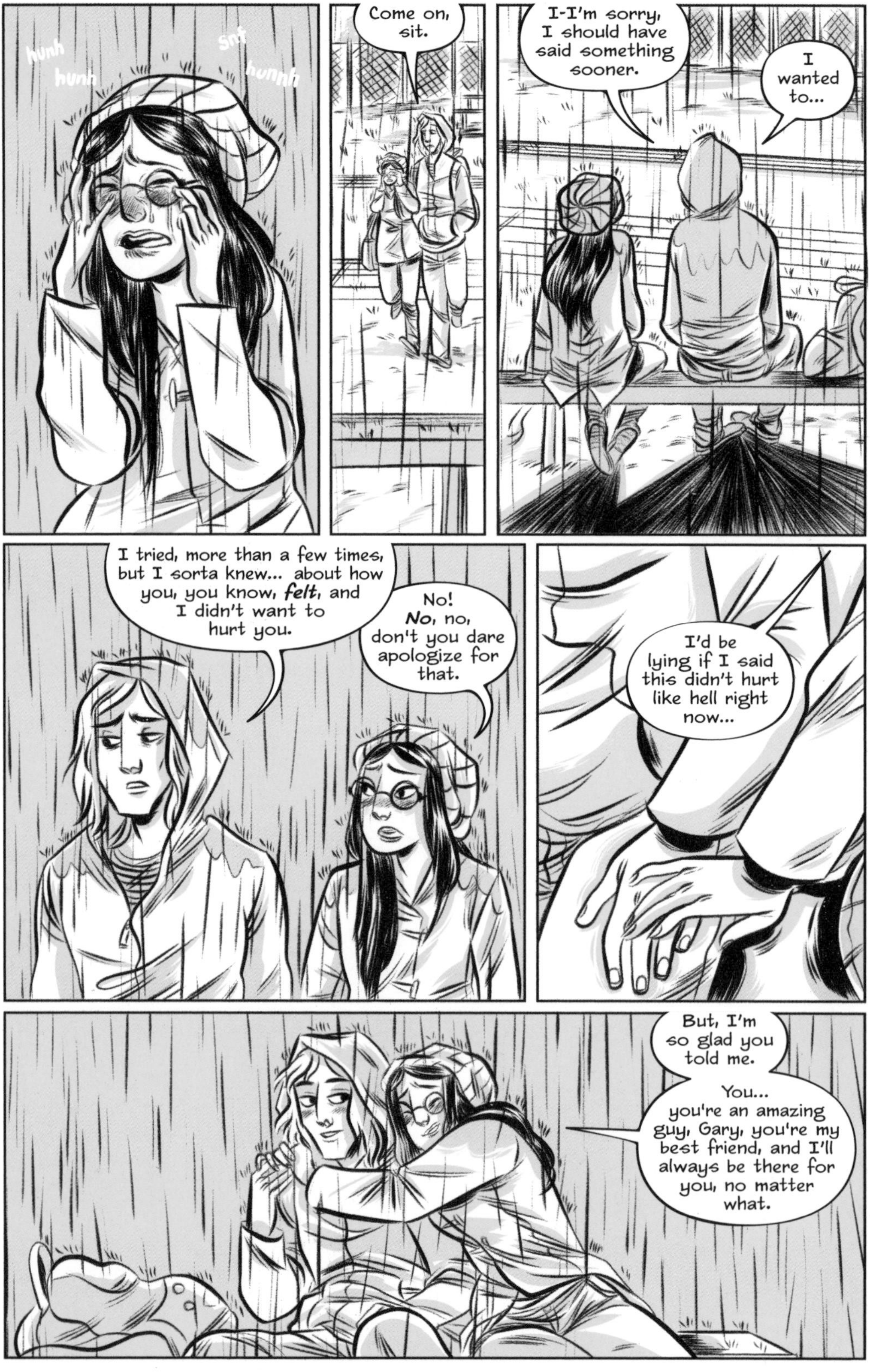
hunh
hunh
snf
hunnh
Come on, sit.
I-I'm sorry, I should have said something sooner.
I wanted to...
I tried, more than a few times, but I sorta knew... about how you, you know, *felt*, and I didn't want to hurt you.
No! *No*, no, don't you dare apologize for that.
I'd be lying if I said this didn't hurt like hell right now...
But, I'm so glad you told me.
You... you're an amazing guy, Gary, you're my best friend, and I'll always be there for you, no matter what.

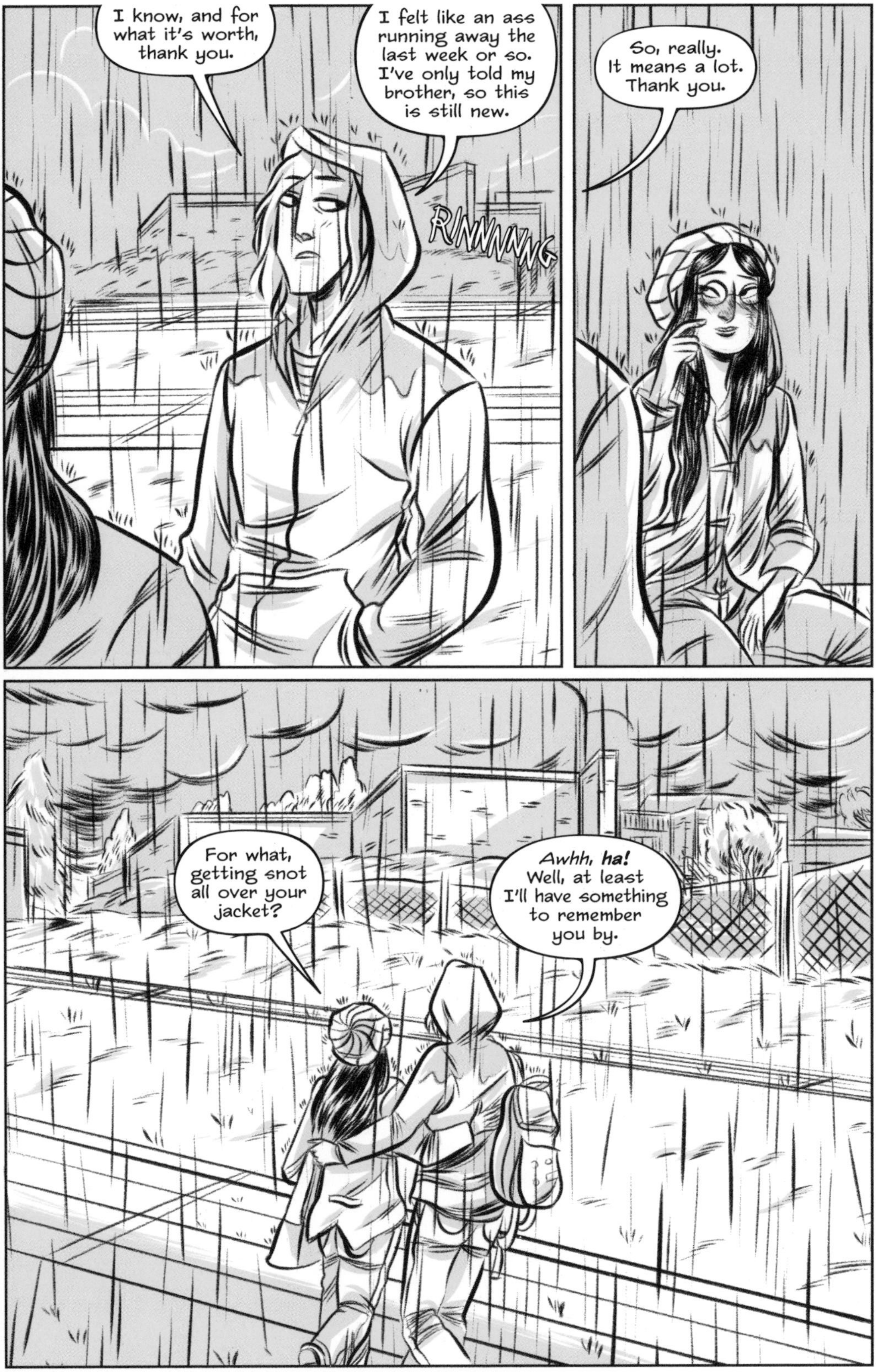
I know, and for what it's worth, thank you.
I felt like an ass running away the last week or so. I've only told my brother, so this is still new.
RINNNNNG
So, really. It means a lot. Thank you.
For what, getting snot all over your jacket?
*Awhh, **ha!*** Well, at least I'll have something to remember you by.

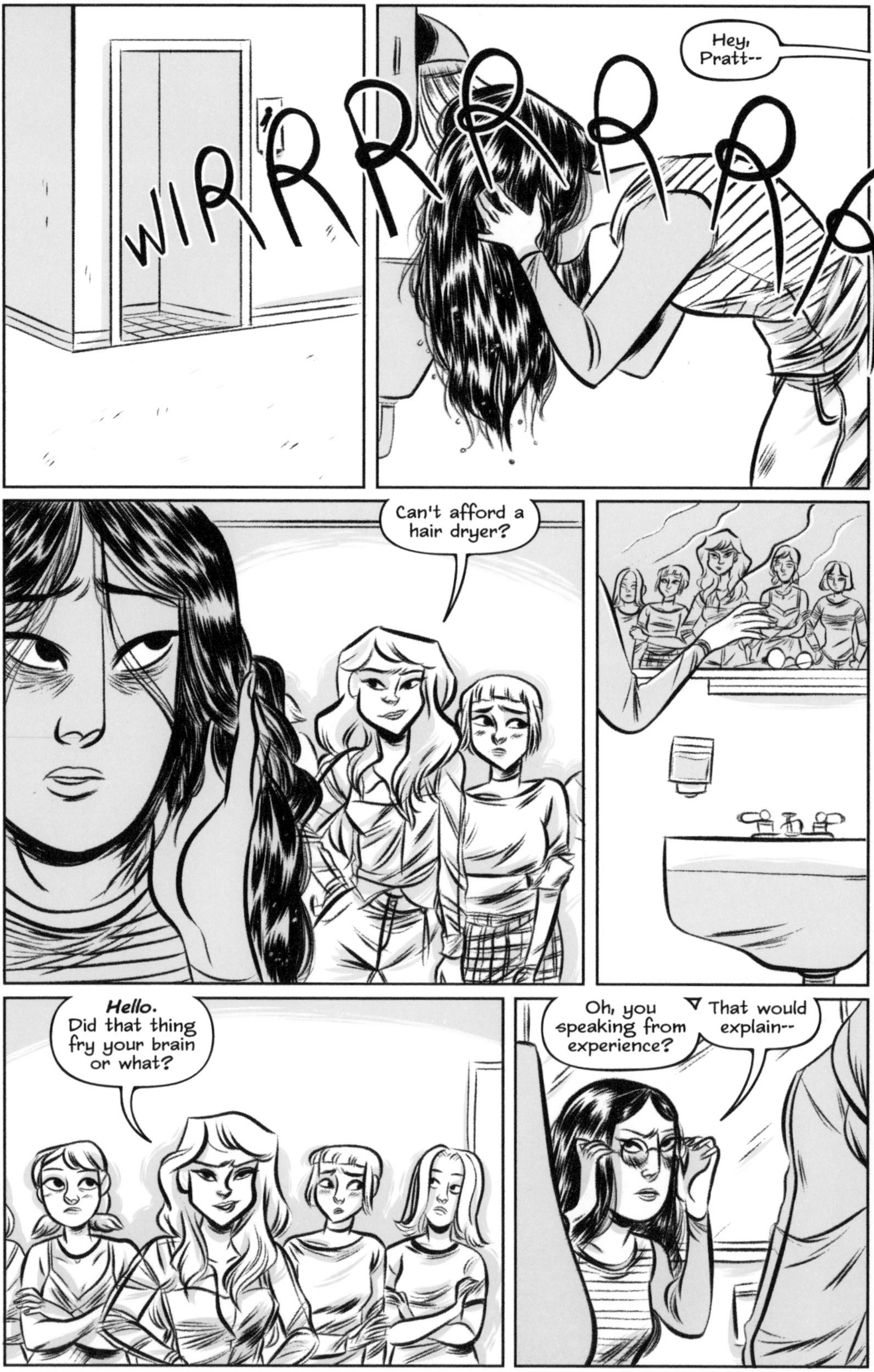
WIRRRRRRR
Hey, Pratt--
Can't afford a hair dryer?
Hello. Did that thing fry your brain or what?
Oh, you speaking from experience?
That would explain--

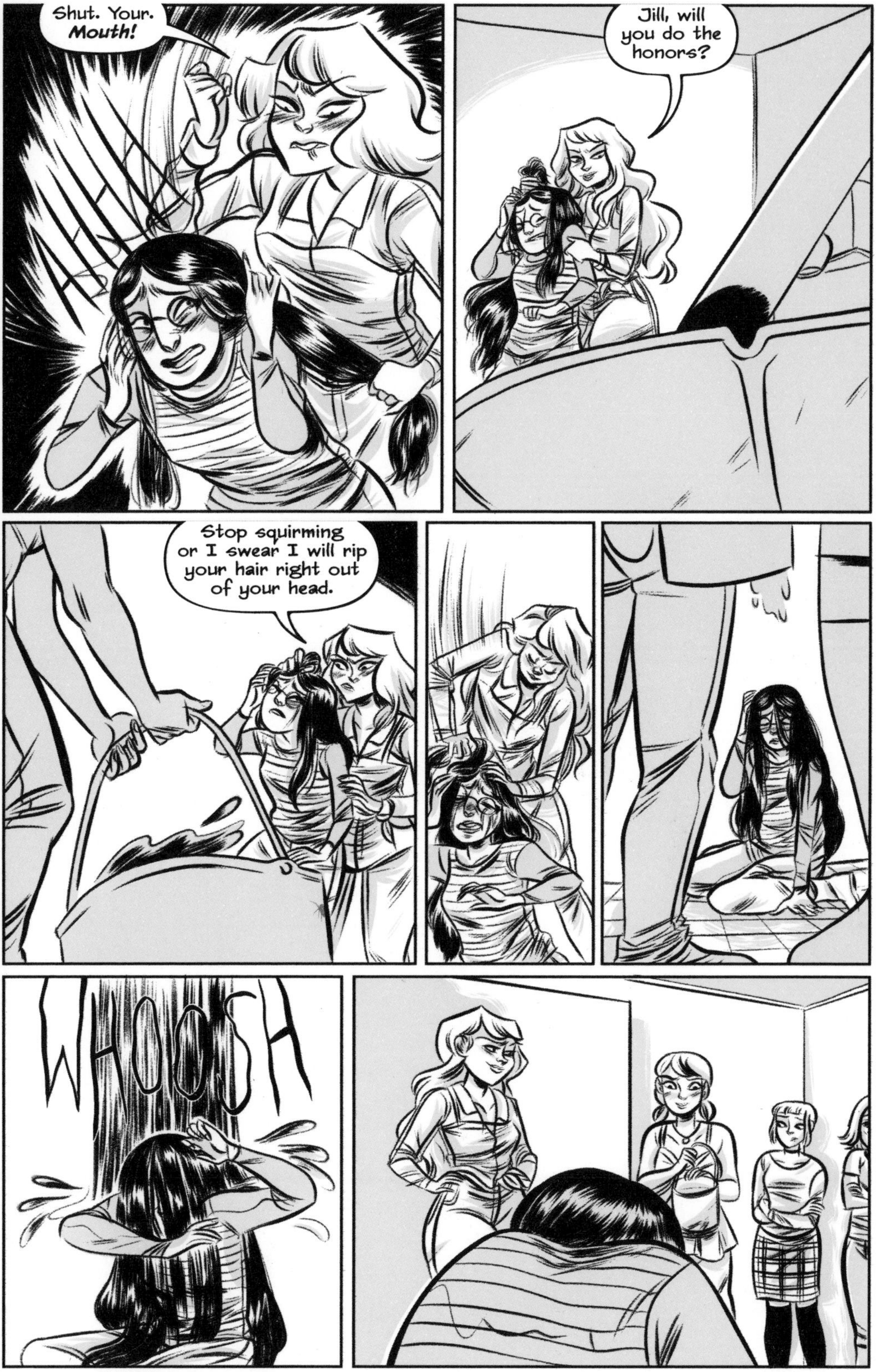
Shut. Your. *Mouth!*
Jill, will you do the honors?
Stop squirming or I swear I will rip your hair right out of your head.
WHOOSH

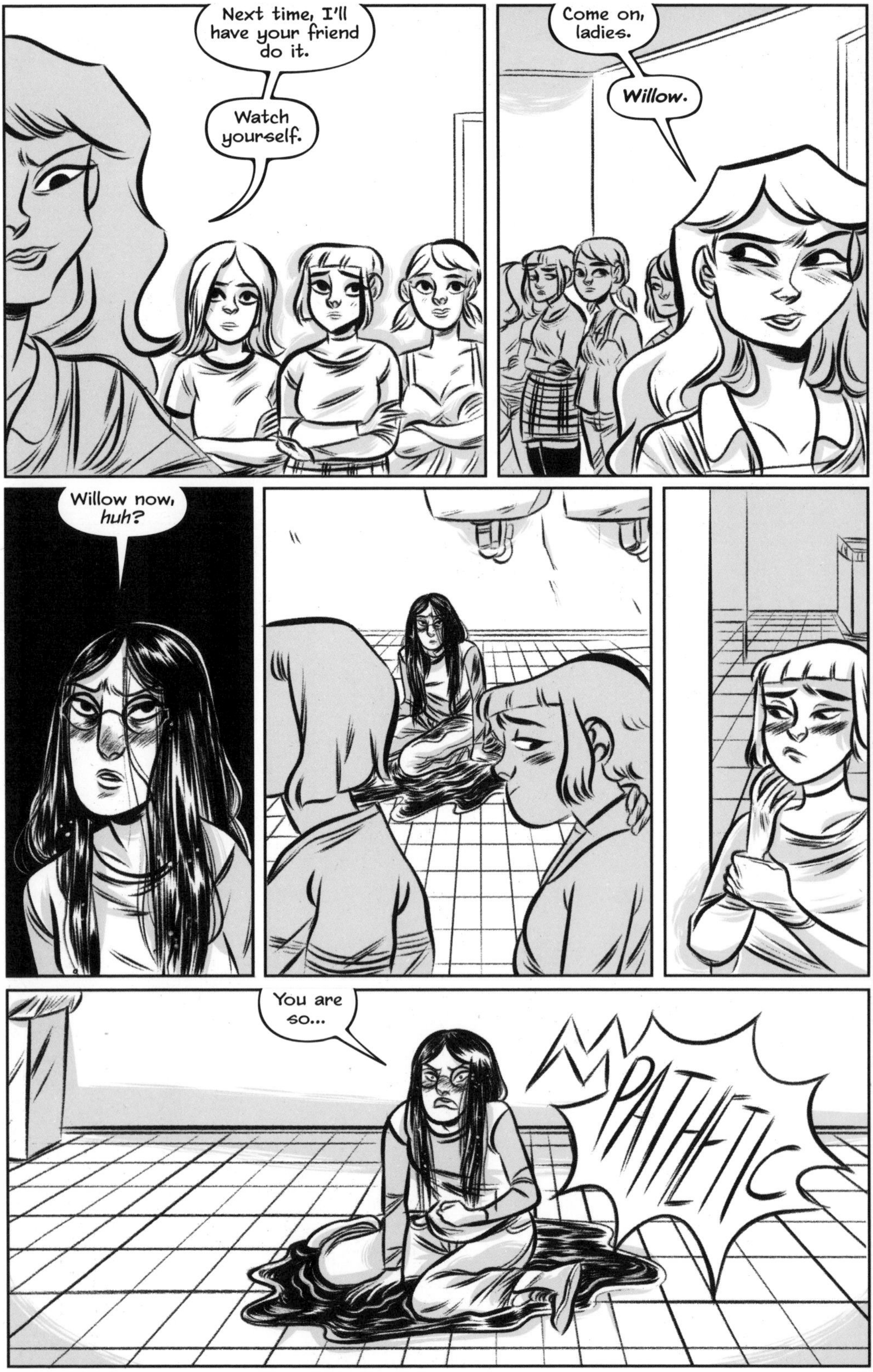
Next time, I'll have your friend do it.
Watch yourself.
Come on, ladies.
Willow.
Willow now, *huh?*
You are so...
PATHETIC

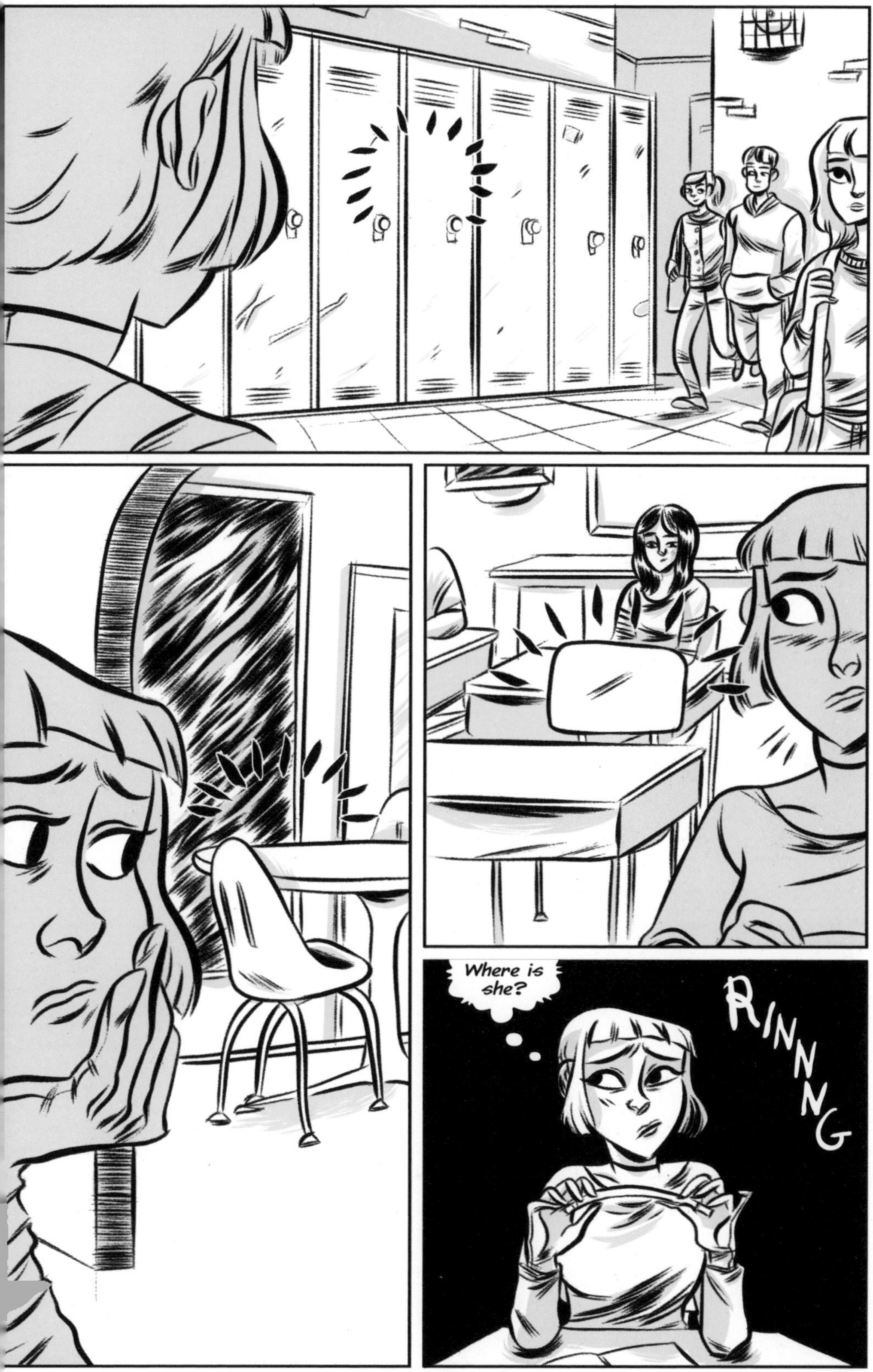
Where is she?
RINNNG

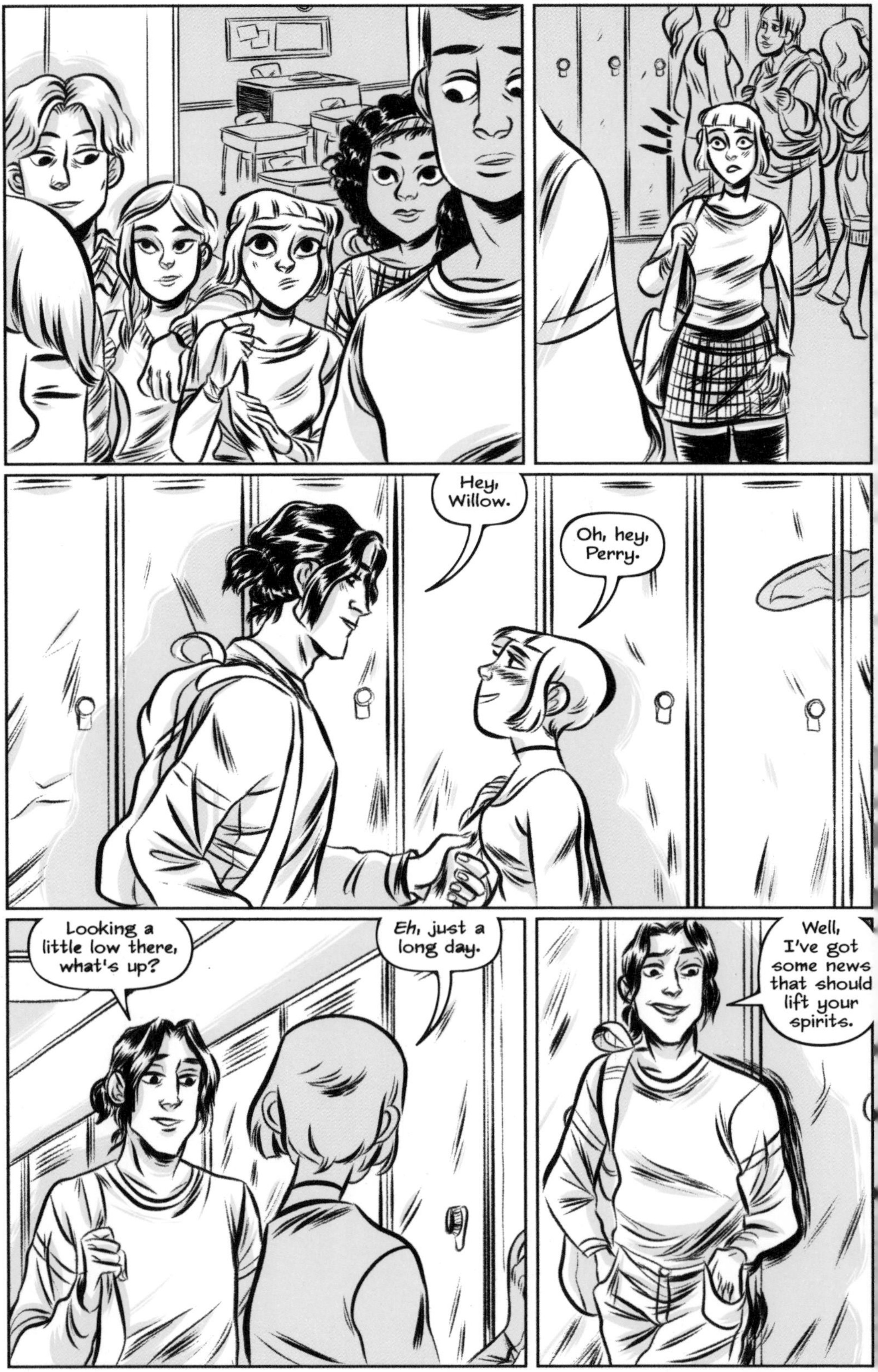
Hey, Willow.
Oh, hey, Perry.
Looking a little low there, what's up?
Eh, just a long day.
Well, I've got some news that should lift your spirits.

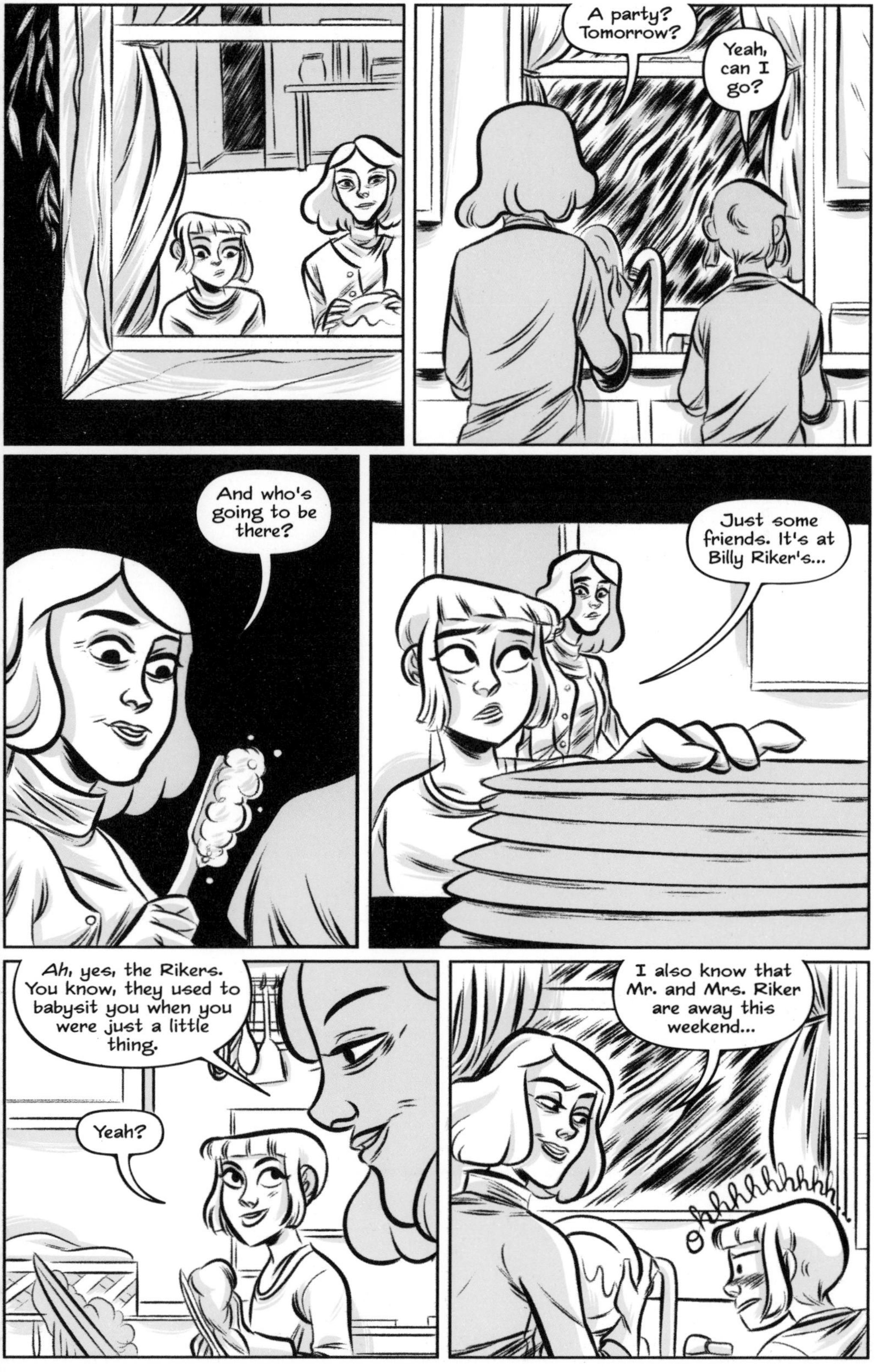
A party? Tomorrow?
Yeah, can I go?
And who's going to be there?
Just some friends. It's at Billy Riker's...
Ah, yes, the Rikers. You know, they used to babysit you when you were just a little thing.
Yeah?
I also know that Mr. and Mrs. Riker are away this weekend...
Ohhhhhhhhh...

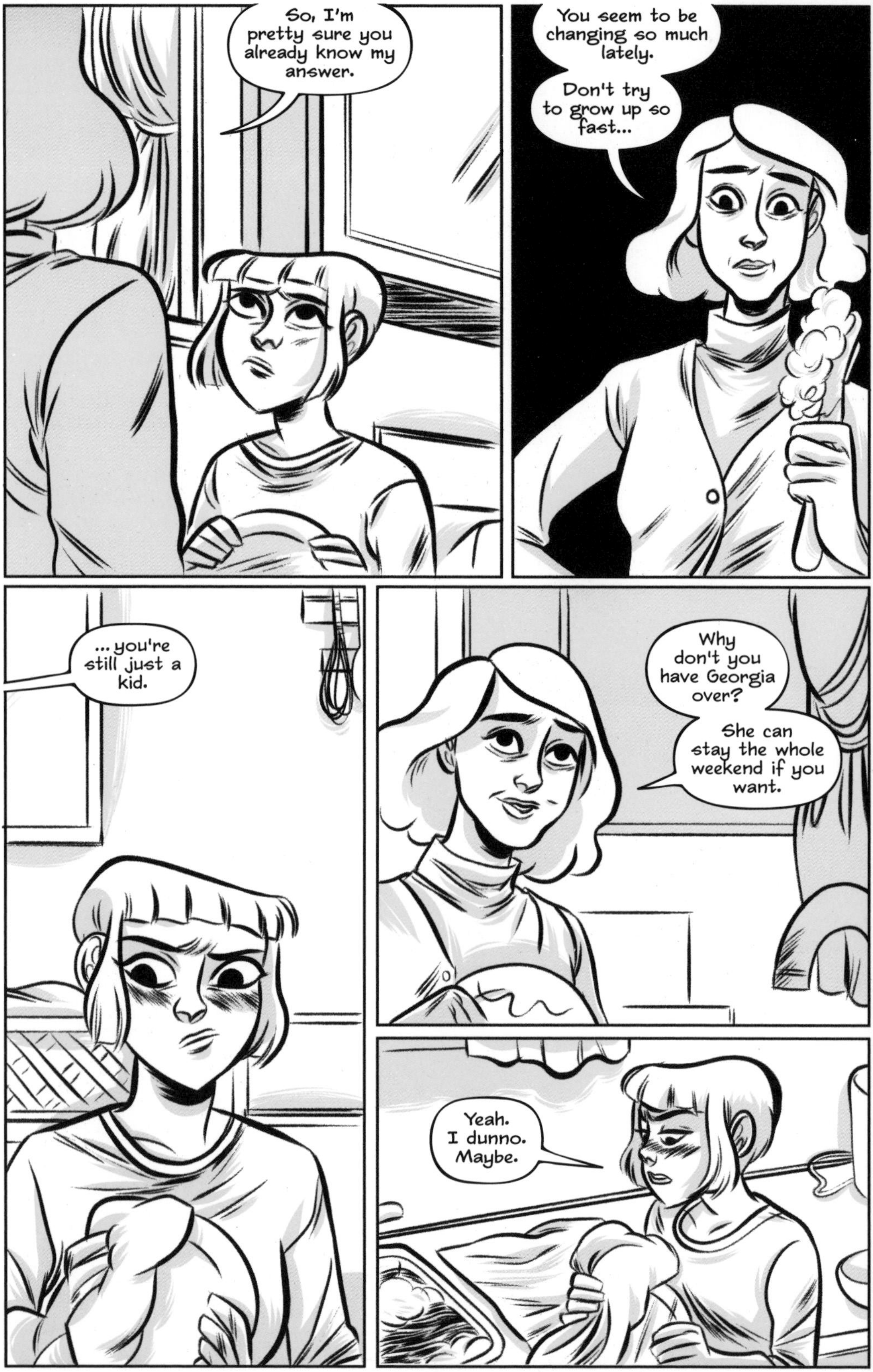
So, I'm pretty sure you already know my answer.
You seem to be changing so much lately.
Don't try to grow up so fast...
...you're still just a kid.
Why don't you have Georgia over?
She can stay the whole weekend if you want.
Yeah. I dunno. Maybe.

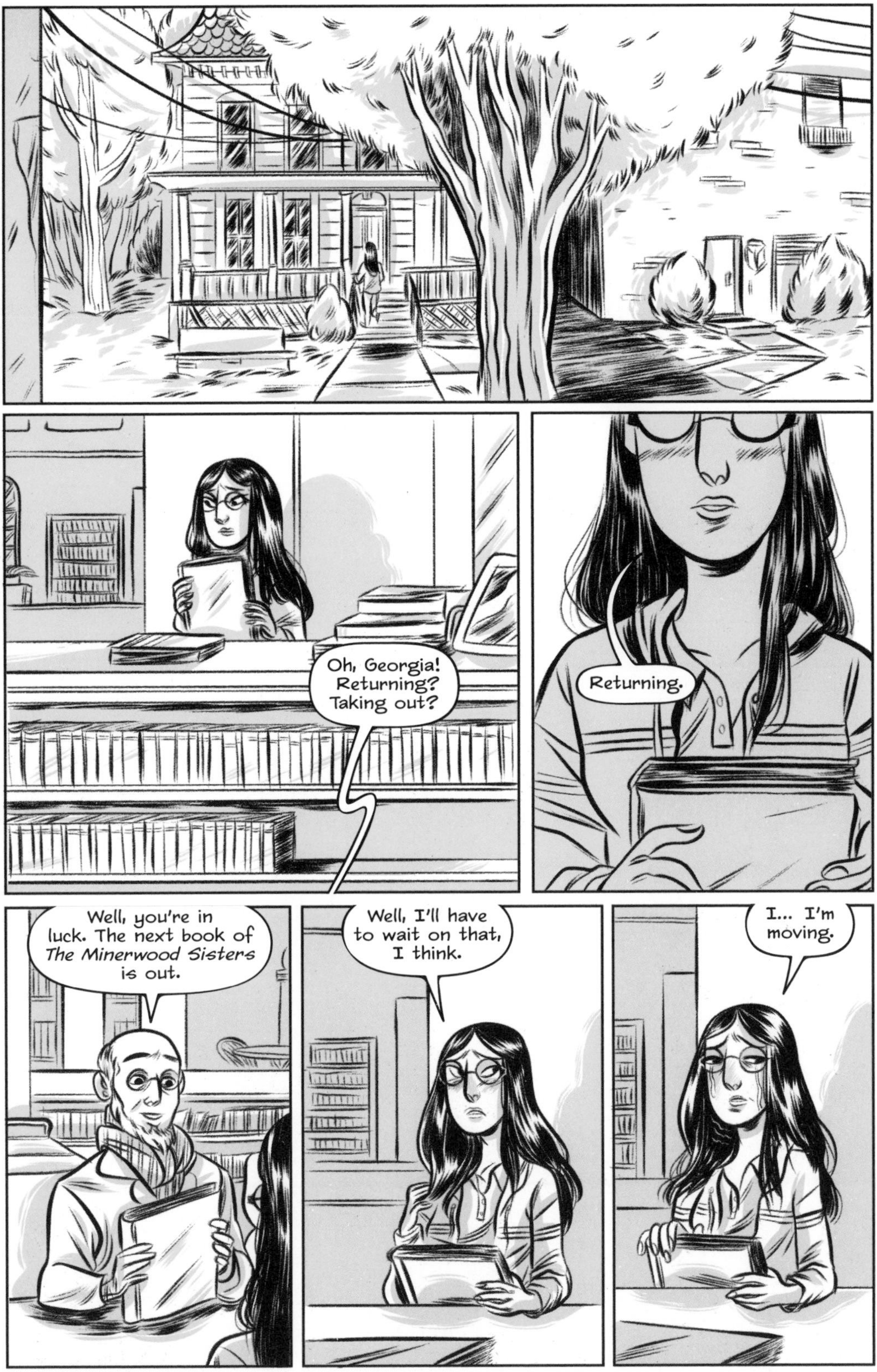

Oh, Georgia! Returning? Taking out?
Returning.
Well, you're in luck. The next book of *The Minerwood Sisters* is out.
Well, I'll have to wait on that, I think.
I... I'm moving.

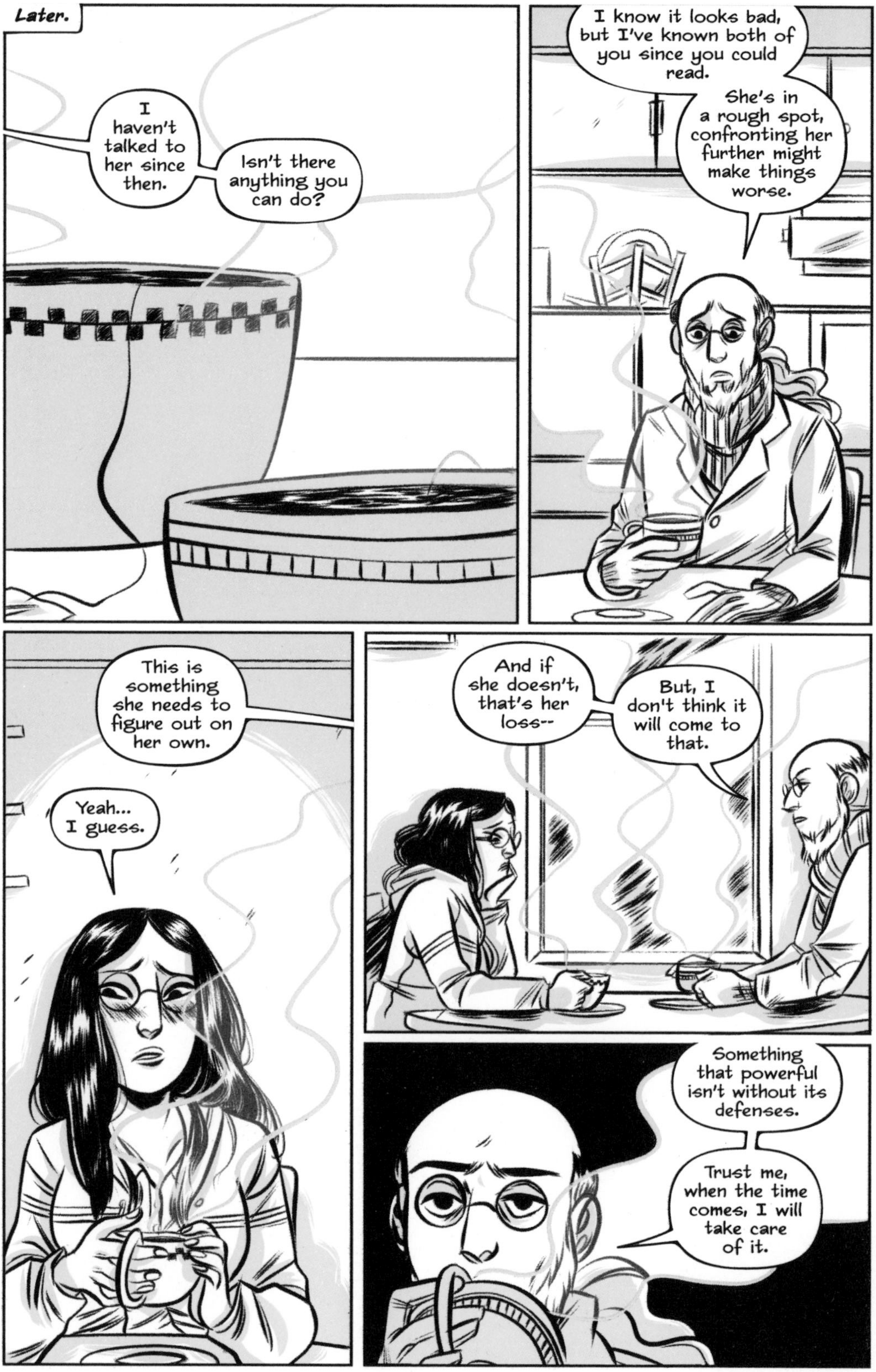
Later.
I haven't talked to her since then.
Isn't there anything you can do?
I know it looks bad, but I've known both of you since you could read.
She's in a rough spot, confronting her further might make things worse.
This is something she needs to figure out on her own.
Yeah... I guess.
And if she doesn't, that's her loss--
But, I don't think it will come to that.
Something that powerful isn't without its defenses.
Trust me, when the time comes, I will take care of it.

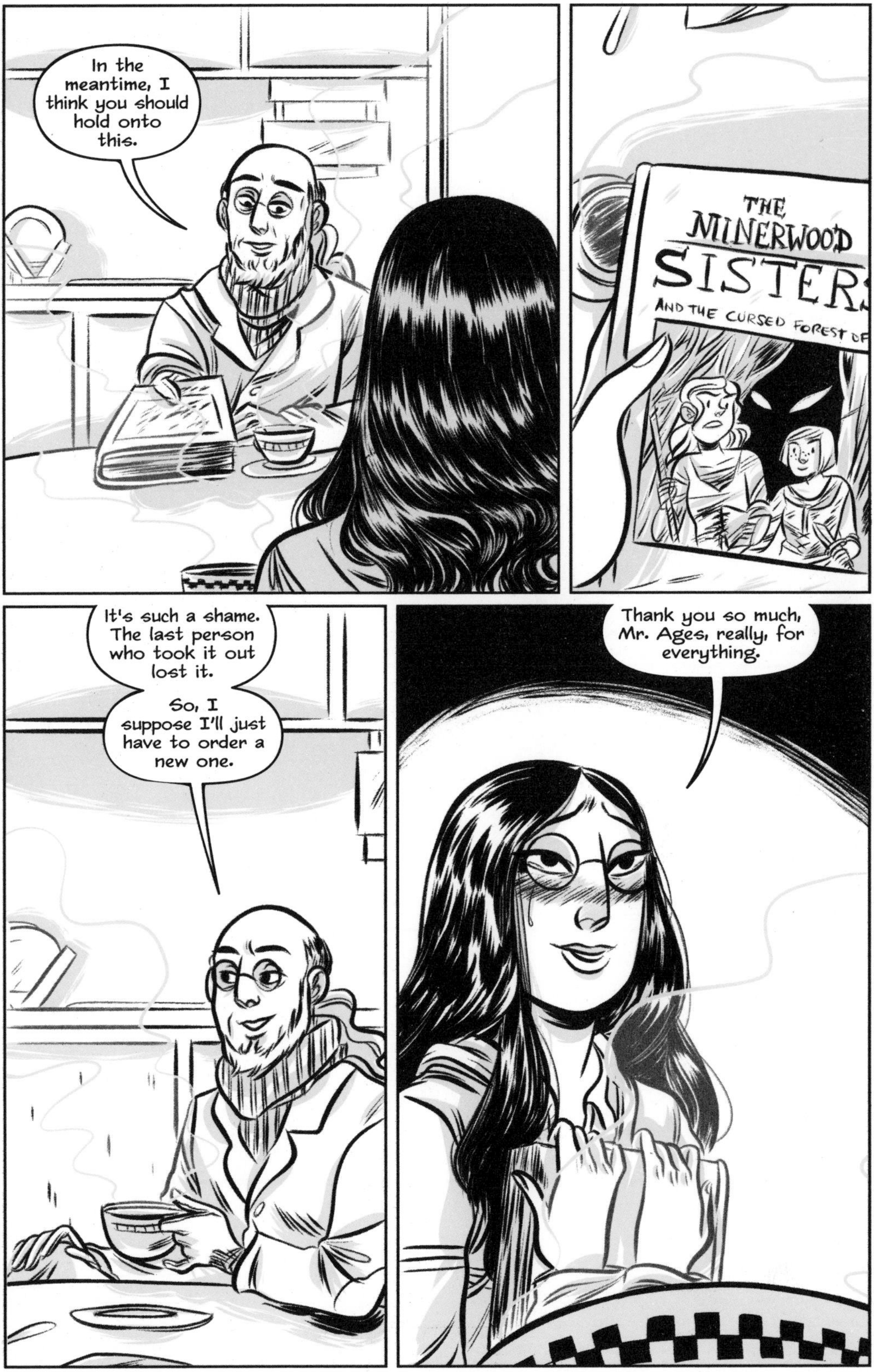

In the meantime, I think you should hold onto this.
THE MINERWOOD SISTER
AND THE CURSED FOREST OF
It's such a shame. The last person who took it out lost it.
So, I suppose I'll just have to order a new one.
Thank you so much, Mr. Ages, really, for everything.

Meanwhile.

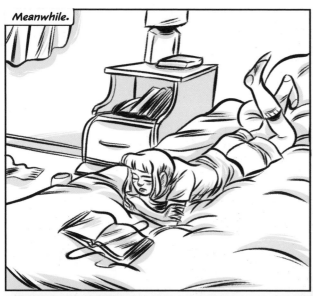

Willow's parents let her go to the party...

Yeah, right, I'm jealous that I can't trick people into liking me.

It's just a party, I'm not tricking anyone.

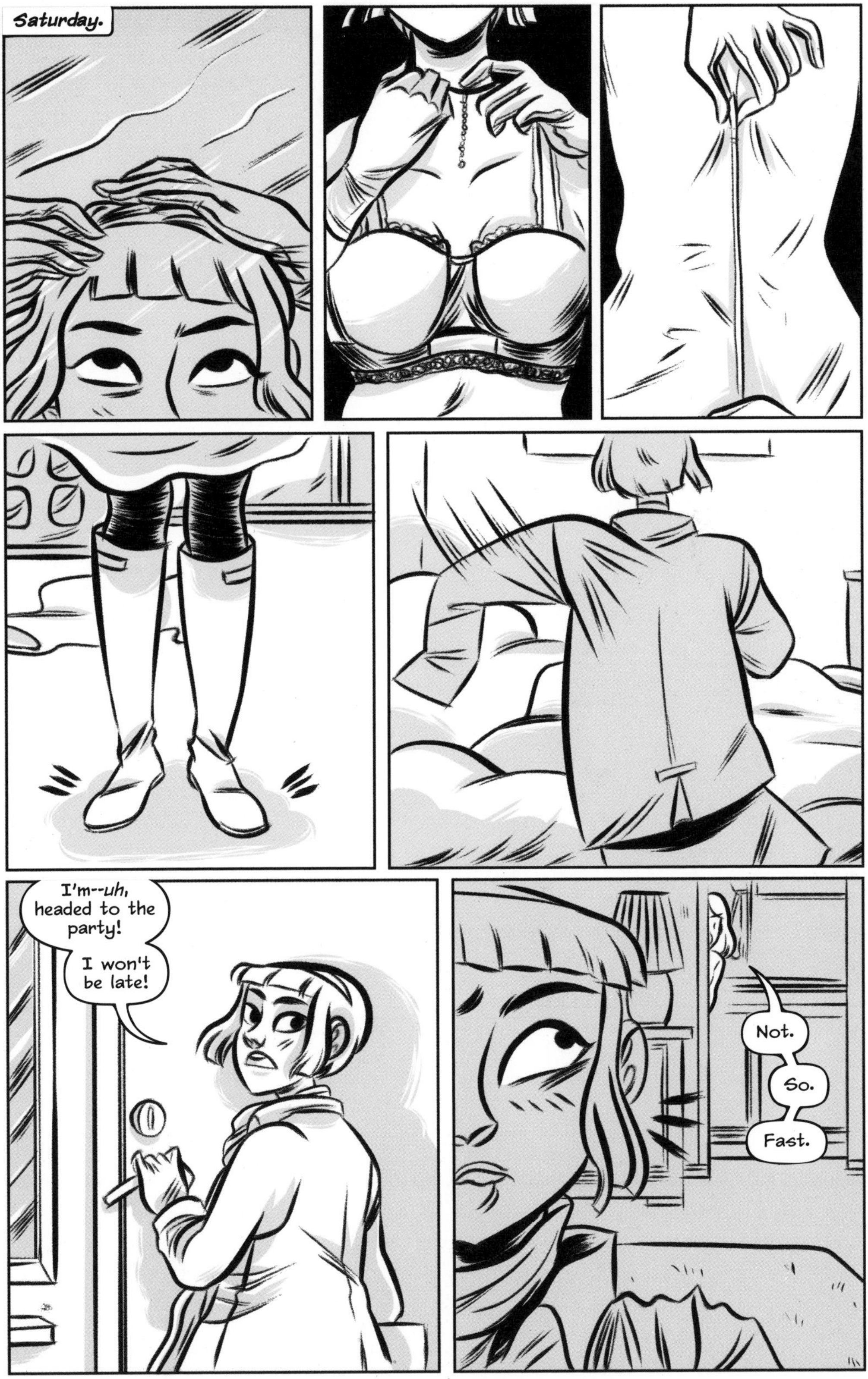
Saturday.
I'm--uh, headed to the party!
I won't be late!
Not.
So.
Fast.

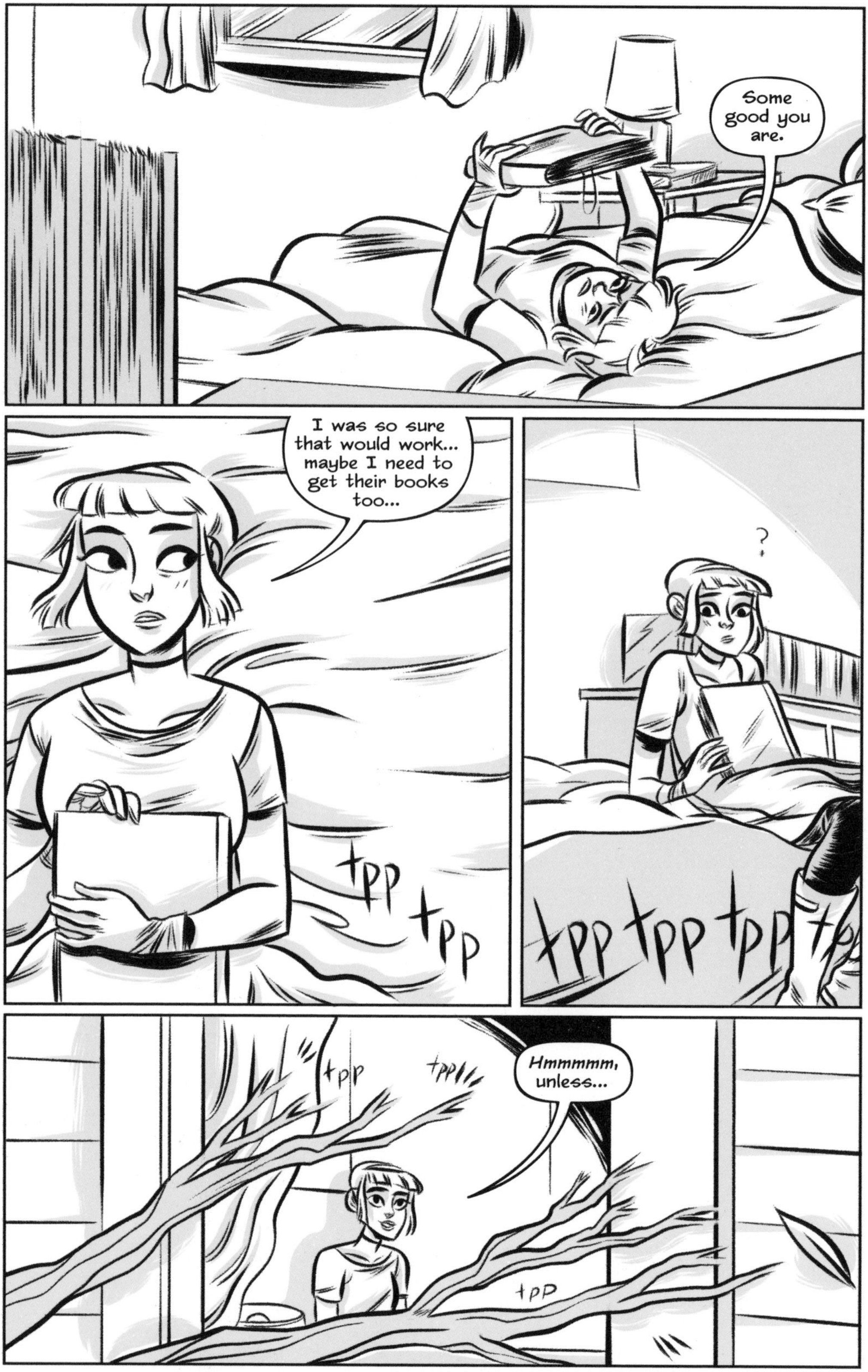
Some good you are.
I was so sure that would work... maybe I need to get their books too...
tpp
tpp
?
tpp tpp tpp tpp
tpp
tpp
Hmmmmm, unless...
tpp

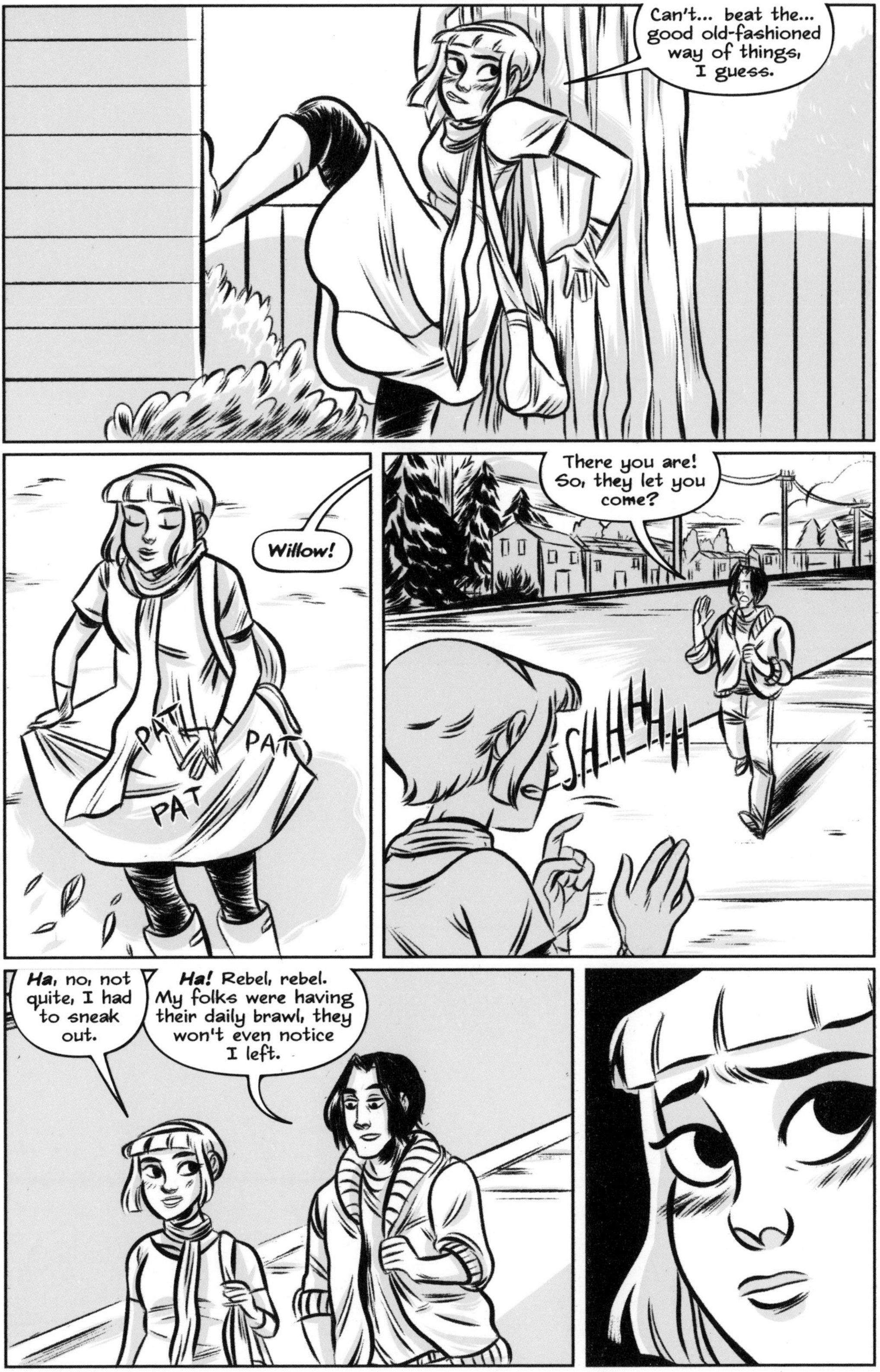
Can't... beat the... good old-fashioned way of things, I guess.
Willow!
PAT
PAT
PAT
There you are! So, they let you come?
SHHHHHH
Ha, no, not quite, I had to sneak out.
Ha! Rebel, rebel. My folks were having their daily brawl, they won't even notice I left.

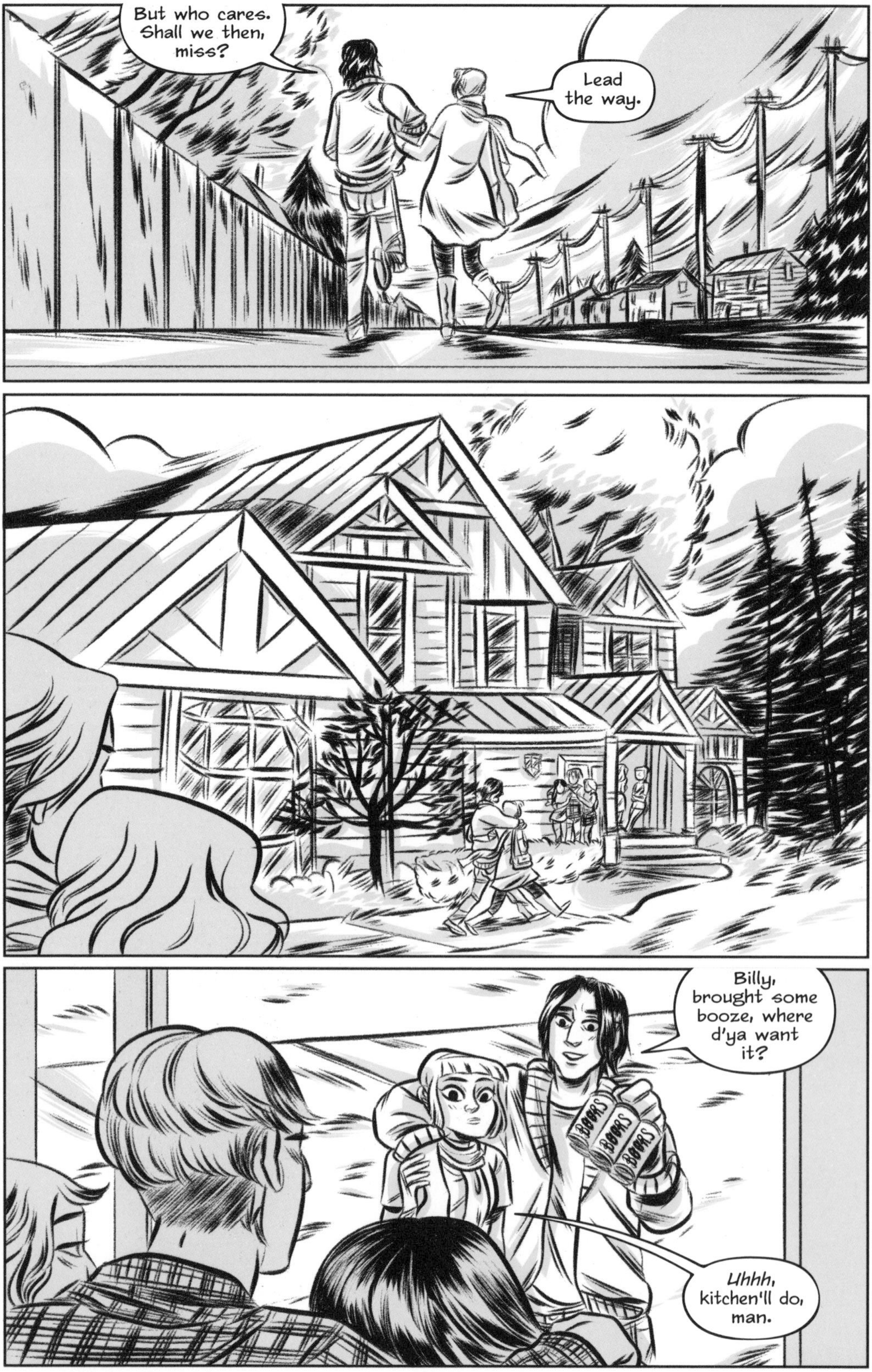
But who cares. Shall we then, miss?
Lead the way.
Billy, brought some booze, where d'ya want it?
BOOZ
Uhhh, kitchen'll do, man.

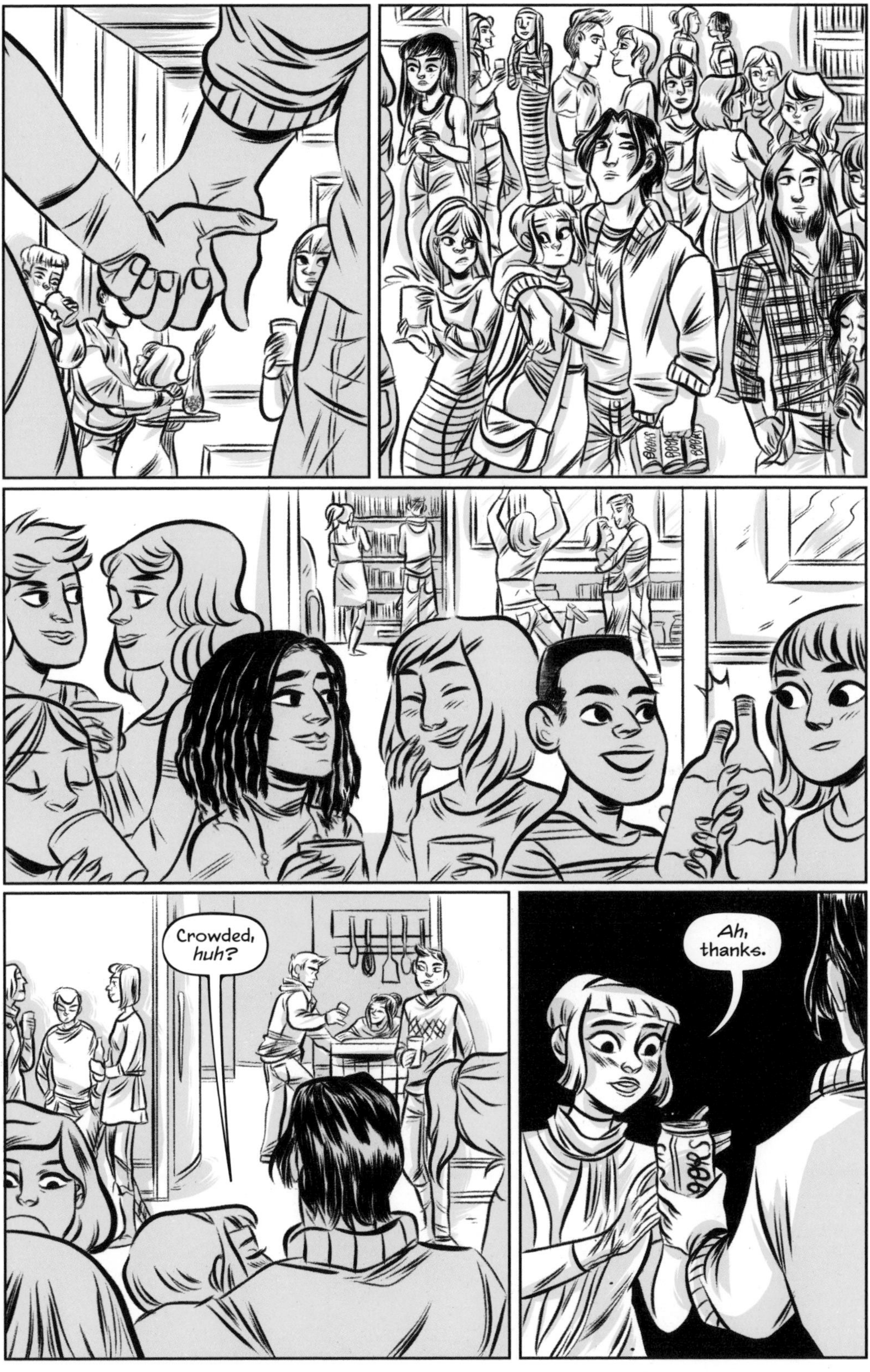
Crowded, huh?
Ah, thanks.

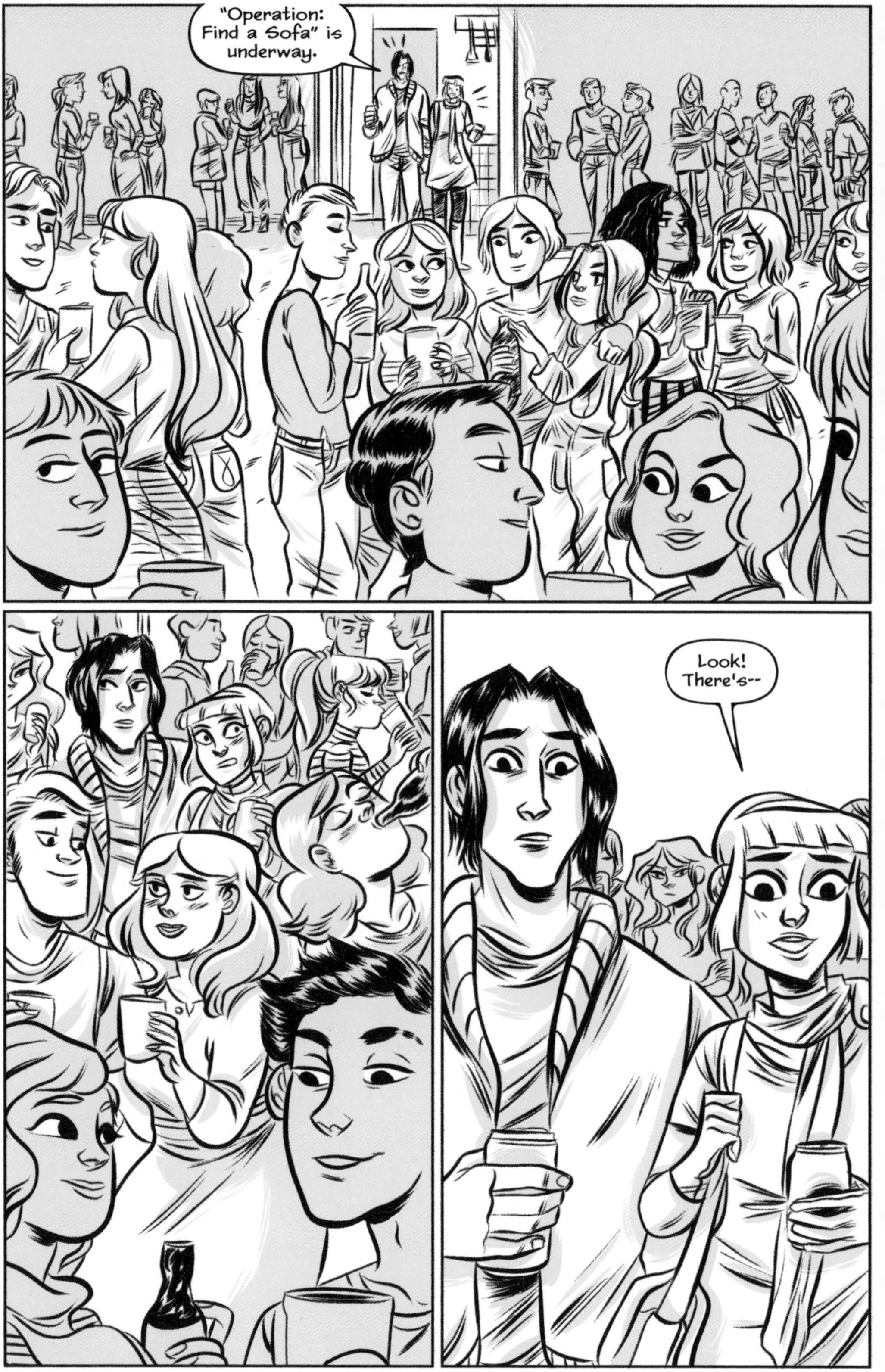
"Operation: Find a Sofa" is underway.
Look! There's--

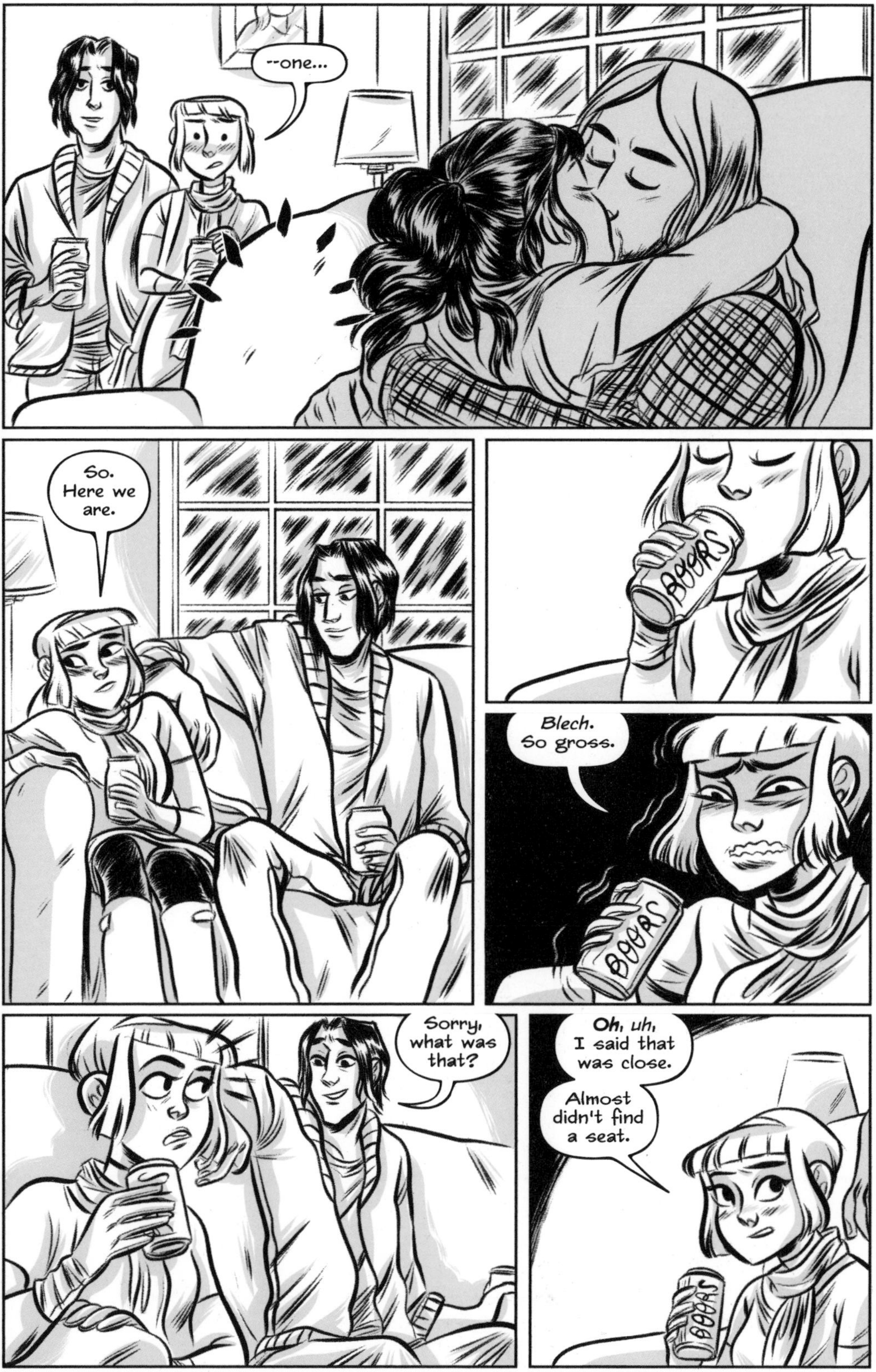
--one...
So. Here we are.
BOORS
Blech. So gross.
BOORS
Sorry, what was that?
Oh, uh, I said that was close.
Almost didn't find a seat.
BOORS

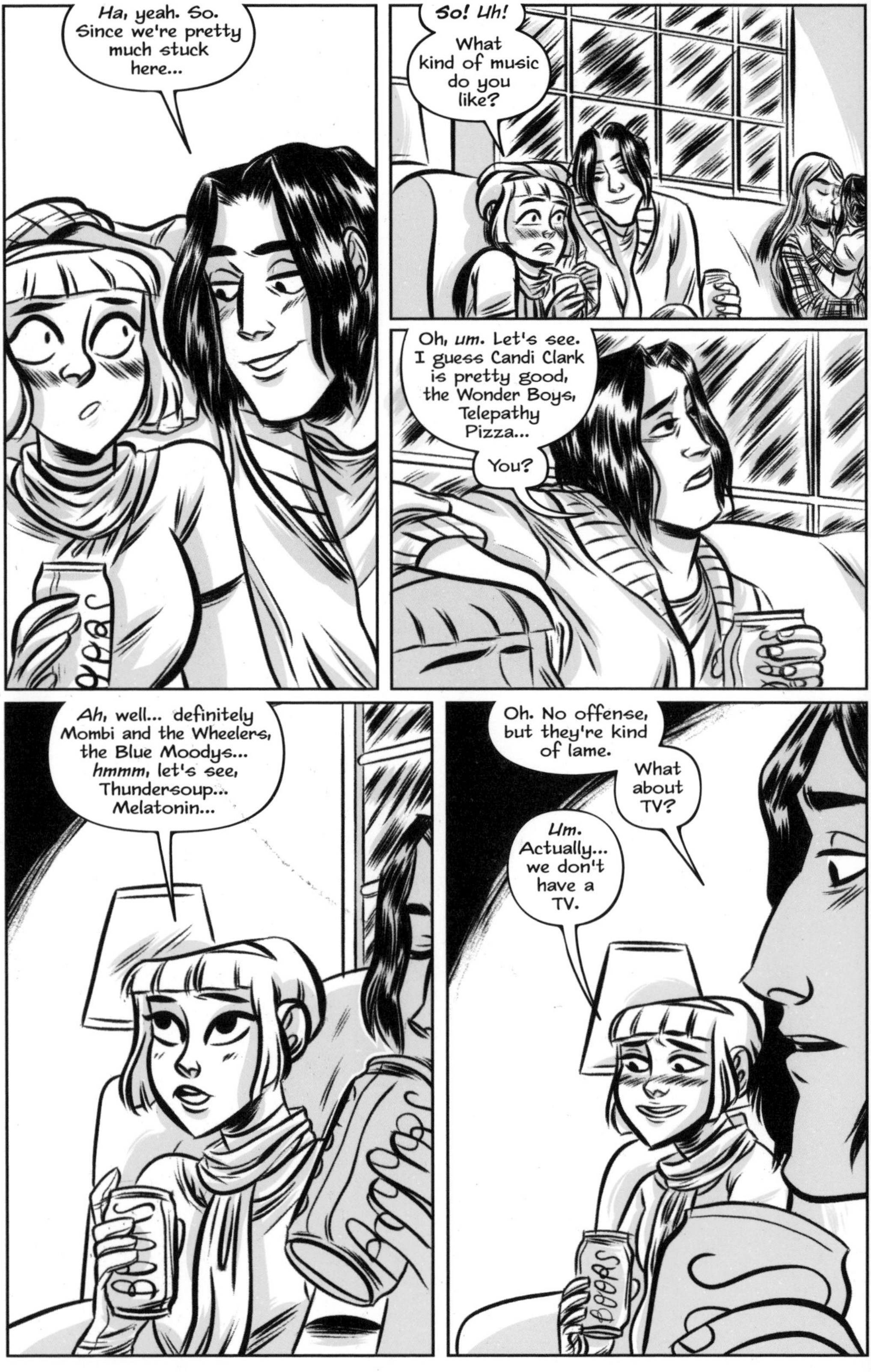

Ha, yeah. So. Since we're pretty much stuck here...
So! Uh!
What kind of music do you like?
Oh, um. Let's see. I guess Candi Clark is pretty good, the Wonder Boys, Telepathy Pizza...
You?
Ah, well... definitely Mombi and the Wheelers, the Blue Moodys... hmmm, let's see, Thundersoup... Melatonin...
Oh. No offense, but they're kind of lame.
What about TV?
Um. Actually... we don't have a TV.

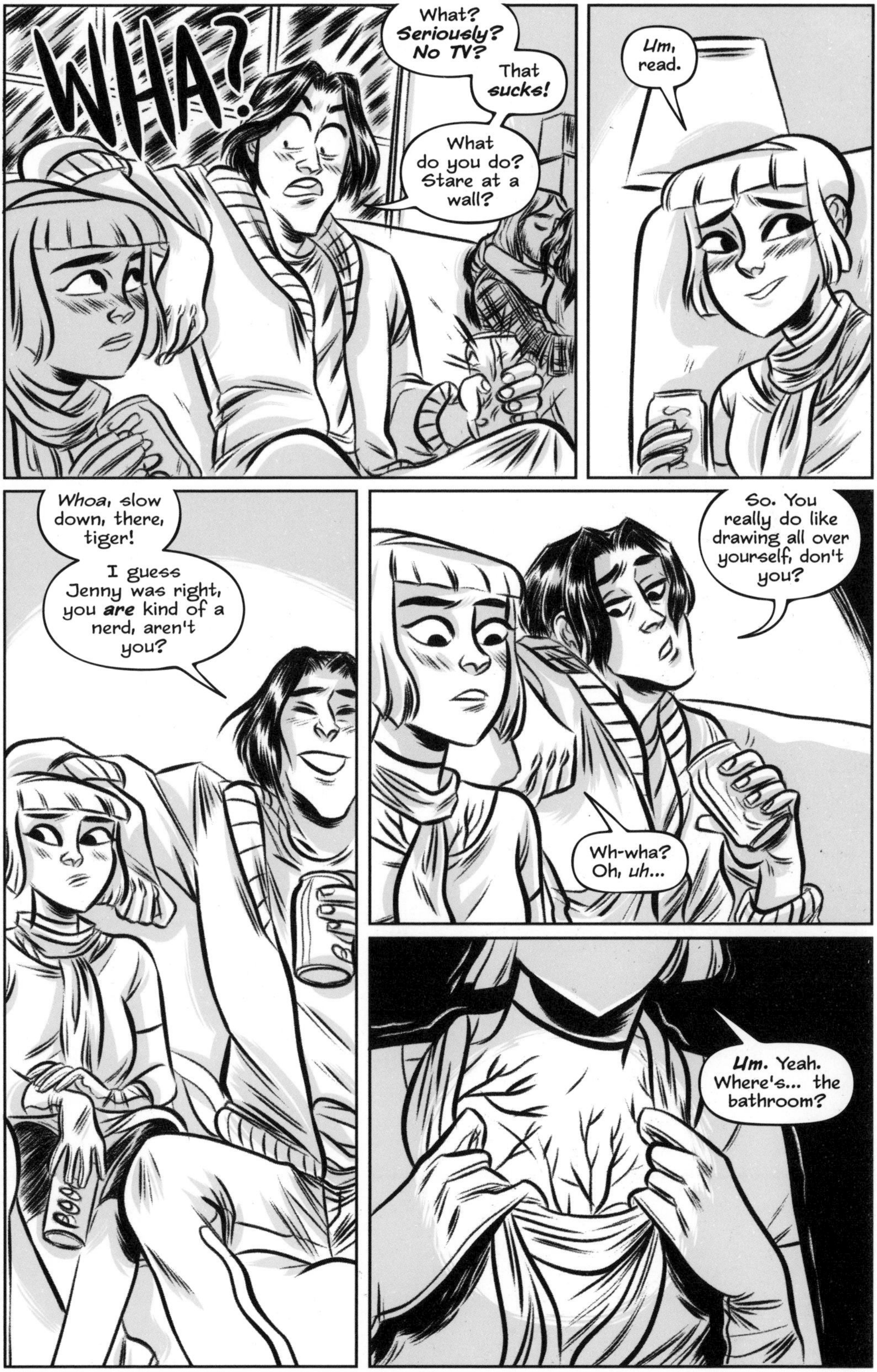
WHA?
What? Seriously? No TV?
That sucks!
What do you do? Stare at a wall?
Um, read.
Whoa, slow down, there, tiger!
I guess Jenny was right, you are kind of a nerd, aren't you?
So. You really do like drawing all over yourself, don't you?
Wh-wha? Oh, uh...
Um. Yeah. Where's... the bathroom?

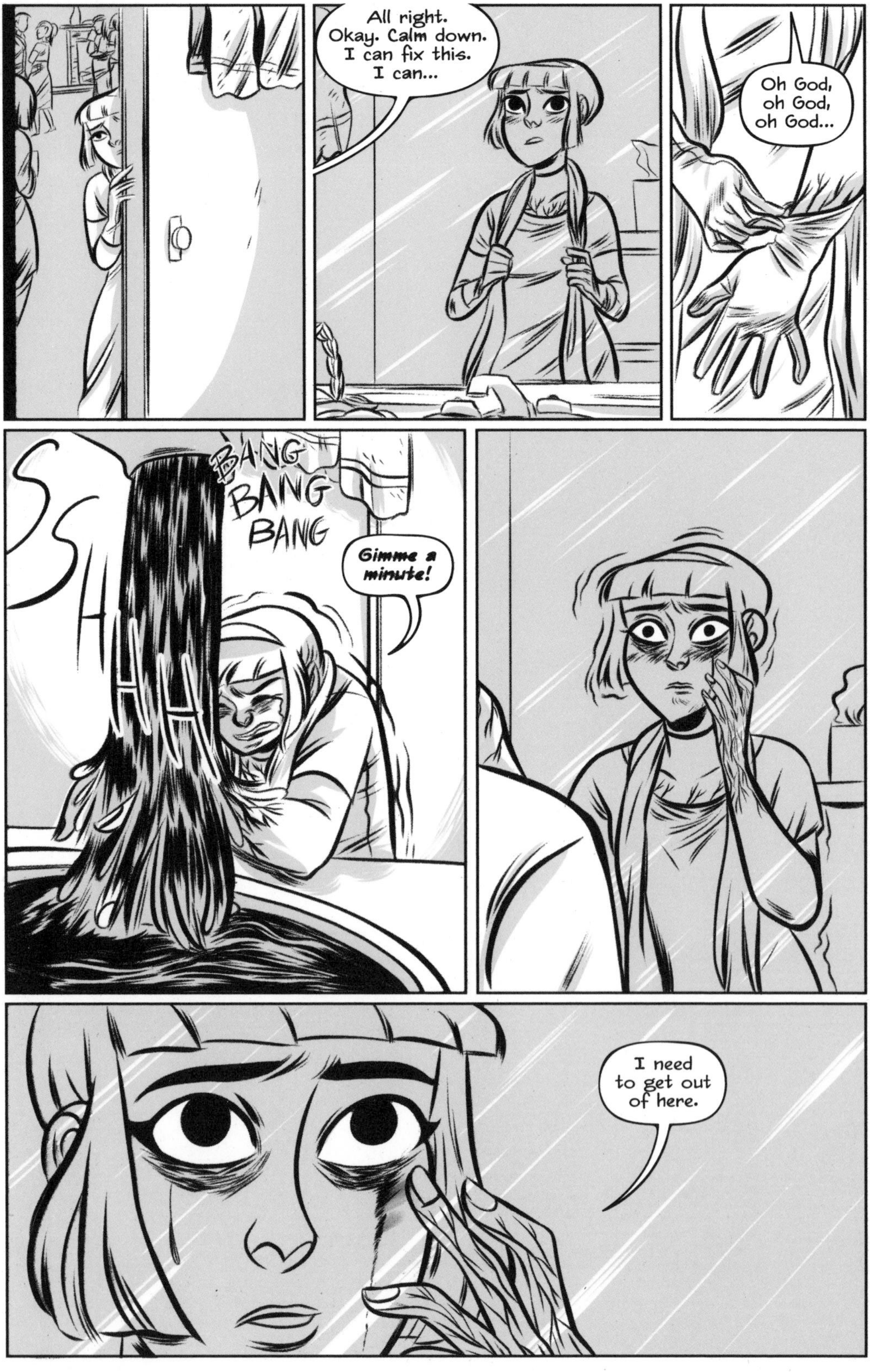
All right. Okay. Calm down. I can fix this. I can...
Oh God, oh God, oh God...
BANG
BANG
BANG
Gimme a minute!
I need to get out of here.

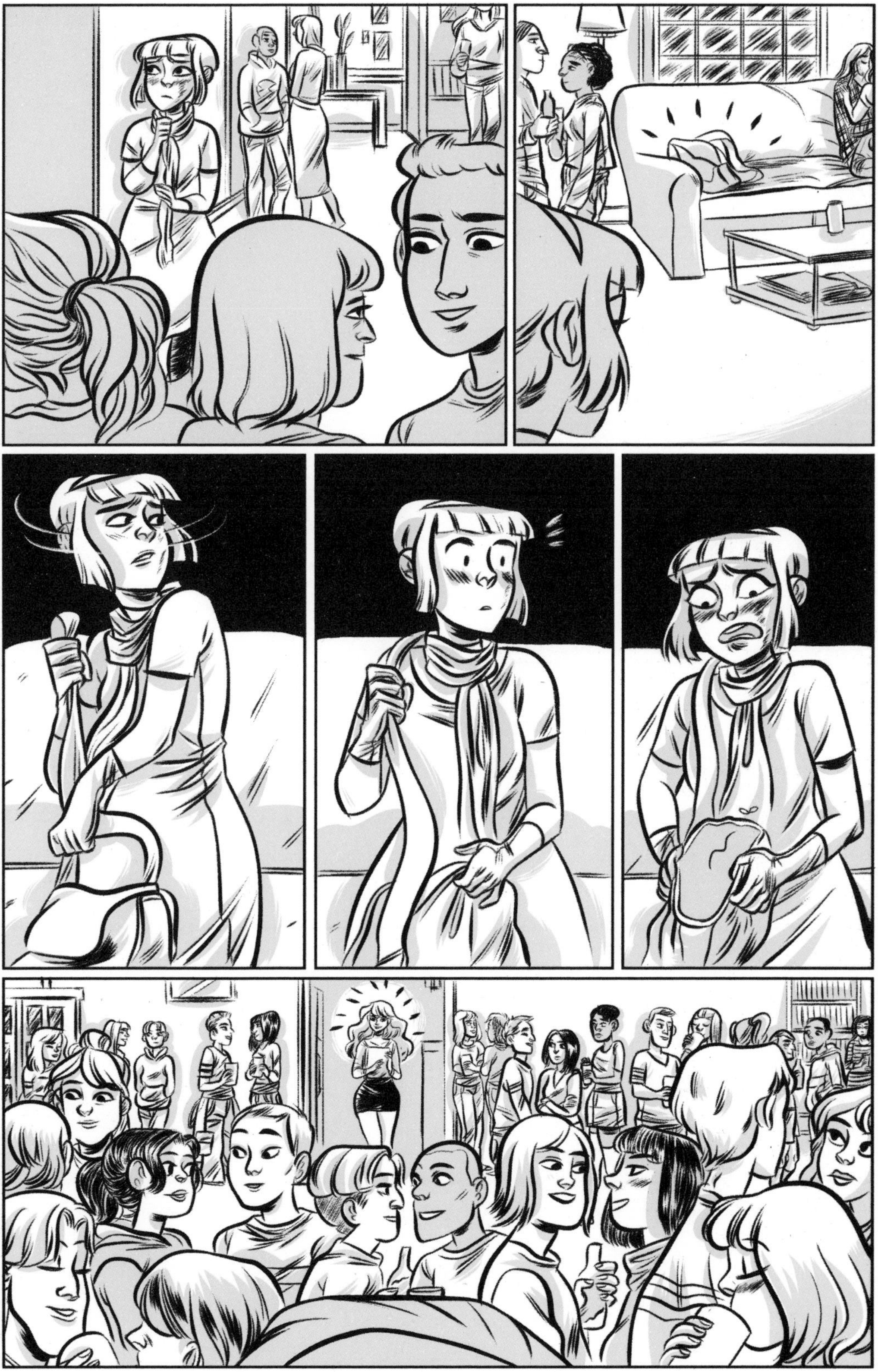

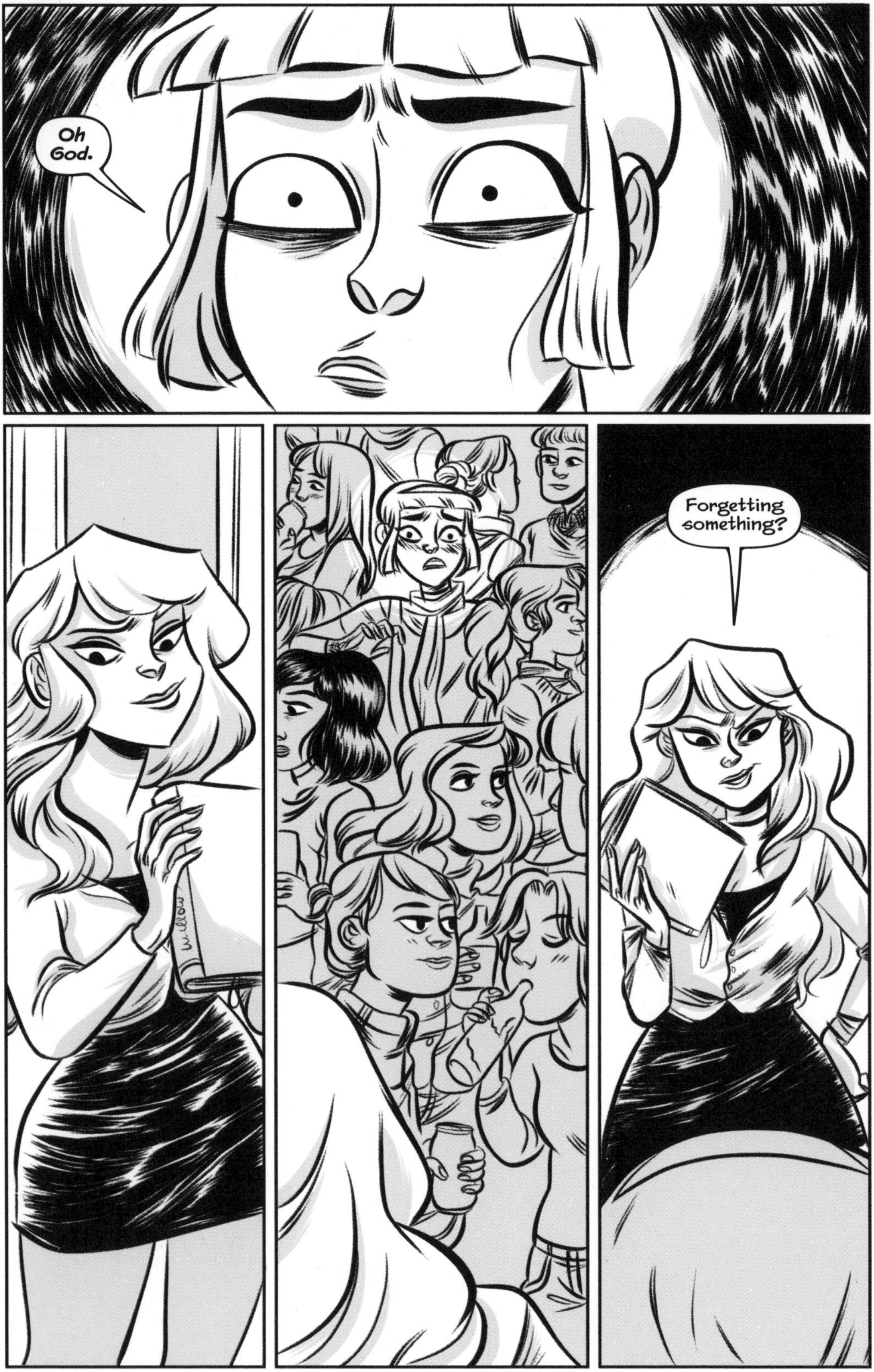
Oh God.
Forgetting something?

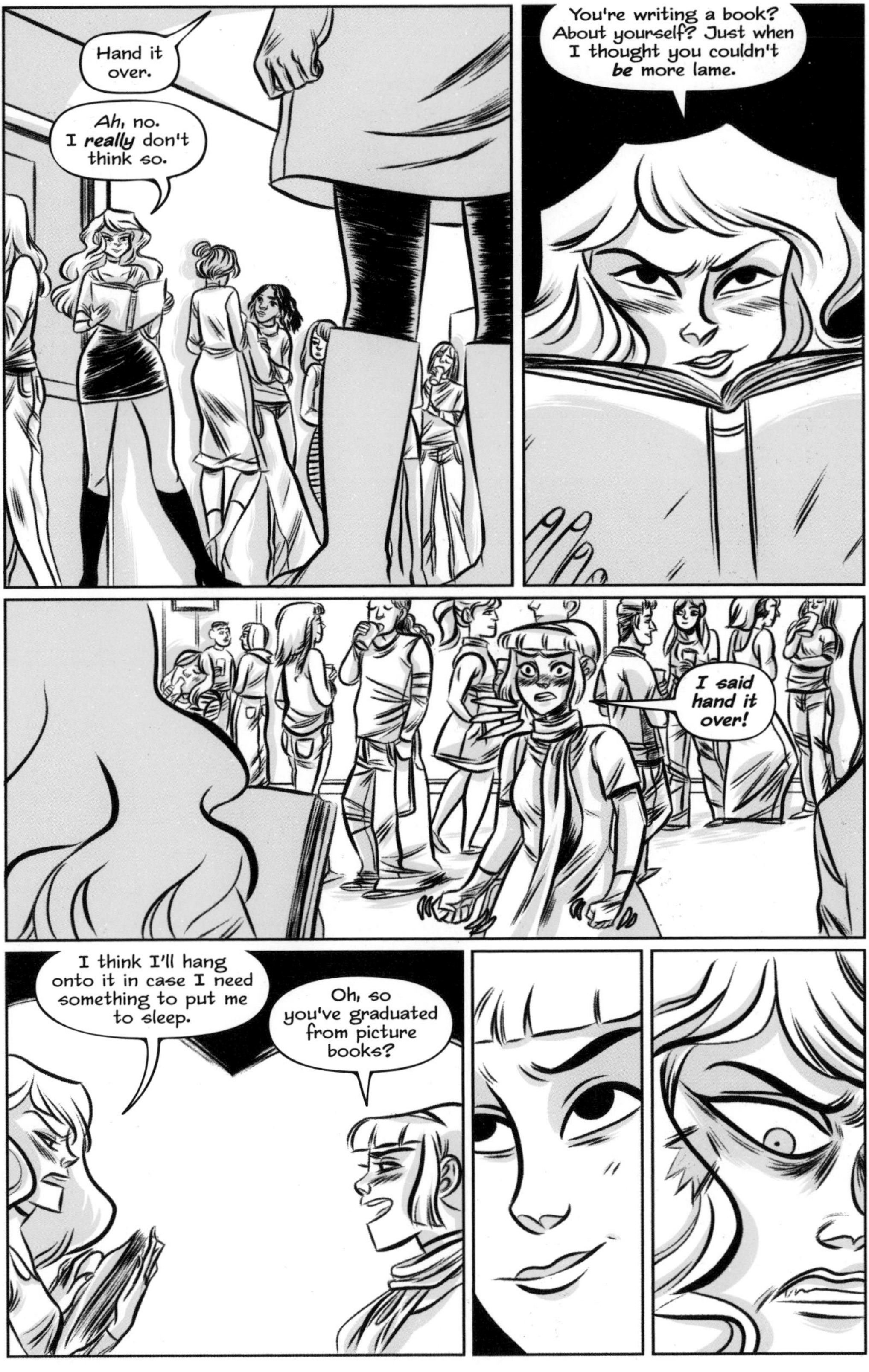
Hand it over.
Ah, no. I *really* don't think so.
You're writing a book? About yourself? Just when I thought you couldn't *be* more lame.
I said hand it over!
I think I'll hang onto it in case I need something to put me to sleep.
Oh, so you've graduated from picture books?

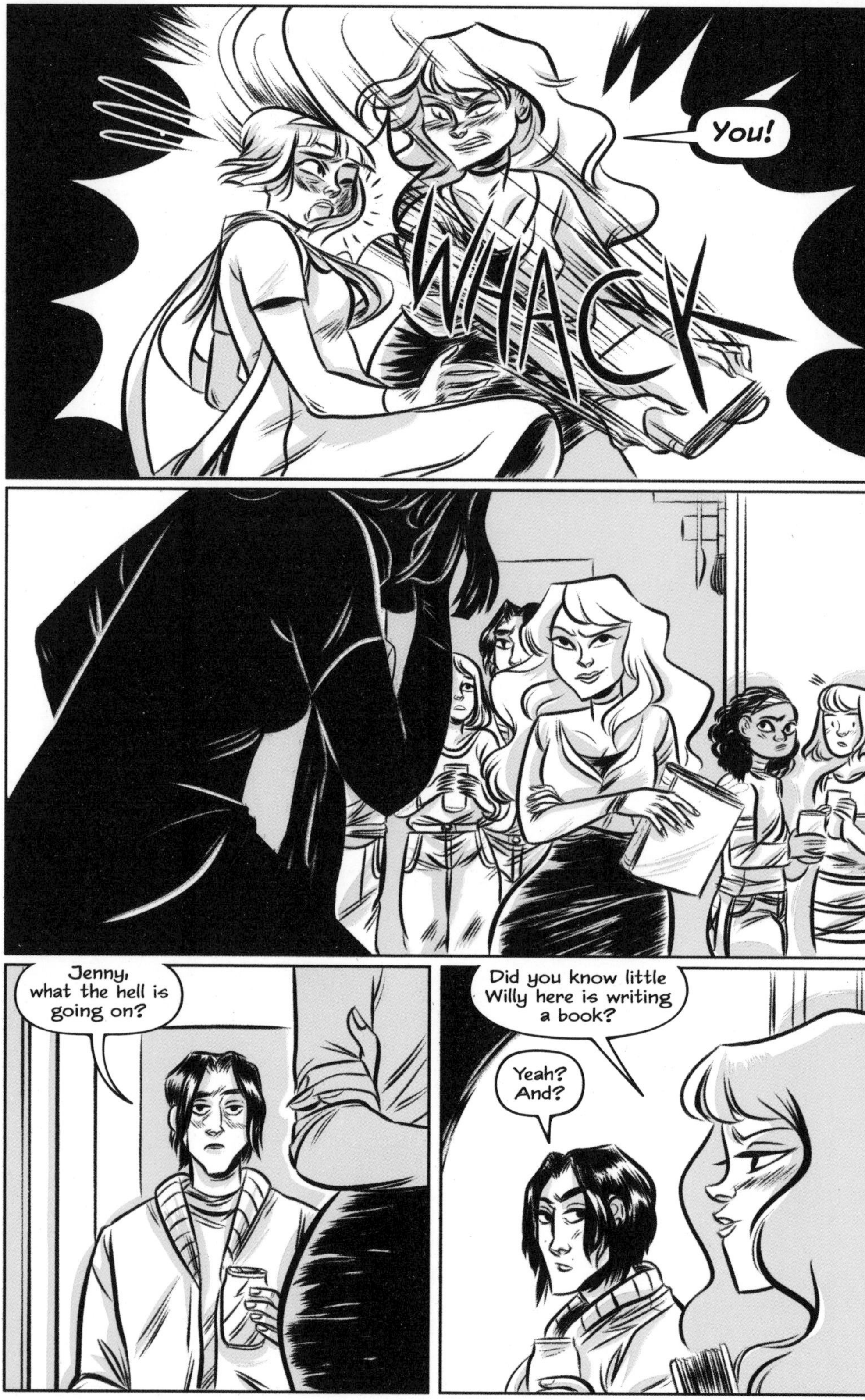

You!
WHACK
Jenny, what the hell is going on?
Did you know little Willy here is writing a book?
Yeah? And?

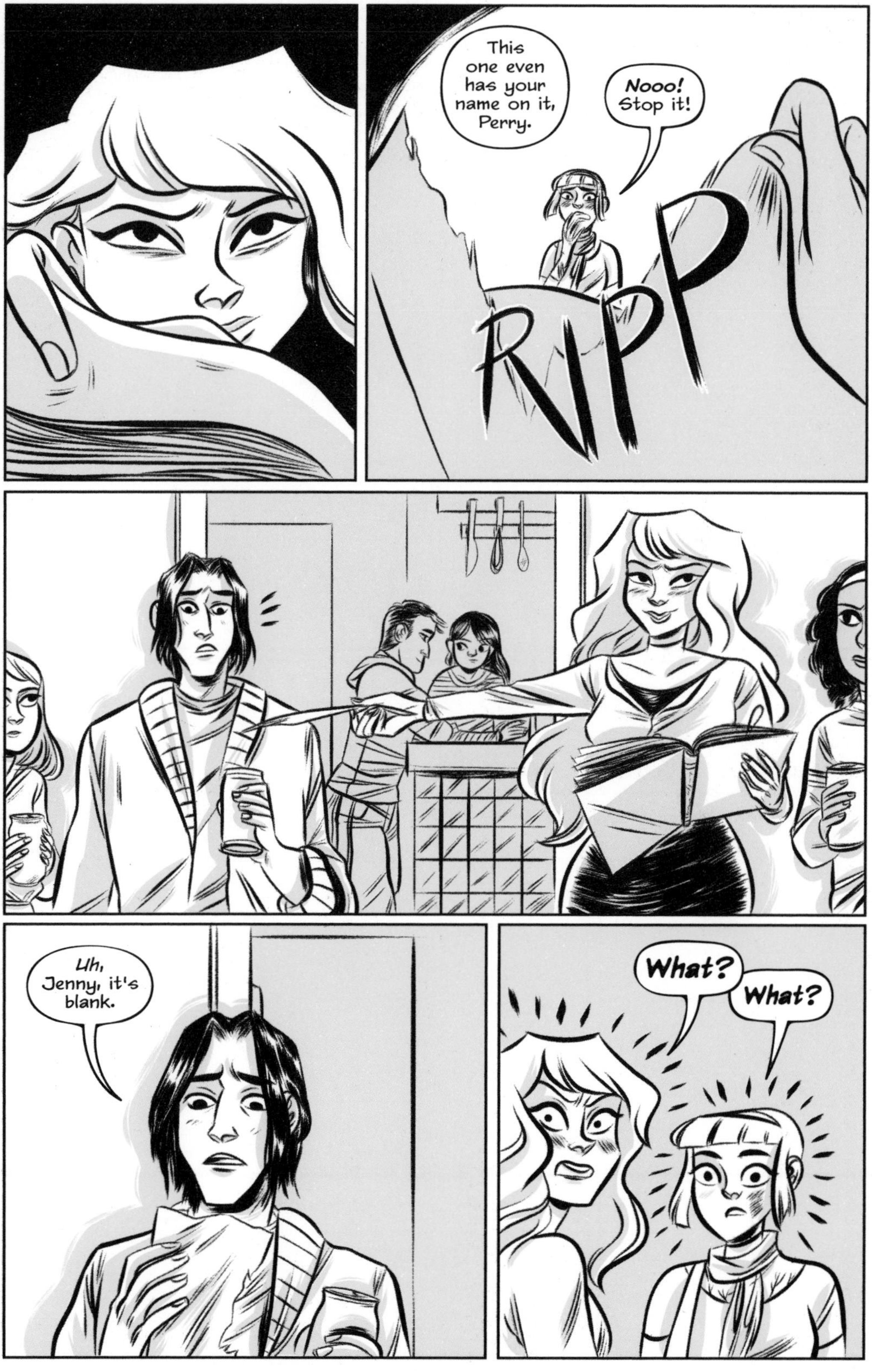

This one even has your name on it, Perry.
Nooo! Stop it!
RIPP
Uh, Jenny, it's blank.
What?
What?

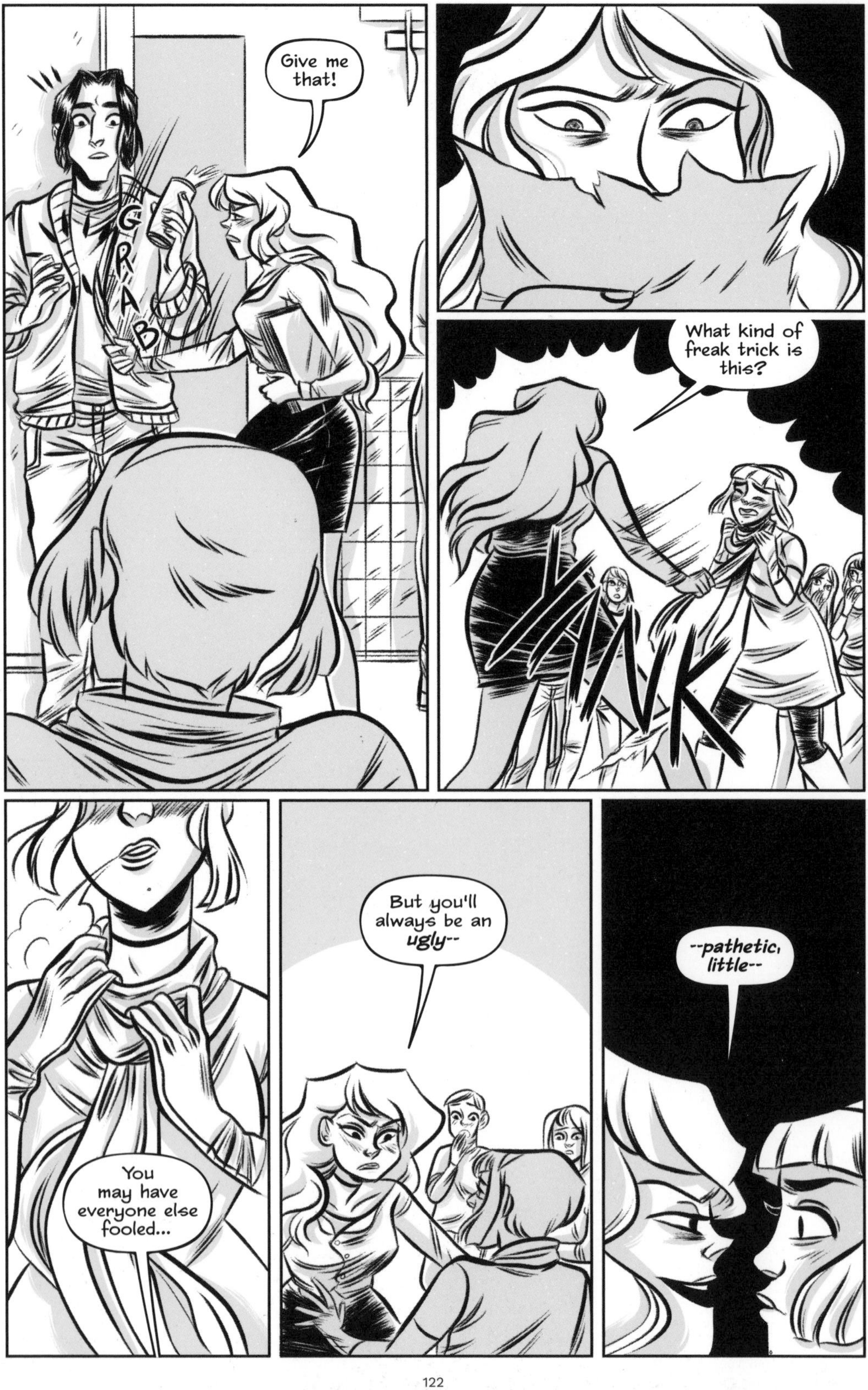
Give me that!
GRAB
What kind of freak trick is this?
YANK
You may have everyone else fooled...
But you'll always be an *ugly*--
--*pathetic, little*--

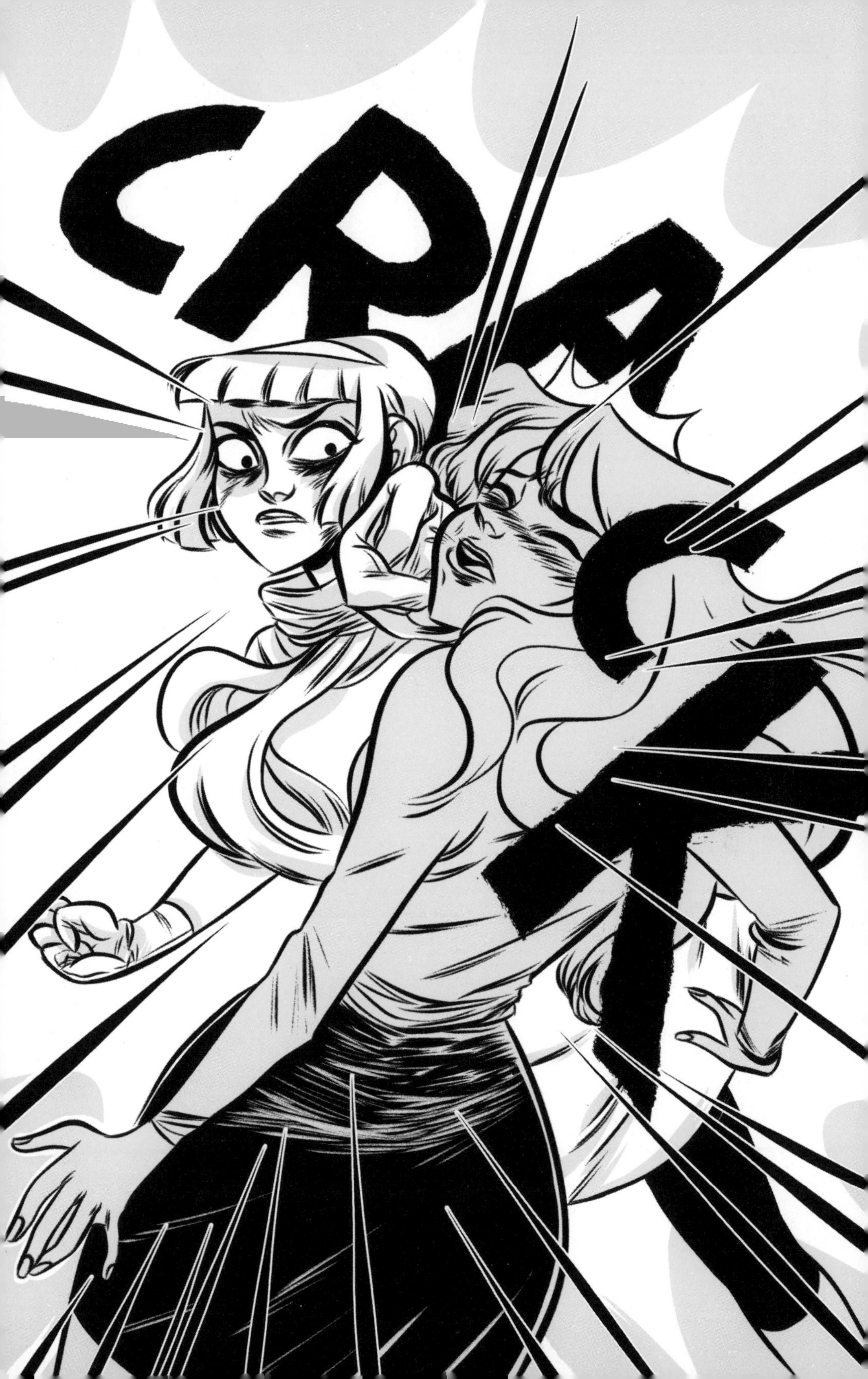
CRACK

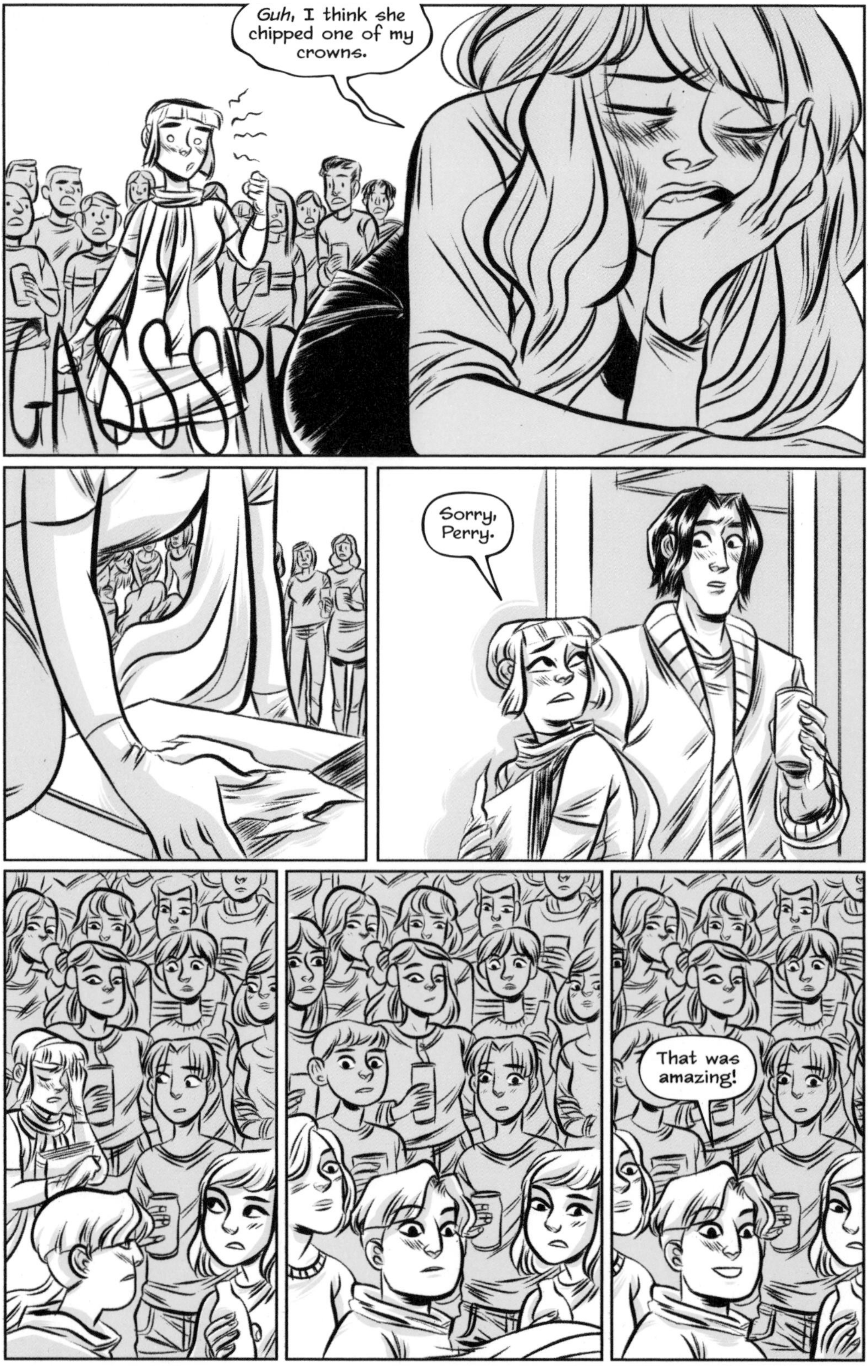
Guh, I think she chipped one of my crowns.
GASSSP
Sorry, Perry.
That was amazing!

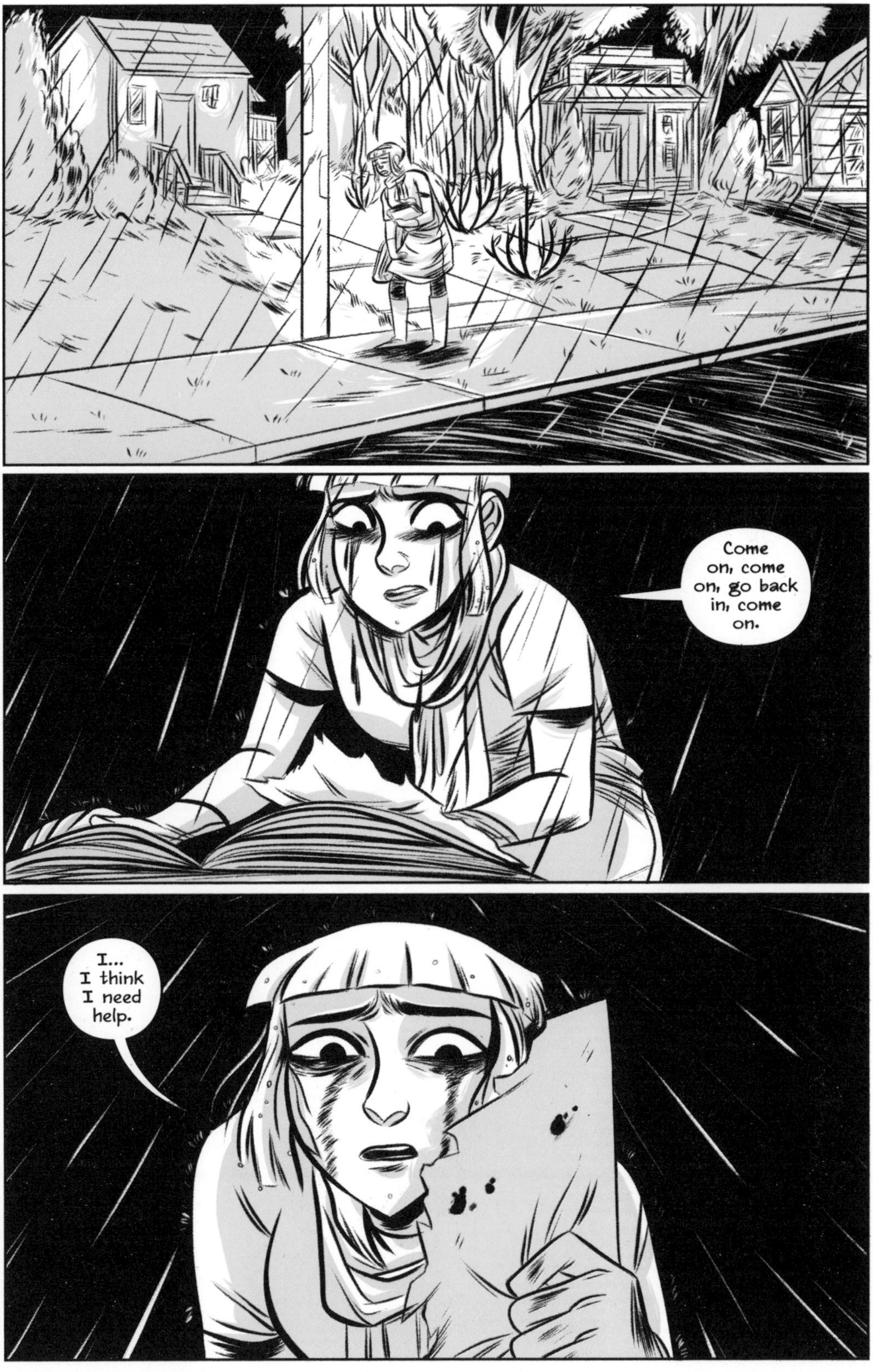
Come on, come on, go back in, come on.
I... I think I need help.

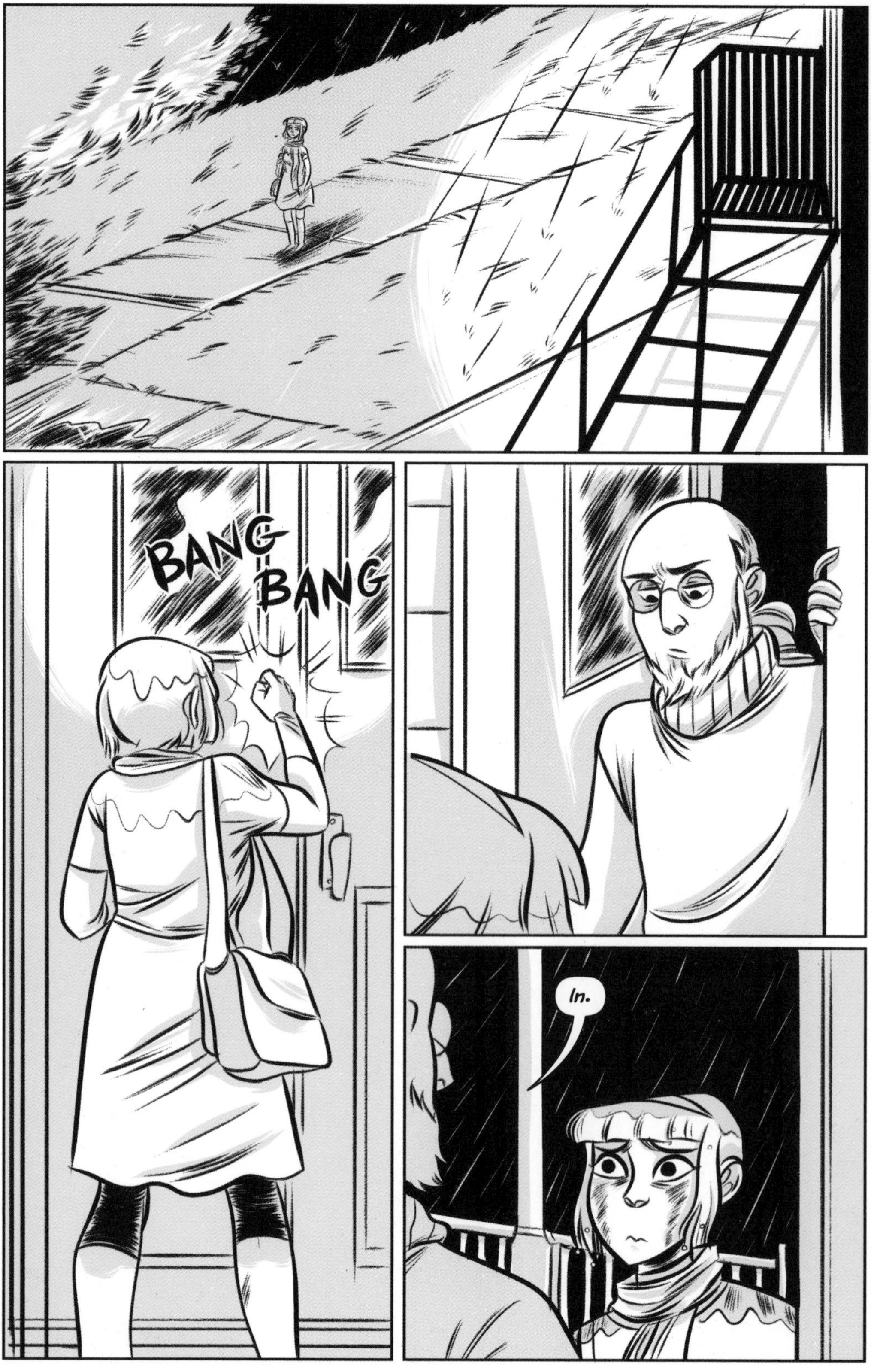
BANG
BANG
In.

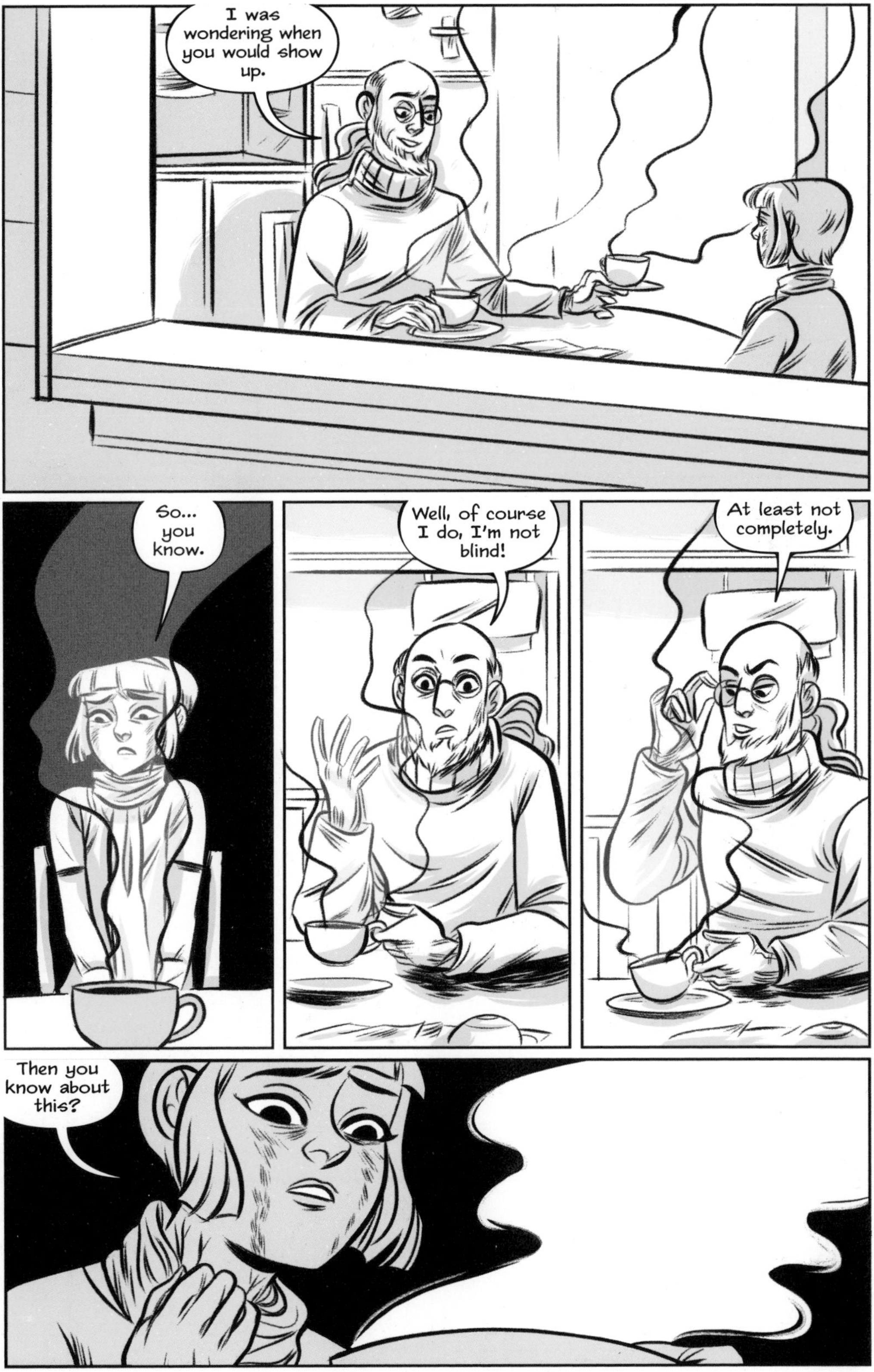
I was wondering when you would show up.
So... you know.
Well, of course I do, I'm not blind!
At least not completely.
Then you know about this?

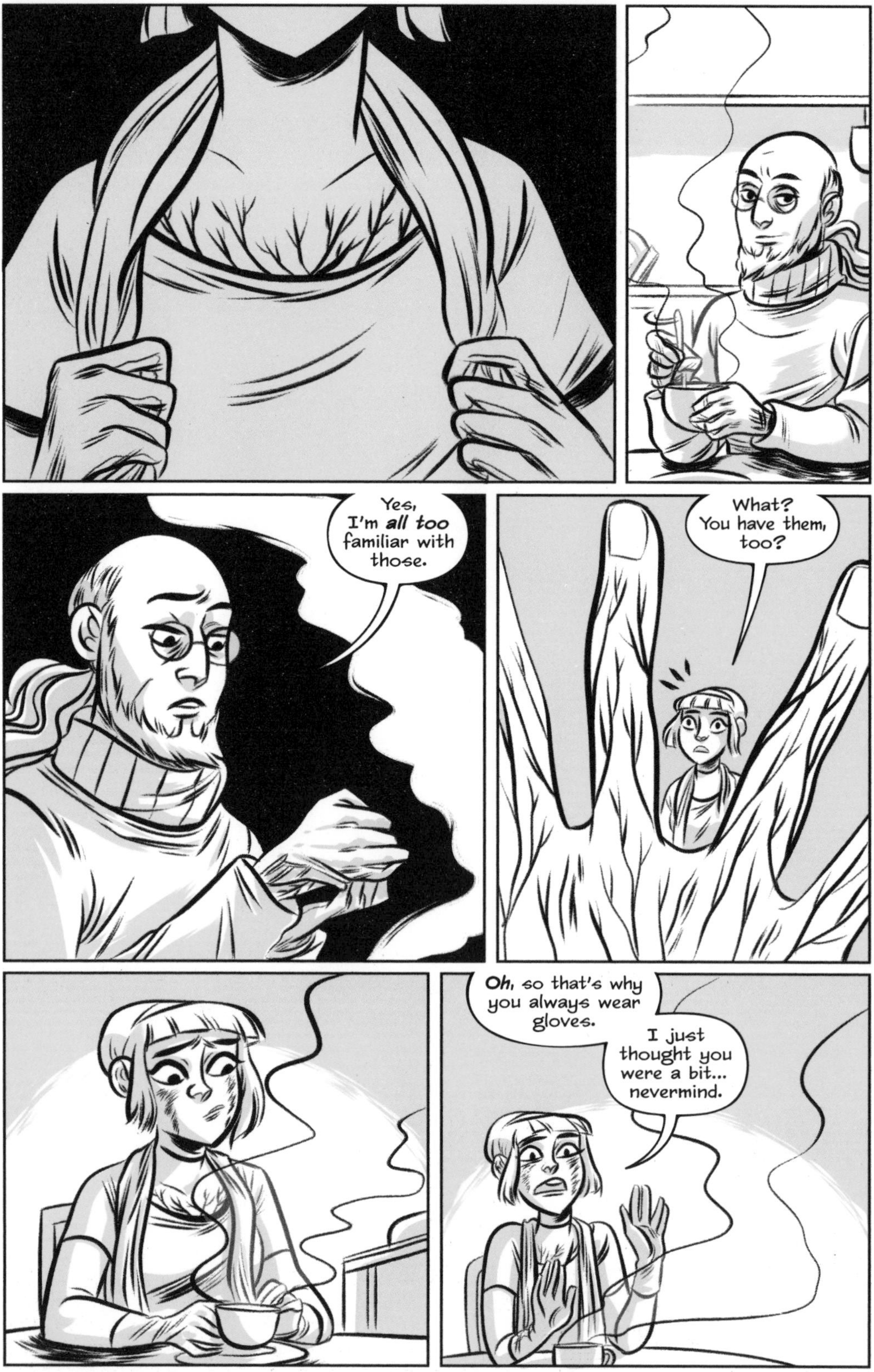
Yes, I'm **all too** familiar with those.
What? You have them, too?
Oh, so that's why you always wear gloves.
I just thought you were a bit... nevermind.

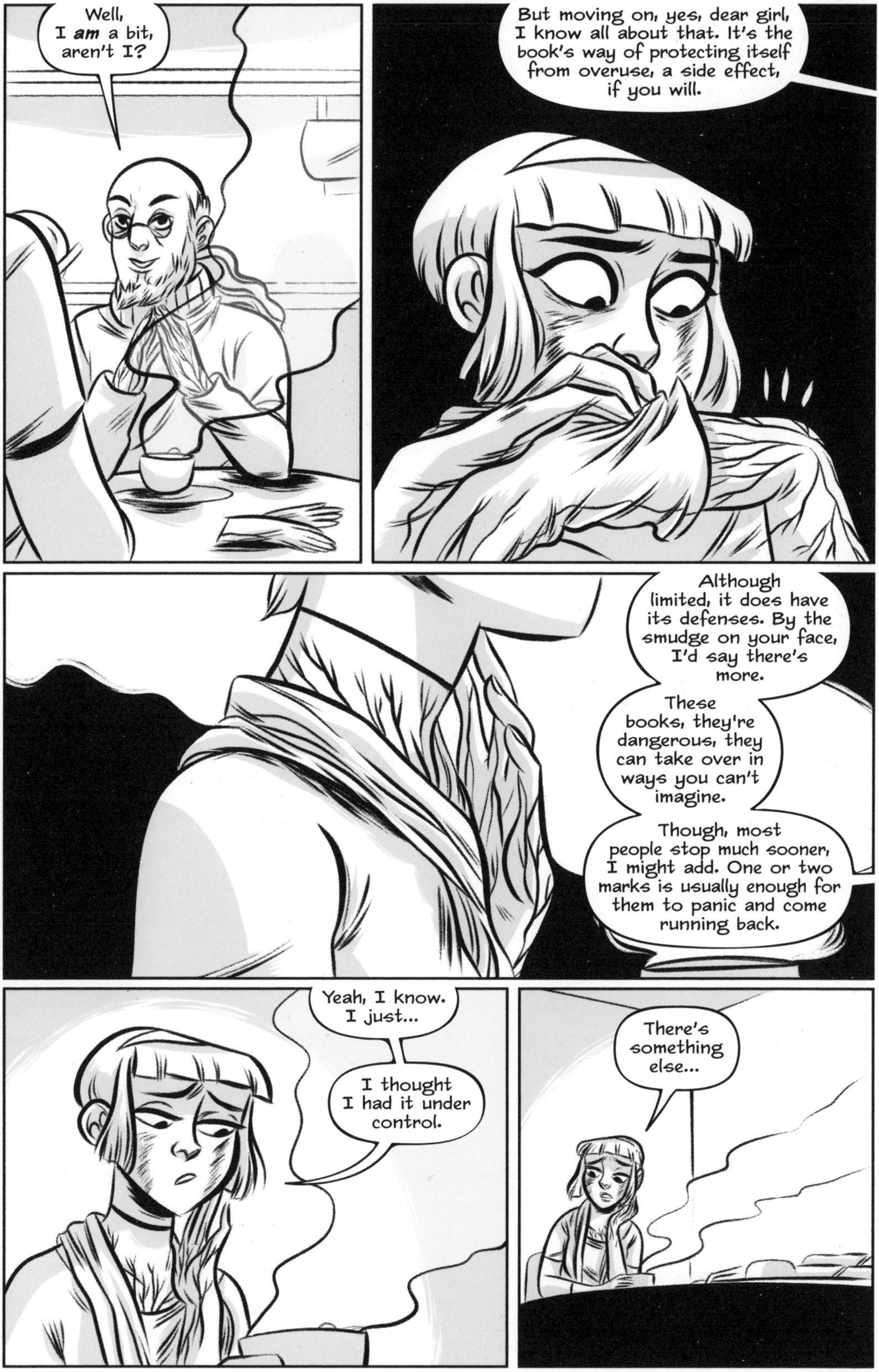
Well, I *am* a bit, aren't I?
But moving on, yes, dear girl, I know all about that. It's the book's way of protecting itself from overuse, a side effect, if you will.
Although limited, it does have its defenses. By the smudge on your face, I'd say there's more.
These books, they're dangerous, they can take over in ways you can't imagine.
Though, most people stop much sooner, I might add. One or two marks is usually enough for them to panic and come running back.
Yeah, I know. I just...
I thought I had it under control.
There's something else...

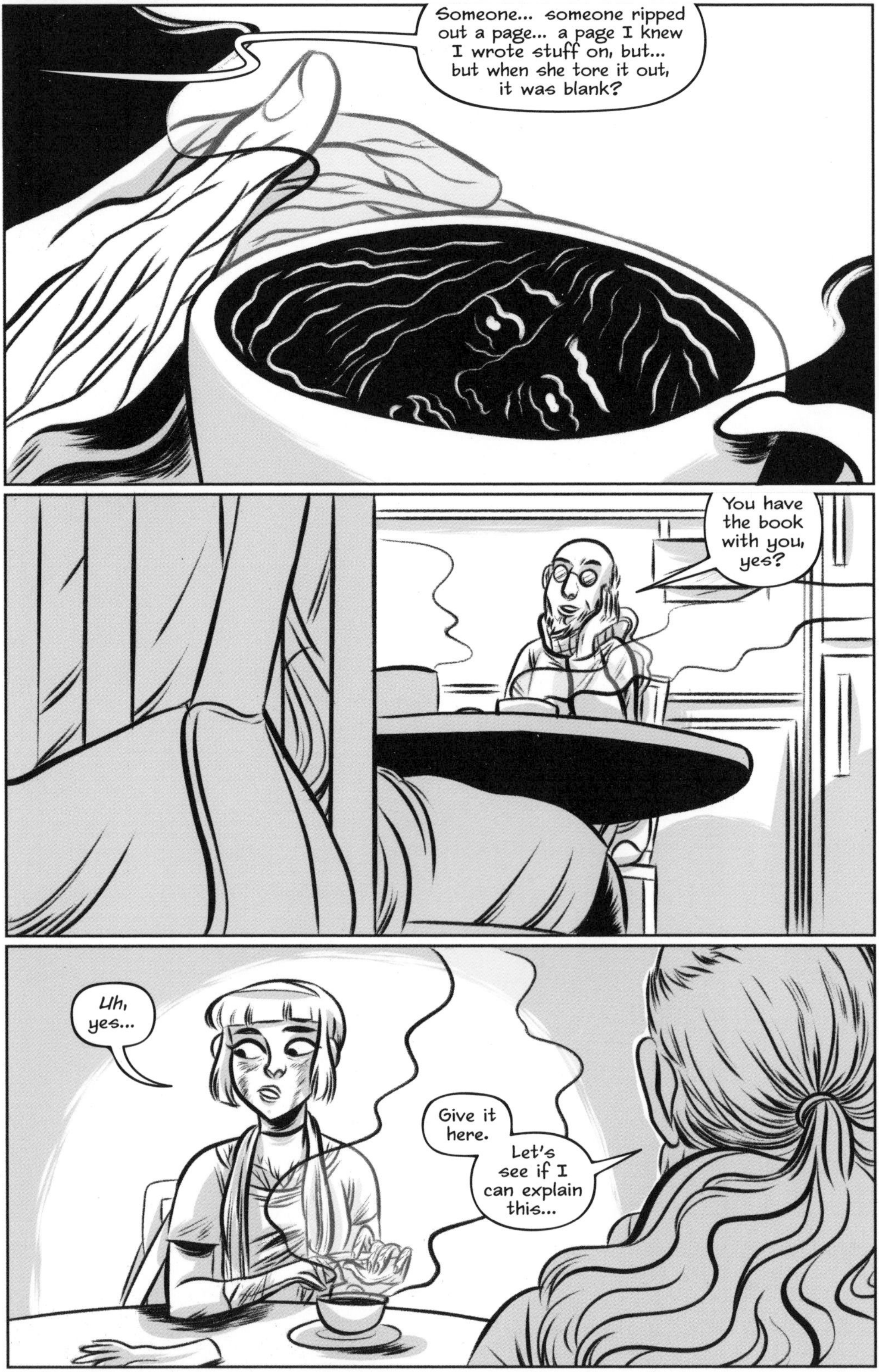
Someone... someone ripped out a page... a page I knew I wrote stuff on, but... but when she tore it out, it was blank?
You have the book with you, yes?
Uh, yes...
Give it here.
Let's see if I can explain this...

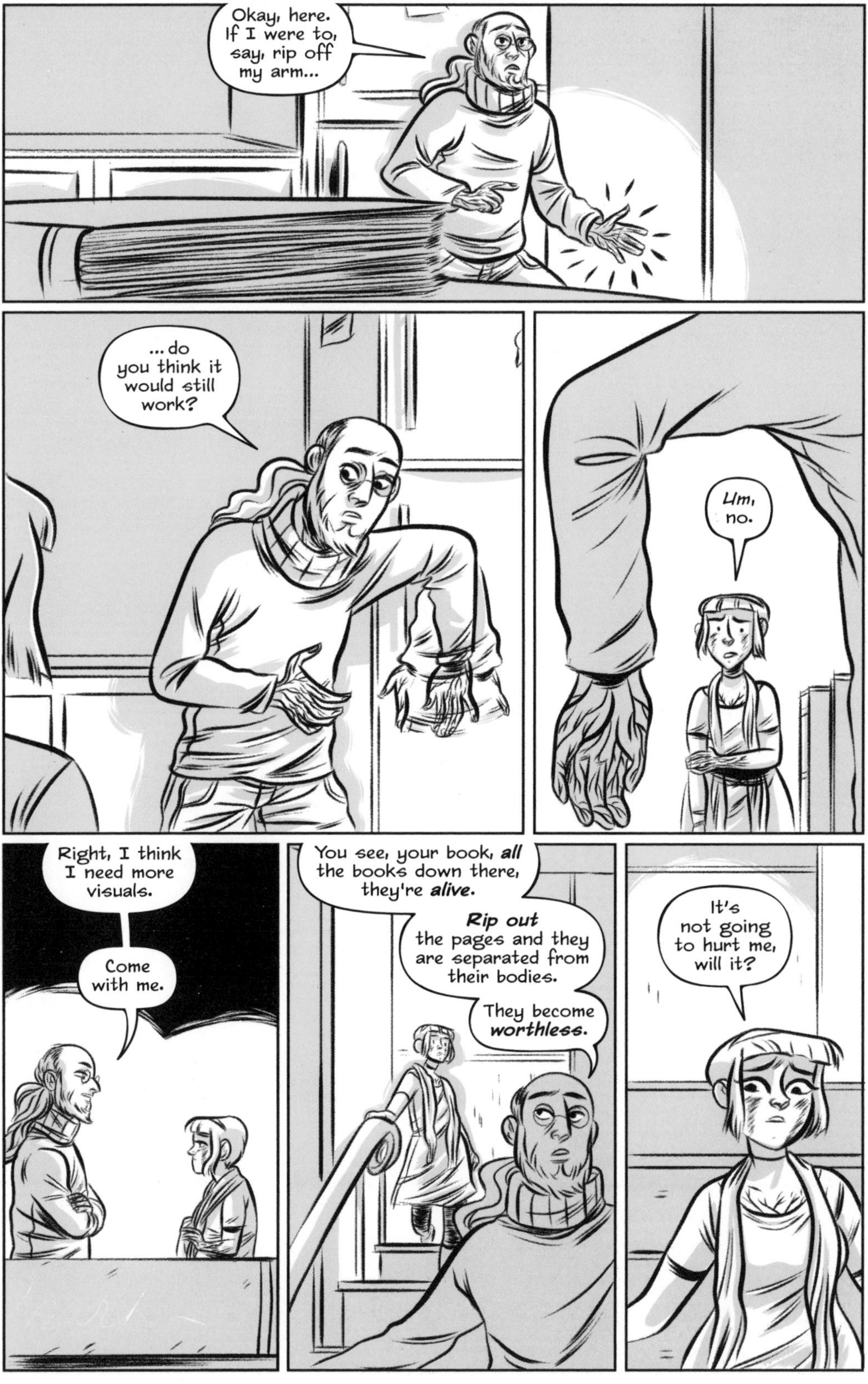
Okay, here. If I were to, say, rip off my arm...
...do you think it would still work?
Um, no.
Right, I think I need more visuals.
Come with me.
You see, your book, ***all*** the books down there, they're ***alive.***
Rip out the pages and they are separated from their bodies.
They become ***worthless.***
It's not going to hurt me, will it?

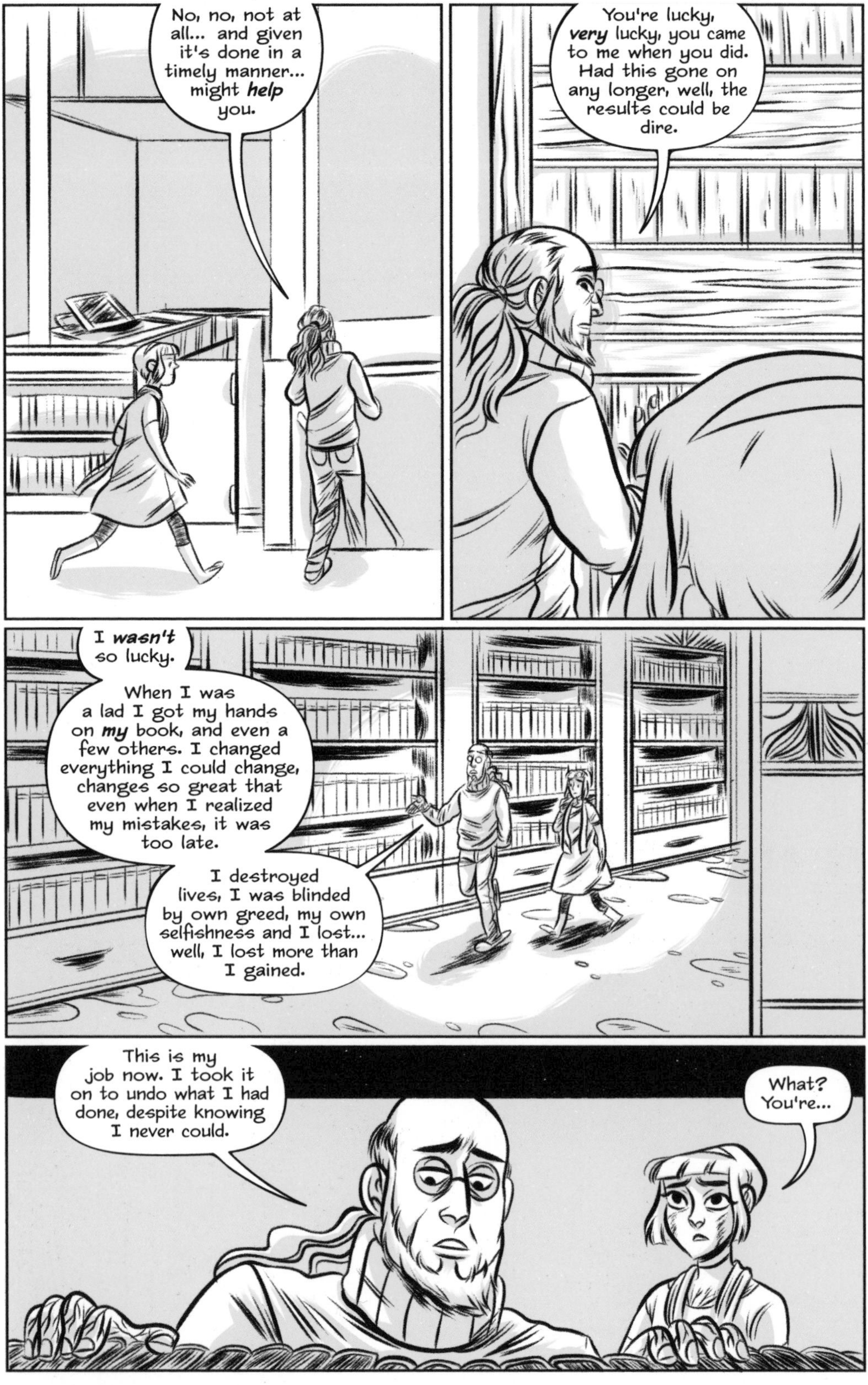
No, no, not at all... and given it's done in a timely manner... might **help** you.
You're lucky, **very** lucky, you came to me when you did. Had this gone on any longer, well, the results could be dire.
I **wasn't** so lucky.
When I was a lad I got my hands on **my** book, and even a few others. I changed everything I could change, changes so great that even when I realized my mistakes, it was too late.
I destroyed lives, I was blinded by own greed, my own selfishness and I lost... well, I lost more than I gained.
This is my job now. I took it on to undo what I had done, despite knowing I never could.
What? You're...

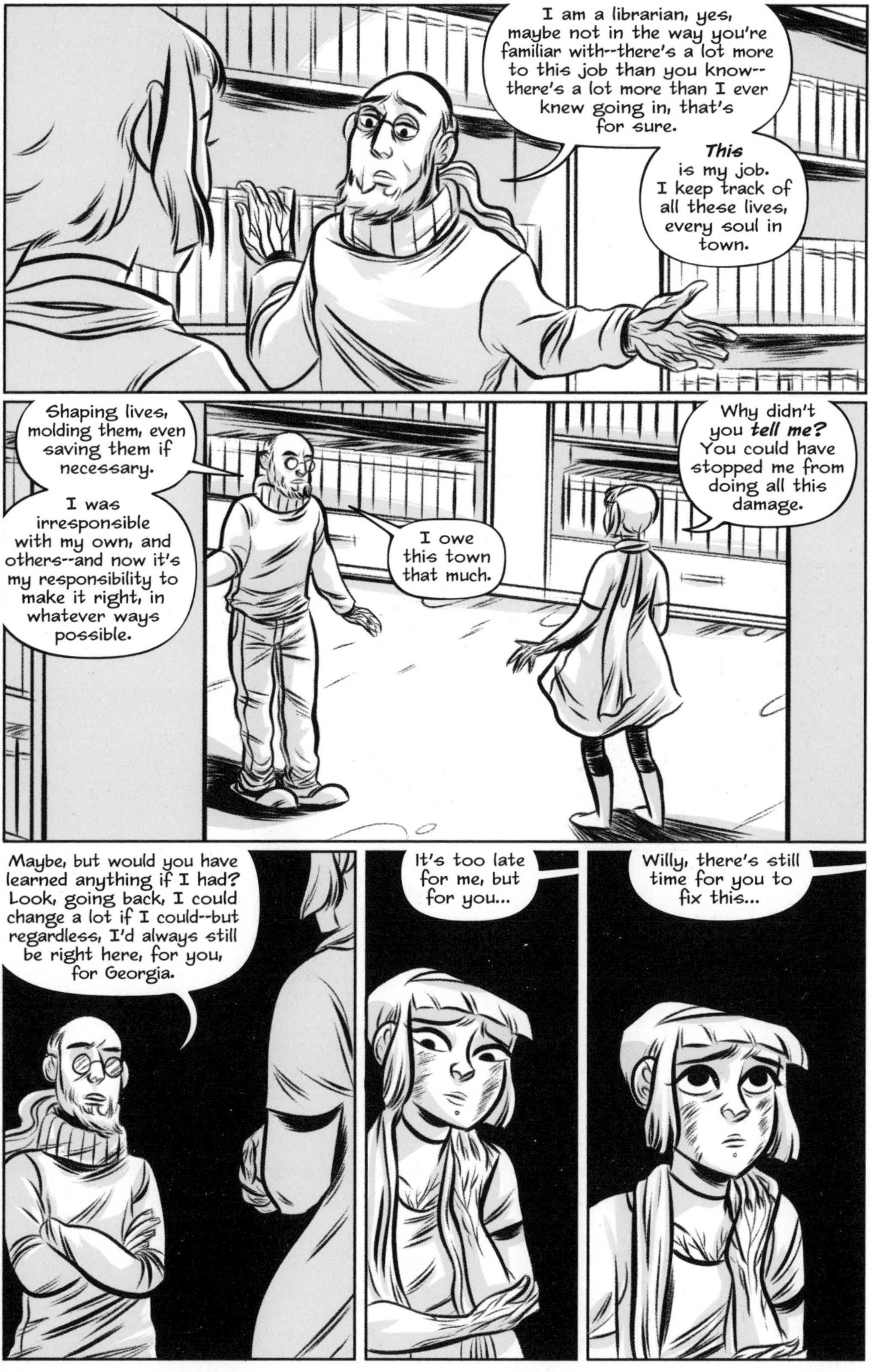
I am a librarian, yes, maybe not in the way you're familiar with--there's a lot more to this job than you know--there's a lot more than I ever knew going in, that's for sure.
This is my job. I keep track of all these lives, every soul in town.
Shaping lives, molding them, even saving them if necessary.
I was irresponsible with my own, and others--and now it's my responsibility to make it right, in whatever ways possible.
I owe this town that much.
Why didn't you *tell me?* You could have stopped me from doing all this damage.
Maybe, but would you have learned anything if I had? Look, going back, I could change a lot if I could--but regardless, I'd always still be right here, for you, for Georgia.
It's too late for me, but for you...
Willy, there's still time for you to fix this...

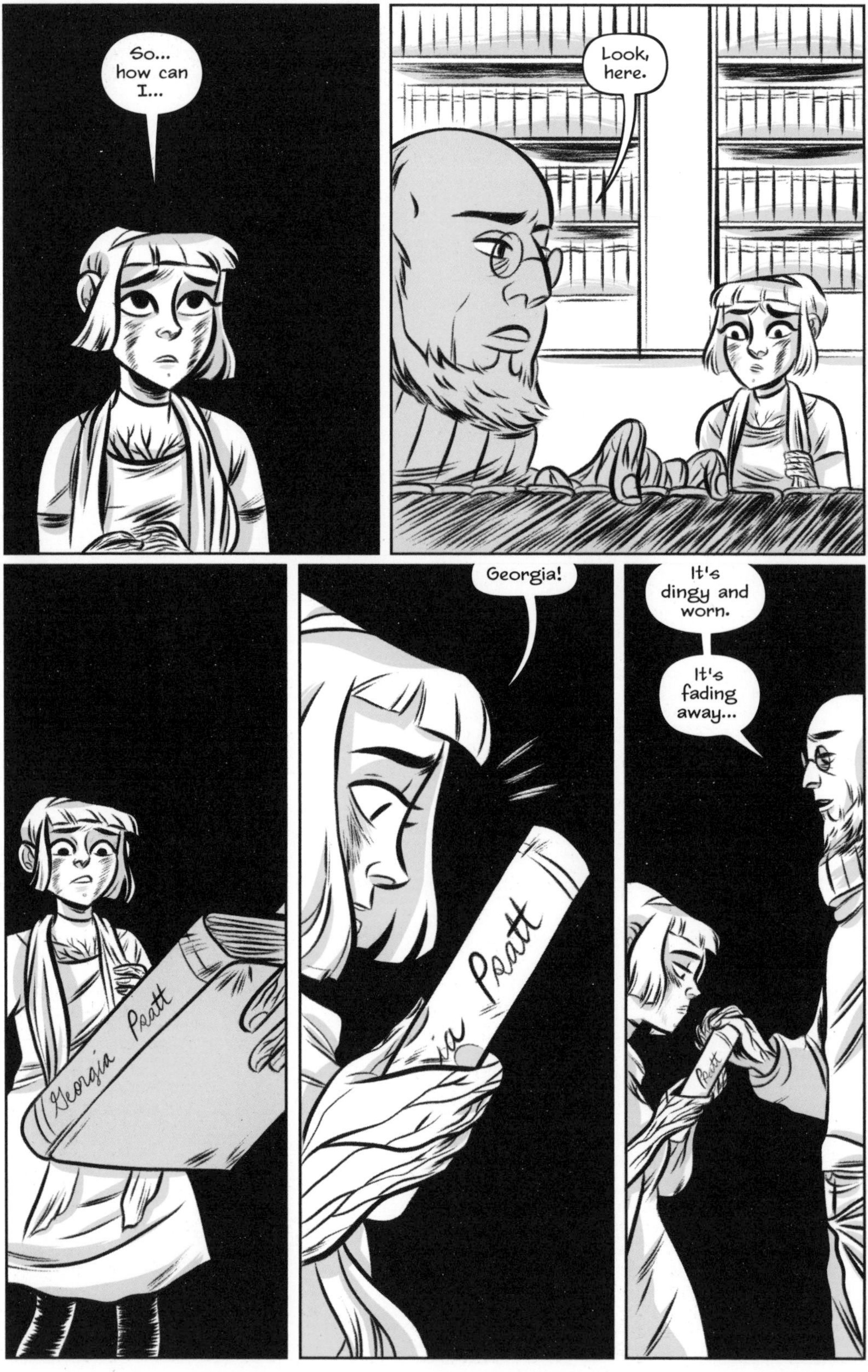
So... how can I...
Look, here.
Georgia Pratt
Georgia!
Pratt
It's dingy and worn.
It's fading away...
Pratt

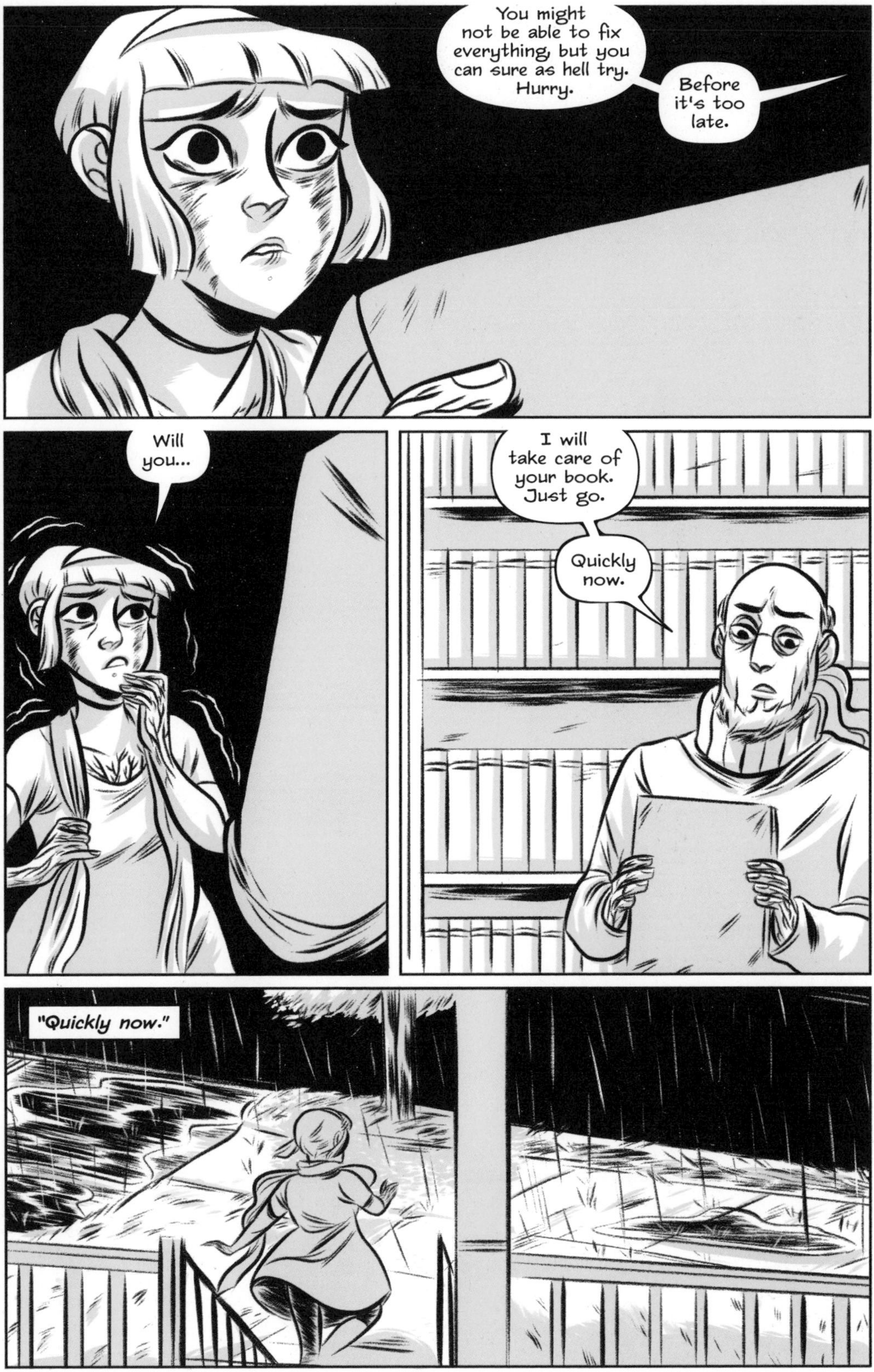

You might not be able to fix everything, but you can sure as hell try. Hurry.
Before it's too late.
Will you...
I will take care of your book. Just go.
Quickly now.
"Quickly now."

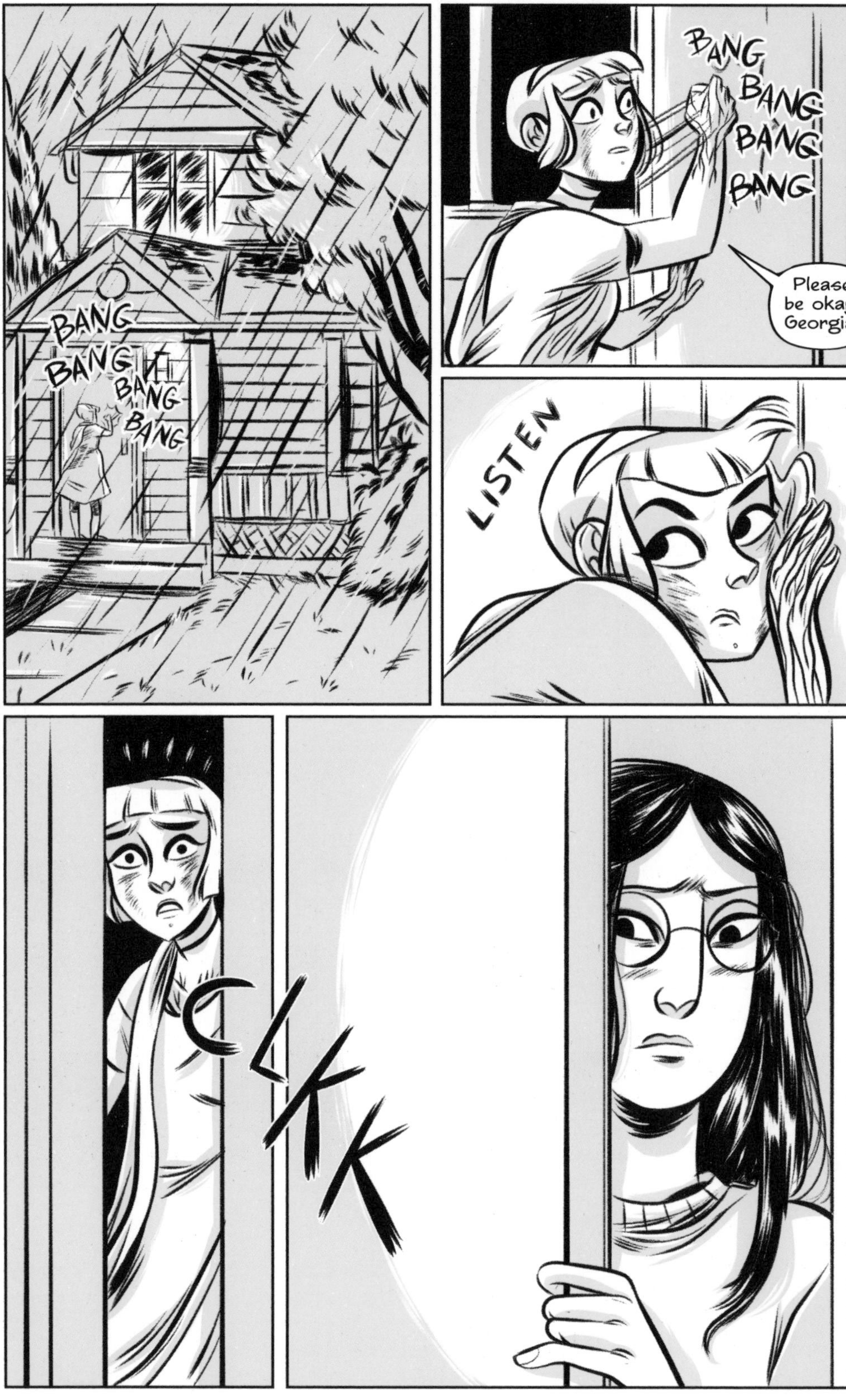
BANG BANG BANG BANG
BANG BANG BANG BANG
Please be okay, Georgia.
LISTEN
CLKK

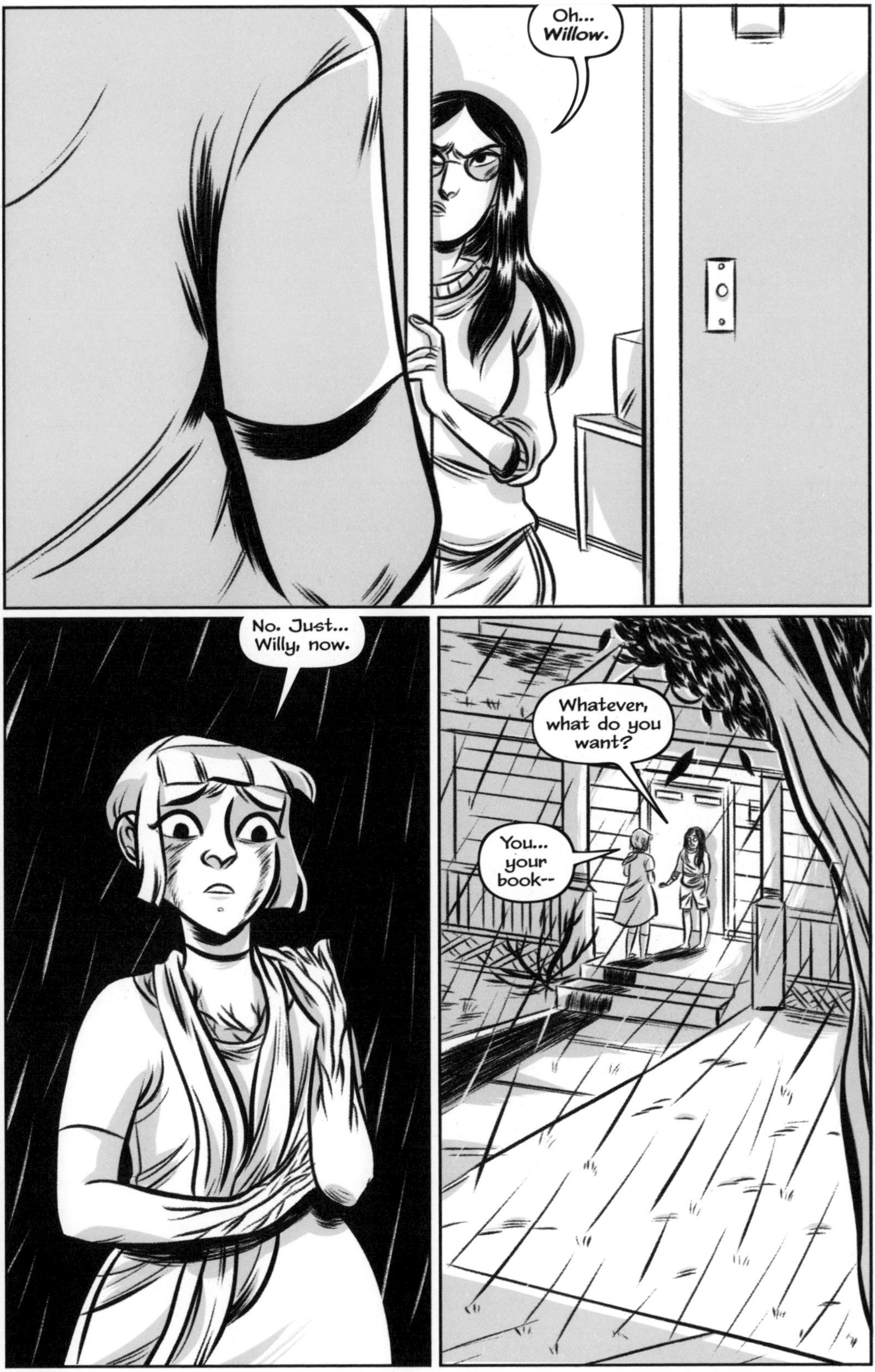
Oh... Willow.
No. Just... Willy, now.
Whatever, what do you want?
You... your book--

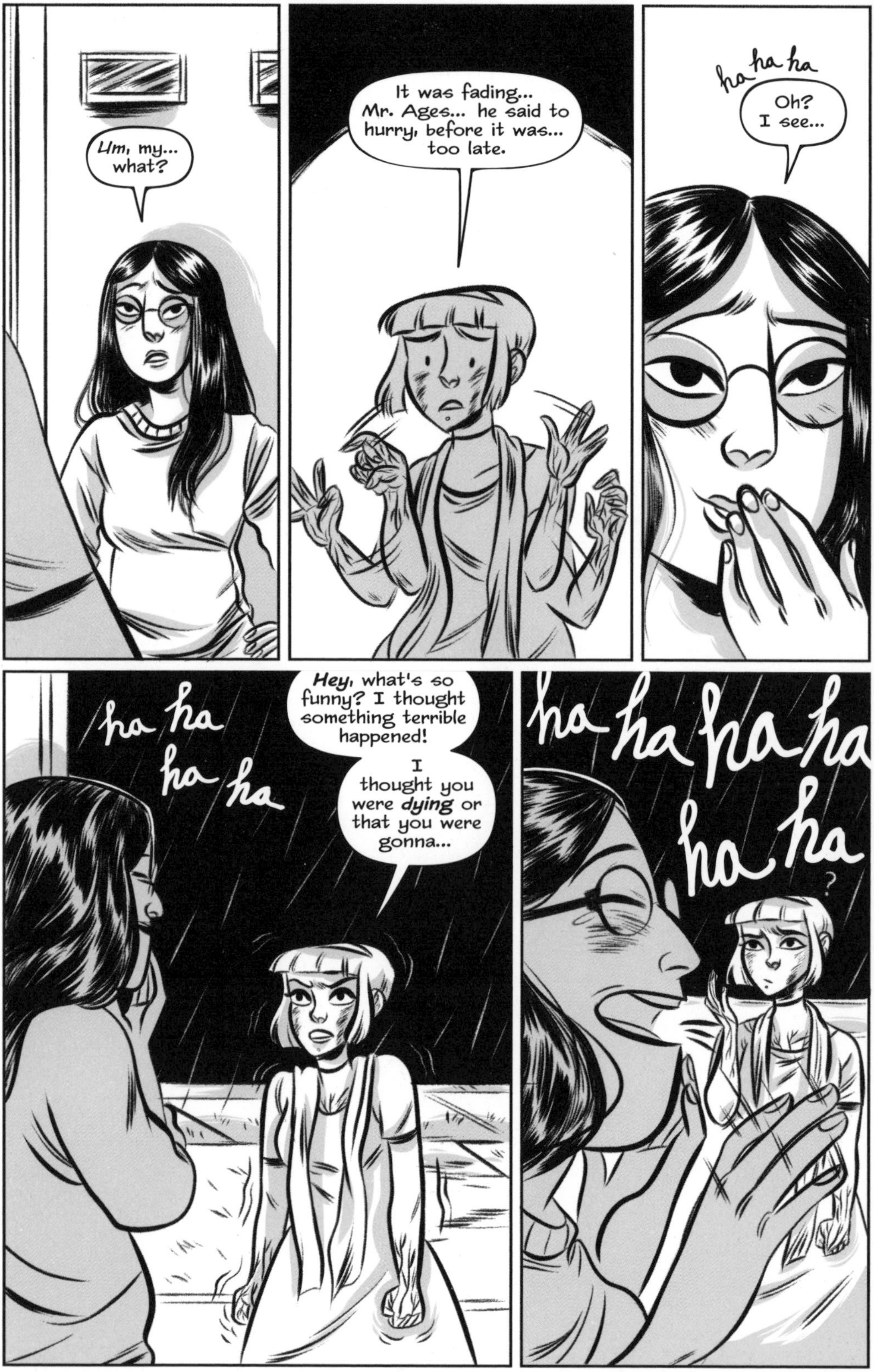
Um, my... what?
It was fading... Mr. Ages... he said to hurry, before it was... too late.
ha ha ha
Oh? I see...
ha ha ha ha ha
Hey, what's so funny? I thought something terrible happened!
I thought you were dying or that you were gonna...
ha ha ha ha ha ha
?

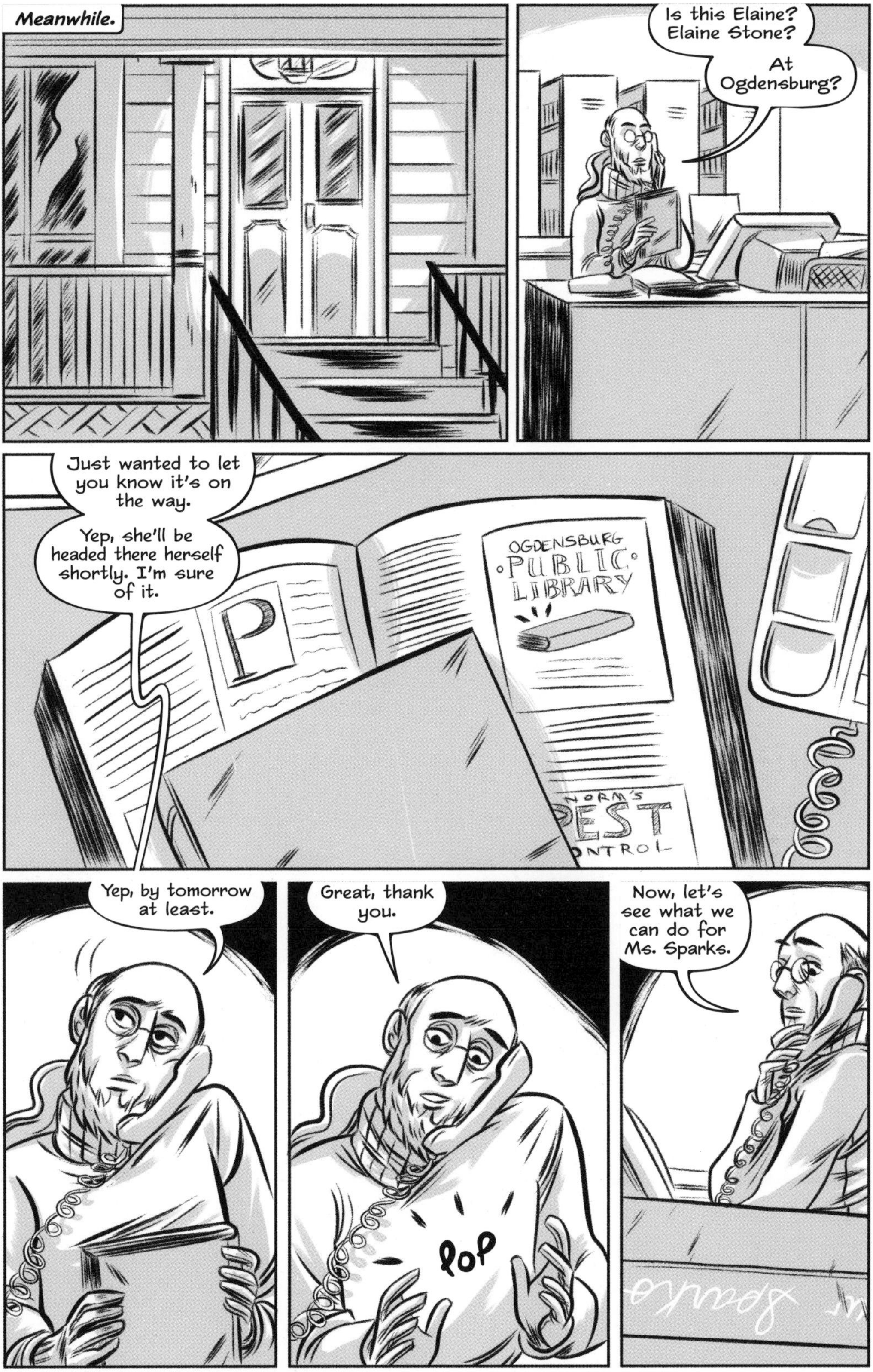
Meanwhile.
Is this Elaine? Elaine Stone?
At Ogdensburg?
Just wanted to let you know it's on the way.
Yep, she'll be headed there herself shortly. I'm sure of it.
OGDENSBURG PUBLIC LIBRARY
NORM'S PEST CONTROL
Yep, by tomorrow at least.
Great, thank you.
POP
Now, let's see what we can do for Ms. Sparks.

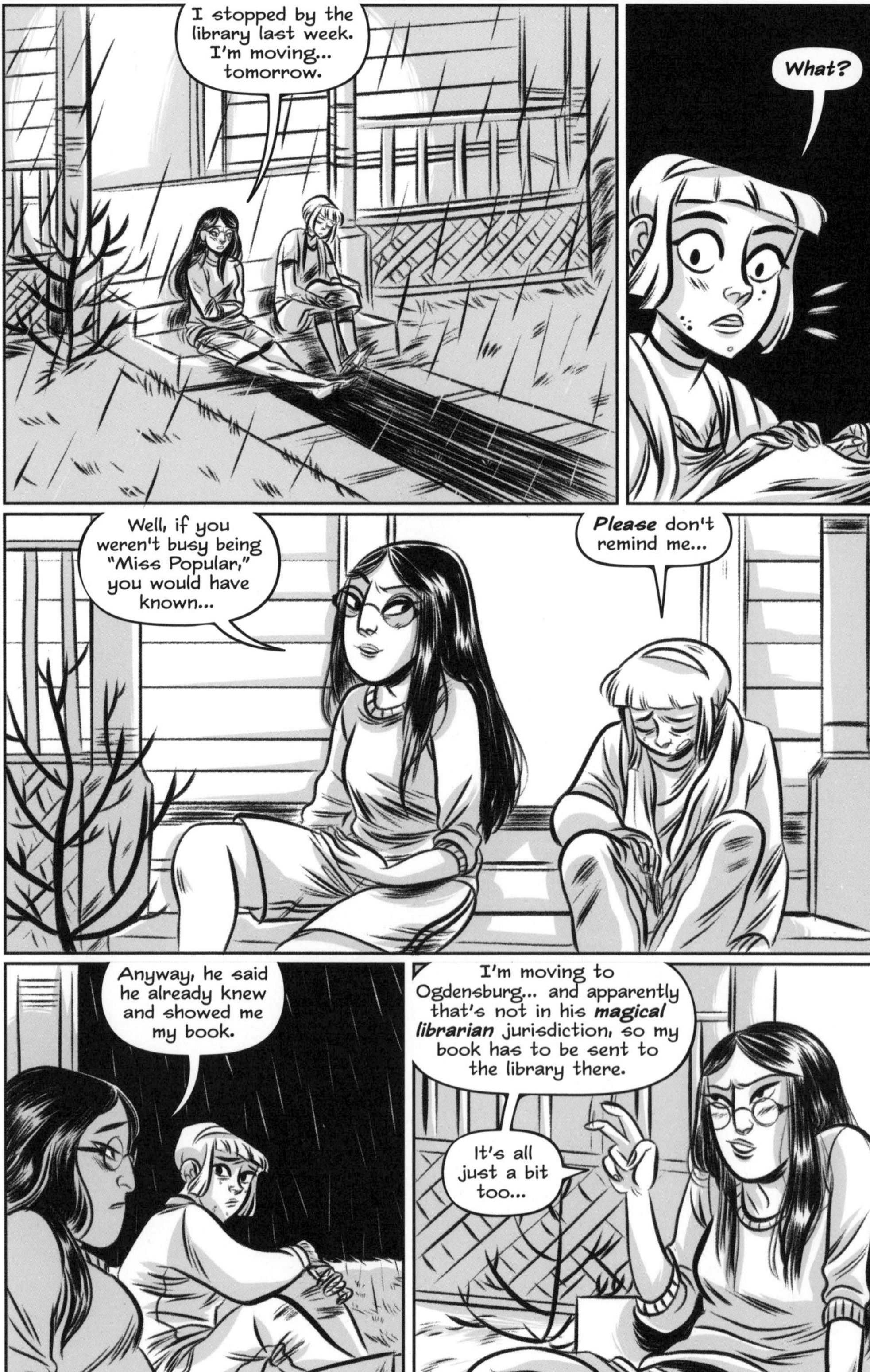
I stopped by the library last week. I'm moving... tomorrow.
What?
Well, if you weren't busy being "Miss Popular," you would have known...
Please don't remind me...
Anyway, he said he already knew and showed me my book.
I'm moving to Ogdensburg... and apparently that's not in his magical librarian jurisdiction, so my book has to be sent to the library there.
It's all just a bit too...

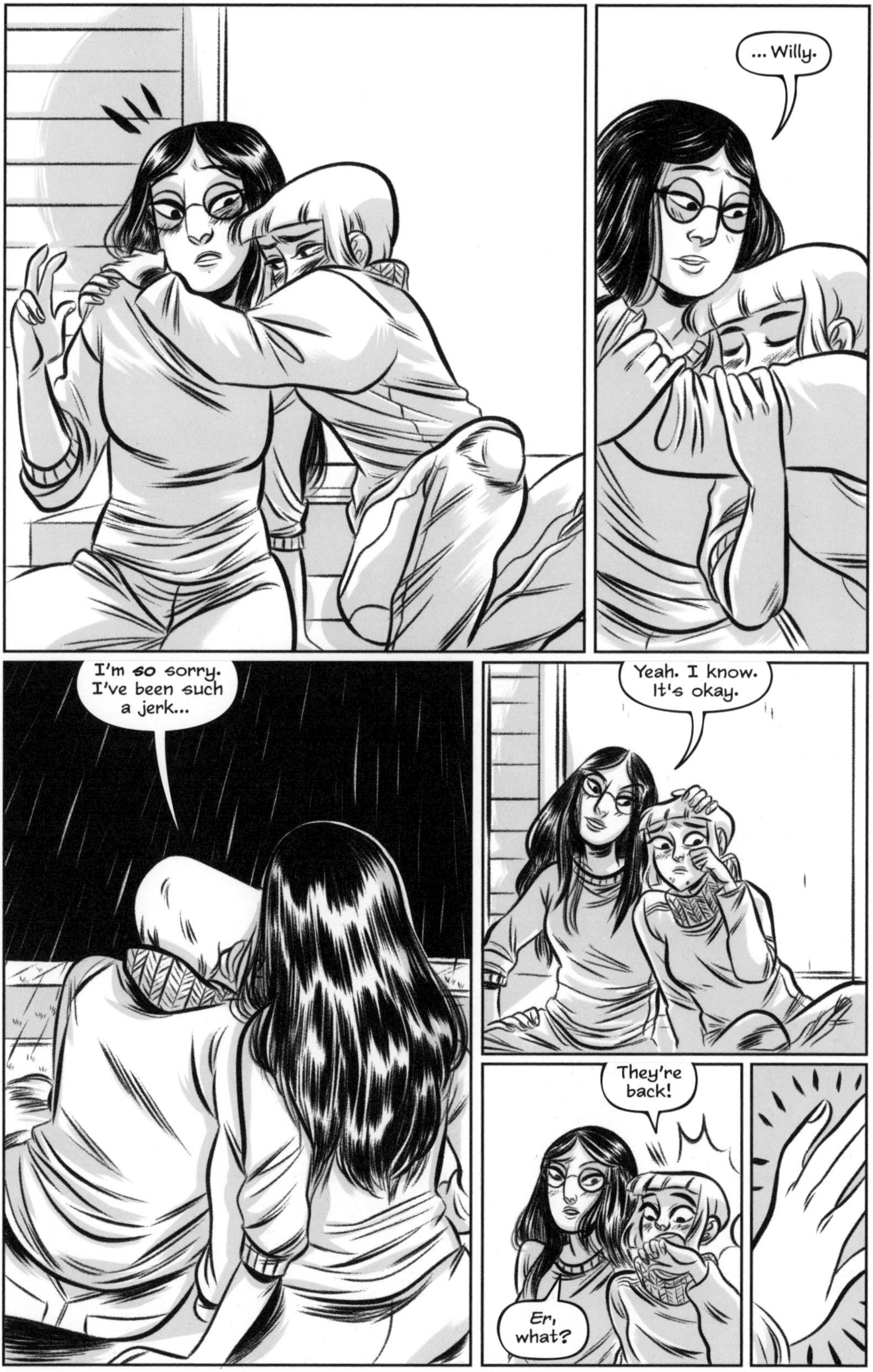
... Willy.
I'm so sorry. I've been such a jerk...
Yeah. I know. It's okay.
They're back!
Er, what?

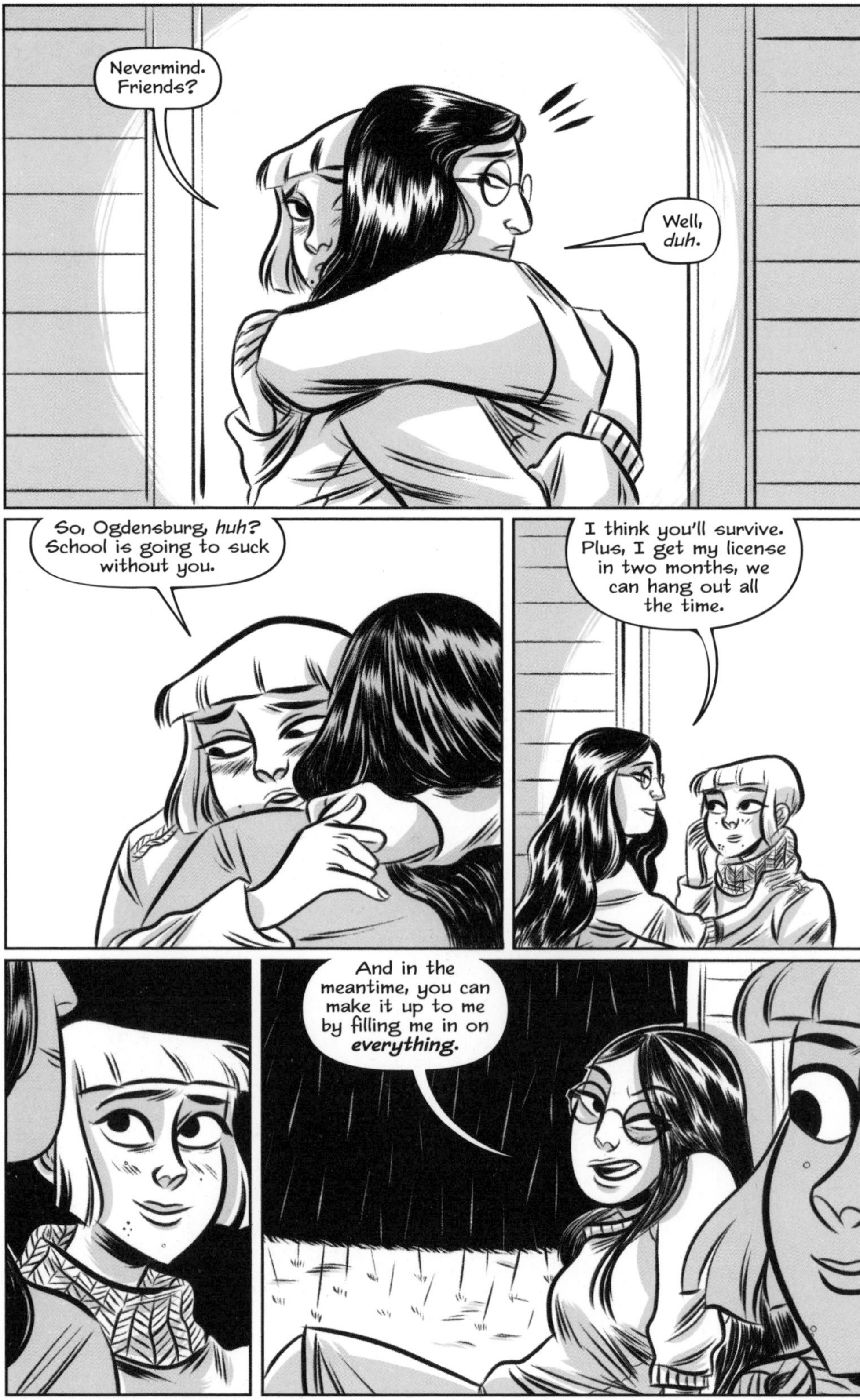

Nevermind. Friends?
Well, *duh*.
So, Ogdensburg, *huh*? School is going to suck without you.
I think you'll survive. Plus, I get my license in two months, we can hang out all the time.
And in the meantime, you can make it up to me by filling me in on ***everything***.

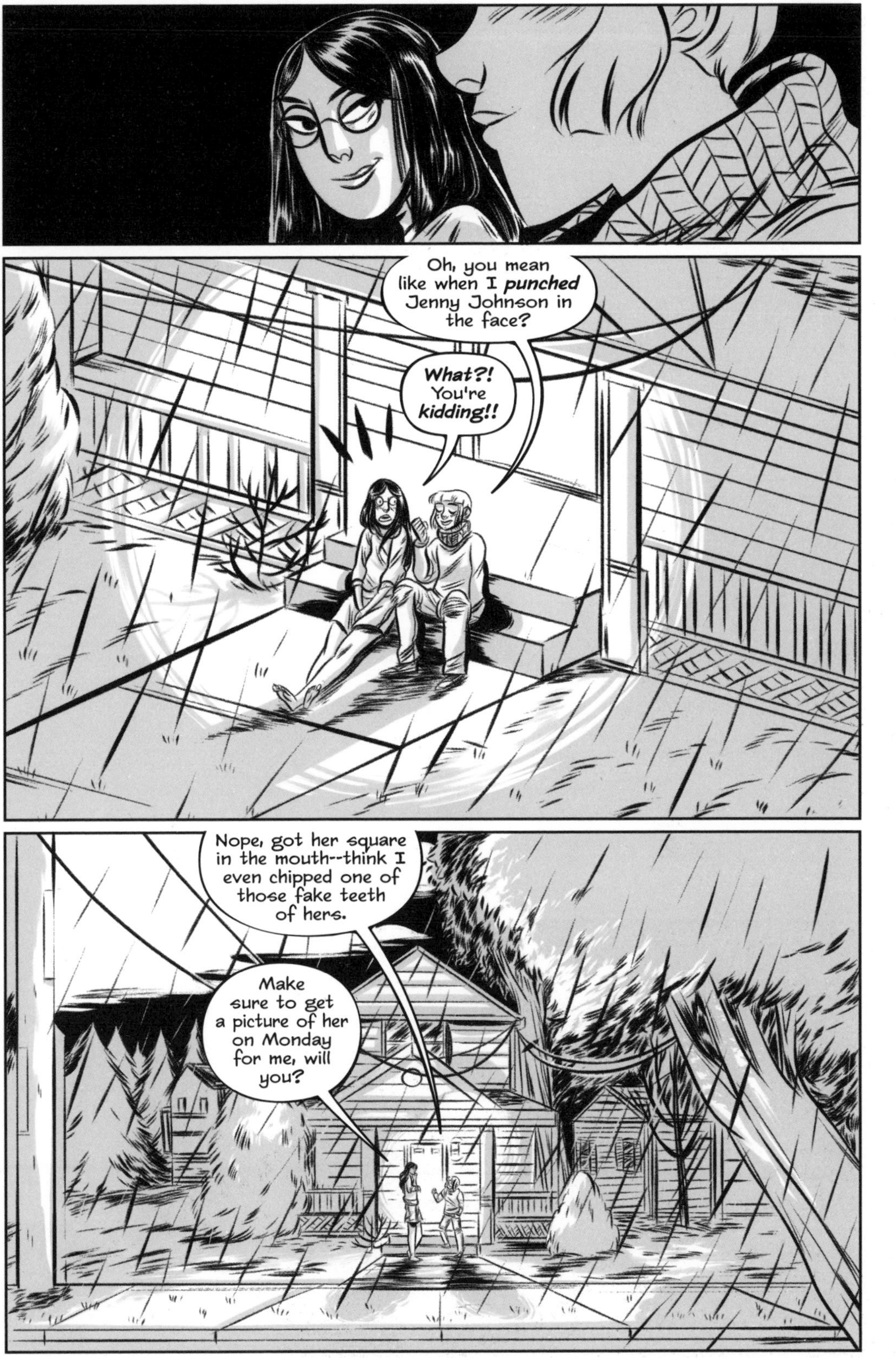

Oh, you mean like when I **punched** Jenny Johnson in the face?
What?! You're ***kidding!!***
Nope, got her square in the mouth--think I even chipped one of those fake teeth of hers.
Make sure to get a picture of her on Monday for me, will you?

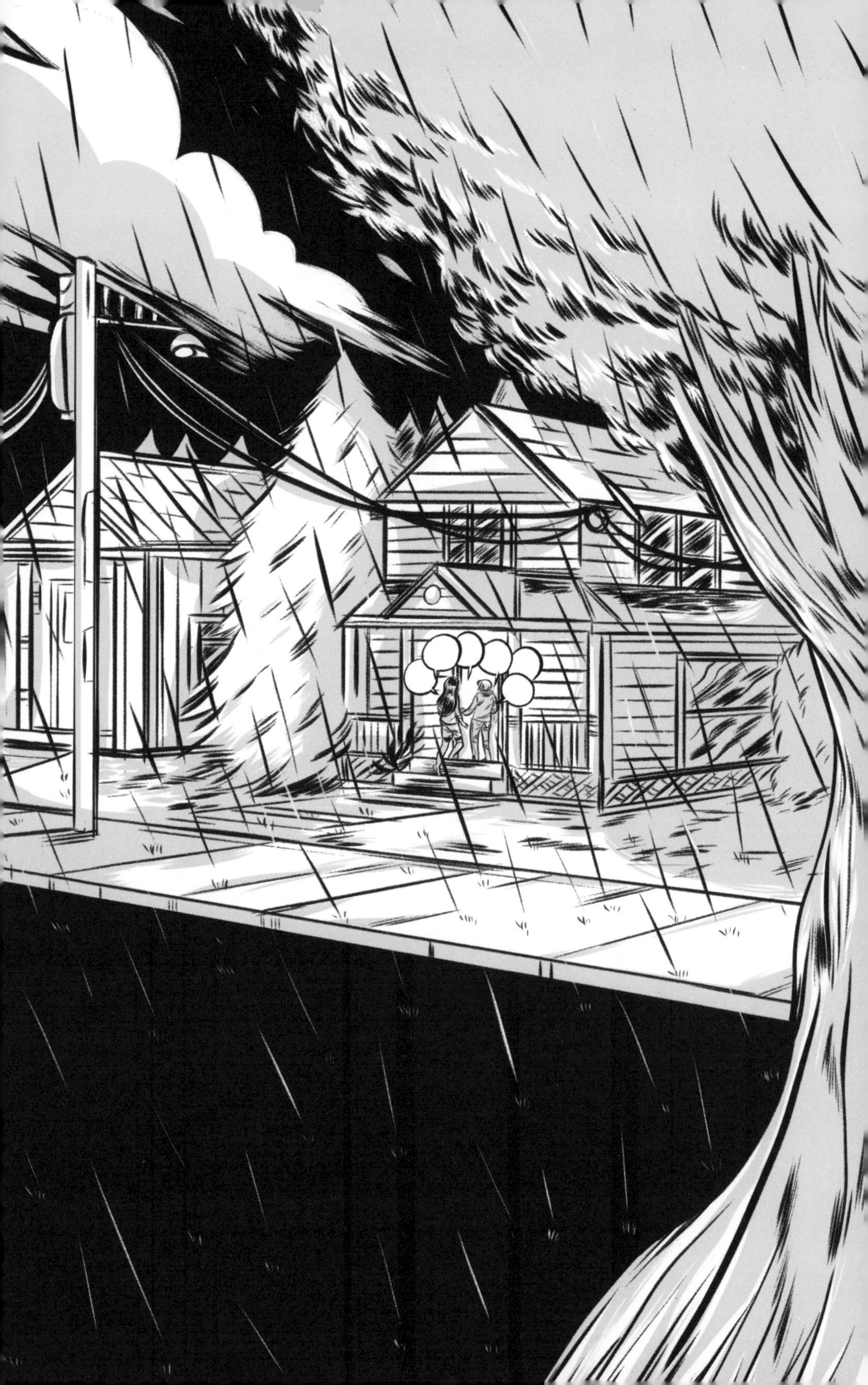

THE CHARACTERS, OVER TIME, WENT THROUGH A FEW MAKE-OVERS. OUT OF EVERYONE, I THINK WILLOW CHANGED THE MOST, BUT EVEN THEN IT WAS ONLY HER HAIR THAT WAS CHANGING.

PERSONALITY-WISE, SHE REMAINED THE SAME OVER THE YEARS. SHE PERSONIFIED SOME OF THOSE TEENAGE FEELINGS OF DOUBT AND SELFISHNESS THAT WE'D ALL RATHER NOT ADMIT WE EVER FELT.

GEORGIA DIDN'T REALLY CHANGE TOO MUCH, BUT I DID FOCUS MORE ON MAKING HER A BIT MORE TRENDY AND STYLISH IN HER OWN QUIRKY WAY.

SHE WAS ALWAYS THE LEVEL-HEADED ONE. I DEFINITELY FELT AT TIMES THAT WILLOW DIDN'T DESERVE HER—WE'VE ALL HAD THAT FRIEND THAT WAS ALWAYS THERE, NO MATTER HOW MUCH OF A JERK WE'VE BEEN. HOLD ON TO THEM!

THE PERSON WHO LITERALLY DIDN'T CHANGE AT ALL THROUGHOUT THE YEARS WAS MR. AGES. HE'S KIND OF A MASH-UP OF EVERY MENTOR I'VE HAD GROWING UP. TEACHERS, FRIENDS, AND EVEN SOME FICTIONAL CHARACTERS HELPED BRING HIM TO LIFE. THE ONES WHO LET YOU MAKE MISTAKES AND FALL DOWN—IN THE HOPES THAT YOU'LL LEARN SOMETHING.

STYLE-WISE I KIND OF WENT WITH A MODERN DAY WIZARD, OLDER HIPPIE, KIND OF VIBE.

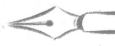

2009

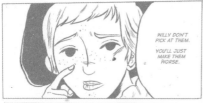

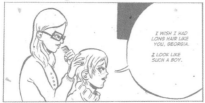

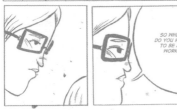

WILLY DON'T PICK AT THEM.
YOU'LL JUST MAKE THEM WORSE.
I WISH I HAD LONG HAIR LIKE YOU, GEORGIA.
I LOOK LIKE SUCH A BOY.
SO WHEN DO YOU HAVE TO BE AT WORK?

2012

Don't pick at it Willy.
You'll just make it worse.
I wish my hair was longer ... I look like such a boy.
It's just hair.
Having long hair doesn't make *me* any girlier, does it?

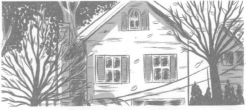

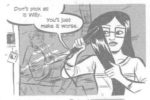

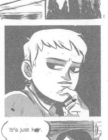

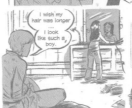

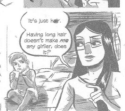

2016

THE ALTERED HISTORY OF WILLOW SPARKS WENT THROUGH MANY DRAFTS AND REVISIONS BEFORE I EVEN PITCHED IT. HERE'S SOME (PAINFUL) EXAMPLES OF THE FEW PAGES I'D REDONE OVER THE COURSE OF 8 OR 9 YEARS WITH THE FINAL, FINISHED PAGE DRAWN IN 2016.

I DON'T NORMALLY CONDONE THE REDRAWING OF COMICS—YEARS OF REDRAWING THE SAME 6 WEBCOMIC PAGES OVER AND OVER AGAIN BACK IN 2006 MADE ME REALIZE HOW FRUITLESS THAT CAN BE—HOWEVER, 2009'S ART JUST WASN'T GOING TO CUT IT—STYLES CHANGE OFTEN, EVEN OVER THE COURSE OF DRAWING ONE BOOK!

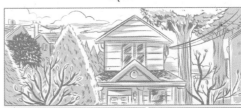

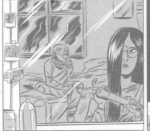

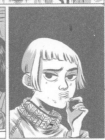

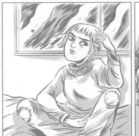

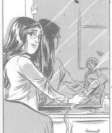

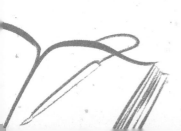

NOTES FROM THE AUTHOR

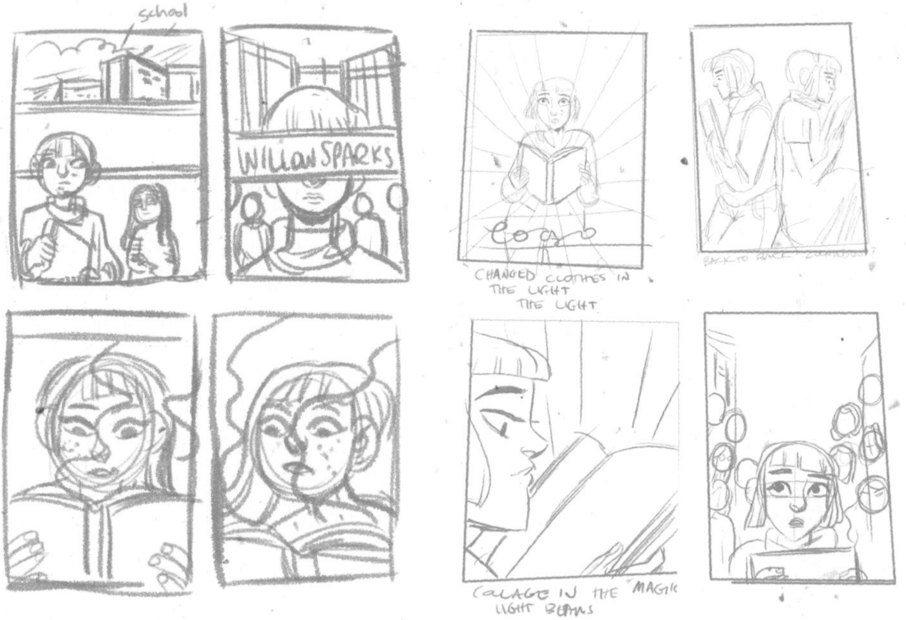
school
WILLOW SPARKS
CHANGED CLOTHES IN THE LIGHT
THE LIGHT
COLLAGE IN THE MAGIC
LIGHT BEAMS

ONCE THE ENTIRE BOOK WAS FINISHED—INKS, TONES, AND ALL—I HAD THE TASK OF TACKLING THE COVER DESIGN. AFTER SELF-PUBLISHING FOR YEARS, IT WASN'T EXACTLY A NEW THING, BUT I DEFINITELY FELT MORE WEIGHT TO MAKE IT THE BEST I COULD. SHOWN ABOVE ARE ONLY SOME OF THE DESIGNS CONSIDERED UNTIL WE FINALLY SETTLED ON THE FINAL COVER (BELOW).

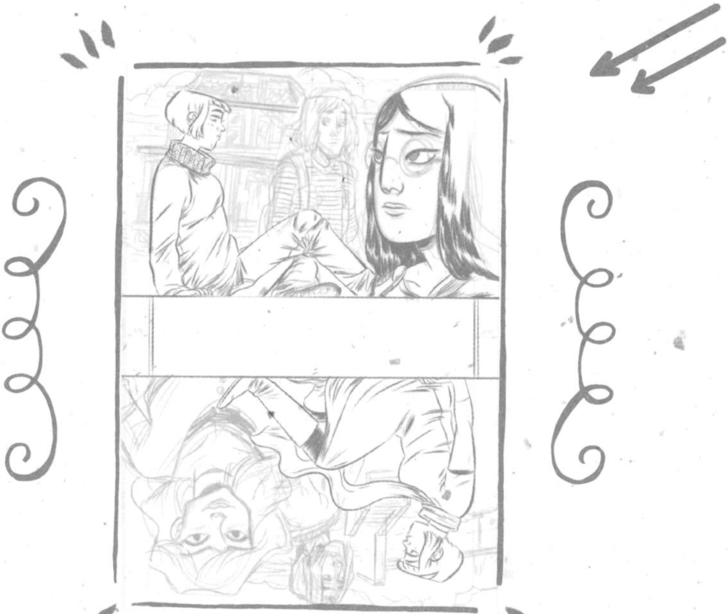

MY ENTIRE PROCESS IS PRETTY STRAIGHT-FORWARD. THUMBNAILS, PENCIL SKETCH, INKS, AND THEN TONES.

FOR THE SAKE OF CLARITY, I DIDN'T INCLUDE MY THUMBNAIL SKETCHES, THEY ARE BOTH TOO SMALL AND TOO MESSY TO BE ANYWHERE NEAR COHERENT. THEY ARE MOSTLY USED JUST TO GET A BASIC LAYOUT OF FIGURES IN THE PANEL, AS WELL AS PANEL LAYOUTS THROUGHOUT.

MY PENCILS ARE FAIRLY SKETCHY AS WELL, AND MOST OF THE FINE DETAIL I LEAVE FOR THE INKING STAGE. THIS IS ESPECIALLY SO FOR SCENES WITH CROWDS!

NOW FOR MY INKS!

I ESSENTIALLY JUST GO OVER MY PENCILS ADDING IN MORE DETAIL AND MAKE SURE I'VE LEFT ROOM FOR TEXT.

INKING IS MY FAVORITE PART OF THE PROCESS BUT IT CAN ALSO BE THE MOST FRUSTRATING—SOMETIMES IT'S HARD TO CAPTURE THE LOOSENESS OF A SKETCH IN AN INKED DRAWING, ESPECIALLY WHEN THE INKED LINE FEELS SO FINAL.

THE ENTIRE BOOK IS AT LEAST 99% DIGITAL—THE THUMBNAILS BEING THE ONLY THING I DID ON ACTUAL PAPER. NOT ONLY IS WORKING DIGITALLY FASTER (FOR ME AT LEAST) IT ALSO TAKES UP LESS OF MY WORKSPACE AND IS CHEAPER (LESS PAPER) IN THE LONG RUN.

NOTES FROM THE AUTHOR

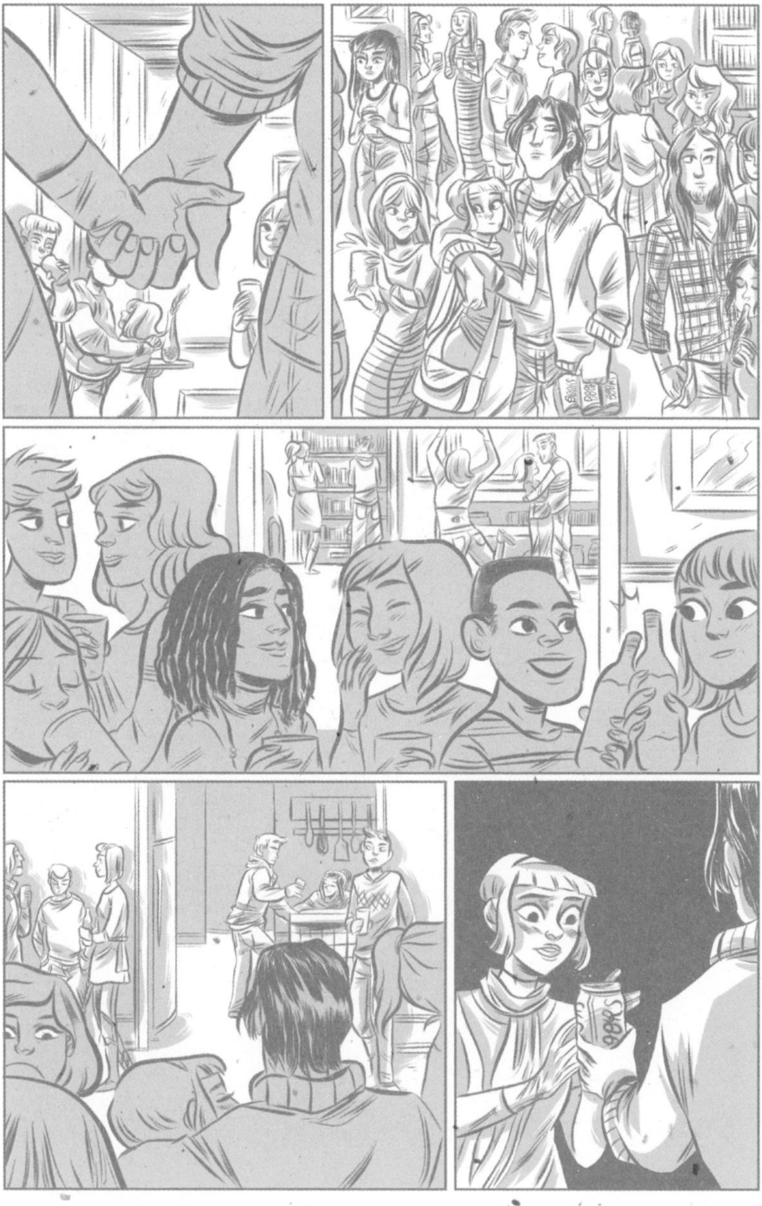

AND THE LAST STAGE IS LAYING DOWN THE GREY TONE! AT THIS STAGE, ON THE ABOVE PAGE, I WAS INKING AND TONING AT THE SAME TIME NEARER TO THE END—IT DID SLOW UP THE PROCESS A WEE BIT BUT I THINK IT WORKED OUT BETTER IN THE LONG RUN. AS FOR SETTING DOWN THE TONES, SOME OF IT IS PURELY SHADOWS, SOME OF IT IS MY AESTHETIC, AND SOME OF IT FOR THE SAKE OF COMPOSITION TO SEPARATE THE FOREGROUND, MIDDLE GROUND, AND BACKGROUND.

OVER THE COURSE OF WRITING AND DRAWING THIS BOOK I WENT THROUGH MUCH CAFFEINE. THE TALLY RESULTS ARE IN:

CUPS OF COFFEE: 1460
CUPS OF TEA: 730
ESPRESSO: 12

I ALSO DREW THIS BOOK WHILE IN TWO DIFFERENT COUNTRIES! HALF WHILE IN IRELAND, AND THE OTHER HALF IN THE STATES.

SOUNDTRACKS

I LISTENED TO A LOT OF MUSIC WHILE SCRIPTING, DRAWING, AND INKING THIS BOOK. HERE'S JUST A TASTE OF WHAT WAS ON REPEAT:

HARRY NILSSON — AERIAL BALLET
WUGAZI — 13 CHAMBERS
GHOST — MELIORA
JETHRO TULL — THICK AS A BRICK
THE MOODY BLUES — DAYS OF FUTURE PASSED
FINAL FANTASY VII SOUNDTRACK
CHRONO CROSS SOUNDTRACK
NEIL YOUNG — AFTER THE GOLDRUSH
AL GREEN — I'M STILL IN LOVE WITH YOU
RUSH — 2112
RY COODER — BOOMER'S STORY
TENACIOUS D — TENACIOUS D
THE STONE ROSES — THE STONE ROSES
LOU REED — TRANSFORMER

— AND SOME — Thank YOUs

A HUGE THANK YOU TO EVERYONE WHO HAS SUPPORTED ME OVER THE YEARS. I CAN'T THANK YOU ALL ENOUGH.

ESPECIALLY: JOHN! I COULDN'T HAVE DONE ANY OF THIS WITHOUT YOUR SUPPORT AND LOVE. AND THANK YOU FOR YOUR HELP TONING SOME OF THE LAST COUPLE PAGES WHEN IT WAS DOWN TO THE WIRE. I LOVE YOU!

TO MY PARENTS, WHO HAVE ALWAYS BEEN SUPPORTIVE OF MY COMICS. WITHOUT THEIR SUPPORT EARLY ON AND BEYOND I WOULD NOT HAVE BEEN ABLE TO GET AS FAR AS I HAVE.

TO MY AWESOME EDITOR, ARI! THIS BOOK WOULD NOT HAVE HAPPENED WITHOUT YOU!

MORE ONI PRESS BOOKS YOU MIGHT ENJOY...

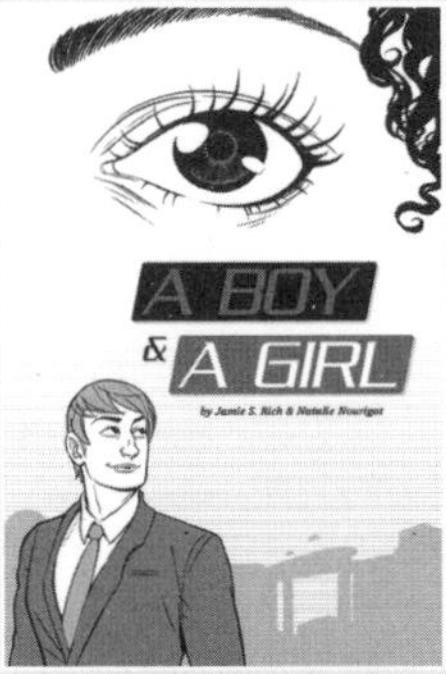
A BOY
& A GIRL
by Jamie S. Rich & Natalie Nourigat

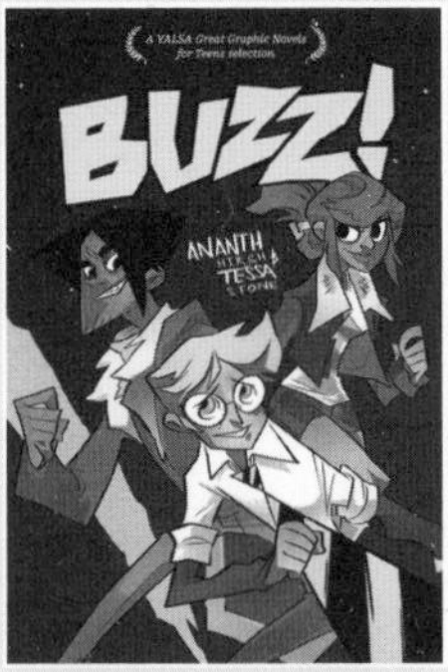
A YALSA Great Graphic Novels for Teens selection
BUZZ!
ANANTH HIRSH & TESSA STONE

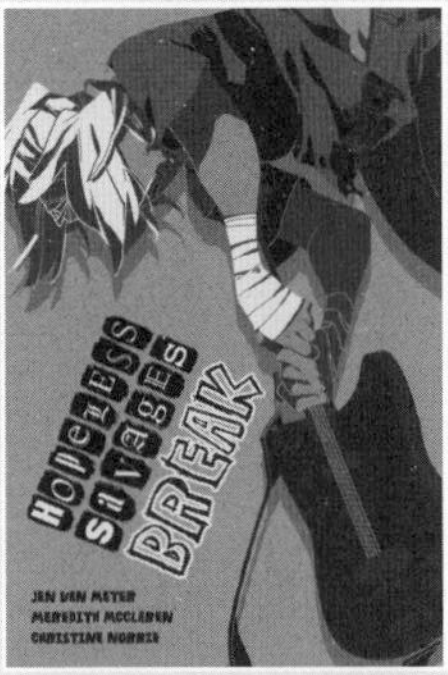
HOPELESS SAVAGES
BREAK
JEN VAN METER
MEREDITH MCCLAREN
CHRISTINE NORRIE

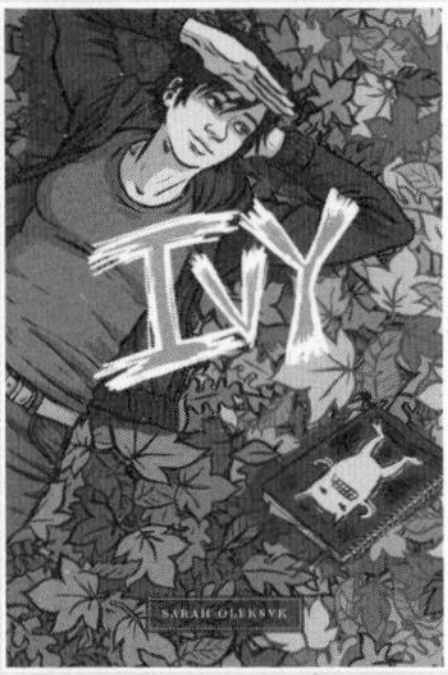
IVY
SARAH OLEKSYK

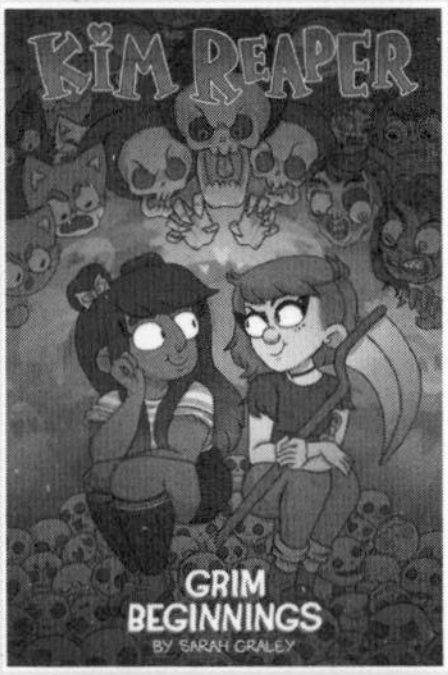
KIM REAPER
GRIM
BEGINNINGS
BY SARAH GRALEY

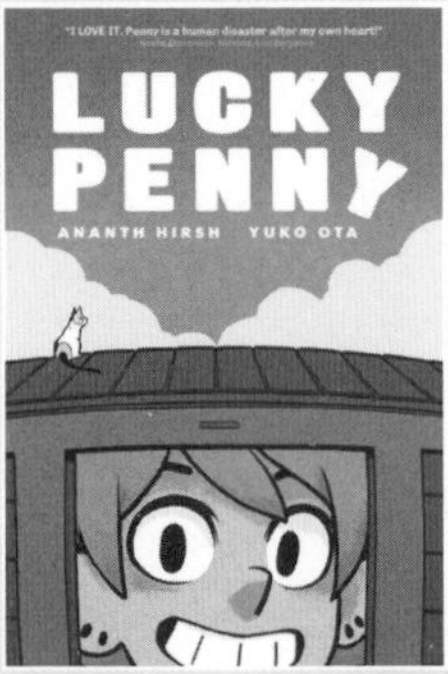
LUCKY
PENNY
ANANTH HIRSH YUKO OTA

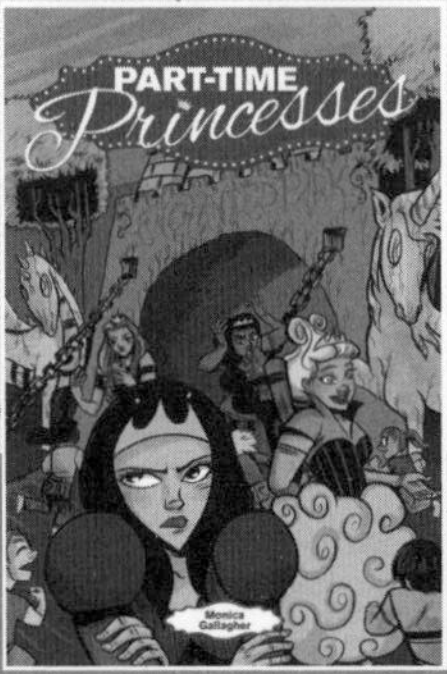
PART-TIME
Princesses
Monica
Gallagher

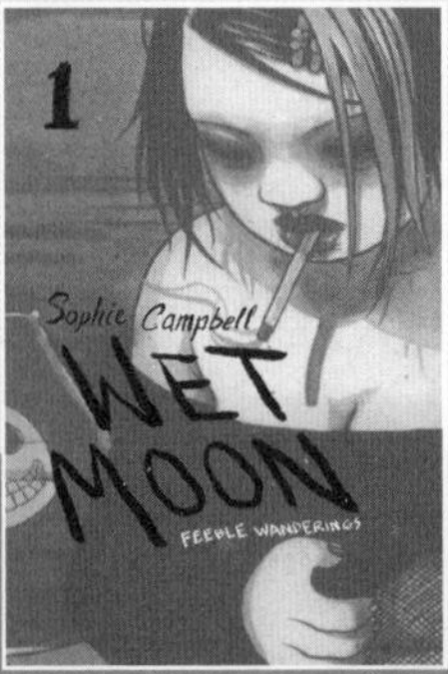
1
Sophie Campbell
WET
MOON
FEEBLE WANDERINGS

A BOY AND A GIRL
JAMIE S. RICH
& NATALIE NOURIGAT
ISBN 978-1-62010-089-9

BUZZ!
BY ANANTH HIRSH
& TESSA STONE
ISBN 978-1-62010-088-2

HOPELESS SAVAGES: BREAK
BY JEN VAN METER,
MEREDITH MCCLAREN,
& CHRISTINE NORRIE
ISBN 978-1-62010-252-7

IVY
BY SARAH OLEKSYK
ISBN 978-1-934964-59-0

KIM REAPER: GRIM BEGINNINGS
BY SARAH GRALEY
ISBN 978-1-62010-455-2

LUCKY PENNY
BY ANANTH HIRSH & YUKO OTA
ISBN 978-1-62010-287-9

PART-TIME PRINCESSES
BY MONICA GALLAGHER
ISBN 978-1-62010-217-6

WET MOON, BOOK ONE:
FEEBLE WANDERINGS
BY SOPHIE CAMBELL
ISBN 978-1-62010-304-3

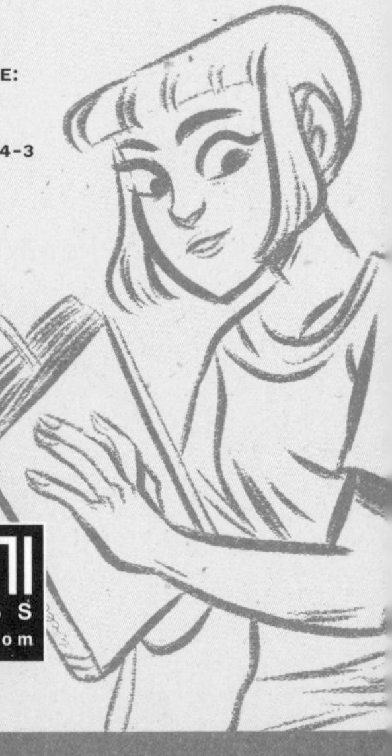

ONI PRESS
www.onipress.com

FOR MORE INFORMATION ON THESE AND OTHER FINE ONI PRESS COMIC BOOKS AND GRAPHIC NOVELS, VISIT **WWW.ONIPRESS.COM**.

TO FIND A COMIC SPECIALTY STORE IN YOUR AREA, VISIT **WWW.COMICSHOPS.US**.